ISLAND
OF
GHOSTS

To Lois, who encouraged me to write
this story, and in memory of the late
Bunny Pantcheff

The action of the story takes place in
the years 1943 and 2000

ISLAND OF GHOSTS

By
RICHARD COX

THORNTON COX

CHAPTER ONE

The two labourers marching at the back of the column were little more than boys, with thin, pinched faces and unnaturally bright eyes. The one called Mikhail was 17 and Wolf 18; but their struggle to survive had made them old beyond their years. That was what the island did to prisoners. They learnt or they died. But these two had not lost hope. They planned to escape. The question was when and also how.

The boys' hair was shaggy, roughly trimmed and already dank from the fog that had welled up in the valley soon after dawn this morning, bringing with it an eerie chill. Wolf shivered. All he had on was a tunic made out of a cement sack, with holes cut out for his head and arms. Miki had on a tattered brown jacket, the same he was wearing when he was seized to be sent here. The torn trousers of both boys were encrusted with grey dust, as if they were scarecrows from a construction site – which in truth was just about what they were – and they both stank of sweat, of tiredness and of fear. Even their mothers might not have recognised them now; and anyway they were a thousand miles from home.

All twenty men in the column wore crudely made wooden sabots on their bare feet. Some had old sacking tied around their legs in place of trousers and all their clothing was coated with the same grey cement dust, which congealed in their armpits and groins, and they all smelt foully. The sabots made a dull clumping on the road as they marched three abreast down the valley, behind the uniformed guard. At the bottom was a bay where they were building a long concrete wall. They marched with the long handled spades for building the wall on their shoulders, as soldiers marched with rifles.

When the wall was finished it would be five metres high and almost two wide and run behind the whole length of the sandy beach. The workers had nicknamed it 'certain death' because so many men had died during its building, either from beatings or exhaustion. The overseer had watched impassively as one man had fallen between the wooden shuttering panels when the concrete was being poured and had writhed, shrieking for help, until he was entombed.

As they marched down Truppfuhrer Kranke, the squad's overseer, shouted at them to sing. 'Sing you bastards, sing!'

The Fortress Commandant liked the labourers to sing. 'They are happy in their work for the Fatherland.' Oberst Grundmann wrote in his reports, using the same ironic, tongue-in-cheek, idiom as the slogan painted on a board at the camp gates: *Arbeit makt Frei*; 'work makes (man) free'. His superiors complimented him on his reports. With luck, as soon as he was promoted, he would soon be posted away from this hellhole.

After a little the singing lapsed and it was then that the boys heard the klaxon, distantly announcing some unexplained emergency. Almost at once they heard a truck's engine revv up and the noise of it speeding off, somewhere out of sight, but not up the road they were marching down. The klaxon's eerie wail continued. They heard more vehicles roar off. They both realised, with a stabbing surge of fear, that their chance had come with this distraction.

'At the corner' Wolf hissed out of the side of his mouth 'by the trees'. They marched on, safely at the back of the column. Wolf had naturally become the leader, because he was older than Miki, but he had nothing like the younger one's assurance. Nonetheless his leadership had emerged, undeclared, from their companionship in their overcrowded wooden hut, where they slept on tiered bunks one above the other.

About one hundred others lived in their hut, mainly Russians, Ukrainians and Poles, almost all from eastern Europe, all *Ostarbeiter*, workers from the east. The entire thousand men in their hutted camp, named Scharhorne, had been rounded up during the previous summer from their home villages, wearing thin summer clothes, and been given no new clothing since.

Scharhorne was both a cruel and a degrading place to live.

Cruel because with food and clothing so scarce, a man could hide nothing securely from his fellows: the smallest hunk of bread concealed in a bunk would disappear. When men died – and two or three died of starvation and beatings every week – they were invariably listed with Germanic exactness as being 'possessed of no personal effects'. Their bodies would have been immediately stripped naked by others desperate for clothing. The bookkeeping also failed to record the 55 pfennigs cash they were supposed to receive each day, but never did.

To the authorities these men, whether teenagers or fifty year olds, were sub-human, what they called *Untermenschen*.

They lived little better than animals, with thin bracken-filled palliases for their slatted bunks, one louse-infested blanket each for warmth, while a single stove failed to heat the 30 metre long hut and anyway was only allowed to be lit after the men returned from their 12 hours of daily hard labour. Their food was a half litre of coffee for breakfast, with sugar or milk, thin cabbage soup at the brief midday break, coffee and a loaf between six men in the evening. Very occasionally they had a tiny portion of meat; while the camp quartermaster grew prosperous on selling the rest of their rations: a fact which the bookkeepers also failed to record.

No man could survive 12 hours hard labour a day on so little food. This and the regularised brutality of the guards had convinced the boys that they must escape.

This morning, after the guards had hammered on the hut's wooden walls with their sticks, shouting 'raus, raus' then bursting in yelling 'aufstehen' and laying about them to beat the nearest labourers, and after they had made what passed for ablutions and paraded, they had been given half a kilo of bread each. This was the ration for three days. With care it could perhaps last longer and when Wolf saw the fog rolling in as they left the camp he had decided that today might be the day.

Miki heard the whisper but did not look round. He felt an acheing mix of fear and hope, envying Wolf's seniority, yet scared by it. He might not make up his own mind until they did reach the corner. Even then he might not obey, except that he would be letting his friend down. He had a rebellious temperament.

The narrow unpaved road ran between earth banks and tumbledown stone walls, but there was a stand of stunted pine trees on the left where its direction swerved. As the column passed this bend the Truppfuhrer would be out of sight in front for a few seconds. Today his fellow corporal was sick and Kranke was the only guard. This, coupled with the fog, had decided Wolf.

Escape from the island was impossible. That was a fact, which the guards impressed upon them. Several had tried, been caught and died in agony from the beatings they were given. One pair had reached the rocks at the foot of the cliffs and been machine gunned from above. Another man, who had dared to resist capture, had been nailed to the camp fence as an example, where the crows pecked out his eyes. The game wasn't worth the candle. The guards told them so whenever anyone tried.

When the singing died away Kranke shouted at them again. 'Sing you bastards, sing.' He flourished his whip as he marched. Its nine thongs lashed the air, beating out the rhythm. 'Links, zwei, drei, rechts, SINGEN!' he yelled, to keep the men in step. Like all the labour overseers of the Organisation Todt he wore a khaki uniform seized from the defeated Czech army.

Kranke wished the Herr Oberst could see him. Then he might be promoted away from this 'arsehole of the world', perhaps to guard a labour camp in France. That was everyone's dream. He heard the klaxon too, knew something bad had taken place, but kept going. Whatever it might be, it was not his business. 'Singen!' he yelled again.

A shrill voice from the back responded with a Russian song. Wolf had reacted fast to the order to sing, even though he only knew the first few words of the verse. He wanted to encourage the others, who were mainly Russians. The more noise, the better. Very soon they would reach the corner where they must make their run for it.

By himself the Truppfuhrer would not be able to do much, even though he had a gun holstered on his belt and the wooden handled cat o' nine tails swinging in his hand. He was not worried that no-one was bringing up the rear today. He could cope. The boys relied on his failing.

The fog swirled up the valley, seeping in more and more thickly from the sea, as soft and concealing as smoke. The pine trees became ghosts, entwined in wisps of chilling mist. The moaning of the foghorn at the lighthouse echoed through the obscurity, three long mournful bellows, followed by fifteen seconds silence, then three more, spaced and deliberate, then a brief silence again.

'Gut!' Kranke shouted, waving the whip, 'Sehr gut!'

The metre-long cat o' nine tails was a great encourager of activity. He had cut his initials into his handle. Its leather thongs were stained with dried blood. It gave him a far greater sense of power than the gun. He could see the fear in men's faces when he raised it.

As the end of the column came level with the trees another moaning sequence from the foghorn echoed up the valley. Wolf broke away and scrambled up the bank, over the low wall and dropped down flat on a bed of pine needles behind.

Miki hesitated, realised that the men alongside him were determinedly not noticing and flung himself up the bank too, scrabbling at the stones to get over the wall. They both lay still, with their heads down, until the clumping of feet and the singing grew faint. They jettisoned their spades close by the wall.

'We must get going.' Wolf said 'When they get to the bay the guard will notice.'

'You know where the boat is?

'It must be beyond the bay, where the women live.'

They had both overheard the guards joking about the commandant's lovelife. Beyond the wall of certain death, somewhere along the rocky shore between the bay and the lighthouse, they knew there was a house where the officers' prostitutes lived. They had seen a group of them once, walking along the beach, and the guards had laughed, talking about how Grundmann fancied himself as a sailor and took them out in a sailboat sometimes. 'Must make a change from fucking!' one guard had commented enviously. Only the officers had a brothel.

So the boat must be kept near that house, in a place where the foreshore was not mined against invasion. Wolf reckoned it couldn't be more than a kilometre beyond the bay. But a kilometre was a long way with so many guards about.

'We'll go round the bottom of the cliffs,' Wolf had explained, when they were planning their escape, 'maybe in fog we could swim past the bay.'

The bay was one hell of an obstacle. The valley led down to it and the long, high defensive wall they were building ran along behind it, between the beach and the road that led to the lighthouse. At least they assumed the road led to the lighthouse and to houses they had glimpsed by the shore. The side of the road was sewn with mines. They had seen the black and white skull and crossbones signs stuck on posts. And beyond them on the rough land stood many high poles, linked by a network of wires, which the boys did not understand.

To complicate things further there was an old stone fort built on rocks in the middle of the bay, reached by a causeway from the beach, where there were always soldiers on guard. So swimming would mean going out to sea, beyond the fort, where the choppy water showed that the tides ran fast. Perhaps it could be done. You would need to be a strong swimmer.

The only alternative would be to wait for nightfall, after the other labourers had been marched back to their camp, and hope to crawl unobserved along the verge of the road. The boys had argued over this in the hut during the evenings, whispering from one bunk to the other, before they fell asleep from exhaustion. They were both fairly fit, in spite of the meagre food, though the longer they delayed the less strength they were going to have left.

But now that they had actually done it, made the break and defied their captors, they felt hugely exhilarated. Fear and desperation would come later. At this moment they could achieve anything.

'The wood.' Wolf ordered 'We can't stay here.'

In the deepest part of the valley, below the road, was a wood, invisible now in the fog. Marching above it, as they had done day after day, it looked dense enough to hide in. Beyond the wood the side of the valley rose again to fields and further beyond must be the cliffs.

They listened for anything coming, then raised their heads gingerly above the low parapet of the wall. The visibility was hardly ten metres and nothing stirred, though soon other work parties would be brought down in trucks from more distant camps. Hundreds of men were employed on 'certain death'.

'Now!' Wolf whispered.

They scrambled back over the loose stones on to the road, ran to the far bank and then scuttled like rabbits down the slope of an overgrown field to the trees, keeping to the side to avoid leaving obvious tracks. A shallow muddy stream ran through the trees. They crossed it and sank down among bushes in the other side, grateful to scoop up water to drink. Miki had cut the palm of his hand on the wall. He washed off the trickle of blood and tried staunching it with grass.

'Wait.' Wolf searched around for something sharp, found a flint and deliberately cut his own flesh below the thumb. Then he made his friend rub their wounds together.

'Now we are brothers.' He said with unexpected solemnity. It was a gesture he would never forget, one that would bind him for the rest of his life.

'Me a Russian and you a Pole?' Miki asked. 'You're kidding.'

'We all had to speak German!' Wolf reacted as if stung. In his region of Poland, close to the border, it had been forced on everyone. 'Anyway you're not Russian.'

Before Miki could answer they heard distant shouts from the bay. And the distant whine of a siren.

'They've found out.' Wolf said, suddenly needing to share decisions. 'Is it the cliff now or the road after dark?'

For a moment their excitement died, their adrenalin drained away. They were two frightened boys, far from home. It was only a few months since Wolf had been seized with a group of other teenagers from their village in Poland, transported across Europe by cattle truck and shipped in the overcrowded, urine-stinking, verminous hold of a coastal freighter to become a forced labourer on this island. Miki's experience had been similar, although he was evasive about his Russian home. What was left of the summer clothes they had on then was all they possessed.

Since the autumn of 1942 both boys had been brutalised pawns in a power struggle for Europe of which they knew no details, slaving to fortify an island they had never heard of before.

No-one told them why all these concrete emplacements were being built, nor for how long they would be compelled to labour twelve hours a day on them. In theory they were paid. In reality they received no money: and anyway there was nowhere to spend it. They had no canteen. On their one rest day each week they were not fed. 'Nicht arbeit, nicht essen.' Was Grundmann's diktat 'No work, no food.'

Gradually, as the weeks had become months and the autumn had turned into winter and the winter to spring they had realised that if they did not escape they would either die here or be crippled for life. But unlike some of the older labourers, they had not abandoned hope. Now, having begun their bid for freedom, they would be hunted down by guards who shot on sight. And they knew it.

'Fuck them.' Miki swore, unexpectedly making the decision for both of them. 'The cliffs.'

CHAPTER TWO

Airlines transported one too quickly into other worlds, and anyway Anna hated flying, so she had taken the ferry. She liked to feel her way into a place, to absorb its atmosphere gradually. But this voyage had only taken an hour and already here was the island, its ochre cliffs rising starkly out of the sea, looking completely unlike the Springtime paradise which Quinn had promised.

In fact it was positively bleak and forbidding, with a cap of cloud lying on its top, although only a mile or so back the ferry had been sailing in sunshine. Perhaps fog suited a man as moody as Quinn. And how would he seem after two years of separation? The same compulsively attractive, totally impossible, artist? Or simply a man she no longer loved, but was still married to?

For the umpteenth time she wondered if it had been wise to come across from Brighton. She had let him talk her into it, though partly because she had her own, private, agenda for the visit: even if it was an agenda which she knew Quinn would instinctively resist. And, completely incompatibly with that agenda, she had come because he was the only person she had ever known who knew how to make her feel wanted and to make her happy.

Well, sometimes he could make her happy. She qualified the memories in her mind as she watched the waves slip by and felt the occasional thump as the bow hit the swell. But not happy enough, often enough, intensely enough, insanely enough for a childless marriage to last. Quinn was so appallingly single-minded, concentrating passionately on one thing at a time, usually a painting, which meant being totally focussed on his own state of mind, his perceptions, his reactions, you name it. And he expected her to be too. Oh God, introspective wasn't in it.

In the old days she used to just patiently clean his brushes and listen. But that had changed, as she had begun to develop her own life. And during those moments when she had been the sole object of his concentration had it really been any better? Flattering and exciting, yes. But also scary.

That was why she had only agreed to come here during the college's mid-term holiday, so giving herself a guaranteed escape clause at the end of a week. Any arrangement with Quinn necessitated a let out, especially when she was taking two risks: one with Quinn himself, the other with the personal agenda of a family mystery which probably wasn't a mystery at all, which she hoped was not, but which had been pre-occupying her more and more intensely.

Could they get together again? That was unabashedly Quinn's hope, although in reality it was a time for decisions anyway, because this separation thing was absurd. They both had new lives. If they weren't going to be together, they ought to divorce.

She watched the day trippers crowding the boat, the older ones chatting, the teenagers giggling and talking. No problems for them. The oldies were secure in knowing they would leave again in the late afternoon after a day spent contentedly criticising the 'duty free' prices in shops, consuming icecreams and cups of tea, and peering like jackdaws through uncurtained windows, while the young girls eyed up the local boys in the pubs.

And there was one thing the brochures all guaranteed. No-one ever came to any harm on this island. The locals didn't even bother to lock their doors, of which the occasional light-fingered visitor took advantage. Quinn had told her some boys were once caught with a town plan, marked up with theft targets.

It sounded crummy if you wrote it down, but she felt herself to be a traveller, not a tourist. For exactly that reason she had not bought a guidebook. She wanted to make her own discoveries; even allowing for the man she was coming to see: and Quinn would want to show her everything as he saw it.

On a boat you might well talk to locals who knew the destination and during the trip she had been looking cautiously around. Certainly there were other passengers who did not look like tourists. A few were presumably residents, laden with shopping bags, discussing the weather in distinctive accents.

Those people looked as though they were returning residents who belonged here, whereas one old man definitely did not. He was in his 70s, at a guess, with a lined and careworn face, perhaps prematurely aged. He was shabbily dressed in a brown leather jacket, shiny at the elbows and the neck, and a flat cap. He had been studying the coastline intently and she could hear him muttering to himself in a foreign language. Suddenly she realised that he was looking straight at her.

She flushed in spite of herself, irritated. Why was this man staring at her? She hated being stared at. She wasn't anything special. When she checked her appearance in the mirror before going out what she saw was just a clear-skinned, quite well-formed face with blue eyes under a thick mantle of light brown hair that fell around her head like a bell. She didn't devote a lot of time to make-up, just gave a brisk brushing to her hair, touched up her lips and made sure she was looking tidy. She had a good enough figure, bosom not heavy, waist slim, hips reasonable, but she knew she was nothing out of the ordinary, so why should anyone stare at her? She looked right back at him, challengingly, and he hastily resumed scanning the seascape.

Not that either of them could see much. The boat was a hydrofoil, Italian designed and fast, but without outside decks, so everyone was forced to stay in their seats and the windows were smeared with salt. She had just about been able to see those ochre-coloured cliffs from a distance. From closer up she saw waves breaking on to outcrops of rock beneath them, while gulls wheeled and soared above like acrobats. One isolated pinnacle of rock seemed to be stained white, until she realised there were hundreds of seabirds crowded on to every ledge, colouring the rock like a *pointilliste* picture, each gull a blob of white paint.

The boat quivered in a patch of rough water as vicious, chopping, waves fought against each other, creating a miniature maelstrom. Could this possibly be the place of Quinn's inspiration?

Ten minutes later they were clear of the tidal race, the sea calmed and became a deep blue, and the whole atmosphere changed.

They passed an old stone fort, standing on a rocky promontory almost in the sea, and a hillside studded with small cottages and bungalows came into sight. The town must be somewhere up there, she thought, and felt a gratifying prickle of excitement as she glimpsed the unusually squat triangle of a church spire. And the light! Even through the smeared windows it was clear that the light was fantastic. The coastline and the houses stood out in unpolluted clarity. She was an artist herself, not in Quinn's admittedly middling league, but still talented enough to appreciate a quality of light that he had told her any artist would sell his soul for.

Rounding the end of an enormously long granite breakwater, the ferry slowed down with a churning of propellers at the entrance to the harbour, set in a wide sandy bay where yachts were rocking gently at anchor. The beach gleamed in the sun. A waterskier traced a foaming trail behind a speedboat. Tall old houses, pastel-washed in various colours, rose beyond the main quayside, like a holiday postcard scene. It was a world away from the forbidding cliffs of a few minutes ago. Even the fog on the hill seemed to have dispersed. Perhaps Quinn was right.

And what would Quinn look like now himself? He said he had grown a beard. Would she recognise him? How stupid! Of course she would. He always had been unmistakably larger than life. Whatever one felt about him there was only one Quinn. That was why he liked to be called by a single all-purpose name, as French actors used to.

'You are with friends visiting?' the old man had moved next to her as they queued up in anticipation of disembarking. He spoke in awkward, heavily accented English.

'Yes.' She said firmly, remembering how jealous Quinn became if she allowed herself to be picked up. Deep down he had always been insecure in their relationship, though surely he could not object to a casual conversation with a foreigner twice her age. Nonetheless she headed him off. 'My husband's meeting me.'

'That is good.' The old man nodded his head approvingly, as though her welfare was somehow his concern. Looking at him she realised that he must have lived through a lot of suffering. His face was gaunt and lined and his eyes possessed the same restrained and patient dignity that she had once seen in the features of an ageing tramp, whom she briefly befriended.

But why should it be good, she almost asked out loud. Why should having a husband be good by definition?

'Have you been here before?' she asked, not wanting to appear rude as they waited.

'It is many years.' He spoke as if this was something he did not wish to discuss, much as the tramp had refused to talk about where he would sleep next. 'You? You come before?'

'This is my first time. I have wait to have money.' He went on. It sounded as though this had taken him many years, though there was no complaint in his voice. He spoke in a completely factual way.

Their stilted conversation was halted by the boat manoeuvring with a jolt alongside a high stone jetty.

A loudspeaker voice announced that passengers could now disembark. Anna gathered her things together and was about to say goodbye when she realised that the old man was already ahead of her. Well, that saved any conceivable embarrassment with Quinn. She waited until the press of people lessened, then took her turn to half stumble up the sloping gangplank, helped by one of the officers, and out on to a sort of landing built into the quay, from which steep steps led upwards. At the top, waiting with a wide smile on his bearded face, was Quinn. He looked remarkably self-assured and she felt that everything was going to be alright, at least to start with.

'Anna, my love!' He enfolded her in a bearhug and kissed her on the lips as though they had never been apart. His beard prickled her chin lightly in a way she had expected to dislike, but found she didn't. Then he held her by the shoulders, away from himself, for all the world as if he was inspecting a doll. It was the sort of gesture actors made in films, theatrically exaggerated.

'You certainly haven't put on weight!'

'Well,' she laughed off the compliment, because she was quite a small person and the loose fitting yellow tunic she was wearing hid her figure. Not that she was in any way fat. But for this trip she had resurrected an old painting smock, one which he had always liked and which would be useful on sketching expeditions, as it had big patch pockets.

'Fat or thin,' she said equably, 'I'm here at last.'

'And as lovely as ever! Welcome to the island!' Quinn kissed her again, his beard rubbing her cheek, then became practical and started looking for her suitcase among the piles of baggage that had been swung up onto the quay in a net.

'Mine's the one with a rope around it.'

The rope did more than hold an elderly but favourite case together. It implied there was nothing worth stealing inside. She stood watching as he searched for it. He had on bright yellow rubber boots, maroon cotton trousers and a thick blue sweater, as if he was a fisherman. That was typical. On a painting holiday in Greece she remembered him in the paint-spattered shirt, old jeans and sandals of a Mediterranean artist. He adapted to his surroundings like a chameleon.

Most of the other men around the harbour had a seafaring look about them and she noticed that they passed the time of day with Quinn in a friendly way. He located her battered suitcase and hefted it up to his shoulder flamboyantly, as if only mere mortals carried theirs by the handles.

'You're travelling light, my sweet.' he commented.

'I am only here for a week.'

'You can stay as long as you like. You know that.' he sounded disgruntled, as if being spurned.

'Only if the college agrees.' she firmly headed off his touchiness. The Head never would agree, because she had asked him not to. 'Never mind.' she said re-assuringly, knowing what Quinn needed: compliance 'I'm longing to see everything.'

Logically, if Quinn wanted a reconciliation, he should have come to stay with her in Brighton. But he had preferred being on his own ground, insisting that she should see the place where he had re-established his life, his 'habitat' as he called it, as if he were some kind of furry animal in its lair. And he had not been even half-joking. It was meant to emphasise his individuality and she reckoned that the recently-grown beard was part of a deliberately created image too. Quinn always had been a bit of a poseur; or rather he struck attitudes to disguise an inner diffidence, like using only the one name. He was Quinn the original, the only Quinn, the mighty Quinn of the old song. It had been hard to achieve that in a cosmopolitan town like Brighton.

If they did get together again, Quinn would be sure to expect her to move over here. But she had her own life now, her own house, and just enough income from teaching art, which she enjoyed. So she had come across entirely at her own expense, not wishing to be in debt to him, yet hopeful that he might somehow become more adaptable. Did men ever really change though? A big question.

'Come on then. Let's go to the car.' he interrupted her reverie and she put those thoughts aside. It was a lovely day and she intended to enjoy being here.

Quinn's 'car' was an old ex-army Land Rover, still in dull khaki camouflage paint. Another bit of image building! Oh glory!

'Useful for carting gear around.' he explained as he helped her in, dumping her case in the back among wicker lobster pots and salt-stained ropes. 'A friend has a boat. Now, would you

13

like the conducted tour before we go home, or after? I'm taking you to the pub for lunch.'

'After, I think. I'd like to see where you live first.' He had told her so enthusiastically about the Victorian fort of which he rented a part that she didn't want to wait. 'Is it the one we passed in the boat?'

'Quite different. There are over a dozen forts. Mine's at the other end of the island, near the lighthouse.' he laughed boisterously, as though he was some kind of medieval seigneur. 'Not that anywhere is very far from anywhere else.'

He started the Land Rover with a clackety roar and they rattled away from the harbour, past the tall houses and the dune fringed sweep of the bay. Children were playing on the sand and there were a few swimmers, even though it was only May; but this a perfect day and a school holiday. The mood was exactly right.

They drove up a slight hill, the slopes covered in gorse and bracken and Anna noticed the fairways of a golf course.

'Where the nobs play' Quinn commented sourly 'at least they think they're nobs.'

Anna smiled, quite unable to visualise him as a golfer even in jeans and a woolly hat. The road continued past some whitewashed cottages and across heathland towards a junction, where there was a low stone built edifice set in the angle where the road divided, with flower beds and memorial plaques.

'What's that?' she asked.

He slowed down, more because of the junction than her question.

'To foreigners who died here.' he said reluctantly. 'Past history.'

She felt sudden apprehension, aware from the way Quinn responded so curtly that there was probably much more to it than just past history. So she dropped the subject. But for reasons she could not put her finger on, she found his dismissal of whatever the memorial meant was disquieting

Soon they reached a smaller crescent-shaped bay, with a clean-looking sandy beach, guarded by forts on promontories at each end. She began to see what Quinn had meant about the landscapes. Every few hundred yards brought a new and unexpected vista. They even crossed a single track railway line, which she would like to have asked about but refrained. The memorial seemed to have made him prickly. He stopped on the road above the bay and pointed to the further fort.

'There.' he announced with pride 'Rocquaine! What do you think of that?'

The fort was not at all like the castle she had imagined. It was long and squat, built of the island's ever-present granite, with no castellated battlements, and seemed to grow out of the rocks of the headland, dominating the wide beach below. There was a low circular tower at one end, while a long line of windows set into the main wall signalled a kind of domestication. Behind and above the main building there rose a single-storey construction, with a wall of windows, like a miniature modernist house.

'My place.' Quinn said with deep satisfaction. 'My habitat. One hell of a view. Now do you see why I sold that poky little house I inherited?'

'How fantastic!' she instantly understood things no letter could have explained. 'What a place to live. And to sketch or paint. I really am going to enjoy myself!'

'Chocolate box, as usual?' he asked, sarcastically.

'Now stop it, Quinn! Don't be beastly. I see things my way, you see them yours.'

She wasn't going to let him slip back into disparaging her work, simply because he considered himself to be the 'true artist', while she was just a traditionalist, a 'stuckist' he used to say mockingly, 'stuck in the past'.

She suffered enough bitchiness at the college, where few of the staff had any technical skills at all; despised them in fact, preferring the easy 'conceptual art' of anything from folded blankets to artfully scattered rubbish. She wasn't going to put up with any of that from Quinn.

'Anyway,' she threw back at him, 'all these rocks are abstract shapes, if you look at them.'

'Sorry, darling. I didn't mean it.' he was taken aback by her vehemence. She used not to be so strong minded.

He let in the clutch again and drove her round to the bay's far side and up a gravel track to a medieval-style stone gateway with the date 1857 carved on the keystone. Inside were a wide courtyard and a grass slope up to the studio, with the fort's main bulk down on the left. He led the way, carrying her case, up to a living room so huge that it completely took her breath away.

15

The room was forty feet long if it was an inch and thirty wide. A massive granite fireplace dominated the back wall, with a coat of arms carved into its high stone overmantel, and green and blue calligraphic mosaics mounted alongside. The opposite wall was mainly a range of sliding windows, which gave a landscape view over the roofs of the main fort lower down towards the sandy arc of the bay. A huge black wrought iron chandelier hung from the ceiling. So this would be her home for the next week. Stunning.

'It's like a filmset' she exclaimed, wondering if all this splendour allowed space for a second bedroom.

'The Lindsays call it the Moroccan room, because of the calligraphy. It's a bit too grand for me. But you should see where I work.' He led her along a corridor to a smaller room directly overlooking the sea.

A series of canvases were propped against the walls, while on an easel was a scene she recognised as the harbour, though in an earlier century. A large steam yacht was moored near the long stone breakwater, accompanied by a host of smaller sailing craft, watched from the shore by a crowd of onlookers and soldiers on parade. Although as yet the people were only sketched in, Anna realised that they were in 19th century clothes.

'Are you into history now?' she asked, amazed at this turnaround, especially after his crack about chocolate box pictures. 'What was this particular chocolate box event?'

For a moment – a very brief moment – Quinn was embarrassed.

'Queen Victoria's visit.' he said, then recovered his poise and became boastful. 'The President has commissioned me to paint a series of historic occasions for the Parliament building. Of course they have to be strictly representational. It's quite an honour.'

'Of course.' Anna smiled, biting back a comment. What a nerve he had. 'Quite a change for you, though.'

'I am the island's tame artist. How could I disappoint the President? Anyway Lavinia would have killed me.'

'Lavinia?'

'She's the heritage expert. She fixed it. Bit of a bulldozer, but a heart of gold. You'll have to meet her.'

'And how old is your Lavinia?'

'Don't get the wrong idea, darling. She's had a facelift and she's sixty if she's a day.'

'And a widow?'

'How did you know?'

'Oh Quinn! Are you really so innocent? Anyway I can see you couldn't possibly refuse.'

She spoke with only a hint of sarcasm, trying not to be bitchy, in spite of all those protestations two years ago that he must leave Brighton – and her – in order to realise his full creative potential. She wasn't at all sure that she wanted to meet Lavinia.

'Now could I freshen up?' she asked. 'It's been a long journey.'

To her relief Quinn showed her to a tiny spare bedroom, also overlooking the sea, then left her to unpack. She knew he would try to drag her into his own bed in the evening, but at least he wasn't taking it for granted. She was determined not to give way to him either, at least not on the first night. Otherwise he would assume that everything about their reunion had been agreed, when it certainly had not. But it wasn't in Quinn's nature to take much notice of female protestations; and plenty of women had responded to the caveman approach, so long as they didn't appreciate the diffidence beneath. She wondered if he actually did have anything going with this 'bulldozer' widow. If so, that would be the final goodbye.

When she was ready Quinn led her down to the fort's main building to be introduced to the owners, a retired doctor and his wife, who insisted on offering them drinks. The doctor was a handsome, suntanned, lion-maned man, who looked too young to have given up work. His name was Henry Lindsay.

'It's not often enough we see an attractive girl like you on the island, is it now?' Lindsay joked, pressing a gin and tonic on her. 'And this is our national drink! How long will you be staying with us, then?'

Irritatingly Quinn answered before she could, saying a week, minimum. But after half an hour's conversation in which she was made to feel fully welcome, she marked the genially hospitable doctor down as someone to be trusted if anything went wrong. It had already struck her that, small though the island might be, Fort Rocquaine was quite cut off. Then Quinn, with rare tact, excused them before they could overstay their welcome, citing their lunch reservation. He evidently held Dr Lindsay in respect.

'We'll see some more of the island on the way.' Quinn announced, as they drove away from the fort by another route, past the lighthouse at the tip of the island. The lighthouse's tower was painted horizontally with broad black and white bands and had a multi-faceted lantern on top, while two monstrous black foghorns were mounted by its base. To Anna they looked like the trumpets the devil might sound at the entrance to hell.

'They must make a terrible noise' she said 'don't they wake you up?

'One gets used to it.'

He drove on up to a vantage point. The sea, she noticed, though azure blue further out, was disturbed and rough close to the island, the water chopped into turbulent white foam against the rocks.

'Strong tides here' Quinn explained 'and when the tide's flowing against the wind, quite dangerous.' On the far horizon a long spit of land stretched across the sea. 'The mainland' he said.

'It looks very close.' She could distinctly see houses, while things glinted in the sunlight, car windscreens perhaps. But this could not be mainland Britain, not possibly. 'Is that France?'

'Ten out of ten for geography.'

'I had no idea it was so near.'

'Nine or ten miles. Very near and yet impossibly far, at least without your own boat. All that wine and cheese and patisserie and we can't get across to buy any.'

'You poor, deprived little boy! Well, you chose to live here.'

She paused, still gazing across. The white triangles of yachts were poised, seemingly immobile, between the island and the French coast, which stretched as far as she could see, with low hills rising behind. The sky over there was heavy with high grey clouds, while here there were none.

'Anyway' she asked 'what about your friend with the boat? Doesn't he take you?'

'I go with him occasionally when he sells his catch. Crabs mainly.'

Now she understood why Quinn's clothes and his harbour friendships made sense. He probably wasn't well enough off to afford a boat, even though he had invested the money from selling his cottage, and she had quickly appreciated that this island was a place one would need to escape from sometimes. Even the Greek islands had proved claustrophobic. This might prove worse, especially with all the unending fortifications. She had caught his frustration in that remark about France.

'Do you really like it here, Quinn?'

He hesitated, then justified himself. 'Fantastic light. Abstract shapes, as you noticed. Boats and bays like Cornwall. All waiting to be discovered. There could be a real artists' colony here, another St Ives.'

'With you as the founder?'

It was unkind, but she was really only teasing. She knew what he meant. His cheeks reddened momentarily above the beard and she knew she had hit home, making her feel instantly contrite. 'Be careful for you tread on my dreams' the poet wrote and now she had trodden on his.

'I didn't mean it.' she said quickly.

A major problem in their marriage had been that Quinn feared he lacked status. Men needed to be respected if they were to respect themselves. Basically unselfconfident ones like him felt they had to be assertive, especially in a sexual relationship. It sounded terribly old-fashioned, but it was true.

Although he had been successful as a graphic designer in England, a career which he always belittled, Quinn's soul was in painting. His problem was not that he had no talent, but that it wasn't really substantial enough. Being a mediocre artist in a sophisticated centre like Brighton left him feeling unrecognised and inadequate. Yet he could always conjure up an outgoing, creative personality for strangers, in spite of that inner diffidence. He knew exactly how to act the artist. He would have been marvellous on TV, all quick-drying exterior gloss with no foundation.

'I do see that it's a marvellous place to paint.' she tried to make up for having been critical

'I hope I can do it justice.'

That was it. He had hit the nail on the head, with unusual honesty. He could be bombastic, yet at heart he was also intellectually honest, which was a redeeming quality. Nor could he embrace the fashionable conceptual art that she so despised.

Because he had this streak of honesty it had effectively defeated him, when he might have easily bluffed his way into exploiting it. He could no more pretend that a pile of dirty washing was a work of art than fly to the moon. To Anna that was his most endearing characteristic: he was that most unusual contradiction in terms, an honest poseur, with a totally genuine passion for art. And very little money.

Anna now realised that here on the island he could be himself, live cheaply, and no-one would worry about his degree of talent. The picture of Queen Victoria's arrival was what people here would appreciate. It was an unkind thought, but this culturally undemanding place might just possibly enable him to develop and paint better. Then he would be fully his own man and a lot more satisfactory for a woman. Anna felt a pang of acute jealousy, in case the bulldozer widow had realised this.

'The big fish in the little pond.' Quinn conceded and drove on abruptly.

The road took them past more bracken covered slopes, dotted with yellow gorse, to a superb vista across a bay towards a much higher headland. Quinn stopped again. In the centre of this bay stood yet another massive Victorian fort, with tiny windows in its granite walls, reached by a causeway from the beach against which the tide lapped gently. Families were picnicking on the beach itself in the lee of a high concrete wall running almost the whole length of the beach, while their children paddled and played, reminding her that it was indeed half term.

'It is the most perfect place.' Anna exclaimed. 'And I see what you mean about forts. They're everywhere. But what on earth is that concrete wall for?'

'Oh, that.' Quinn seemed disconcerted again, as if she ought not to have noticed it. 'The Nazis built it in the war to stop troops from landing. Quite useful as a windbreak for sunbathing. Thoughtful of them, in a way.'

'The Germans were here? I didn't know.'

'During the war. Bloody krauts.'

'Was that what the memorial was about?'

Anna felt another prickle of worry even as she asked. Sooner or later she was going to have to tell Quinn about her private agenda, something she had barely got straight in her own mind yet, an aspect of her ancestry she had not known about when they were together. She was half-German herself. The loving parent she remembered from childhood had not been her father at all. Until this moment she not imagined that Quinn might resent her having German blood. The last war was so long ago and they were all Europeans now. Suddenly she feared he might.

'For five years they were here.' Quinn continued resentful indeed. 'Not a subject people talk about much, although God knows the place is littered with bunkers and gun emplacements to prove it. Concrete remnants of Hitler's thousand year Reich. They built to last, alright, those krauts.'

'Then you can't ignore it.'

'But it gives me a problem historically. Do I paint the SS Commandant inspecting the concentration camp in 1943? Or the slave labourers building this wall? Would the President hang those alongside Queen Victoria at the harbour? The hell he would. The only answer is to pretend that 1940 to 1945 never happened, which in a sense it didn't.'

'What do you mean?' Now he was being typically difficult. 'It is history. Thousands of people still remember the war. Or if they'd don't they've read about it. Churchill and all that.'

'Not here. The islanders were all evacuated to England. There is no folk memory. They weren't here.'

'How strange.'

Anna was disconcerted. Quinn's answer only posed more questions. If the Germans had been here, then things must be known, there must be records. She didn't like the reference to a concentration camp either and felt she was getting out of her depth very rapidly. Did the island have two characters, a dual personality, like some kind of historical schizophrenia? She felt relieved when Quinn revved up the engine and drove on.

'They're keeping a table for us at the pub. Let's get going.'

They drove past the bay and up a shallow wooded valley, along the other side of the golf course and soon reached the town. Here everything changed and Anna was immediately entranced.

The main street was cobbled, with pretty Georgian cottages. Red, white and blue bunting was strung overhead, criss-crossed between the houses. Tourists with rucksacks congregated by the blue-doored Post Office. Young boys pushed bicycles and mothers wheeled prams up and down the narrow pavements. Everything was happy bustle. People said hello to Quinn and smiled at her.

The pub was called the Victoria and Albert. A Union Jack hung from a pole above the entrance. Inside it was compact and friendly, with a bar on one side and dining tables round a fireplace on the other. A tall, pleasantly open-faced woman in a smart print dress welcomed them.

'I've kept a table in the garden for you, Quinn.' she said 'it's such a glorious day.'

She beckoned them through to the back and as they followed her Anna glimpsed a colour print of Queen Victoria's visit to the harbour over the mantelpiece. She wondered if Quinn was copying it. Ten to one he was. But there was no time to look more closely.

In the garden they sat at a table under a huge, striped umbrella, which advertised Beck's Bier. The menu was chalked on a board, with lobster, crab and seabass prominent, all three expensive. Quinn's historical paintings for the President were unlikely to support a lobster diet. She let him choose first and followed his fish and chips order with a prawn salad. However, she did welcome his asking for a bottle of chilled white wine and when it came they touched glasses and toasted her safe arrival.

'To the future!' Quinn said, smiling and gazing into her eyes, clearly implying 'together'.

She smiled back, seeing less of the old uncertainty in his face and wondering if she was failing to give him a proper chance. But she needed to keep her distance at the beginning, or he would jump to all the wrong conclusions. And there was her own agenda.

'The future' she answered non-committally.

CHAPTER THREE

The boys crouched among the bushes by the stream, trying to decide what to do. It was one thing for Miki to say 'go for the cliffs', Wolf thought to himself, but which way? With the fog swirling around, so close he could have snatched handfuls of it, neither of them had any real sense of direction.

'Keep still and listen.' he suggested. 'No panic.'

Gradually they began to distinguish sounds, although the fog seemed to distort noise. Occasionally a bird sang or they heard a light rustling as some small animal disturbed dead leaves in the undergrowth. A rabbit hopped out into their range of vision, saw them, stopped, stared, and loped cautiously away again. Then they heard the first human sound, and it was an unexpected one. Someone was striking metal with a hammer and it sounded dangerously close. Both boys froze.

'That way.' Miki whispered, jabbing his thumb up the slope of the track.

'But we saw trucks at the bottom.'

The road down which they marched to work every morning had a lane leading off it towards a hill, with a roofless barn close by where they had seen army vehicles.

A further sequence of dull hammer blows striking metal floated up to them, followed by a more distant shout.

'Sounds like a workshop They're mending something.' Miki said. 'We can't use the track.'

'The fields, then.' Wolf re-asserted himself. 'Come on.'

They moved carefully out of the bushes, crouching, then straightened up and walked away from the stream.

In front of them was a wooded bank, thick with bracken, brambles and dark green ferns. They tackled it slowly, to avoid being scratched, and emerged at the edge of a field. Another barely visible line of stunted trees, just coming into leaf, ran at right angles to the bank, up the field, like ghosts in the fog.

They walked across and began following this treeline, always steeply upwards, until perhaps fifty metres further on it joined another series of trees running straight across their path, leading along a ridge. They sat down, panting, as if by mutual agreement, the adrenalin rush of escape suddenly gone. The sheer exhaustion which had enabled them to sleep at night in the camp seemed to have seeped into their bones: that plus the chill of the fog and an unspoken edge of fear.

'We're a lot higher up.' Miki said. 'This has to go to the cliffs.'

As if in confirmation, the foghorn's three blasts came to them, distant and disembodied, giving no sense of direction. They had not heard the foghorn down among the bushes, though neither had thought about that at the time. So now they must be higher up.

Even more distantly they heard another sound, the one that signalled an emergency, the sound that had prompted their making a run for it. The klaxon wailed from far away, its tone rising and falling, not always audible, but full of meaning. Whatever had happened must have been serious.

'Is that us?' Wolf asked nervously.

'Can't be.' Miki said with a confidence he didn't feel, 'We're not that important.'

Their clothing was soaked from sitting by the stream and Wolf felt cold all through his body. The safe discomfort of their wooden hut and plank beds seemed immeasurably long ago. He had never imagined he would regret losing the camp's barbed wire, the shouting guards and the constant fear of being beaten for no reason. But if you'd kept your head down and did as you were told you could survive.

'Aren't they after us?' Wolf asked again.

Miki considered this once more. 'How many of us on the island?' he asked, almost rhetorically, 'hundreds? No! Must be a thousand just where we were.'

'Several thousand then.'

'And they'd sound the alarm for two? Something bigger's happened.'

Wolf considered this thoughtfully, slightly comforted. and unexpectedly prepared to take the younger boy's word for it. Without rationalising it, he knew he was no longer the leader.

'That's good.' he said. 'If they're busy, I mean.'

'Doesn't mean we can hang around.'

Miki jumped to his feet and led the way along the new line of trees, sometimes stumbling over the gnarled and twisted roots projecting from the hard ground, until the treeline abruptly ended. The fog eddied around them, revealing only the grass of the field. They could see perhaps ten metres, sometimes less. But the upward slope was clearly to their left. They headed that way and after a few minutes came to a path, which took them uphill along the side of a tumbledown stone wall. Bracken and gorse grew thick on the other side.

'What's that?' Miki demanded, looking to their left, where small trees half concealed a darker patch of vegetation close to the path. They deviated cautiously to look, tripping over thick strands of brambles, and found a small disused quarry pit, perhaps five metres deep, thick with undergrowth and surrounded by stunted trees.

'Could be useful.' Miki said.

'Why?'

'Don't ask me. It just could.'

They returned to the path, which followed the wall and soon began to rise less steeply. The noise of a truck's engine starting up made them stop and drop flat on the ground. They listened. It sounded close, although noises were so distorted by the fog that they could not be sure. But one thing was certain. It was roughly in the direction the path was taking them.

'Must be at the castle.' Wolf whispered.

The castle reared up above the bay, at the end of the hill, seeming to grow out of the steep sides, around which a narrow road ran. The boys had only ever seen this hill from a distance, as they marched down the road or laboured on the wall. But they had never been able to study this horizon, only glance furtively towards it when they had their midday *Bunkersuppe*

However they had observed that at the top the ground was more level and concluded that the cliffs were beyond. To be safe, they needed to head for the ground to the right of the castle, up above the fields they had just crossed. And now the view was totally obscured by fog. They could only assume that this path led to the castle. A moment later the truck confirmed it.

The invisible driver gunned his engine and ground the gears as he moved off. The noise diminished.

'He's going down to the bay.' Wolf suggested, instinctively trying to regain his lost authority.

'We're too bloody close.' Miki said. He gestured at the bracken on the other side of the wall. 'Let's get up there.'

Miki was definitely making the decisions now. Not that Wolf disagreed. It was easier to fall in with the other's plans. They waited a little longer and then, when there was no further sound, climbed over the disarranged, half-fallen stones of the low wall and plunged into the bracken and long grass, immediately slowing because of the noise they themselves were making. The bracken might be wet, but it crunched audibly underfoot.

After a few metres they saw a sign and stopped dead. It was the sign they feared.

'ACHTUNG MINEN!'

The sign was on a white board nailed to a wooden pole and had a black skull and crossbones stencilled below the warning. The pole was held upright by wires staked into the ground. It stood almost as high as them, poking up out of the bracken, explicit and menacing.

They looked at it, confused in spite of understanding the warning. They'd heard the guards say that some of the minefield signs were fakes, because there weren't enough mines. The guards were not army, they worked for the Organisation Todt, Hitler's labour corps. Although they wore uniforms, theirs were plain khaki and different to the grey of the real soldiers. But that wouldn't make any difference. They would still know about the mines.

The boys were pretty sure the minefield warning signs inland of the coast road behind certain death were real, because apart from a piece of land used as a cemetery, most of it had poles with wires strung between them. The guards said this was to stop enemy aeroplanes landing on the flattish ground. But up here, where all that this scrub led to was the cliff edge? Would anyone have bothered?

'We have to chance it.' Wolf said, briefly asserting himself again. 'They can't be real up here.'

They began to continue along the path past the sign, but cautiously. Although they would never see anything buried in the undergrowth, both boys were still cautious.

Their movement flushed a rabbit out of the bracken ahead of them. It broke cover and shot off along the path, changing direction in a zigzag way towards the cliff, its white scut bobbing among the bracken and ferns until it vanished.

Seconds later there was a deafening explosion. Both boys threw themselves flat, just in time. Fragments of metal sliced through the bracken above their heads, sprinkling them with shredded foliage. They lay there for several minutes, panting with fear, almost wretching. Then Wolf raised his head and found himself staring at the rabbit's corpse, caught high up in a yellow-flowering gorse bush and dripping blood. The blast must have thrown it back towards them. The drips gradually covered a frond beneath, making it a dull red.

'Miki' he hissed 'are you okay?

'Jah.'

They both continued to lie there, keeping rigidly still, listening. All the excitement and stimulus of their escape finally collapsed and died. They were no better than hunted animals, ringed in by minefields and barbed wire, and they knew it. After a while they sat up.

'Christ that was lucky.' Miki said, but not in an accusing way. He had followed Wolf this time, after all. They were in this together.

'One of the jumping kind.' Wolf said knowledgeably, trying to sound calmer than he was.

The guard had told them about the mines, partly to intimidate them and partly boasting of his knowledge. The guards were always conscious of being inferior to the army and so tried to bolster their own importance. It sounded odd that they would trouble to impress mere slaves, especially when they had whips and guns, but human vanity is a curious thing. So the boys knew what the rabbit had saved them from.

The mine had been of a kind that jumped in the air when pressure set it off and then exploded at waist height, lacerating its victims, tearing flesh, maiming limbs and blinding eyes. It was an 'anti-personnel' type. This one had been three or four metres away: just far enough for them to drop below its blast in time. As they lay there the rabbit's bleeding remains overwhelmed the gorse branch and dropped out of sight.

'We can't go to the cliff.' Wolf whispered as though afraid of being heard, remembering too late that the signs at the fake minefields were a different colour, which they were not supposed to know, except that the boasting guard had mentioned it. Still cautious, he peered through the bracken and then stood up. At ground level the fog was as thick as before, but directly overhead there was a patch of more luminous white. At a guess – neither boy had a watch – it was around nine o'clock. Before long the sun would burn through and they would be nakedly exposed on the hill.

'The bang means a patrol will come.' Miki joined him standing up, trying to think straight and stay calm. 'We must get back to the wood.'

Wolf considered this. Their plan had been to climb down the cliffs, which they had never seen close up, and then negotiate their way among the rocks and coves of the shoreline until they reached the bay. The topography was all supposition – two words they would not have understood – but the idea sounded okay. Then, with a lot of luck, they would swim across the bay, passing outside the fort on the causeway, and go ashore again to find wherever the dinghy was beached. It was one hell of a plan, given the ferocity of the tides, but it was the only one they had.

And now it was impossible. If the fog did lift they would have to hide until the working parties were marched back to the camp, so Wolf knew that Miki was right. They must go back to the wood, or perhaps to that small hidden quarry, and wait until dark or a return of the fog, before trying to reach the bay. The fog often rolled in again at dusk.

'We can't stay here.' Wolf agreed. 'They'll find us for sure.'

So they retreated the way they had come, more shaken than either would admit. But for the rabbit they would have lying maimed up there in the bracken, waiting for the guards to find them and be shot.

'What if they bring dogs?' Wolf was suddenly frightened. They had not thought of that before.

'We go down the way we came up. We make different tracks.'

That would be easy along the path, less so across the fields. They were thinking it through when they reached the overgrown quarry. The scent of the route they had followed before had deviated to the edge, returned; and continued on down the hill to the field, as well as up. That should confuse a dog.

'Let's try it.' Wolf agreed. 'At least we'll be out of sight.'

They could see from the wet grass exactly where they had walked before and when they reached the edge they used a tree branch to swing right up off the ground and lower themselves via another tree into the pit. They found a tiny pool of water and scooped it up with their hands, though it was muddy. But they disciplined themselves not to touch the bread. It was all the food they had to last them to France. Then they settled as comfortably as they could in the undergrowth to wait.

'We were lucky with that mine.' Wolf said nervously, trying to get back his composure and speaking quietly. He had been badly shaken.

'I am lucky.' Miki said, aggressively.

'Then why weren't you with the other Russians on the boat that was shot up?' Wolf had wondered about this for a long time. Now he asked. There was something he didn't trust about Miki's story 'Was that luck?'

They had heard about a cargo boat bringing labourers that had been strafed by Allied fighters a few months before. The same guard who boasted about his knowledge of the minefields had told them, presumably to impress them with the terrible things that could happen. He was a rough character, a Serb who seemed to be despised by the other German guards. So he boosted his authority by frightening the labourers. At the same time he could not risk being thought to be fraternising with them, so his remarks were always brief and often interspersed with blows from his whip. From him they learnt many things.

'I wasn't on that boat because I <u>was</u> lucky.' Miki said shortly.

'Where do you come from in Russia?' Wolf insisted.

'The Ukraine. We were taken last summer.'

'Us too.' Wolf agreed. He knew from others in the camp that labourers had been rounded up from all over Eastern Europe. 'Everyone over 16. We went to Frankfurt first in cattle trucks. Did you go there?'

'We were taken to Frankfurt too. Then France.'

'How come you speak German?' Wolf knew why he did himself, having been raised in a part of Poland close to the border.

'I learn fast.' Miki said, a bit too defensively. 'We were moved around Germany for months before we came here.'

'Okay. I believe you.' Wolf said, relenting, aware that he knew he was asking too many questions at the wrong time. He wasn't sure he wanted to know too much about Miki anyway. The important thing was that they were in this together now. He changed the subject. 'When we get to France we'll get clothes.'

'And eat.' Miki said, with feeling.

'Meat and things.' Wolf agreed.

After this burst of confidences they both fell silent.

An hour or so later it was lighter, but the sun had still not come through and they could still see swirls of fog drifting past above. Then they heard men coming down the path.

'He doesn't find anything.' A man's voice said, evidently referring to a dog, which the boys soon heard panting 'They must have been killed.'

Another voice said 'God, I need hot coffee. It's too damn cold.'

There must be two guards together. That was normal. The boys cowered back in the undergrowth of the pit.

The voices came closer. Then the dog growled.

'He's on to something' said the first voice.

The boys stayed absolutely still, down below the trees, afraid even to look up, hoping the distance they had swung outwards on the branches would leave a gap in their scent. They could hear the dog sniffing and nosing around in the grass above the pit and imagined it pulling on its leash. Then it barked, but with what sounded like a lack of certainty, barking at someone it knew must be there, but could not smell.

'Probably went in there for a pee.' The second voice suggested, as though two runaways would bother with such privacy. But his idea must have carried conviction.

'Let's get back for that coffee.' number one agreed and called out to the dog.

'Genug, Caesar. Kommt hier.'

The dog growled in protest, unhappy at being pulled away, but it knew all about obedience and about punishment too.

The boys listened as the footsteps retreated, muffled by the wet grass of the path.

'We can't stay here.' Miki said. 'When the fog goes we'll never get away.'

By mid-morning the fog usually cleared, sometimes in just a few minutes. It was unpredictable, untrustworthy, as though it had a malevolent character of its own. They had to rely on it, but they couldn't.

'Better we go in the wood.' Miki said, almost as an order 'And nearer the bay. Let's go.'

Scrambling out of the overgrown quarry was not as easy as getting into it. They were both scratched and bleeding when they emerged on the path again.

The fog swirled past the wall and the fields in uneven eddies, sometimes concealing everything within a few metres, sometimes clearing to grant a glimpse of the wall running down the hill and the field they had crossed before. For the first time they realised there was a gun position further down by the wall, the gun's long barrel poking out above a low emplacement. Then it vanished again. And at that moment they heard other soldiers' voices.

CHAPTER FOUR

The fog enveloped the island's rugged coast, cocooned it, wrapped it in a shawl of chilly damp wraiths like drifting smoke.

Anna was woken in the middle of the night by the booming of the foghorn. The sudden noise alarmed her and she sat up in bed, clutching the duvet close around her, listening to those three mournful beats, a sequence followed by a brief silence, then repeated in a chant that seemed unending, a loop of depression.

She kept hoping that the fog would disappear and the short silence endure. But it never did. Then she became aware that there was bright moonlight outside, penetrating the thin curtains of her room. That seemed strange in fog. She slid out of bed and went quietly, almost on tiptoe, to the living room, anxious not to disturb Quinn. It had been difficult enough keeping out of his bed last night. He had lost none of his old persistence and if he found her wandering now, he would invent all sorts of excuses to try to persuade her there again.

Drawing back the curtains, she peered out towards the bay. The landscape was clearly lit by the moonlight and somehow the fort was above the fog, which now lay all around below like a sea of cotton wool, making the next headland invisible, although she could clearly make out the central hill of the island, where a scattering of lights shone yellow in windows.

The scene was insubstantial and eerie, a children's fairy story illustration. It made her feel spooked and incredibly alone. Telling herself not to be silly, she went through to the kitchen and foraged for tea bags and a mug. Ugh. He had told her that a cleaning woman came once a week. Once an hour was what Quinn needed! Then she returned to the living room and sat in a big armchair thinking.

Yesterday had been a day she was unlikely to forget. Not that much had actually happened. Yet Quinn had a capacity for investing everything around him with drama, or at least a sense of the intriguing. So when the lunchtime white wine at the pub had mellowed his mood, and the warm sun out in the garden made them both a little drowsy, he had told her about a whole catalogue of island 'characters' whom she was going to meet: and who sounded suspiciously like the supporting cast of his life.

It seemed a good moment to raise the subject of her hidden agenda. Quinn might react badly to his not being the sole reason for her coming, but she had to risk that.

'There's one thing I would like to do while I'm here,' she had said 'no rush or anything. My uncle may have lived here for a time after the war. He must have died long ago: my mother completely lost track of him. I know terribly little about my mother's family. Perhaps I could look him up in the parish records.'

'I suppose we could.' Quinn had been every bit as unenthusiastic as she had feared. He didn't like anything that threatened his own centre-stage position. 'On Monday maybe. The vicar's pretty busy at weekends.'

'Which you know from personal observation?' Somehow she couldn't help being sardonic. He was about as likely to be found in church as at the Women's Institute.

Quinn had bridled. 'You know damn well it isn't. I'm not a Jesus freak.' Then he relented. 'The vicar is pretty approachable, though. Needs to be in a place like this.'

She had apologised and further softened her crack about religion by adding tritely 'I'm glad you've found such a nice place to live.'

'For both of us to live.'

'We'll have to see. I've only just arrived, my love.'

Why did Quinn always have to rush his fences? He only ended up getting hurt. And why had she gone and called him 'my love' when she didn't mean it?

At that moment a girl in jeans and a 'Victoria and Albert' tee shirt had broken the tension by bringing their food.

After lunch Quinn had driven her around the rest of the island, stopping near the south cliffs for a stroll along a cliff path. The path led through bright yellow blossoming gorse and tall cow parsley, while the turf edges of the cliff were thick with wildflowers; giant daisies, rock samphire, sea campion and exotically red and purple flowered 'kaffir figs', their fleshy dark green leaves carpeting the ground. Anna had been delighted at this lush, almost tropical flowering.

'I never imagined anything like this.' she had said happily.

'We have a micro-climate here, on the edge of the Mediterranean zone, even though we're hundreds of miles north.'

But at the same time she had not been able to help noticing what looked like a concreted trench close to the bank of flowers, and they had passed all kinds of half-buried grey concrete shapes amongst the undergrowth, which she realised must have been German.

'Bunkers.' Quinn had admitted grudgingly. 'All over the bloody place.'

There was a simple wooden bench set on top of one these cliff top emplacements, bearing a small plaque commemorating someone who had loved the view, and they had paused to gaze across the sea towards France themselves.

'If it's like this again tomorrow,' she had said 'I must come here sketching. We could bring a picnic.'

'Unfortunately I have to spend the morning with Queen Victoria.' Quinn had grimaced, making a show of deploring such hack work, 'I can give you a map, though.'

'I liked that bay with the causeway and fort. I might go there.' She wouldn't have to draw the concrete wall.

On the way back Quinn had driven up a steep hill overlooking that same bay, from where they could see the whole end of the island, with the lighthouse at the tip. There had been yet another Victorian military looking building atop the hill; though a more domesticated one.

'The Monastery' Quinn had explained, 'not that it ever was one. There's a lot of legend here. It's apartments now.' He had pointed down to the fort in the bay, with its long causeway approach snaking out through the sea. 'That fort you liked is Drake Castle. Sir Francis Drake was supposed to have anchored here after defeating the Spanish Armada in the Channel. Don't imagine he did for a moment, but there is the site of an Elizabethan gun position on the bay and a sunken galleon out to sea, so it's a natural for a historical picture.'

'In the series?' Anna had prompted tactfully this time, doing her best.

'People really go for period costumes.' He had become unaffectedly enthusiastic. 'And as there are no contemporary records I can invent what I like. The bay's named after Drake too. It was the island's original harbour, in Roman times.'

'I'll come up here, then.' she had decided, gazing down at the squat stone fort in the bay, at the clear water around the rocks and the long curve of the grey concrete wall, with sand dunes piled up behind it. 'It makes a marvellous composition.'

'You could walk it from Rocquaine in 20 minutes.'

Quinn had pointed out the low outline of his home, just visible across the other side of the island, to the left of and beyond a hill with a monstrous concrete tower on its top. She had wondered what the tower was, guessed it belonged to the Nazi era and held off asking in case she upset him.

Overall she was beginning to feel that the wartime past hung over the whole island like a shadow. Those grey bunkers crouched half-concealed like primeval monsters in the undergrowth, while lookout points and gun positions were still dominating the landscape they had originally been built to defend.

'Or I can drive you up here.' Quinn had added. 'There's a caff at the bottom where you could get something to eat.'

'I'll take sandwiches' she had said, recording a mental picture of where everything was so she would not get lost. She noticed with a slight sense of foreboding that the distant coast of France, so clearly outlined before, had now vanished. A low bank of fog lay across the calm sea, which had become a pearly colour, merging into the hazy sky, leaving no discernible horizon. She had felt a sudden, irrational, fear that the fog would drift in and swallow them both up.

'That's the trouble with these early summer days.' Quinn had explained 'The air is warm, but the sea's still very cold, so the moisture in the air condenses into fog over the water.'

'Quite peculiar.'

Anna had not been much interested in the meteorological explanation, but was fascinated by its results. A yacht which had been sailing out there in bright sunshine a moment ago abruptly disappeared, as if snatched away from the world.

'Horrid for sailors.' she said.

'The locals made a living for centuries off wrecks on the rocks. Not that radar makes much difference. Every now and then a drunken crew steams straight into the island. Either drunk or fast asleep. There was a ship hit right by the lighthouse itself a few years ago. On a clear night, too. Shall we go home?'

35

That evening Anna had found herself offering to help with dinner and, inevitably, cooking it.

'Living alone hasn't made you any more organised.' she had commented, almost as a knee-jerk reaction, although the apartment was not as untidy as it might have been.

'I get by. The Lindsay's housekeeper "does" for me.'

After they had eaten he had tried, as she had known he would, to start a replay of their lunchtime conversation, saying how they ought to get together again, this was the ideal place to make a fresh start, surely she felt the same way or she would never have come? 'Etc, etc' she thought.

'Please Quinn,' she had tried to be firm, 'don't rush me.'

But when they were clearing up she had unintentionally brushed against him, her breast briefly touching his arm. He had stopped, still holding a wineglass in each hand, gently held his encumbered arms upright around her and kissed her hair.

'You're more lovely than ever.' he had said, then swung away to put the glasses down, leaving her feeling physically disoriented, her stomach a jelly, her mind a blur. 'I love you, darling.' He had come back beside her. 'I always have done. I love you and I want you. Most terribly.'

'Not tonight, Quinn,' she had insisted. 'Not all at once. Softly, softly. We have a whole week.' She knew all his old routines of seduction. In a way she loved him for them, but sleeping with him was not going to be a foregone conclusion. No, no, no.

'If you say so.' he had agreed, with rather a bad grace, and had eventually showed her to the little guestroom, catching her one last time in the doorway and kissing her on the lips.

'Goodnight, Quinn.' she had returned the kiss briefly, then pushed him away and closed the door.

Having finished her mug of tea, Anna went back to bed and slept fitfully until after seven, when she got up and pottered around, wondering if Quinn was still as reluctant to rise as he used to be. He always dressed up his laziness as needing to 'refresh the spirit', which wouldn't have fooled a schoolboy, let alone a wife.

She stood by the long windows gazing down at the carpet of fog, hoping it would clear when the sun's warmth developed, so that she would be able to go sketching. But it seemed to be doing the opposite, gradually embracing more of the hillside until, quite suddenly, it enveloped the fort itself and she could see nothing.

Surely this fog must clear! Perhaps Quinn would blow it away, she joked to herself. After all, he did only want her to see the light and cheerful aspects of 'his' island, like the flowers and the pub and the bright sunny landscapes.

The long moans of the foghorn continued, inexorable, unstoppable, the very voice of despair.

This was an island of extraordinary contrasts. Those forbidding cliffs contrasted with the pretty pastel-painted Georgian cottages in the town, just as the German bunkers did. She realised that Quinn would have liked to prevent her seeing the Nazi legacy, half-concealed though most of it now was, lurking like ghosts, and she wondered if new houses had been built on top of bunkers too. How could you hope to hide such grim evidence of the past? When would Hitler's Reich become mere history, like Napoleon? In a hundred years? In a thousand years? Did concrete ever decay?

She remembered reading how during the Napoleonic wars nannies used to frighten errant children by warning 'Boney will get you!' But at least Boney built magnificent memorials, the Arc de Triomphe among them. The Greeks had built magnificently throughout their ancient world colonies, the Romans even more so. But Hitler's legacy? Ugh. There ought to be a moral in this somewhere, could it be a Christian one of forgive thine enemies? Did she believe in that herself? Her thinking was becoming muddled. Would she herself forgive and forget if she had been born on this island? Perhaps with a little help from a bulldozer.

She was speculating somewhat philosophically about all this, but restless for the day to begin, when she noticed a small magazine on a coffee table. It was called the 'Island Journal' and was illustrated with rather grainy black and white photographs.

The picture on the front showed a group of sober-suited people, including three priests in their robes, standing in prayer by a wide stone memorial, decked with flowers, which she recognised, though she was not sure where they had driven past it. The caption beneath the picture read 'WARTIME MARTYRS REMEMBERED'. She flicked through the pages to find the story.

'Only four of the surviving wartime slave labourers have been fit enough to make their annual pilgrimage to the island this year for the service on Sunday. But the welcome for them will be as warm as ever, with a service at the memorial to commemorate those who died here (last year's ceremony pictured) and a *Vin d'Honneur* at the Island Centre.'

The youngest survivor would now be in his mid-70s, Anna calculated. Eventually the pilgrimage must peter out. Perhaps, she speculated, that would be the moment when the recent past fell off the shelf and did become 'history'. Suddenly it occurred to her that perhaps the service was why the old man on the boat had come.

The article also took her mind back to the mystery of her uncle and when he could have been here. During the war? Hardly, because he would only have been 18. Perhaps soon after? And what had he been doing? The solicitor who told her about this uncle, when going through her mother's will, had been distressingly vague.

She had not even known she had an uncle until after her mother's death, three months ago, let alone that her mother had been born in Germany, not England. The shock of this discovery had not been made less by the way the nervous young solicitor had explained it to her.

'Er, Mrs Quinn,' he had said, facing her across an antique mahogany desk, which could have been his grandfather's in the small town law firm, and fingering his striped club tie. 'There is something else she wanted you to be told. It may come as a bit of a surprise.'

She had burst into tears when he explained.

Her mother had been sent to England as a child refugee from Hitler's Germany just before the war. She was adopted by the English family she was housed with after they learnt that both her parents had died in a concentration camp, incarcerated because they were politically opposed to Nazism. When her mother married an Englishman she had apparently decided to airbrush out her origins. For good domestic reasons, Anna now realised.

Anna's adopted grandfather had served in the British army during the war, fought in North Africa, come home with a ration of medals and a shattered knee. To his dying day he regarded the Germans as 'bloody krauts'. She herself had grown up to regard her grandfather's attitudes with tolerant amusement; like many of his generation he didn't exactly hate the Germans, but he certainly didn't like them. Anyway she was still a teenager when he died and Britain had joined the European Union. The war was the past.

The solicitor had fumbled with some other documents. One day he would learn how to deal with the bereaved. He had not learnt yet.

'Your mother wanted you to have these after her death.' he said and handed two items across the desk.

One was a letter on coarse and discoloured paper from the International Red Cross, unevenly typed on an old machine, deeply regretting to inform Mr and Mrs Ryrie that the parents of their foster child Anna had died in the Sachsenhausen concentration camp in August 1944. The other was an old photograph, in black and white and slightly out of focus, of a boy in uniform with close cropped hair and the bland features of a teenager, standing stiffly at attention between his parents.

The letter, which was dated in November 1947, had taken the breath right out of Anna's body, leaving her totally confused.

The Red Cross official had added that the family's neighbours said the son Johann had disappeared when his parents were arrested in 1942. It was assumed he had been called up into the army, as he was nearly 16. The next year the neighbours had received a postcard from a former school friend of Johann's saying, in very guarded language, that they were both on the same island. The neighbours had since lost the postcard, but remembered about the island, which had a strange name.

Anna had sat in the solicitor's office and read the letter twice, then once again. So she had a totally unknown relation; an uncle who had survived the war and been in the island where Quinn had inherited a cottage. If he had been 16 or 17 in the war he might still be alive today. He could be. As an old man.

So why hadn't her mother tried to find him? Perhaps it was too expensive. After her father had been killed in a car crash they had been very badly off. He had not been adequately insured and the blame for the accident was disputed. They could no longer afford a car, her mother had to get a routine job as a secretary and Anna had to wear second hand school uniforms. Maybe that was the reason.

Then again, perhaps her mother hadn't tried to find out because she would hardly have remembered her older brother and was just not interested. But surely when your parents had died in the gas chambers and you had no other relations, surely then your brother must be worth locating, even if he had been ten years older? Perhaps he had been the family black sheep. There were too many 'perhaps's'. And no relations to discuss them with.

The unfortunate young solicitor was embarrassed by Anna's questions and fumbled for answers. He had been given this task because the inheritance involved was miniscule and it was useful practice for a junior. The sooner the interview was over, the better, so far as he was concerned.

This was the real reason why, when Quinn had pressed her to make the trip, Anna had agreed. She wanted to find out about this mystery uncle before it was too late, before he was likely to be dead, even knowing how much Quinn might resent her search.

Sadly Quinn clearly was going to resent it. He was so dreadfully single-minded, concentrating passionately on whatever dominated his thinking at the time. This characteristic could be flattering and exciting if it was all about her; but it could also be scary, which was why she had engineered an escape clause.

And if she was honest with herself, she already knew she would not want to stay on with Quinn, though she dared not tell him. Not while she was here. She would say so later in a letter, cowardly though that was. Her mind was still buzzing around all this, and over whether she minded being half German herself, when Quinn appeared, dressed only with a towel around his middle.

'Have you been up long?' he asked, as if her being up when he himself was not constituted some kind of transgression, an infringement of his rights.

'I couldn't sleep. It was the foghorn.'

'Well, we'd better have some breakfast.'

'Let me do it.'

How obvious Quinn's hints were and how easy it was to fall back into the old ways, although in fact she preferred to do the cooking! And Quinn responded, as he always used to, by going off to get washed and dressed. She wondered how often he cut his new beard. That was not a task she would be volunteering for. He had heavy complexes about his appearance.

After breakfast she insisted on going sketching, which seemed to relieve him. He muttered something about Lavinia being along soon to check up on his progress, so he ought to do some work. Anna made no comment, not at all sure that she wanted to encounter his dominatrix widow yet. She felt certain that Lavinia would do her best to spoil this visit. Then, with miraculous timing, the fog began to clear.

An hour or so later Quinn drove her up to the Monastery on the hill and dropped her off there. She took a small picnic basket, with a bottle of mineral water, her sketching pad and box of watercolours. She preferred to be self-reliant, insisting there was no need for him to fetch her from the restaurant at the bottom of the hill later, she would find her own way back.

When they set out the fog seemed to be almost gone, but from the top of the hill the horizon of the sea was still obscured by haze and almost indistinguishable from the sky. Then, as inexplicably as before, the fog rolled in again across the bay below, not a solid bank, but in drifting wraiths.

Never mind. Anna told herself 'it's still beautiful up here.' She settled down to draw the bay, using the top of a drystone wall to support her pad. Yet, although she could fill in details bit by bit as the fog shifted, the light was different and curiously tricky. There were not the same helpful contrasts of light and shade as there had been the previous afternoon, when the sun was behind her. There was also more going on around the long concrete wall behind the bay than there had been. Men were working on the wall. She was not very good at drawing people, much better at landscapes or buildings, so she only roughed in the tiny figures, who were anyway ant-sized in the distance.

After she had completed her sketch, she drank some water, and allowed herself to think about last night. She had so nearly ended up in bed with Quinn: much too nearly. She must keep her distance. Otherwise she would fall back under his old spell and make promises she would regret. Quinn certainly did possess a dangerous allure and she speculated on how far it was attracting Lavinia. If there was one thing she abhorred, it was a man who tried to keep two women at the same time. She would not have made a successful Mormon.

When she had finished she packed everything back into the basket and began to walk away from the Monastery towards the cliffs. Quinn had told her there was a cliff path. In practice there were several paths through the gorse and bracken, none wider than sheep tracks.

Her eye was caught by a delightful valley of hayfields, with woods at its foot, over to her right, though there were a lot of ugly concrete remnants up here too. Skirting round them she reached the edge of the field, encompassed by a low and largely broken-down stone wall. The patchy sunlight was where she needed it now, half behind her. She settled down, again using the wall as a support, and began to sketch this unexpectedly rural scene. The island had very little countryside in the usual sense, of farms and pastures, woods and streams.

Then there was a minor intrusion on the landscape. A man was trudging slowly along the far edge of the field, by the wall, his back bent. He was exactly what her composition needed, the labourer in the vineyard, the human who adds point to the story. She sketched him as best she could before losing sight of him, then went on drawing.

'You make pictures?'

The man had come up behind here unobserved and his voice so startled her that she dropped her sketching pad, her thoughts jumped to mugging or rape, and she scrambled round, ready to scream for help. Then she realised who he was.

It was the old man from the boat, in the same worn and shiny leather jacket and flat cap. He backed away immediately, seeming as frightened as she herself had been a moment before.

'I am sorry' he said in his accented and awkward English, 'I have not meant.' He bent down to pick up her pad and return it to her, a gesture which cost him effort, as though he suffered from arthritis, and glanced at her drawing before handing it back. 'Is good! Is your work?'

'Yes.' Then she realised he was not so much asking if she had done it herself, but whether painting was her profession. 'I am an art teacher.' she explained. 'How odd meeting you again.'

'For me also'.

'Unexpected, I mean.' Anna flushed, embarrassed and wondering how much English he really understood. She no more owned the cliff walks than he did. But he did seem unsure of what he was doing.

'I learn English in night school.' he said, reading her thoughts. 'But not so good.'

'You have been here before?' she asked, trying to mask her initial surprise and alarm with politeness. He was really quite a harmless old man. And she felt as though she already knew him from the ship, even though they spoken so little.

'Correct.' he agreed in the same heavy accent. 'I look for cliff.'

'That's what I was going to do.' she pointed. 'The cliffs are over there.'

'Yes.' he echoed her with worried seriousness. 'I think I am in wrong place.'

Without actually agreeing to go with him, Anna picked up her basket and ambled alongside the old man away from the field, following a track through the bracken in the direction of the cliffs. She was only wearing sandals and the undergrowth scratched her feet. But she felt an odd certainty that she must accompany him, that she somehow had to. The fog started to drift in up here, drifts of it obscuring where exactly the cliffs were, although she occasionally caught sight of a gull, wheeling and soaring above, telling her that they were close.

As they walked she tried to make helpful conversation, discovering that his name was Tadeus, and his friends called him Tad, but learning little else. He moved cautiously, as though the path was hazardous, and kept looking to either side. Then, abruptly, he gripped her arm. His grip was not strong, but insistent.

'It is bad here. Very dangerous.' he said, pointing in apparent fear at a red-painted sign on a pole sticking out of the bracken.

The sign bore a skull and crossbones, with underneath the words 'Rodent control.' and a warning in smaller letters saying 'poison' and advising that dogs should be kept on a leash. She could feel Tad shaking at the sight of it and his hold on her arm intensified.

'It's only against rats.' She assured him.

'Shhh.' He put a finger to his lips.

At this moment a rabbit, which must have been sitting tight in the undergrowth, bolted out of the bracken and down the path ahead.

'Halt! We go back.' Tadeus tried to pull her back the way they had come. He kept muttering 'meenen', which she did not understand. He absolutely would not walk past the skull and crossbones sign. She thought he must be ill and decided the best

43

thing to do was to take him down to the café by the bay, where he would be able to sit down and have a hot drink.

But when she tried to guide him towards the Monastery and the road – or rather where she thought the Monastery must be, because the fog was closing in fast – he was again reluctant.

'Is danger.' He insisted. 'We cannot go'.

'Don't be silly.' she became annoyed. Why all this drama? After all, it was he who had approached her, interrupting her painting. Now, as the fog thickened, she began to feel shivery and strangely alone. 'I came up that way.' she said crossly 'It's perfectly safe.'

The sharpness of her tone seemed to bring him round, like a cold douche, freeing him from some personal nightmare.

'You think?' he asked, anxiously.

'I know. And I don't want to get lost in the fog either.'

She took his arm firmly in a reversal of the way he had been grasping hers and guided him back along tracks to the road and so to the hill. Walking down, they emerged into a clear space below the fog, which had lifted a little, although strands of it were still blowing around the fort at the end of the causeway, while the long concrete wall was in hazy sunlight.

She noticed without particularly thinking about it that the men she had seen working there had all left. Probably their lunch break, she thought. The only people were a family on the beach, whose children were playing and building a sandcastle.

Tad made her halt halfway down the hill, while he gazed at the partially shrouded bay below, as if being granted some divine revelation.

'Have you been here before?' Anna asked, feeling slightly ridiculous at playing the guide when she knew so little.

'Is called Long Bay, I think.'

'I thought it was Drake's Bay.'

'I not right, perhaps.'

But he sounded unconvinced and she saw that something about the landscape fascinated him; in fact more than that, held him spellbound. He just stood there on the grass verge of the road looking down at the bay and muttering to himself. Eventually he agreed to continue and they reached the restaurant.

The Drake Manor restaurant was a single storey building, clearly adapted from an old barn, but with a courtyard garden cascading with flowers both on trellises and in huge pots. Anna guided Tad to a table and tactfully offered to get him something. When they had talked on the boat yesterday he had sounded decidedly hard up. 'I wait to have money.' he had said, in his heavily accented central European voice and the awkward phrase had stayed in her mind. Luckily she had enough cash with her, although he asked only for coffee and she had to talk him into having a ham sandwich.

He was dreadfully thin. Accepting the ham meant that he could not be Jewish, which she had thought he might have been. A vague theory about him was creeping into her mind; a theory which she wasn't at all sure that she liked.

'What is your friend?' he asked politely, when the coffee had been brought, 'I see him by harbour.'

'Oh, he's an artist, too.' She smiled. 'A serious one. You?'

'Me?' Tad seemed surprised at being asked. 'I am pensioner. I work machine tool factory in Poland. Foreman.' he added with pride. 'I can pay for visit.'

'Poland's a long way. Are you on holiday? '

Tad gave this question careful consideration. 'I have money for one week.' he eventually said, unemotionally.

After a little sympathetic prompting, because conventional small talk seemed all wrong in the context, and anyway difficult, he told her that he had saved three years for this trip. It had been hard to do on an eastern European pension when prices here were so high.

'My wife agree. She is Olga.'

As before, he spoke with such intensity that she could not help regarding him analytically, as a nurse might a patient. This time he did not remind her so much of an old tramp as he had on the boat. True, he had the same worry and work-worn pale skin, the same crinkled old man's neck with its V of tendons straddling his Adam's apple. But in his eyes and the set of his mouth there were determination and spirit. Something really is going on inside there, Anna thought. But what?

'Olga agree.' Tad repeated quietly, in a tone which made her understand just how much the visit must be costing them in material terms. 'I stay in guest house.'

'You have no friends?' Somehow she had assumed he would have some contacts.

He shook his head. 'I have name.' He dug into his pocket for a leather wallet, shiny with age, and removed a slip of paper. 'Mackinnon' he said, experiencing great difficulty with the pronunciation. 'You know him?'

'I'm afraid I don't know anyone here, except Quinn.'

'He help me?'

'What with?' As she spoke Anna knew she had fallen into a trap, not a deliberate one, in fact a totally innocent one, but a trap just the same. 'Quinn's very busy this week.'

Her reaction sounded mean and unwelcoming, which she had not intended, even though it was doubly justified. Quinn was inherently unlikely to respond to the old man, while the Queen Victoria painting was a looming threat to his time. Lavinia again!

'I look for something.' Tad said apologetically. 'Mackinnon help.' Evidently he was relying on whoever this Mackinnon person was.

'What exactly are you looking for?'

'Where I was. But is not same.'

'And you came all the way from Poland? It must be very important.'

She was probing unashamedly now, because intuition told her that the old man was researching the past in a way that might parallel her own prospective search.

He placed his cup down very carefully on the saucer, as though the coffee was precious and he feared to spill any. 'Is important, yes. Before too old I find out.'

'Find out what?'

'A friend die. May be my...' he struggled and found the wrong word, 'problem. I think so. I no remember.'

'How dreadful.' her reaction sounded trite, but it was not intended to be. 'You really don't know?'

For a moment she could not imagine being unsure about a thing like death. Then she thought of mountaineers losing their grip and fellow climbers, roped to them, falling also; of speedboats hitting swimmers; of fatal mistakes in hospitals. Such things happened all the time. You only had to read the tabloids.

'Strangely enough,' she said, again aware that she might be making a commitment of which Quinn would disapprove, 'I'm looking for something too. My uncle lived here once. I want to know when. And where.'

'Ah.' His interest was aroused, then as quickly diminished again. 'Not be the same time. Not the war'

'It might have been.'

'I think no. I was in war.'

'Oh.' Now she was seriously taken aback. Quinn emphatically would not want her to be involved. 'Well, I might help you find Mackinnon.'

'And you walk with me sometime again?'

Anna's natural generosity made it impossible to refuse.

'Alright,' she agreed, 'I will tomorrow, so long as I can stop to make sketches.'

'Thank-you' he said gravely.

How on earth she was going to explain this to Quinn she did not know. She wrote down the name of Tad's guest house, left him to take the afternoon bus back to the town, and began the walk to Rocquaine, her head buzzing. What on earth had she let herself in for?

When she reached the fort she realised that the fog had vanished as mysteriously as it had crept in.

CHAPTER FIVE

Returning to the fort, Anna heard voices as she walked up the sloping lawn above the wide interior courtyard, once a parade ground for soldiers. At the door of the studio apartment she called out tactfully 'Are you there, Quinn?' already knowing who she was going to find with him.

'We're through here.' came Quinn's voice, sounding less than at ease.

She continued through the vast sitting room and up the half flight of steps to the studio overlooking the battlements where he painted, bracing herself mentally for the encounter. At least he's not trying to hide Lavinia under the bed, she thought, catching sight of the intruder's reflection in the full length studio mirror and realising with a slight shock that this was not the overweight, dumpy, middle-aged busybody she had imagined. Not in the least. If the mirror on the wall told the truth, Lavinia was tall and elegant, straight out of a fashion magazine for elderly women.

When Anna entered they were both standing in front of the Queen Victoria picture on its paint-spattered easel, either absorbed by details or else pretending to be. Propped up on a hardback chair was a print similar to the one in the Victoria and Albert pub. Lavinia turned to face her, looking haughtily surprised, as an actress playing a 'grande dame' might.

Lavinia was undeniably impressive. She had thick, carefully coiffured white hair, a high cheek-boned face, albeit drawn slightly tight from the facelift and with a touch too much compensatory make-up. She was wearing a tailored linen suit which talked a lot about money and might have just returned from morning church and be on the way to a lunch party. She smoothed the jacket down over her hips and let her hands linger there, while she looked Anna up and down.

'May I introduce you to Anna.' Quinn cut in, with nervous and uncharacteristic formality. 'Anna, this is Lavinia Wildeblood.'

'How nice to meet you.' Lavinia said, her palms still resting on her hips in a genteel version of a fishwife's arms akimbo confrontation. 'I've just brought our poor dear artist a little refreshment.' Anna now noticed a slender-necked bottle of hock on a table. 'He does need looking after, you know. Well, all men of course, but artists especially.''

Holding back an impulse to reply 'pleased to meet you, too' in a deliberately common voice, Anna held out her hand. 'Quinn's told me all about you.' she said. Two could play at being patronising.

'Would you like a drink?' Quinn intervened hastily, noticeably not calling her 'darling', and pouring a glass of wine as he spoke.

You bloody so and so, Anna thought, and again had to restrain herself, this time from demanding a gin and tonic, which he would have had to leave the room to fetch.

'So you were Quinn's wife?' Lavinia asked, a chilly smile on her face, a totally unconvincing and thin smile.

'Am, actually.'

There was dead silence. Anna met Quinn's eyes, saw only irresolution in them, and felt completely hollow inside herself, defeated and stupid in front of this usurping woman. How could he have begged her to come, protest his undying love, tried to bed her; and then reveal this?

'We're very definitely still married, aren't we darling?' Anna threw Quinn a lifeline, gave him a final chance. This was the moment when he had to be honest or it really was all over; the moment when all the hundred or more widows on the island learnt that he was not up for grabs. Or else that he was.

'Of course we are.' Quinn said, though it sounded a reluctant admission, rather than a positive affirmation, and Anna really did not know if she was relieved or sorry. He turned to Lavinia, wearing his schoolboy confession look. 'Anna's come across to see if we can't get together again.'

'I see.' Lavinia said in a chiselled voice, clearly implying that she saw nothing of the sort. 'Well, my dear, you have a very talented artist on your hands. We're lucky to have him here. I hope you're not going to whisk him away again.'

'Quinn's career matters a lot to me.' Did it? Well, so far as this bitch was concerned it did.

'And to all of us.' Lavinia's permafrost smile melted a degree or two. 'I was so pleased to be able to arrange this important commission from the President.' She emphasised the adjective 'important', immediately using it again. 'Sensitivity to the island's historical ethos is so important, don't you agree? Empathetic ethos' she turned to Quinn, 'your guiding principle.'

'I'm sure it is.' Anna focussed on the fresh brushwork of the painting and saw that Quinn was copying every last detail of the print. There was no touch of originality present. 'Do you help him with reference material?' she asked innocently.

'Lavinia is Chairperson of the Heritage Committee.' Quinn cut in.

'Chair and Founder.' Lavinia corrected him. 'None of the islanders understood how much was at risk before. Centuries of history. All they ever want is more bungalows. They're almost as destructive as the Germans.'

Having thus established her own status, she launched into none too tactful probing. 'I suppose you feel the same way as we do about the Germans – not that we're supposed to say so nowadays.'

'As it happens my mother was German.'

'You never told me that!' Quinn was visibly alarmed. 'I thought your mother was English!'

'No, Quinn. She was sent to England as a child, just before my grandparents were sent to a concentration camp. She was six at the time.'

'You mean your family was Jewish?' Lavinia became incredulous. A German Jew, she was thinking, Oh my God!

'No. Just German.' Having had the pleasure of shocking Lavinia to the core, Anna kept careful control of herself. 'My grandparents were against Hitler. My mother never saw them again. She was given asylum and later adopted by an English family. When she was grown up she married my father, who was English, of course. For reasons I don't know, she never told me.' But what had those reasons been? Shame? Who knew? It was none of this woman's damn business anyway.

'My dear,' Lavinia sought salvation in condescension, 'what a simply awful story.'

'After my Mother's death the solicitor told me I had an uncle and that he'd been here at some time.' To emphasise the point, she added. 'My uncle was here, Quinn. Here in this island. And I never even knew he existed.'

'There were only Germans here in the war.' Quinn insisted 'All the islanders were evacuated in 1940.'

'My uncle was a German. Remember? '

Lavinia's permafrost returned. 'Well this is a morning of revelations!' she said, as if trying to reconcile herself to bad news, whilst keeping a safe distance from it. 'And now you're trying to find out!' She tut-tutted. 'I suppose he was a Nazi?'

'I told you,' Anna bit back her anger, 'my family hated the Nazis. Anyway my uncle would only have been a teenager. He probably came here after the war.' She decided to skewer this appalling hypocrite. 'You must remember the 1940s well, Mrs Wildeblood. Things must have been pretty hard for the women.'

'My dear, I was hardly born. In any case, I'm not an islander.' Lavinia gave her a furious look and told Quinn she must be going. 'A little more research is needed on those costumes,' she gestured at the painting, 'otherwise it's coming on quite well.' As a parting slap in the face to Anna she added 'I'm afraid the Germans aren't everybody's favourites here.'

After she had gone Anna reached for her glass of wine. 'So that's your patron! What a pain.'

'Did you have to be so foul?'

'Did she? Anyone would think I had swastikas all over my face like chicken pox. And she despises the islanders, when one of them's worth ten of her. She's an absolute "grockle" herself.'

'How do you know that word?'

'I saw a sticker on a car. It seems to mean gawping tourist. When did she come here?'

'About ten years ago. For God's sake, Anna. She gets me work. Don't you dare antagonise her.'

'And she tries to treat the Occupation as a non-event. Which is why you do. What a crassly silly party line to take! History is history is history. It happened. You can't change it. And as for being born after the war!'

'What's that to do with it?' Quinn protested, and then weakened. A man should never get between two women quarrelling. If he does, they will both inevitably turn on him: rule numero uno in the wise man's self-preservation handbook. 'Alright, she is older than she looks.' He admitted. 'Her husband died four years ago.'

'Another honourable tax evading settler?'

Quinn's cheeks coloured. 'Stop it, you're being a bitch.'

'And she's suffering from what Simone de Beauvoir called "The ridiculous problem of how to kill time". So she kills it with committees. We have widows like her in Brighton too, always interfering and scheming because they have nothing else to do, in other words no men.'

'Stop it!' Quinn began to shout. 'You're being a bitch and Lavinia means well.'

'That's pretty rich after what she just said. What would she have done if I was a Jew as well as a German? Fainted? Thrown up?' She glared at him. 'Don't tell me she means well, either. You're a virile, good-looking man and she's got you nicely in hand. Or imagines she has. The last thing she wants is a wife appearing out of the woodwork. I suppose you told her we were divorced?'

Quinn burst out laughing, a poseur's laugh, but effective. 'I do believe you're jealous!' he took Anna by the shoulders and looked straight into her eyes, while she tried to dodge him, but couldn't free herself. 'By God, I believe you are.' he said, with sudden gentleness.

Still holding her tightly, he kissed her on the mouth. She could taste the wine on his lips. When she managed to push him away, she was more disconcerted than angry, realising that Quinn really did love her. Damn the bloody widow.

'Have you slept with her?'

'With Lavinia? Don't be absurd.'

'Have you?' Lavinia had been far too protective of her protege. 'She's not bad looking, facelift or no facelift.'

'No my love, I have not!' Quinn almost succeeded in convincing himself that he wouldn't have wanted to. He gripped Anna's arm again. 'But for that I'm taking you to bed.'

'You most certainly are not.'

Anna knew that trick of old, it was one she had first fallen for years ago; the quarrel followed by the passion. And she was not at all sure that she believed his denials. Half of Quinn's world always had been fantasy: often beguiling, but largely invented.

'There's really nothing between you?' she demanded again.

'What if there was?' he was more relaxed now, prepared to challenge her, realising it was only a matter of time before she did come to bed. He let her go.

'I'd be on the next boat out.'

'Not the next flight? Fear of flying?'

'You are the original male chauvinist pig.' she said, well aware of his literary allusion and moving away to sit down on the sofa. 'The original.'

'And since when have you been a fan of Simone de whatnot?'

'Why shouldn't I be? You don't have to be a militant to be a feminist. The people I hang out with these days understand that.'

She didn't admit that she had only heard of de Beauvoir in those awful classes. Or say how her recent friends were more open-minded than the ones he used to have in Brighton. But that was what she meant, because Quinn had always kept her fenced into his own small social circle, which was absurd in a town where so much was going on.

'Wasn't she Sartre's girlfriend?

'So you do know who she was! Why do you have to put women down all the time?'

Anna choked back a retort about Lavinia being at the right intellectual level for him and changed the subject. 'I do seriously want to trace my uncle.'

Quinn sighed, facing a reality he would have preferred to avoid. 'Alright. We'll call on the vicar tomorrow.'

'There's something else too.' She might as well get everything over with at once. 'I met an old man today who came over on the same boat. He's someone who definitely was here in the war.'

'How did you meet him?' Quinn was suspicious at once..

'I was sketching. He was walking near that Monastery place. He's trying to find someone called Mackinnon. I said you were bound to know.'

'Yes, I know Jack.' Quinn seemed reluctant to admit this. 'He's the local expert on what happened in the war. At daggers drawn with Lavinia, as you can imagine.'

'I can. Presumably he knows a lot more than she does.'

'Got it in one. She just doesn't want to know about the Nazi occupation. For her it never took place. And I have to be on her side. No option. Cash. No pictures, no pounds.'

That was it, Anna reflected. Money. People said women would do anything for it. But men were worse.

'So what exactly did you promise this man?' Quinn demanded.

'To find Mackinnon and to go for another walk. He's about a hundred years old, for God's sake. You've nothing to get uptight about.'

'I thought,' Quinn said after a very deliberate pause 'that you came here to see me.'

'I did.' she almost added 'darling', to soften the situation, but stopped herself just in time. There was going to be no 'darling' about it until the Lavinia situation was clearer. 'So I did. But now you have your work with Lavinia, remember? This old man is trying to rediscover the past. Like me.'

Ridiculously this was becoming like a game in which outwitting your opponent was the aim. It was not what she had come here for.

'Do you have to help him?'

'No. But I'm going to try, because he's old and he's frail and he needs someone.'

Far from being understanding, Quinn put on his familiar expression of wounded sincerity, an expression which together with wordless grunts of displeasure made him infuriating at times. Could she possibly live with him again? Love him, perhaps. But live with him, that was quite another question. And hadn't she already decided anyway? But in the heart or in the head?

'You know something, Quinn.' She said, 'Women always fall in love with artists. But what they have to live with isn't the artist, it's the man. That's the problem.'

CHAPTER SIX

'Lucky we saw that.' Wolf whispered, as the shape of the big gun was momentarily revealed in the drifting mist, and they dropped flat on the path by the low stone wall.

'We <u>are</u> lucky.' Miki whispered back.

They badly needed to believe they were lucky after the near-miss with the mine. If they did not stay lucky they'd be finished, dead meat under the blows of rifle butts. If there was one skill these German guards had fully developed it was beating slaves senseless with the maximum amount of brutality and pain.

Not being inhibited by having any civilian population to observe them, because the entire population had been evacuated a week before the Germans arrived, the guards had lost any scruples they might have had as civilians themselves only a few years before. Although they despised this place as 'the arsehole of the world' they also took a sadistic pleasure in comparing it to Devil's Island, from which no prisoner had ever escaped and few returned.

The boys had known they must get back to the wooded valley soon: whatever happened they had to get away from the area of the little quarry before the fog lifted. Otherwise they would be trapped there until it was dark and they would have lost a whole day. Their bread would soon be finished. There was no water, except for stagnant puddles.

Worse still, they knew the guards with the dog would be back. Even Miki's common-sense realisation that the klaxons they had heard in the distance could not be due to their escape gave them no comfort. They could only guess that they had more luck than they knew.

Lying on the path, listening for what the soldiers might say, they tensed themselves to get up on their hands and knees before trying to retreat. The fog tendrils parted briefly and they saw the upper parts of the great gun again, its mountings cloaked in armour plate, its thick long barrel elevated, ready to fire. From the noises they heard they reckoned the crew of the gun, several soldiers at the least, were lounging around out of their sight, most likely sitting on groundsheets on the wet grass. The men must have moved up to the gun position while the boys were on the hill. But mercifully the gun itself was on the far side of the crumbling stone wall and the crew had not yet seen them.

They smelt coarse tobacco smoke and heard a man's guttural voice say 'Hear that bang a few minutes ago, Helmut? Just another damned rabbit most likely. No point going to look in this bloody fog.'

'Richtig.' the other answered 'What's the use of being on standby when you can't see a pig's arse at five metres. I'm going for a pee.'

The boys flattened themselves tight against the foot of the wall, hardly breathing, while the disgruntled gunner strolled towards it on the other side, unbuttoned his trousers and began pissing against the stones a few feet away, staring vacant-faced into the nothingness of the fog. Had he looked over the wall he could not have failed to spot them. But he was so concentrating on the physical relief of urinating that he saw nothing. Many a soldier has been shot by a sniper when his pants were down.

They heard the tiny splashing cease and caught an acrid whiff of urine. The soldier flicked the last drop off his penis, stuffed it back into his trousers with a grunt of satisfaction, and wandered off again towards his mates. When the boys next heard his voice he was much further away.

They crawled back up the path on their bellies and the moment the fog rolled across again stood upright and ran off into the field. Again they enjoyed tremendous good luck, almost tripping up over the roots of the first tree in the stunted row they were trying to find. From there it was simple to find the fence further down the slope and scramble across the overgrown bank down to the track and the stream. No-one challenged them. There was not a single soldier around.

Once in the valley they trudged along the narrow trickle of muddy water to wipe out their scent, heading downhill and away from the vehicle park, until they were satisfied that their trail could not be followed. The bank to their right had become higher and steeper and more densely overgrown. Staring at it they thought they saw a darker patch behind the underbrush and saplings and cautiously investigated. The patch was a hollow in what was actually a rock face, presumably part of yet another abandoned quarry.

'Looks okay.' Miki said. Wolf agreed. They would be able to see out through the curtain of vegetation, yet be hidden in deep shadow themselves. Except that it was away from any water, it was ideal.

The other snag was that they had no real plan, beyond waiting for the end of the day, when the working parties would have finished at 'certain death' and they might be able to worm their way to the end of the track and get past the bay. How to do it, they had no idea. They lay down and went to sleep on the damp leafmould which carpeted the recess.

While they slept the fog evaporated, though more quickly on the hill than around the bay where the slaves laboured, while it still hung over the pearly ocean in a low bank, as if waiting its chance to sweep in again and reclaim the island. The foghorn continued to moan its warning.

Gradually the sky brightened and became a clear blue, with only a few high clouds which did not interfere with the increasingly warm sunshine. Not that the sun penetrated to where the boys hid. With its overhang of trees, the valley was in permanent shadow.

Down by the wall Truppfuhrer Kranke had counted and recounted his squad, as though doing so would somehow make the numbers right again. He cursed his luck. His thirty men were not the only group of workers. There were more than a hundred in all, tasked to concreting different sections of the wall. When the supervisor came round at the start Kranke had confessed to his loss and been roundly sworn at.

'They won't get far, Mein Herr.' he had tried to assure his immediate supervisor, the Hauptruppfuhrer, but his boss only grunted and swore at him some more.

Both guards were relative juniors, despite their ages, in one of the most hierarchically structured organisations of Hitler's Third Reich – and the Third Reich was nothing if not hierarchical.

The labour organisation created for the Fuhrer by Dr Todt had many gradations of rank. Kranke himself had struggled for promotion from Vorarbeiter to Truppfuhrer by administering more beatings than his colleagues, because perceived merit was intertwined with brutality in all the camps the Organisation Todt ran, here or anywhere else in occupied Europe. But with two labourers missing, his past diligence counted for nothing. Supervisors could be reduced to workmen for less, exchange their khaki uniforms with the red swastika armbands for mere overalls.

'You will report to the Frontfuhrer in person at noon.' the Hauptruppfuhrer ordered. 'Today I will expect fifty percent more than the usual daily work. I will deal myself with the search for the criminals.'

Kranke knew this curt reprimand spelt inevitable demotion and punishment duty, because even with the fiercest beatings 28 men could not achieve one and a half times the normal work of 30. Even if their midday 'bunkersuppe' was denied them and they continued straight through the hour's break, it was impossible. But 'impossible' was not a word in favour here.

Then, just before eight, Kranke heard the klaxons again. Very soon word reached them that a ship loaded with 300 Russian slaves had hit rocks in the fog and sunk. All available men were called to the rescue of the German crew. This did not affect Kranke himself, but did result in the soldiers manning defences round the bay leaving hurriedly in trucks from the old farm barn that was the transport centre for Long Bay.

The Russians might drown and probably would, if they were locked in the holds as usual. That did not matter. They were only *Untermenschen*. German lives were a different matter. Within minutes the area of Long Bay was devoid of service personnel. With no-one to observe him, Kranke beat his slaves mercilessly with his cat-o-nine-tails, as if this would miraculously spare he himself from punishment.

Up in the wooded valley it was after midday when the boys were woken by a dog's growls. They sat up and listened. Then they saw an Alsatian through the foliage. And it saw them. It stopped growling and faced them through the bushes. When Miki made a move it instantly snarled disapproval and came closer.

'There will be a man.' Wolf whispered, causing the dog to bark. 'What do we do?' They could see it was muzzled, so could not bite, but if it barked surely a guard would come running.

Stay still.' Miki said, with more confidence than he felt, 'it has been trained to wait.' The master at his school used to have a shepherd dog to frighten off burglars and trained it that way..

They both tried to see more through the screen of fresh green leaves and tree branches, but while the foliage concealed the shallow cave, it equally obstructed their seeing out. Only if men came down the path would they have a decent chance of spotting movement. And none did.

For minute after long minute nothing happened. Miki tried moving forward a step. The dog growled viciously.

'Don't make it bark.' Wolf urged.

'I'm not a fool.'

The stand-off continued. Any movement set the dog going and at one time it did bark. Wolf tried to work out what was going through its mind. As Miki said, the dog's training must have been to hold suspects until its handler deal could with them. It would only attack if ordered. So where was the handler?

After about ten minutes, which felt like an hour, the Alsatian became impatient. Things were not proceeding as it expected. It looked round increasingly often and they noticed that there was a short length of frayed leather lead attached to its wide, studded, collar and to the thick brown leather muzzle

'Shit,' Miki said, 'the bastard broke away. There is no handler.' That meant there was no-one to call the dog off.

Hearing him, the Alsatian barked, as if in confirmation.

'He'll hear the noise. Wherever he is.'

Miki took no notice. 'Have you got the knife?' he asked.

Wolf felt for it in the patch pocket he had sewn inside his cement sack jerkin. It was a 15 centimetre kitchen knife that he had managed to steal in the camp, while Miki had purloined a length of thin wire and coiled it around his leg below the knee for concealment. Wire, like string, always had a use.

Wolf drew the knife out. The dog objected to the movement by snarling aggressively. It moved closer, sensing both trouble and the boys' nervousness.

'They can smell fear.' Miki said. 'You know how to use a knife?'

'I know.' Wolf said, trembling a little in spite of his nickname. He had never before used a blade for anything more bloodthirsty than skinning a rabbit, but he knew what was coming. He and Miki were two metres apart, on opposite sides of the cave. It was too dangerous to try passing the knife across, even to throw it to Miki, because the dog was gradually closing in. He would have to kill the dog himself, while Miki distracted it, which would mean acting extremely fast.

Miki examined the cave floor, methodically scanning the dead leaves and twigs for a weapon. Almost hidden by debris there was a small rock. He lowered himself into a crouching position, his eyes on the Alsatian, feeling blindly with his hand. The dog growled and tried to bark. Its instincts were accurate. Miki's left hand fumbled, gained a hold on the rock and he began rising to his feet. The rock was unexpectedly heavy and came close to unbalancing him. The dog either recognised what he had picked up, or felt threatened by the raised arm. It let out a furious snarl and sprang straight at his throat.

Still off-balance, Miki succeeded in slamming the rock on to the Alsatian's nose. It recoiled, but surged forward again. Wolf already had the kitchen knife in his hand and lunged forward to drive it into the side of the dog's neck. He felt the resistance of thick fur, then the tip penetrated and he thrust the blade in deep. Blood spurted everywhere.

After a terrible struggle the animal collapsed sideways Caught off balance, Wolf fell on top of it. The dog still struggled powerfully, pinioned by his body, while he desperately continued pushing on the knife and Miki rolled clear sideways. For a few seconds it tried to twist its head back and bite. Then Miki crashed the rock down its head again and it went limp.

Wolf struggled up and put one foot against the dog's neck to pull out the knife. The body twitched. The two boys staggered back, anxious to be out of the way in case it was not dead. Wolf's hands were covered with blood.

'Are you okay?' Miki asked.

'I think so.' Wolf began examining himself. His legs had been deeply scratched by the dog's claws, but he was basically unhurt.

They both sat down on the leaves, trembling and exhausted. The dog's corpse lay beside them. For several minutes they said nothing. From further up the valley came a voice, calling out and giving sharp whistles.

'Caesar. Hier! Caesar! War ist der verdamt hunde. Caesar kommt hier.'

The boys shifted themselves into the very back of the shallow cave and lay flat on the leafmould. They heard boots tramping the path and then more shouts for Caesar, which diminished as the handler passed down towards the barn and the bay. It was only one man, because there was just one voice.

'If he'd found us we'd have had to kill him too.' Wolf said.

'That is an idea.' Miki said reflectively. 'Jah.'

'Thank God he didn't stop. We'd better bury the dog.'

'First we eat. Give me the knife.' Taking it Miki discovered that the end had broken off against the dog's neck bones. Clumsily he sliced two chunks from the animal's haunches and trimmed off the fur and skin. It was difficult with a broken knife. Neither of them had tasted meat since being brought here.

Thanks to Kranke selling off half their miniscule rations their meals had consisted of coffee and bread at daybreak, half a litre of thin cabbage 'bunkersuppe' at midday at the work site, and another half litre in the evening. Occasionally they were given a sliver of sausage or cheese. Very occasionally. They never received the food the official records showed. So they had become used to devouring anything they chanced upon, from raw mussels to rotten turnip, gorging themselves and often becoming miserably ill within hours.

And to do that was perilous. If there were SS men around they shot any slave seen scrounging food.

The bleeding chunk of warm dog flesh was too much for Wolf. He forced himself to chew a slice, then spat out his second mouthful and retched. Miki swallowed his with bravado. This had been his idea. Their mouths and faces were now smeared with blood, as were their sacking clothes.

'Hey!' Miki said, greatly cheered up, 'we look like werewolves.'

'I'm going to wash in the stream.' Wolf said 'I've got to.'

'Fat lot of good walking through the water did us.' Miki commented. 'Didn't put the dog off at all. We'll have to bury it.'

They dug down into the earth floor of the cave with the knife and with their hands and managed to inter the Alsatian. The body took up an astonishing amount of space and the task took them an hour. Because the knife, broken and blunted, was now so little use they left it in the cave.

'Now what?' Wolf demanded, after he had risked going down to wash his face and hands in the stream.

'Wait for darkness. Or fog again.' Miki looked at him with a mischievously boyish, yet hardened, grin. 'Or a guard.' Their success with the dog had given him a definite idea.

CHAPTER SEVEN

'I'm afraid there is no trace of a Johann Eberhardt marrying or dying here since the war, Mrs Quinn'

The vicar pushed the last bulky leather bound volume of parish records aside. He was a tall, angular man, very thin, with a bony face and a smoker's rasping cough. His angularity was emphasised rather than concealed by his severe black cassock, buttoned high at the neck. But his appearance was misleading, because he had cheerfully undertaken this tedious and lengthy search through the registers.

The immediate post-war volume dated from when the first islanders had returned in 1945 after the occupation, but had yielded little. Alone among the entries was the marriage of one man with a German name to a local girl. That was all.

'If you've been to the Court offices there's really nowhere else to try, at least not on the island.' The vicar closed the book.

'I did warn you, sweetheart. 'Quinn said, with an undertone of self-satisfaction.

Trying to dig up information here had been like trying to catch handfuls of fog. Apparent facts shredded into allusions and gossip, to hesitations, then referrals to some other person 'who just might know' but never did.

'When we arrived to live here' the woman at the Court office had told Anna. 'we came to report our arrival and all my predecessor of that time said was "So what?" I don't think there were any electoral rolls until 1947 or 48.'

In spite of this, Anna insisted to the vicar that there must have been some records. Coming from an English county where everything had to be notified, not just birth, marriage and death, but countless other personal details, she could hardly believe there was nothing. Yet if the vicar's answer was unavoidably unhelpful, he did try to explain a few things something about the island.

He steepled his fingertips together, rested his elbow on the table around which they were sitting and began.

'By inheritance the islanders were smallholders, fishermen, privateers and wreckers. Survival was a struggle. The last thing they wanted was some official ferreting out information that might later be used by the Customs. Baptism and marriages and deaths were about the limit. That kind of traditional reticence dies hard.' he smiled at Anna. 'Except that each family's strips of land were meticulously marked on the maps and attributed to each family in rather flowery copperplate handwriting, because there are strict Norman inheritance laws and land had to be divided between sons. Beyond that, If what you did was done in the sight of God, that was enough and the devil take the bureaucrats.'

'How about this Mister Mackinnon?' Anna asked.

'Ah, I wondered if you'd ask. Jack Mackinnon is an original, a one man authority. He's our venerable Bede, our unofficial archivist of everything about the war and its aftermath. He is probably your best hope; if not your only one.'

'The island's guru,' Quinn cut in, 'as I told you.'

'Not the most accurate description', the vicar suggested, in a tone which implied he didn't much like Quinn. 'Your average guru is a sage, who gives guidance, for instance on what days or hours are most propitious for decision making. Jack would never claim such powers, but he does have a deep understanding of the human condition, which is rather more useful.'

'Anyway,' Quinn said, disliking being corrected, 'he's the best bet. Can we phone him? We're a bit short of time.'

This was untrue. Quinn simply wanted to get the quest over with and preferably have it fail, but Anna let that pass.

Half an hour later they were outside a low-built unpretentious, whitewashed cottage, set in a garden full of flowers and honeysuckle. A tiny orchard, its apple trees dappled with sunlight, was laid out to one side, beyond which lay a vista of the harbour and the sea. Baskets of pink geraniums hung on either side of the front door. Quinn touched the bellpush.

'This is like something out of a story about when life was good.' Anna exclaimed while they waited. 'It's gorgeous.' This typified the island she had hoped to find.

The door was opened by a white haired, broad faced, elderly man, wearing bifocal spectacles. He had on a short sleeved shirt for this warm day and Anna noticed, when he greeted her, that his forearms were deeply tanned. He must have spent time abroad. He grasped her hand firmly and she found herself looking, through his rather owlish glasses, directly into very pale blue, narrowed and watchful eyes. She realised with a jolt that, for all his cherubically benevolent appearance, Jack Mackinnon probably didn't miss a single trick. Would he help her?

'Mrs Quinn? Glad to meet you.' he said warmly. And you, old chap. How's the art world?'

Quinn muttered something about being busy.

'I imagine Lavinia can be a hard taskmistress.' Mackinnon laughed knowledgeably, though not unkindly. 'Come on in both of you. My wife's out shopping, but I have coffee on the go.' He led the way down a short passage to a low ceilinged, chintzy sitting room. 'The islanders were short in stature in the old days and this is one of the oldest houses. Do sit down.'

He left them and quickly returned with a traditional silver coffeepot and cups on a tray. 'I gather you had an uncle who was here during or just after the war?'

'After the war, I suppose.' Anna hesitated, afraid of pushing him towards a wrong conclusion. 'He was German.'

Mackinnon's interest was aroused. She could see that from the sharp glance he gave her. 'Well,' he said, perhaps to gain a little time, 'before we go any further do you take milk and sugar?'

When this was settled he began a gentle interrogation. 'So when your mother was sent to England in 1938 he was not allowed to go too? When had he been born?'

'1926. He was a lot older than her.'

'So he was 12? Just too close to military age. Hitler knew a war was coming, was planning one, and wasn't going to let potential cannon fodder out. Do you have any details?'

Anna delved into a large ethnically patterned shoulder bag which Quinn always joked contained enough junk for an auction sale, and eventually produced a creased manilla envelope.

'This was among my mother's papers.' She drew out the Red Cross letter and the photograph and handed them across.

The small photograph showed three members of the family. The boy was standing rigidly to attention between his parents, who were in heavy overcoats, but he wore a uniform consisting of shorts with a shiny leather belt, a military style shirt with a swastika armband just visible and he was bareheaded. His hair was close cropped and Mackinnon noticed that his wideset eyes were similar to Anna's, though his face had the unlined, smooth features of a teenager.

'Hitler Youth get up.' Mackinnon commented, handing back the photograph, which he had observed bore a 1941 date on the back in gothic script, 'I wouldn't worry about that. Every schoolchild had to join, both boys and girls.'

'It doesn't mean he was a Nazi?' Anna began to let her fears show.

'I bloody well hope he wasn't.' Quinn exclaimed.

'That was not a very helpful observation.' Jack said in a voice of sudden steel. 'Why don't you go for a short walk, Quinn. Come back in an hour.'

This was an order. Quinn got to his feet reluctantly, then made a show of nonchalance by blowing a kiss at Anna and saying 'See you later, my love.'

'Why is he so uptight about the Germans?' Anna asked. 'He never used to be.' She was relieved that he had gone, though he would probably make her pay later for having been dismissed like a schoolboy.

'He's gone a little too native.' Mackinnon shook his head. 'What the Germans did still makes me deeply upset, even though not all Nazis were evil, let alone all Germans. There is huge pressure to conform under any totalitarian system.' he spoke with the measured consideration of a judge. 'I sent murderers to execution after the war and would do so again. But to hound old people now, simply because they were in the Wehrmacht – the German army – would be absurd. Like accusing islanders of being collaborators decades later.'

'Quinn told me there weren't any islanders here.'

'Not quite every one chose to be evacuated.' Mackinnon temporised, as if not wishing to tamper with accuracy, 'one couple did stay and collaborated. But they left pretty quickly after the rest came home.' He shrugged his shoulders 'That's history now. We have to live in the present; and the present includes German tourists, whose money the island needs.'

'Quinn doesn't think so.'

'I imagine Lavinia has got it into his head that the island was a paradise before the occupation wrecked everything, not that she knows anything about it. The island wasn't a paradise of course. Far from it. I used to come here as a small boy just before the war. But what I think I remember is largely what my uncle told me. Anyway there was no mains water, most houses had rainwater cisterns, there was no electric light – oddly enough the Germans installed that – although there was a gasworks. The shops were primitive; quarrying was a major source of employment.' he smiled 'The islanders were literally selling the granite they lived on. Lavinia would have loathed the life here.'

'She has an awful lot of influence over Quinn.'

'She's a very manipulative woman.' Jack smiled at Anna impishly. 'May I let you into a little secret? You must never mention it to your husband.'

'I promise.'

'Lavinia's attitude to the Germans has a rather personal orientation. You see, during the war the island's commandant was a certain Colonel Grundmann, who was very fond of what the French call "a little bit on the side". Normally the German army organised prostitutes for both officers and men, but the island was underprivileged in this respect.'

Anna laughed politely, slightly put out at this turn of the conversation, and trying to guess what was coming next.

'So the gallant Colonel imported some girls himself from France and installed them in a house near Drake Bay. Nor was he selfish in his enjoyment. His friends were allowed to join in. He rather enjoyed group sex, or possibly watching it.'

'You can't mean Lavinia was one of the girls!' Anna was fascinated by his dry humour.

'What a delightful thought.' Mackinnon chuckled. 'Alas, no. Her involvement only began when her late husband bought that very house and she decided to redecorate.'

'And made discoveries.' Anna started to giggle, now able to guess what might be coming.

'Exactly. Some most imaginative murals were revealed, while a pit in the garden yielded a selection of sex aids. The Germans were more advanced in their practices than we realised. Personally,' he winked at her, 'I felt Lavinia should have donated it all to the museum.'

'But she didn't? Anna managed to stifle outright laughter at a vision of the fragrant Lavinia using rubber gloves to examine the Colonel's collection.

'She did not! She was outraged at the idea. She had the walls replastered and the rubbish dumped at sea. Happily her late husband allowed me to take some photographs first, for which she has never forgiven me.'

'Why doesn't she sell the house?'

'It has a superb situation by the sea.'

Anna was still helpless with amusement when it occurred to her to ask how he knew so much about the sex-starved Colonel.

'He was interrogated after the war.' Mackinnon became serious again. 'As Commandant he had been ultimately responsible for the deaths of hundreds of labourers here, mostly Russians. He explained about his House of Joy, as if it excused everything else. Under the Allied agreements of the time he was handed over to the Soviet government and hanged.'

The matter-of-factness of this account was frightening. One moment Grundmann was ridiculous, with his girls and his murals, the next he was on the scaffold.

'You mean he was a murderer?' Anna asked

'Not personally. But he gave the orders and encouraged the brutality. When a labourer escaped, which happened occasionally, he ordered the man to be hunted down and shot. That happened several times around the shoreline below the cliffs.'

'How terrible.' Anna's mood changed abruptly as she realised that if Tad had made an escape, as she suspected he had, he too would have been hunted like an animal. Was that what he was remembering?

'In reality,' Mackinnon continued, in a quite different tone of voice, dismissively cynical. 'Grundmann wasn't executed at all. He ought to have swung. But he probably bought off his Russian warders. In those days five cigarettes bought a woman for the night. He died in his bed in Germany in the late 1970s. That only emerged quite recently.'

'How do you know about it?

'I was in intelligence myself.' He hesitated, as if he had been indiscreet. 'Well, it's hardly a secret now. As a young man I became involved with following up the war crimes here.'

Anna wondered if, although he was retired, Mackinnon was still a professional pursuer of Nazis, like that famous Jewish investigator of the Holocaust. 'Are you still looking out for information?' she asked.

'Very much so,' he admitted frankly 'any fragment helps with the jigsaw, which is why I am curious about your uncle. 'Not', he added firmly, 'that there is any justification for harassing later generations when their parents will soon be dead, if they aren't already. There is a divide between witch hunting and genuine morality. But I would like to close the files about this island before I too pass on.'

'So what about my uncle?' she was sure her mother must have unearthed something so bad she dared not put it on paper. 'Could he have been in the SS. What was the SS anyway?'

'The SS.' Mackinnon glanced at her quizzically. 'You really want to know? Well, Hitler never trusted his own armed forces. So he created the Schutzstaffel, a word in which 'Schutz' means 'protection' and 'staffel' means 'echelon'. The black uniformed SS, with its silver death's head badges, became huge and, just to confuse things, also had its own military units.'

'So what did it do?'

'Carried through Hitler's 'final solution' of killing the Jews. The SS also dealt with his political opponents, some of whom were distinguished soldiers whom they dared not kill. A mixture of Jews and "unreliable" Germans was sent to a concentration camp here. Not, incidentally, a death camp like the one your parents were murdered at. But still pretty brutal.'

'They held Germans here? That sounds odd.'

'And it was complicated. Devilishly. Officially there were no SS were here. They were on the books of a concentration camp at Neuengamme, near Hamburg, while this was Neuwerk. So there were no records here and officially no atrocities, no beatings, no killings. That was the impression they hoped to leave behind when they hastily dismantled the camp and shipped the labourers out in June 1944, shortly after the Allied liberation of France began.'

'You mean they all got away?'

'They couldn't get out fast enough in 1944. But our people caught up with some of them.'

'Could my uncle have been one?' This was what she most feared and why she had asked about the notorious SS. She was getting close to the crunch and almost trembling.

'Your Red Cross letter is dated November 1947. There were still German prisoners of war here then.'

'You mean he could have been just an ordinary soldier.'

'If he was here in 1947, that's more likely.' Mackinnon understood her fears, though he didn't want to be dishonest. 'He was very young at the end of the war. Too young for the SS, I'd have thought. Anyway they were dealt with differently if they were caught. None were kept here as prisoners of war.'

'Why were any prisoners kept here?'

'The island was in an unbelievable mess. Many houses had been stripped of floors and staircases for firewood. Others had been demolished. Rats and rabbits had taken over the farmland. There were coils of barbed wire all along the cliffs and 30,000 mines. As you've seen, there are fortifications everywhere. The Germans may have installed mains water and electricity. They also destroyed. So prisoners of war helped put the island to rights.'

Mackinnon smiled a little wickedly. 'They were made to test their own mine clearing by walking over the areas afterwards. A few got blown up. After that they became more thorough. An officer I later worked for ordered it. I would have approved.'

Anna gasped. There was naked steel behind Jack's white hair and benign appearance. Then she realised that this was good. Here was a man she could trust all the way, who would never dodge inconvenient facts, a Mr Christian for truth. She went for the next question.

'Could my uncle have died here?'

Mackinnon considered this, his broad and balding brow slightly creased. 'Possibly. But you won't unearth much, forgive the pun. After the war all the German military dead were exhumed and re-buried at a war cemetery in France.'

'So I can't find out here?' Her mood swung again and she felt like bursting into tears at the frustration. The Court, the vicar, now even this expert. No sooner did a new lead open up than it was closed again. 'This place is impossible!' she almost screamed, then apologised. 'If only my mother had talked about it!'

'I'm sorry, my dear.' Jack Mackinnon became positively avuncular. 'I can tell you where to look in France. And there are files in Germany at the Bundesarchiv. I'll check through my own papers, of course, though the name doesn't ring a bell. Tracing ancestors isn't simple as TV programmes make out.'

'That's very kind of you.' Now she felt ashamed of her outburst.

'There might be something in the archives at St Mary's too. Their records are much more complete.'

'I caught the ferry from there.' Anna remembered the attractive town, with its Georgian houses ranged up the hill behind the harbour. 'Yesterday.' Was it possible that she had only been here for one night and a single day?

'It would be worth a try. And easier to get to than Germany' he changed the subject, 'I hear you met old Tadeus.'

'Yes.' She was cautious because the question sounded too casual. 'I met him on the boat and then again near the cliffs. He wanted to find you.'

'He succeeded. He came round yesterday evening.' There was a reticence in the way Mackinnon spoke which puzzled her. 'He told me you were going to walk with him again.'

'He seemed so frail and alone. He was here during the war, so that gave us a sort of bond. But I couldn't make out what he was really looking for.'

'The past.' Mackinnon said shortly. '*A la recherche des temps perdus*'. He paused. 'He says he was one of the forced labourers here and escaped, but only one man ever did, and that was by bluffing his way on to a ship. All the others who attempted it were shot. Or worse.'

'But he's alive and here. How could he be inventing it?'

'Not logically.' Mackinnon now seemed as puzzled as she was. 'He thinks he got away in a small boat. I can't quite believe that. True, all the labourers were shipped to France in the end and a few did escape there when a train was shot up from the air. But they didn't escape from here.'

'Well,' Anna's innate practicality asserted itself. 'He may be gloomy. But he very definitely is alive now, what next?'

'There is to be a commemoration service on Sunday for the labourers who lost their lives. At the memorial. You may have seen the memorial, quite striking. In theory he has come for that.'

'I read about it.' Now she understood better why Tad's wife had approved his spending their savings on the trip.

'But it's more than that.' Mackinnon went on.' He's afraid he was responsible for a fellow labourer dying. He's trying to retrace everywhere he went on the day they escaped.'

'He certainly looked as though he'd been seeing ghosts. He was dreadfully agitated.'

Mackinnon hesitated, then said very deliberately. 'It may not be wise to walk with him.'

'You mean he might attack me?' She recalled Tad's forcibly pulling her back from the cliff path.

'Oh no. I'm sure not.' Mackinnon assured her. 'Anyway he's old and quite frail. 'No' he repeated and then became

70

cautious again. 'But if he did rediscover something disturbing he might drag you into it.'

'How could he?' Anna felt a tremor of the same apprehension she had felt when the rabbit ran out on the cliff path by the skull and crossbones sign. 'You mean he's seeing things that I can't see?'

'I do not believe in ghosts, Anna.' For someone who didn't Mackinnon was being very earnest. 'But I suspect he does. Or, to be more exact, he believes it is possible to relive the past, if he can manage to remember it intensely enough. Not merely emotional memories, but actual experiences.'

She considered this. The idea sounded plausible, even if it was bordering on the supernatural. 'Should I back out?'

'Well. Let's just say that whatever happened to Tadeus isn't going to have much bearing on your uncle.'

'You think not?' This felt like giving up a possible clue and she needed every clue she could find, given her lack of time.

'If your uncle was just an ordinary young conscript, which sounds the most likely situation to me, he would seldom if ever have been in contact with the labourers.'

Mackinnon was clearly trying to dissuade her and for a moment she went along with him.

'Quinn doesn't like my meeting him either.'

This seemed to cheer Mackinnon up, as though he had won his case. His rather morbid sense of humour returned.

'If your husband doesn't approve, that can only be because of Lavinia and, if I may be so bold, provides an excellent reason for taking no notice of me.'

'Oh, but I would do. It's just....'

'That you don't want to abandon any leads?'

'And I'm sorry for the old man, being all on his own.'

'Well, it's your decision.' Mackinnon smiled. He liked her spirit. 'Just be careful of old men's fantasies. And I mean his, not mine.' He smiled again 'If there's any hint of trouble, run. Don't hesitate. Oh, and please call me Jack. And come to see us again.'

CHAPTER EIGHT

'It's such a glorious day,' Anna suggested, 'why don't we have lunch outside when we get back?'

She was hoping to ameliorate Quinn's foul mood, which had resulted from his being excluded from the conversation with Mackinnon.

They had stopped near the cricket pitch on the way home from Jack Mackinnon's cottage and she felt she must shake off a growing depression. She was becoming more and more afraid that her uncle might have been in the reviled SS, if he had been old enough. In 1943 he would have been 17. Or had he never been here at all? Could the postcard the neighbours received have been from somewhere else?

For her own peace of mind she had to find out, because she was beginning to face a moral dilemma as well. Should the present generation be accountable for the sins of the past? Or should past crimes be airbrushed out of history? It was hardly a new topic, in fact a staple for columnists. But it never had personal meaning for her before. Meanwhile the two contrasting aspects of the island, the sunny holiday resort and the grim concrete fortifications looming out of the fog, were increasingly disturbing.

How would those holidaying families whose children played happily by the wall at Drake Bay feel about the story of the wall if they knew? Would the campers be aghast that they had pitched their tents on the very site of a slave labour camp? Or would it simply not worry them? Perhaps most people simply did not feel the aura of evil here in the way that she increasingly did.

She had seen books about the occupation with lurid titles on sale in the town, such as 'The Island of Dread' and 'Hitler's own Torture Island.' Perhaps visitors read them without making any emotional connection, the way reports of murders in the tabloids were basically titillation, unrelated to the readers' own lives. But the walk with Tad had made her involved, as if he was somehow linked to her lost uncle, not that he could be.

She had been taught by her mother that the Nazis were the epitome of evil, people with whom there could never be an inch of common ground. And even today the term 'Nazi' was a standard, knee-jerk reaction, pejorative used by liberals against their opponents, along with words like 'obscene'.

Anna was an instinctive liberal herself, but she never had liked the indiscriminate use of 'Nazi'. Perhaps if she had been brought up in Germany, there would be other ways to cope with it. The Belsen concentration camp had even been turned into a tourist attraction. Did that exorcise the ghosts? She doubted if it could.

She needed to talk all this through dispassionately with someone. But who? Not with Quinn, whose view was so distorted by Lavinia's prejudices. And was she over-dramatising the issue? In whom could she confide? The obvious answer was Mackinnon.

And beyond that a husband was supposed to provide emotional support. If in practice he was unable to do so or even to sympathise, what future was there with him?

She put these worries aside. At this moment her need was to enjoy the sunshine. Perhaps her thoughts would be clearer by tomorrow.

'It really is beautifully warm.' she told Quinn 'We must make the most of it. I'll get a picnic together.'

'That would be nice.' Quinn agreed, though hesitantly because he had to meet Lavinia at three. A picnic could drag on, especially since he would want to doze on the beach afterwards. 'We could always eat on the lawn outside the studio.'

Now it was Anna's turn to hesitate. She guessed Lavinia might be coming round.

'The courtyard lawn isn't exactly private.' she said.

'Nor is the beach.'

'Either way I'll have to do some shopping.' She didn't want an argument. 'All you seem to have in the house is baked beans and pasta.'

Quinn laughed and agreed. He liked being looked after. He missed her domestic thoughtfulness. But he was still basically selfish, because in the past he had never reciprocated with help. If challenged he would have claimed meals were a woman's job.

He had parked the Land Rover by a largish area of grass, known locally as the 'plateau', with a cricket pitch marked out in the centre, and from which there was a stunning view of the harbour and the sea, even better than from Jack's nearby garden. Sailboats dotted the blue water. Fluffy white clouds drifted past in stately procession. A cuckoo sang its two echoing notes and Anna spotted it flying in its lolloping way to perch on a telegraph pole. The church bells began to peal, announcing a wedding.

'Small wonder tourists like this place.' Anna remarked, deliberately praising the scene and putting the island's dark side out of mind 'Everything's so uncomplicated, like a Dufy painting.'

'Until you get involved with politics.' Quinn said, as if determined to puncture her enthusiasm, which he had failed to notice was actually slightly forced. 'We'll have to get a move on or the shops will shut. We'll leave the mighty machine here.'

On the short walk to the main street they passed some overgrown ruins, which Anna had not noticed on the way down. A low wall had gaps for a semi-circular driveway, beyond which a tangled confusion of brambles and weeds swallowed up what had once been a building. The driveway was littered with beer cans and windblown shreds of paper and plastic. An old red saloon car without wheels stood on cement blocks. A bicycle lay abandoned.

'Not another German bunker!' Anna said, trying to make a joke of it.

'For a change, no.' Quinn quickly struck a pose, bowing theatrically with one arm outstretched, as if introducing her to royalty. 'Allow me to present the grand entrance and ballroom of the Island Palace Hotel.'

Anna gawped at the dereliction. 'You're joking.' she said, while actually horrified. 'Did the Germans do that?'

'Wrong again. An arsonist. And nature reclaims its own pretty quickly here.' He stepped back and gestured again. 'I'm thinking of using the Palace Hotel in the 1930s as one of my paintings. You know, brilliantined young men tangoing in tailcoats, flappers dancing the Charleston.'

'Surely the Charleston was in the twenties? And was the island ever as sophisticated as that?'

'The 1920s then.' Quinn was not going to be put off. 'Pleasure Island. Cricketers in white flannels. Girls in cloche hats. Lavinia is very keen on.....' He cut the tactless explanation short, but too late.

'She probably still has dresses of her own from the 1950s she could model for you.' In the same breath Anna regretted being bitchy, when all she really wanted was to have a nice relaxed day. 'Sorry, but I do hear rather a lot about your patroness.'

'Since the subject's come up,' Quinn attempted bravado, 'I have to meet her this afternoon.'

'At her place or yours?'

Anna deliberately did not say 'ours'. She had already guessed that Lavinia was behind his rejecting the picnic idea.

'At the Museum.'

'Then you can drop me off and I'll walk with Tadeus.'

'If that's what you want.' he agreed grudgingly.

'Tadeus needs help. He's very frail.' She gazed again at the overgrown and rubbish strewn remains of the grandly named hotel. There was something terribly melancholy about it. For once she fully understood Quinn's nostalgic ideas.

'They had a pianist every evening, right up to the last night.' Quinn spoke as though he remembered it, which of course he could not have done.

'It's spooky. I don't like ghosts, even of dancers. Let's go and do the shopping.'

They made their purchases and then Quinn drove her back to the fort the long way, past Drake's bay, stopping to look across at the French coast, where the headlands stood out in the same astonishing clarity as they had on the day of her arrival – goodness, had that really only been yesterday! She felt as though she'd been here a week already. This time she noticed a substantial group of white buildings, with tall chimneys, on a hill in France. They were catching the sun and seemed to float above the landscape.

'Bloody nuclear plant,' Quinn commented. 'A nice long way from Paris but far too close to us. Trust the frogs to let our water pick up their radioactive waste.'

'Remind me to go for a swim later.'

'Actually the French claim very little gets into the sea.' Too late, Quinn tried to reassure her. 'And the prevailing wind takes the smoke towards them, not us.'

'Radioactive smoke too? Even better. Did I tell you I've joined Greenpeace?''

Why, she thought angrily, should this island be plagued by malicious interventions all the time? The Nazis, this nuclear plant. Was it just the result of being offshore, or did something about it bring out the worst in people?

'Sorry Quinn,' she said 'but that kind of thing makes my blood boil. Let's get on with our lunch.'

They continued to the fort and Quinn set out a table and chairs just off the sloping lawn, where a wall created a suntrap, while she got together a salad and cold meat, with French bread and camembert. He opened white wine and brought her an old straw hat for the sun. They ate in such contentment that she reached across impulsively and squeezed his hand.

'It can be so lovely here. I do understand what it does for you.'

'Could you live here? I could make you very happy.'

'I'm still thinking about it, Quinn. Give me time.'

'Forget about your uncle. He was probably only here after the war. If Jack Mackinnon has no record of him, nobody will.'

Quinn tried to sound confident, though he now appreciated that if Anna got it into her head that her uncle had been in the SS she would never stay. 'Forget the past. It's the future that matters.'

But Mackinnon had told her that the SS not only kept no records of its personnel here, many of them they were given cash and false identity papers at the end of the war and slipped off to South America.

'Forgetting is easier said than done, darling.' Anna gently released the tips of his fingers. 'You do understand, don't you?'

'Yes, of course I do.' He said testily, not exactly brushing her aside, but impatient. 'Where else you can search is another question.'

'Jack Mackinnon did suggest St Mary's.........'

A shrill feminine voice interrupted her in mid-sentence 'Anyone around?' Lavinia emerged on to the grass from the entrance arch. 'I was lunching with the Lathbury's so I came here rather than the Museum.'

'We've just about finished ours.' Quinn assured her hastily, earning himself a daggers drawn look from Anna, who was incensed at being interrupted at such a crucial moment.

Lavinia intercepted Anna's look and said with transparent insincerity. 'If this is a bad moment I can always go on ahead.'

'No, no, no!' Anna insisted, equally falsely, 'I wouldn't dream of upsetting Quinn's private arrangements. They are so important.' She deliberately stressed Lavinia's favourite word, 'I have plenty of time. I'll walk to Drake Manor. You go with Lavinia, Quinn. I have to sort out my sketching things anyway.'

Caught in the crossfire, all Quinn could do was ask feebly 'Will you be alright?' as if she risked being assaulted or raped.

'Don't be silly. Of course, I'll be okay. Now off you go, both of you.'

Lavinia flushed. She did not like being given orders by anyone, least of all by the younger wife of a man she was interested in. But the fort was now indisputably Anna's turf.

She made the best of it by saying proprietorially to Quinn 'I'll go ahead and meet you there, dear boy.' then turned elegantly on her heel and stalked unhurriedly back to the entrance, having successfully got in the last word. They heard her car start up and the scrunch of gravel.

'You, Quinn, are a louse. And as for her!' Anna stormed back to the sitting room to collect her things. If she'd been a horse she would have whinnied and bucked.

CHAPTER NINE

At the Drake Manor Anna found Tad standing outside the restaurant entrance and knew he had not wanted to go inside and waste his little money on ordering anything.

'I hope I haven't kept you waiting.' she said, even though she was slightly early. 'Let's just sit down for a moment.' she guided him to one of the tables in the garden, a table in the shade because the sun was hot. 'Coffee?'

'Water only.'

She ordered coffee for herself and prepared to be very patient over her gentle questioning.

'You haven't told me what happened to you in the war.' she said at last. 'Were you here long?'

'This man,' Tad indicated the proprietor 'he ask me. And I do not know.' he seemed amused by this.

'When did he ask?' Anna was unaccountably alarmed, as if she didn't like her own questions being pre-empted, though that was illogical. She had no rights of possession over the Pole.

'It is yesterday. I wait for bus. He like to talk, when I not…know….' Tad searched for the word.

'Remember?' Anna prompted.

'Yes.' Tad laughed; a dry, coughing laugh that reminded her of the vicar. 'Some things, jah. Not important thing.'

'Tell me what you can. How did you escape?'

At this moment the owner, Brian, brought the drinks. 'So, what are you telling this lady today, young man?' he demanded in his jocular and mildly offensive way, speaking with a strong Yorkshire accent. Tad sat silent, supposing this was some kind of English joke.

'Well, tell us all about it then?' Brian insisted.

'I am for honour come, not talk.'

Despite his stilted English, Tad said this with such dignity that Brian had no choice but to back off and Anna hastily paid the bill. Then, quite unexpectedly, Tad began to come out of his protective shell.

'I with friend and we find boat. I think is near bay, but I not know how…. I remember fog.' He rubbed his gaunt and stubbly chin perplexedly 'I think friend is kill because in France not there. I worry. Is my fault?'

'So you are trying to find out where you went?' It might be as Mackinnon had suggested. If Tad had lost consciousness at some point in the escape then he could have suffered from amnesia afterwards, yet still have lurking suspicions of a death.

'Where went?' Tad was having language problems 'What is that?'

'The way you escape.' she explained what she meant.

'Jah, jah! And I fear what is there. Ich muss kennen. Olga agree.' He looked at Anna anxiously, fearful that she might not want to go with him. When agitated he lapsed into German.

'No problem.' Anna reassured him, though he had not explained things to her, at least not properly. She thought of Mackinnon's warning to be careful. And then she thought how unkind it would be not to help this old man, who had no friends here and whose wife had self-sacrificingly consented to spending their savings on a trip that was so quixotic. In any case, how could recovering his memories possibly harm her?

'So long as we walk in daylight,' she offered, 'and I can do my sketching. Where do you want to go this afternoon?'

'On hill. After I think we were in wood. After...' he rubbed his forehead with both palms in puzzlement. 'I look.'

By the time they had completed the steep climb up the road to the Monastery it was half past three. Anna would have liked to stop and sketch, but the fog was starting to creep in again, hiding the view of the bay below. Furthermore Tad, who walked only laboriously, was urging her to go straight to the place where they had seen the skull and crossbones sign.

She understood now why he had believed the two of them were walking into a minefield, because Mackinnon had shown her a photo of a wartime black and white danger sign. No wonder Tad had become so agitated, even though the real minefield signs had been black, not red.

The cliff path was rough and eroded, so she took his arm to steady him. Up here the fog was patchy, drifting as before like smoke, though rapidly filling the valley to the side where she had meet Tad originally. How long ago was that? It seemed an age. Actually it had been yesterday, Sunday, her first full day on the island. An awful lot was happening on this trip.

When they reached the spot where the rabbit had leapt off into the bracken or somewhere very close to it, she felt Tad's muscles tighten. He stopped and began casting around in different directions, as if he was a gundog tracking a scent. Abruptly he began pointing to another path which led down obliquely towards the big field.

'We go there.' he insisted.

'Isn't that where you came up yesterday?'

'We go there.' This was all the explanation he offered. The terrain was rough, the path ran through tussocky grass and between gorse bushes, and on several occasions she had to save him from tripping up. They passed a row of ornate Victorian cast iron railings, serving no apparent purpose in the middle of the scrub, then the path came alongside a broken down stone wall as they began descending the side of the valley, now completely shrouded in fog. Anna shivered in spite of herself. It was both eerie and chilled.

Suddenly Tad stopped dead, swaying as if he would fall. Looming out of the white murk ahead of them and alongside the wall was an old combine harvester, an angular hulk of rusting metal casings and wheels, painted in fading green. The foot-thick pipe that had once disgorged threshed grain stuck out from its side like a monstrous cigar, pointing into space and held up by bracing wires. Like a cigar. Or like something more sinister.

A simple pipe was how Anna saw it. Tad obviously saw something different and menacing, because he looked frantically round for an escape route. He would have collapsed on the path if she had not held him up. She clasped him by the waist, felt him trembling violently, and began to be scared herself.

'Run!' he cried out. 'Run.'

Still supporting him, she looked at that long pipe protruding from the rectangular bulk of the machine and suddenly understood. What he saw, hindered by poor eyesight and the mist, was the barrel of a huge gun.

'It's alright,' she assured him, 'it's only an old harvester.'

But Tad did not believe her. He struggled to free himself, making her more and more infected with his fear and not knowing what to do.

'Everything's okay,' she kept repeating, unable to understand his mutterings, but fully comprehending that he was reliving a moment of absolute terror. 'It's all right. It's not a gun. It's only a farm machine.'

Eventually he accepted what she was saying and began to recover himself, as though emerging from a nightmare.

'Thank-you,' he said shakily, 'thank-you so much. I have thought a gun. There was gun. And soldiers. We hide by wall.'

When he had calmed down Anna looked at the combine harvester again, ghostly in the fog, and could even imagine the soldiers of the gun's crew standing around. It seemed unbelievable that Tad and another boy had hidden behind this tumbledown, grass grown wall, hardly four feet high, when there were Germans a few yards away. They must have been frightened out of their wits. Then, inevitably, she wondered if her uncle had been one of those soldiers, and felt completely frozen inside.

'We go on.' Tad urged at last, to her relief.

He wanted to plunge straight across a field, but Anna felt the visibility was too poor and so they agreed o compromise by continuing down the path to a large semi-derelict house and from there along a muddy track, bordered by a trickle of water, which led down through a wooded valley. The ground was marshy and the fog seeped between the trees, making Anna keen to avoid the track and get back to the restaurant. She was feeling more and groggy, without any explanation she could think of.

Tad remained insistent on exploring the wood. 'I go there.' He kept repeating. So, with some hesitation, she let him. Again, for reasons she could not put a finger on, she was becoming increasingly apprehensive and stood watching his stumbling figure disappear into the fog with dismay.

While he was gone a man walked past and told her that in fact the muddy path led down to Drake Manor, while the metalled road to Drake Bay was only 50 yards away out of sight. They had walked around three sides of a square.

After less then ten minutes Tad emerged, his cheap shoes muddy and squelching, his clothing snagged with small twigs and burrs. She immediately felt guilty at having abandoned him. However, his worn and pinched expression was triumphant.

'We come this way.' he announced. 'I know. But then there is dog and we hide again.'

Anna tried visualise them but could only conjure up a vague image of two bedraggled youngsters.

'There is cave.' Tad said. 'I show you.' He set off ahead of her, somewhat unsteadily, and this time she had to follow.

The valley was thickly overgrown. The muddy path soon narrowed, where it ran among taller trees, while a low cliff rose on their right. Although Anna could hear cars on the tarmac road out of sight, this was a completely secluded and secret place.

'Is it there?' Anna asked, pointing to the cliff, anxious to get this over with.

Tad stopped, surveying the small trees and underbrush at the base of the cliff, then began pulling branches apart to get through. Weak and old he might be, but he was as determined as a terrier after a rat. She had to help him and was thankful to be wearing jeans, which gave her some protection against the nettles. Even so, she was about to give up when they glimpsed a low overhang of rock, showing dark behind the undergrowth. What with the fog shrouding the trees it was very gloomy.

'There!' Tad exclaimed excitedly. 'Is there.'

The shallow, low ceilinged cavern looked dank, dark and thoroughly uninviting. She didn't want Tad suffering a seizure deep in there and he was getting so excited that she thought he might. Reluctantly she took his hand and let him half pull, half guide her to the entrance. He was stronger than she expected, transfused with febrile energy.

'Hier!' he declared with excited conviction, 'we hide hier.'

'How long for?' She more and more desperately wanted to get out of here again, but to stir up his memories might be the quickest way. 'We ought to have a torch.' she suggested, knowing that would mean going to fetch one.

Tad took not notice. 'We here many hours.' was all he said.

Releasing her hand, he stooped low to enter beneath the overhang. As she followed she felt something hard beneath her left foot, a lump beneath the sole of her trainers. She groped around for whatever it was in the thick carpet of leafmould on the cave floor and came up with the rusted remains of a knife. Holding it to the dim daylight, she saw it had a blade about five inches long, with the tip broken off, while its handle had disintegrated, leaving only fragments of rotten wood.

'Look at this.' she said, holding it out. Tad examined the rusty blade. He was trembling and fingered it agitatedly, speaking abruptly 'We come tomorrow. Now go.'

When they reached Drake Manor ten minutes later – the distance was quite short – they were both soaked and muddy. It was extraordinary how wet the valley was even on a warm day.

We both need a hot drink.' Anna decided, taking command again, and they went inside, getting skew-eyed glances from the voluble owner, Brian.

'And what have you been up to, my darling.' he asked, 'mud wrestling? Better get cleaned up before you wreck my best chairs.'

Anna did not to deign to answer. The owner of the Drake Manor seemed to enjoy being offensive. When they had washed and been brought a pot of tea she asked him to call a taxi.

'No need for that, sweetheart.' he said 'The bus to town goes in fifteen minutes.' he winked at her. 'Passes your lover boy's studio too.'

'Quinn's my husband, thank-you.' Anna replied curtly. The gossips could jolly well know that. Not to mention the predatory widows.

'No offence meant, I'm sure.' Brian backed off, but of course he had meant every word.

While they waited for the bus Anna asked for a ferry timetable and discovered that the boat to St Mary's operated tomorrow, which was Tuesday, and also on Friday and Sunday. Tomorrow would be her third day! And she had barely made any progress at all. She thought about this over their tea, though Tad's mind was evidently still focussed on the cave.

'I go again.' Tad insisted, giving her a curious smile, like a fellow conspirator, which she realised she was fast becoming. 'I know more now. Miki is frightened by gun, but after not so bad.'

'Miki?' she picked up on the name instantly. 'Who was Miki?'

'We together. We brothers. When escape we take each other's blood.'

'Blood brothers?'

'Richtig.' he again slipped into German. 'This why I go cave tomorrow.'

During the brief bus journey Anna warned him that tomorrow she would be busy. She had her own searches to make and could not walk with him again until Wednesday. He said, disappointed, that he also had little time. He could not afford to stay longer than Sunday and the remembrance service. In fact he was so downcast that she promised to telephone his guest house when she got back from St Mary's tomorrow. On the bus she gave him the rusty knife, which he was hesitant about accepting, but finally did put in his jacket pocket. After all, it must have been his.

It occurred to her that he certainly would go to the little cave again, now they had located it, even if she wasn't with him, though to go alone would be foolish. If he had an accident no-one would ever find him. In the end she left that unsaid, got off the bus at Rocquaine Bay and walked round to the fort. With luck she could change into clean clothes before Quinn got back. The fewer explanations she had to give, the better.

She felt so drained by the afternoon's experience that she rested briefly on a bench in the lee of the fort. By one of the freaks of local weather the bay was now in brilliant sunshine, while fog still lay over most of the island. There was a south westerly wind and, the bay being on the north, she supposed that was why it was clear, if the fog came off the sea. But it was not a question to which she gave much thought.

She leant back on the bench and relaxed in the warmth. Now she understood that cliché phrase 'shell-shocked'. Being with Tad by the ancient combine harvester had been like having a bomb go off beside her. She did not doubt that it was worthwhile helping him. But that did not do much for her own search. In fact it was all very well for Tad to lean on her, but who did she lean on? Quinn? Hopeless, when he was under Lavinia's thumb. It was an annoying problem, which could become serious.

To her surprise, when she walked up through the stern imitation medieval archway, Quinn was already back.

'Where on earth have you been?' was his inhospitable greeting as she entered the Moroccan room. But she was unexpectedly relieved when he enfolded her in an affectionate bear hug. 'Are you all right, darling.' he asked solicitously 'you're soaked through!'

'Yes. No. Well, I suppose so.' She stayed there for a moment in his arms. Perhaps he could be the mainstay she needed after all. 'It's hard to explain.'

But when she tried to recount the afternoon his sympathy first dwindled and then evaporated. 'All this stuff about the war. You ought to forget it.'

'I can't. How could I?' she detached herself. 'My uncle was here. Somewhere. And the old man needs help.'

'From your description he looks after himself pretty well.'

'He is tougher than he looks, in spite of his age.' she admitted. 'He's been through a lot. A slave labourer here as a boy. Then the Communists jailed him in Poland after the war just because he had been a prisoner of the Germans. There wasn't much justice in that. It's a sick joke, Quinn.' Seeing she was making little impact she changed the subject and tactfully asked 'How did you get on with Lavinia?'

'She's gone off the Elizabethan idea.'

'Because I liked it?'

'Probably.' Quinn grinned and tried to hug her again, only half succeeding. 'Stuff Lavinia. She's a cow.'

'A witch.'

'Women know best.' he conceded.

'It takes a witch to know a witch.'

'Let's go out tonight, sweetheart. The hell with cooking.'

'I didn't know you were planning to cook.'

He lent across and kissed her cheek. 'You're too bloody fast by half. When did I ever cook dinner?'

'When I wasn't here. Baked beans. You can't fool me.'

They had suddenly hit such a blessed rapprochement, such a restored meeting of minds, that she put off mentioning her St Mary's plans. Until, that was, he revealed, apologetically, that Lavinia had exacted her pound of flesh for letting him off early this afternoon. She required him to 'discuss themes' all tomorrow.

'No problemo. I'll go to St Mary's for the day.'

'St Mary's? What for?'

'The archives there. In some library.'

Quinn was about to object, then realised he could not. This was her holiday, her money, and he was being kept busy with – of all things – another woman, albeit professionally.

You do what you like, darling. Just lay the ghost of your uncle. That's all I ask.'

He made this sound more of a concession than it actually was. But she kissed him none the less. 'Thank-you, Quinn, I appreciate that.' Perhaps he might yet become a reformed character, after all. But not enough for her to sleep with him tonight, which was the reward he would undoubtedly press for.

'By the way,' he added, reinforcing his new, sympathetic image. 'How did your sketching go?'

'Would you like to see?' This was indeed a change, because Quinn usually took the patronising view that he, the professional, was on such a totally higher plane than her, that it was barely worth looking at her work. She was the amateur who taught because she couldn't really paint.

'Yes, I would.' He put as much enthusiasm into the words as he could. She went and fetched her drawing block.

'I wasn't able to do anything today. Tad took up all my time. But I did these yesterday from the hill above Drake bay.'

She laid out on a table the two pencil sketches she had done as the fog drifted around the bay and the fort at the end of the causeway, although the long wall with all the men was in clearer light.

'I couldn't quite get the effect of the fog.' she explained, 'I would like to have made it spookier. It might be more effective with watercolour.'

But Quinn hardly heard. He was staring at the drawings with a worried expression on his face, almost one of alarm.

You copied all this from one of those books about the Occupation, I suppose.' he said.

'No. Of course not.' she didn't understand. 'Why should I do that? I drew the bay as it was, though when we got down there again all the men had left.'

CHAPTER TEN

'It's none of my business, of course.' Lavinia smiled considerately at Quinn, as one concerned colleague might confide in another, exactly as she had rehearsed it. 'But Anna's visit is rather distracting you from your work.'

They were sitting side by side at the table in his studio, with various sketches laid out in front of them. And Quinn was losing this particular skirmish, if not the whole battle.

Hardly today.' he protested, making two irreversible errors in the same breath: one in consenting to discuss Anna at all, the other by tacitly admitting that Lavinia was right. 'Today is one hundred percent yours.'

Theoretically they were exploring the 'conceptual theme' of Quinn's historic sequence of pictures. In practice Lavinia was exploiting Anna's absence to nail him down about his future and to express her reservations – in the nicest, yet iciest, possible way – about his annoyingly intelligent and attractive wife. Her underlying attitude was roughly that of a loyal spouse who has just discovered that her husband is a bigamist.

Lavinia had dressed carefully for the occasion in designer jeans and a crisp white cotton shirt, with a dark blue and gold Hermes scarf loosely knitted around her neck. As Anna would have said, she 'reeked of money', specifically of Arpege. She had the figure of a woman half her age, slimmer than Anna's in fact, and knew precisely how to look coolly professional, yet seductive.

She often told herself that anywhere else a woman with her distinction and poise would have been on the Boards of half a dozen companies and constantly photographed in the glossies. If only her late husband had not insisted on moving to this god-forsaken island to avoid capital gains and inheritance tax! That had been a disaster. And now she felt trapped. The only faint silver lining to her predicament was Quinn.

'And why <u>has</u> she gone across to St Mary's?' Lavinia demanded, as though it was her business and she had caught Anna in flagrante delicto.

'To search the archives.' Quinn felt obliged to defend his wife. 'She needs to lay her uncle's ghost, as it were.'

As he spoke he recalled Anna's disturbing drawing of the bay. Perhaps she knew too much about ghosts. At the same time, that she should have perceptions of the island which were denied to him was irritating. Intensely so. He decided that, whatever she pretended, her sketches could only have been inspired by one of the many books about the Occupation. Overall it riled him more than he would ever have admitted to Anna. He was the island's artist, for God's sake. It was he who had the historic insights essential for Lavinia's project.

'This obsession of hers is not at all healthy in my view.' Lavinia continued to chisel away at her rival's character. 'One German's as bad as another. She should walk away from it all.'

'I've tried to tell her that.' Quinn felt increasingly trapped. He loved Anna, but depended financially on Lavinia. And Lavinia knew full well how to exploit that dependence. 'Anna feels she could never live here without knowing the truth.'

'Live here? I never knew that was on the menu!'

'We're talking about getting together gain.' Quinn squirmed on the harpoon of his patron's acidity and made yet another error by saying 'I thought I told you.'

'Not that I can recall.'

There was a vibrant silence. This was not Quinn's day.

'Well,' Lavinia said eventually, radiating the hauteur of a Duchess who has been mistaken for a maid, 'if you had made that clear from the start I would never have spoken. She's utterly the wrong woman for you, of course, but that's your affair.' she allowed herself the briefest of stage managed pauses. 'And, if I may say so, you are devoting time to her, which she is hardly reciprocating.'

'Anna's entitled to her own life.' Quinn was almost pleading now.

'My dear man,' Lavinia changed tack completely, laying a sympathetic hand on his knee, 'you are simply too talented to be losing sleep over a failed relationship. You and she really are two very different kinds of animal. And she doesn't hesitate to rush off when it suits her.'

'She had to go to St Mary's today'. he completely forgot that Anna had chosen today because he was going to be tied up with Lavinia. 'She is actually a very genuine person.'

'And I shall be very "genuinely" upset if our project gets behindhand.' Lavinia reverted to being acerbic, as if he had deliberately provoked her. 'I assume you do want to continue?'

'Of course I do' Quinn realised there was going to be some further price to pay and piled on his devotion even more thickly. 'It matters enormously to me.'

'Then I absolutely insist that you allocate enough time to it. Without distractions. Quality time.'

'Quality time.' he echoed the meaningless phrase, knowing he would now have to sacrifice the few days he had meant to spend with Anna.

Lavinia had brought a plastic folder with her. She extracted a sheet of paper and handed it across.

'We need to get our working relationship completely clear.' she said in the brisk, businesslike way that would have kept Board members on their toes and regularly did intimidate members of the Heritage Committee. 'So I drafted this. Then there will be no misunderstandings. And after that I should like to see your conceptual drawings.'

Quinn examined the document. It was headed:

'ISLAND HISTORICAL HERITAGE PROJECT
MISSION STATEMENT'

He read through its five pompous paragraphs, noting grimly that they contained nothing about payment, only an insistence on 'satisfactory completion within the appropriate holistic framework and in the spirit of interpretative empathy'.

'Brilliantly expressed.' he stroked his beard as he imagined the great Rembrandt would have stroked his in such circumstances, if Rembrandt had a beard, which he could not remember, and if the Master ever got in a hole with a patron, which he also didn't know. Who on earth had cooked up all this shit for her? 'No-one could have put it better.' He enthused.

'Thank-you, Quinn. I'm so glad we understand each other.'

Having won conclusively, game set and match, she could afford to be the indulgent patroness again.

'We all know you have the talent, Quinn. You merely lack guidance. Next I should like to look through everything you have done so far. And after that I have a little reward for you, not that you deserve it. We are lunching at my house with the President.' Lavinia smiled her most patronising smile. 'When I heard that Anna deserting you for the day I thought to myself 'I really must feed the poor man. And luckily dear Charles Cabot was free to come too.' She touched the back of Quinn's hand with delicate fingers, their nails a glossy, pearly pink. 'I do have your interests at heart, you know.'

Tad took the bus down to the bay, counting out the unfamiliar coins for the fare carefully, in case he paid too much, and getting off at the stop near Drake Manor. The bus was full of excited children going with their mothers to the beaches further round the island, although some went to the beach by the wall on Drake Bay – still Long Bay to him.

He walked slowly past the entrance to Drake Manor, struggling to recall how it had looked during the war. Before his and Miki's escape he had only ever glimpsed it as the guards marched them along the road. He had a vague memory of soldiers and parked trucks by a ruined and roofless barn. Today the muddy path from the wooded valley emerged inconspicuously from among bushes right opposite the restaurant's driveway. But he was sure the path had been more of a road then. And how had they succeeded in getting past the vehicle park unseen? The shapes of extreme violence haunted him.

Then, as he started up the valley path from the restaurant end, looking for 'his' tiny cave, a much larger opening in the overgrown cliff face caught his eye. He negotiated ferns and saplings to discover the entrance to a substantial tunnel in the rock, more than high enough to stand upright in.

Half buried in the earth outside the entrance lay the rusted chassis of a small wheeled vehicle. It even had the remains of an engine. And just inside the tunnel were railway lines. He was about to use the flashlight he had borrowed to investigate further when he checked himself. No recollections of this tunnel stirred in his mind. He must stick to his search or he would lose too much time. His so expensive week was passing fast. He had a duty not only to himself and the memory of Miki, but to his wife. He continued trudging up the path.

Tad was convinced the valley had not been as overgrown as this in the war. And the distance seemed much shorter than he recalled. But it was the right time of day. Around noon. The fog had cleared, just as it had all those years ago, and above the trees he could glimpse blue sky, although the valley remained in shadow. Indistinct memories began to coalesce in his mind.

When he located his cave again it was as dim as it was dank, even on this midday of bright sunlight. With no real difficulty he thrust aside the branches, just as Anna had helped him do yesterday, reached the cave and took out the flashlight. He had the rusty old knife in a pocket, but left it there.

The knife worried him, because it was such tangible evidence of the past, and he knew intuitively that its moment of revelation would come. He had wrapped a strip of cloth around the rotted handle, in case he had to use it. The fear of being hunted down still made him tremble, even now. He had a feeling that Miki and he had used something, perhaps the knife, to carve their initials on the rock while they waited in the cave for whatever would happen next.

He started shining the flashlight around the shallow circumference of the cave. The low roof glistened darkly from the wet. And there, on the roof, expected but still a shock, he saw the crudely incised initials WM, Wolf and Miki.

He had known yesterday that this was the cave, because of the knife. But the initials were the final proof. And why was it so identified in his subconscious with bloodshed and violence?

He was struggling to recall exactly what he had done here when there was a furious barking from outside. He was still scrutinising the roof and almost fell over as he swung round to face this enemy, realising that he was trapped, just as he and Miki had been all those years ago. A large black dog was barking as it thrust towards him through the undergrowth. Without really thinking about it he snatched the knife from his pocket and stood in the cave entrance, confronting the attacker.

The woman in a blue dress walking her Labrador down the valley had taken off his lead and let him run free. He had scented the man, run him to ground and was barking his head off.

'Peter!' she shouted angrily, assuming her dog was chasing a rabbit and might vanish, 'Peter. Come here! Heel.'

The Labrador broke into a crescendo of barks and as she ran down the path to catch it she saw the hairs on its back stiffen. Tad was holding his ground, knife in hand, facing the dog. He had no alternative. Somewhere behind there would be a guard. The Labrador moved closer. Not normally an aggressive animal, it sensed the unusual and reacted furiously when it saw that the man was holding something threatening.

'Peter! Come here!'

The woman was forced to plunge into the undergrowth herself and was grabbing the dog's collar when she saw what had excited it and flinched.

A few feet ahead of her, standing in a rock opening, was a man in a leather jacket and a cloth cap. She did not realise that he was old. All she saw, with horror, was that he had a knife in his hand and the knife was pointing at her. She screamed.

In the next moment the man slumped sideway against the rock, pitched forward onto the ground and lay motionless. This time she did not scream. She snapped on the dog's lead and dragged it away to look for help.

'And what exactly is this, may I ask?' Lavinia held up an unframed oil painting that she had routed out from amongst Quinn's canvases. It was a portrait of a woman.

Quinn tried to take it back from her, but she resisted. They had agreed the absurd 'conceptual theme'. She had examined his preliminary sketches. Their business discussions were over and they were about to drive to her house for lunch. Then, without reason or asking his agreement, she had delved again into the rack of his unfinished work. Like a wife suspicious of infidelity she now confronted him.

'And who sat for this, I should like to know? It's obviously new.'

'No-one.' Quinn was being strictly truthful. There had been no sitter. But he was not defiant enough. He should have told Lavinia straight out that it was none of her damn business. Because it was not. This was a portrait of Anna done from memory and from photographs and Lavinia knew perfectly well who it was. He had painted it a few months ago when he was missing her badly. On account of a quite unaccustomed reticence, which he could never have explained, he had not yet shown it to Anna herself. He knew it was good, one of the best he had ever done. But he was nervous about it, perhaps because of what it revealed.

'It's Anna, of course,' he admitted, annoyed at Lavinia's pretence of not recognising the subject, 'but she never sat for it.'

'Well, well, well. How quite extraordinary! So it is!'

Lavinia carried the canvas across to the easel and placed it in front of the Victorian harbour scene. She saw, to her extreme annoyance, that it was both a fine portrait and, more importantly, a loving one. Every wave and highlight of Anna's bell of soft brown hair, the tiny crinkles of amusement around her mouth, the deep compassion in hazel eyes which gazed openly and directly at you; every single detail added up to a portrait of surprising depth. No wonder Quinn could not paint with such power and authority for her when he was still in love with Anna.

'I didn't recognise her at first.' Lavinia lied. 'Of course her hair is actually mouse-coloured.' she scratched her brains for a way to be more derogatory. 'I must admit that the old trick of making the eyes seem to follow you can be very effective. You ought to use it in the Drake portrait.'

At this moment, to Quinn's relief, the phone began its insistent buzzing. The call was from the police. The Polish visitor, Tadeus, had collapsed after being attacked by a dog. The dog's owner was counterclaiming that he had threatened her with a knife. It was thought that Mrs Quinn knew him. Could she go at once to the hospital?

'She's across in St Mary's today.' Quinn was conscious that Lavinia, who had moved away in a pretence of courtesy, was listening avidly. 'I'm pretty sure the old man is staying at a guest house in the town. Mr Mackinnon might know. He particularly asked for Anna? I'm sorry, but she won't be back until this evening and I don't where she is in St Mary's. Except that she will be at the ferry later. Yes I'll tell her.'

'Not another drama!' Lavinia made it an exclamation, not a question. At the same time she contrived a small, despairing gesture with her hands. She had obviously heard every word.

'An old Polish man who came for the memorial service next Sunday has been taken ill. Anna had befriended him.'

'Not another throwback to the war! Why does she have to get herself so *involved.* Anyone would think she'd been personally saving Jews from the Holocaust herself.'

'I'm sorry, Quinn,' Lavinia realised she might have been a touch too bitchy, though she still spoke as if wearied by all this 'but your wife is getting herself mixed up in some very odd things. No wonder you're not able to work properly yourself. Anyway there's absolutely nothing you can do about that little drama. Let's go for lunch. Thank heavens Rachel is doing the cooking.'

Lavinia absolutely abhorred the dishevelled, smoke-smelling and spartan interior of Quinn's Land Rover, so she drove him in her own sleek, metallic blue BMW round the end of the island to her house between the lighthouse and Drake's Bay. Quinn had been there often enough before, but its setting never failed to excite him.

The house was close to a rugged, rocky shore, looking towards the French coast. A round towered stone fort was perched on some offshore rocks, only accessible at low water, though neatly completing the view. Built for the Victorian soldiery, its most recent occupants had been the Germans, who had added their tithe of concrete emplacements and gun slits. Since the war it had been abandoned, though it was not yet in ruins. The tides swept past it with a racing, churning venom, creating overfalls and small whirlpools among patches of apparent, but delusive, calm. Quinn had often tried to capture the contrast between the picturesqueness of the fort and the treacherous sea around it. He had usually failed.

By some minor miracle of nature or the tides a little cove close to the house had retained a tiny triangle of sand, with rock pools alongside, while above at each side reared miniature headlands of close turf, alive with tiny blue alpine-like flowers at this time of year.

Lavinia regarded the cove as her private beach; and indeed no strangers would have known it was there unless they stumbled on it. She had planted mint and borage in the headland turf so that if she picnicked there it would be available for garnishing the drinks of ice-cold Pimms, which she gave her guests from a giant thermos flask. She felt that this detail showed style.

In total contrast, her house was almost suburban. It was an enlarged bungalow, originally built in the 1930s, with upstairs dormer-windowed bedrooms in the shingle tiled roof, and a flat roofed extension at the front with wide sliding glass doors, giving on to a patio which commanded a splendid view of the fort and far off France. The view alone, the agent who sold it to her husband had declared, was worth the value of the house. She hated being there by herself.

Inside, all the rooms were painted off-white with white carpets and oatmeal coloured curtains of a textured material. Quinn suspected that Lavinia was terrified of colours, in case she chose badly. The white carpets, with an often muddy garden outside, were an unspoken challenge to the rest of the world. The pictures were mainly conventional sporting prints, although in the sitting room there hung a large portrait in oils of Lavinia herself as a young wife, in a shimmering ice-blue silk gown, a magnificent diamond necklace and earrings, plus a tiara, unsmilingly regal.

Quinn suspected, from the house's only photograph of her much older husband, that she had definitely been a trophy wife, even if the phrase had not been invented in those days. She had certainly been an expensive one. She still sometimes wore the huge diamond ring that she sported in the portrait.

After she had ushered him in, Quinn bade a friendly hello to Rachel, a buxom, bustling doctor's daughter who made a part-time profession of cooking for people she regarded as her social equals and who would therefore join them at lunch. Or rather, luncheon, as his hostess liked to call a formal meal.

Lavinia had fixed ideas about etiquette, taught her by the titled lady whose personal secretary she had been and who had introduced her to Gerald Wildeblood, largely for amusement. Lavinia had always believed that this employer, who was a lady-in-waiting at Court, would engineer the peerage for Gerald which they both so badly needed. Unhappily the titled lady had failed. Or perhaps had never really tried, reckoning she had done enough by introducing a very beddable, young blonde to a rich industrialist twice her age.

'G and T or wine?' Lavinia asked Quinn and without waiting for an answer poured him a glass of red. 'So much better for you than spirits.' she prodded his belly playfully. 'Less sugar. Someone ought to put you on a diet.' She believed in controlling the men in her life. Firmly.

The island's President, Charles Cabot, arrived. He was a tall, wiry, lanky man with short-cut greying hair, dressed in a blue suit and white shirt, while his tie had a silver griffin embroidered on it. He spoke in a clipped, military voice and the griffin with its curled tail seemed oddly exotic for such a conventional person. In fact it was the island's heraldic symbol. He frequently quoted the New England joke about 'the Cabots speak only to God', but was only distantly related to the famous American family. Although far from being island born, his parents had retired here, as he had now done, and Quinn supposed that he had been elected because he had been a Brigadier with a rack of medals and people were impressed by his rank.

'I am very glad to say, Charles,' Lavinia announced after some small talk, 'that our little project is well under way.'

She took the Mission Statement off a side table to show Cabot and was in full flow when Rachel appeared to say she was wanted on the telephone.

'Really, people do ring at the most inconvenient times.' she complained, but left to take the call, while Rachel stayed.

'She driving you hard?' Cabot asked Quinn with genial sympathy. 'There's no need. I'd rather get the pictures done properly than rush them. D'you have any problems, apart from all that ghastly jargon?'

'Not really.' Quinn wasn't going to call him 'Sir' or admit to difficulties in painting technique. 'I do have one question. I assume you would want me to leave out the war?'

'Funny you should ask that. I've been thinking about it too.' Cabot frowned, as if trying to reconcile conflicting pieces of evidence. 'Thought about it a lot. As a soldier I don't think you should leave it out. The Occupation's part of the island's history. Can't pretend things never happened. On the other hand....'

'Lavinia's dead against it.'

'Many islanders would be too. They'd rather blot out that bit of the past. Against that it was an island family who created the memorial, wasn't it? Difficult problem all round. You know something, Mr Quinn, you ought to come to the service on Sunday. There won't be many more. Might give you some ideas.'

'You mean they haven't all died yet?' Rachel chipped in, avid for gossip as usual. 'I suppose they will have soon. It's umpteen years since the war. I heard there's some old Polish guy here though?'

Quinn was far from sure what to say, so stayed silent.

Seizing advantage of Lavinia's continued absence, Rachel asked in the hasty, breathless voice of the born scandal-monger. 'Do tell us. Was this the room where the porno paintings were?

'I believe they were all over the downstairs.' Cabot chuckled. I suppose the house hadn't been extended then. There probably were a few in here. There's a set of photographs in the Museum, I believe.' he remembered his official position and issued a disclaimer. 'Haven't ever seen them myself, of course.'

Tell me another, Rachel thought.

'Was it the officers' brothel?' Quinn asked only semi-innocently. He suspected it had been.

'Oh absolutely!' Rachel knew that for sure. 'They had a high old time. Kinky old farts.'

'Not all the murals were pornographic.' Cabot corrected her. 'The German character has a strongly romantic side. I'm told there were scenes of a Rhineland castle and a small sailing boat, probably out there.' he gestured towards the shore. 'Must have been calmer water than usual. Or wishful thinking. But, yes, apparently some of the other paintings were, well, exuberant.'

'How fascinating!' Rachel enthused 'And then they were covered up?'

'Twice.' Cabot seemed to be something of an authority on this. 'Wallpaper the first time. Then painted over, pronto, after our hostess rediscovered them and was not amused. My wife was helping her. She wasn't amused either.' He evidently had been.

'Gosh, I'd love to have seen them.' Rachel exclaimed with girlish enthusiasm. 'Those sexy old krauts! What a laugh! Oh, help. I must get back to the hot stove or I'll be in trouble too.' She refilled her glass of wine and hurried out. She had private catering sewn up in an island where no local wanted to be a servant.

'Are the murals the reason why Lavinia's so anti-German? Quinn asked the President.

'Better ask her yourself.'

Quinn laughed. 'Not bloody likely.'

'So what's the big joke?' His patron had reappeared. The two men looked at each other. 'Don't tell me there wasn't one!'

'Just something Rachel said.' Quinn ducked the issue.

'That girl may be a brilliant cook, but she has a mind like a sewer. I suppose she was talking about the wretched murals.'

'I'm afraid so.' Cabot admitted, quickly escaping from the issue in a way he knew would assist Quinn. 'And talking of paintings, so far as I'm concerned there's no rush for Mr Quinn to complete his "mission". Rather he got it right.'

'Of course. But an artist has to paint when he's in the swing of it. Which is now, isn't it Quinn, dear?'

Lavinia was not going to be distracted by any advice that might prevent her sabotaging Anna's visit and Quinn was forced to fall into line meekly.

Having defeated that initiative, she reverted to the murals, making a mental note to revenge herself on the wretched Rachel, perhaps by denigrating her cooking.

'Some people find the whole business desperately funny. I'm afraid I don't and personally, having had relations blown up by a flying bomb when I was a baby,' she laid as much emphasis on the word 'baby' as she would have done had Anna been listening 'I have no love for the Germans. Any of them.'

Noticing the men exchanging glances, she changed the subject. 'Now, would anyone like a refill before we go in?' One thing the titled lady had failed to teach her was never to ask if someone wanted 'another' drink, but simply a drink

The lunch was uneventful, though excellent. Rachel's delicately flavoured *sea bass en papillote* reminded Quinn of how pleasant it was to eat well, while Lavinia easily persuaded Cabot to rubber stamp her project plans.

'And we cannot delay,' she insisted, 'we must not lose any more time.'

After the coffee Cabot excused himself and Rachel retired to clear up.

This left Quinn alone with Lavinia, who had consumed several glasses of wine and become, if not full-bloodedly amorous, at least feeling like going further than merely undermining Quinn's relationship with his wife.

'My dearest Quinn,' she said, pulling him towards a sofa and then, continuing to hold his hand, went on 'you are a most attractive man. Has nobody told you that?' She pulled him down. Feeling obliged to respond, and not unwilling, he kissed her lightly on the mouth.

Then, alarmingly, he became aware that her fingers had strayed to his groin and sat up abruptly.

'Lavinia my love,' he said, knowing he could now be in real trouble, 'Rachel not only has a mind like a sewer, she has the ears of a bat and she is the queen of gossip. She'll be back for something she "forgot" any moment now.' He nuzzled her cheek before standing up determinedly. 'I think I'll get a breath of fresh air before she does come in.'

He slid open one of the glass doors to the patio and walked determinedly down a path through the shrubbery to the shore. He didn't really know how to cope with this situation, except by escaping. A low wooden gate gave access to the shoreline path. The turf was short and springy underfoot. The characteristic tiny wildflowers grew everywhere.

He stood and looked down into the cove, really no more than a fifteen foot cleft in slabsided rock formations, tilted at the steep angle at which they had been thrust up by the earth's movements a hundred million years ago. Although covered with lichen they remained jagged and sharp. It was low tide and the triangle of sand was exposed. He made his way gingerly down the rocks – he had enjoyed a few glasses of wine himself and was unsteady – and sat down on a large rounded boulder, gazing out to sea. He needed to think.

But Quinn's first thought, perhaps subconsciously evading the real issue of his relationship with Lavinia, was that the girls from the officers' brothel must have swum and sunbathed here in the cove's seclusion. The sailing boat in the mural was likely to have been kept here. Some unknown soldier artist during the war had conjured up a scene of innocence and happiness at this spot, little knowing that he would create a connection with someone many decades later.

He watched the white sail of a yacht dipping on the swell out at sea and began to understand why Anna was so persistent in her search. It was hardly an original thought, but life was a continuum. Whatever he did now could affect his children yet unborn, just as she was affected by her uncle.

And that jerked him back to his basic dilemma. What the hell was he doing, hoping to tempt Anna to live with him here when his only dependable income came from a small investment – and Lavinia.

Of course he could always sell watercolours of local scenes to tourists. He would never starve. But it was a mediocre existence if it promised no serious recognition, an existence in which, for all his talk of artistic freedom, he was not so much liberated as trapped.

He might kid himself that Anna would play the loving Tahitian girl to his Gauguin. But that would be nonsense and an illusion. The outward show, the beard, the Land Rover, were fine for the islanders. He had to offer something more for her. And all he'd been able to do so far on this lousy island was trumpet his artistic libido and get entangled with a witch.

He clambered back up the rocks feeling something akin to hatred for Lavinia, with all her scheming and possessiveness, her "interpretative empathy" and her self importance. What she actually wanted was a toy boy, a decent looking younger escort who would do as he was told. He was only under consideration himself because there were so very few unattached men on the island, with too many women after them. And he was not unattached.

Good God, he thought. Lavinia was twenty years older than him and he'd let her kiss him on the sofa after half a bottle of wine. Okay, most of a bottle. It made him feel like a pet poodle. Worse, he knew he would never dare to say so, just have to zip it all up inside, because he needed the work. And he worried because inside the bearded façade he knew he was not a great artist, just a very ordinary man.

Lavinia could have told him, had she chosen, that an ordinary man was what most women wanted. But she didn't, because what she was after was an affair, not a marriage. And Anna could have told him too. But he had never asked her.

CHAPTER ELEVEN

Visiting St Mary's was a trip to another world. The town's stuccoed Georgian houses clung to the steep hillside above the busy quaysides, guarded by an ancient castle. Yachts lay moored in marinas, while small ferries creamed their way to other islands visible on the horizon. A giant white-hulled cruise liner lay at anchor offshore, its tenders shuttling tourists to the duty free shops. Spires and towers decorated the skyline. Surveying the sunlit scene as her ferry slowed down before docking Anna realised where this place reminded her of: Portofino in Italy. Not the same climate, of course, but a comparable charm.

The contrast with the single shopping street, sleepy harbour, fierce tides and jagged cliffs of Quinn's home was intense, although she had already been warned that bad weather could envelop St Mary just as quickly. And, of course, this much larger island had also suffered German occupation. But its population had not been evacuated and Jack Mackinnon had assured her that the archives were far more complete.

In fact Mackinnon's backing was to be the key to her researches here, although initially she did not welcome his arrangements. The last thing she wanted was what he'd fixed up.

As she stepped off the gangplank a small, fair-haired man in a sweater and jeans came up to her on the granite quayside.

'Mrs Quinn?' he asked, 'I guessed you must be from Jack's description. My name's Dick Carey. I work for the St Mary Gazette.'

'You're a reporter?' she was far from sure that she wanted to talk to the media. And anyway her visit was hardly news. So why had Mackinnon told this man she was coming?

'Don't worry.' Carey grinned broadly. 'I am after a story, but not about you. I've been researching a series of pieces for the Gazette about the war years. So I can introduce you to the archivist and I've also got a collection of memorabilia myself.'

Anna thanked him politely, but remained suspicious. 'Just what kind of story are you after?'

'Jack tells me there's an old Polish man who was on the island as a slave visiting you.'

'Not me particularly. But there is one. He's called Tadeus.'

'I'd really like to interview him, though it may have to be on the telephone. The Gazette isn't over-generous with expenses.'

Anna made a quick decision. This mid-30s, casually dressed and quite attractive reporter was being straight with her. No subterfuge. What was more, he seemed ready to help.

'Tad's very shy.' she said 'And he doesn't speak English at all well. But I'll ask him.'

'Thanks a lot. That was all I wanted. There can't be many of the slaves still alive, so his memories would be worth recording. I only hope the Gazette will pay the fare. Now I think you need to get to the reference library.'

'Is it in walking distance?'

He glanced down at the shoes she was wearing and was relieved to see they were trainers. The current girl in his life liked to wear shoes that were completely incompatible with walking.

'Easily,' he said 'it's not much of a climb.' Then he asked, as they made their way up a steep, stiletto-defeating, cobbled street to the Reference Library. 'What brought you out here?'

'I had a relation who was on the island after the war. He's not been heard of since.'

'What was he doing?'

'That's exactly what I don't know.'

The library was in a handsome stone built Victorian house on the edge of a park, once its gardens. At the entrance they passed a receptionist, ensconced in a cubicle by a security gate designed to prevent the theft of books, and Dick led her up a wide, grandiose stone staircase to the top floor. The family who had once owned this mansion lived in some style. A photograph of them, with the top-hatted paterfamilias seated on a chair among his brood, hung on the stairs. And there was a wartime photo of a jackbooted German soldier standing outside too. Another reminder, Anna reflected.

Inside there was a high-ceilinged room equipped with desks for readers and a large photocopier. Anna knew immediately that she would feel comfortable working here.

Dick introduced her to the chief archivist, who occupied an adjoining office and was also named Carey. 'There are a lot of us around.' Dick joked and the archivist replied, reluctantly and in a pained voice, 'All related, alas.' He must be close to retirement, Anna judged, and wore a Fair Isle patterned pullover over his shirt and tie, which fortified the elderly impression. He spoke pedantically.

'So you know Jack Mackinnon? He told me you were coming. How can we assist you?

Anna hesitated, not wanting the reporter to hear. With unexpected tact, Dick offered to withdraw and wait for her. She appreciated that and, once the door was closed, explained all about her uncle.

'So he would have been 19 or younger in 1945? Not that it helps much. Even 12 year olds were conscripted at the end. You see, Miss....'

'Anna Quinn. Mrs.' she didn't go much for the 'Ms' title, except at the art school, where it was virtually compulsory. A surprising number of her married friends didn't like 'Ms' any more either.

'I do apologise' he glanced at her left hand, but did not ask why she was not wearing a ring. 'Well, Mrs Quinn, you must understand that our archive, and it numbers some million and a half documents, is entirely concerned with relations between the civil administration and the wartime Occupying Power. The German military government was known as the Feldkommandatur and took its orders from a higher headquarters in Paris.'

This kind of detail was of zero interest to Anna. 'Can you look up a person's name?' she asked.

'Not as such. A subject, yes. If you want to know about requisitioned bicycles or directives to fishermen, that's easy, and then you will find names.'

'What about German servicemen who were kept on as prisoners of war afterwards? Weren't they given jobs to do?'

'Now there you could have a starting point, Mrs Quinn.' The archivist spoke as if she had proposed some new way of opening a chess game. 'They were indeed allotted tasks; lifting mines, removing barbed wire, clearing rubble.'

'And some were sent to our island for that?'

'Yes indeed. As were civilians.' He rose to his feet. 'Let me fetch you the files. Will you mind working in the main room?'

'It is rather a personal search. Can I come to you with questions?'

'Most certainly you may. Any friend of Jack's is a friend of ours.'

Ten minutes later the archivist and an assistant came back with their arms full of document boxes and cardboard file covers, all bulging and dusty, making Anna realise why the men wore sweaters that could be washed, rather than jackets. They deposited their burdens on a table, where Dick was waiting patiently.

'You may find it useful to mark any documents you need to have photocopied.' the assistant handed her some slips of paper. 'We'll do the copying for you.'

'You've got yourself a job and a half there.' Dick commented cheerfully.

'These are only some of the relevant files,' Carey said, with pride, 'I have endeavoured to be selective.'

'You're going to have to excuse me now.' Dick apologised and stood up. 'I have to write an obit. But we could meet for lunch. I could collect you at twelve thirty.' Not 'shall collect you' she noted with relief, but 'could collect'.

'Are you sure? I mean don't feel you have to.'

'I'd like to know how you've got on. It's my own hobby too.'

'Then I'd love to.'

By twenty past twelve, having been hospitably provided with unofficial coffee during her labours, Anna was forced to accept that her uncle had probably not been among the POWs kept on in 1945. The name Johann Eberhardt did not appear in any list. She knocked on the archivist's door to thank him.

'Did you have good fortune?' he asked.

'Not so far. During the war would he have been able to send a postcard home to Germany?'

'Until the Allied landings in June 1944, most certainly. Ships carried supplies to and from the mainland all the time. After D Day, of course, the islands were under siege.'

Anna wished for the umpteenth time that the Red Cross had attributed a date to that solitary postcard. It must have had a postmark.

'And, as a German, what might he have been doing here?'

'An 18 year old? Hardly a skilled technician. A ranker in the army, navy or air force is the obvious answer. Or...' he seemed embarrassed. '...one of Hitler's special organisations. The Todt Organisation, which built the fortifications, was run by engineers, but it had ordinary guards, many of them young.'

'I know a little about that. One of the forced labourers is back in the island now.'

'And' Carey cleared his throat, confronting the worst possibility, 'the SS were in your island, though not here.'

'How can I find out?' Anna's own throat was becoming dry, perhaps only from the dusty files, and her body felt tense. She steadied herself on the edge of his desk. 'Is there any way?'

'I'm afraid not here. The Nazis tried to destroy anything incriminating before they surrendered. Have you asked Jack?'

'He sent me to you because he had nothing.' Was everything going to continue in circles just like it had before, constantly preventing her from reaching the truth? The feeling of desperation began to grip her again.

Observing her distress, the archivist tried to console her. 'At least you now know he was not a POW.'

'Yes.' she agreed dully. 'Could he have come as an ordinary visitor?'

'Immediately after the war? Most unlikely. He would not have been at all welcome.'

Somehow this reminded her of Lavinia and she wondered what exactly she and Quinn were doing at this moment. Drinking more of that endless white wine, probably, damn them.

'If you will excuse me,' Carey said. 'We have to close now for lunch. I can leave the files on the table if you are returning.'

'Thank-you so much, but I don't expect I will be.'

What was the point? She thanked him warmly and walked back down the grand staircase to find Dick waiting in the lobby. He took her to a small Italian restaurant in a narrow cobbled street in the old town. The trattoria was as genuine a place as one could hope to find outside Italy itself, with red check table cloths, giant pepper mills and a lengthy menu.

'Quite a few Italians have settled here.' Dick said. 'They've transformed our eating out.' He handed her a menu. 'First, what would you like to drink?'

'Please, Mr Carey.' she blushed, which she did not do often. 'Alright then, Dick. Let's go Dutch, shall we? I don't imagine you can put me on expenses. And I'd like some Frascati.'

Two can play at enjoying white wine with a companion of the opposite sex, she thought vengefully, and then was puzzled at

105

how completely Lavinia had managed to get up her nose. But she certainly had. And even after ordering local fish with prawns in a, guess what, white wine sauce, she was still wondering what Quinn was eating, certain that Lavinia would have invited him to lunch.

'Please tell me,' she asked to break her own mood, 'what is an "obit" and did you get it written?'

Dick laughed, an unaffected, genuine laugh. 'Obituary. Total hack work. At least this time the dead politician's family wanted one published.'

'Don't they usually?'

'It's amazing how often they don't. Either the husband died in the wrong bed or he was deep in some dodgy deal and the widow refuses to talk. Rather hush everything up. Then it's back to the cuttings library. Talking of which, how did you get on?'

'A dead end.' She told him about her morning.

'There were thousands of German troops in these islands,' Dick explained 'and they weren't even frontline ones. Most were conscripts who were horrified at what went on. How old would your uncle be now?'

'Seventy plus. Probably 73. He's probably dead by now.' She didn't want to talk about her fears. 'What got you interested in the Occupation, Dick?'

'German officers requisitioned the house next to ours. My Grannie was forced to do their laundry. They said if she didn't they'd throw her out of her house and all of us out of ours too.'

'Not very nice people.'

'No.' There was a silence, during which the food and wine were brought. Then Dick said very earnestly. 'Look, I've been lent a diary written in your island in 1943. It was found in the rafters when a house there was being redecorated. The stupid thing is, although I've had it for two weeks, I don't know what's in it.'

'Why not?'

'I can't read French. Can you?' She nodded.

'If I let you have it, would you promise to give it back?'

'Of course I would.' She realised this might be a breakthrough 'But can't you follow any of it?'

'I did show it to a friend who knows French. He thought it must have belonged to the girlfriend of one of the German officers. Some of the entries were pretty explicit. If you like I could bring it to the ferry.'

'I would like, very much indeed.' The more insight she could get into what had gone on during the war, the more she would understand. She had almost given up on her uncle. Perhaps that was premature.

'Back to the archives?' Dick asked sympathetically, when their meal was over.

'No' she shook her head decisively. 'I'm going to take a look at the town. A little retail therapy. I might never come here again.' For a moment she had hoped he would offer to show her round, but remembered he had a living to earn. He would have been a nice man to go around with. 'I'll see you at the boat. And thank-you for a most enjoyable lunch.'

Within moments of saying goodbye she was kicking herself for not suggesting he should show her round, even if he might have declined. It had been a pleasure being with an uncomplicated person. Anyway, she thought, consoling herself, I could use an hour or two with no strings attached.

In the streets and alleys near the trattoria there were antique and curio shops. Anna browsed, wishing she had enough money to indulge in serious retail therapy. But the restaurant menu alone had made her realise that one thing success as an offshore financial centre does not bring is low prices and, judging from the many brass nameplates announcing the offices of foreign banks, St Mary was extremely successful.

She ventured further and briefly investigated a rock tunnel near the port, which had been turned into a museum of the German Occupation. It seemed to her to be all helmets and guns, although the tunnel had originally been an underground hospital. The soldiers must have lived like troglodytes half the time. It was dreadfully depressing and she did not stay long.

At 3.45pm she was waiting to board the ferry when Dick arrived, carrying a very small parcel.

'Here you are.' he said. 'Take care of it. It'll be of real historical value one day, if it isn't already.'

She thanked him, stowed the diary away in her capacious sack and was about to say good bye, when he said something that caused her instant alarm.

'The newsroom just heard that the old Polish guy is in hospital. Seems he collapsed when he was attacked by a dog, but the dog's owner claims he threatened her with a knife.'

'Oh no!' Anna gazed at him with horror. She didn't need to be told what had happened. Tad had returned to the cave alone and things had gone desperately wrong.

'He's in your hospital with a police guard.'

'Police? But that's crazy. He's far too weak to attack anyone. He's just not physically strong enough.'

'I'm so sorry, Anna.' Dick was sympathetic, but he was a newsman. 'That's what we've heard. I might be sent across for this. Sounds like a good story. All depends on the Editor.' He saw her distressed expression. 'I promise I'll keep you out of it.'

Anna clutched her sack, feeling completely hollow. The very last thing Tad needed was publicity. And then she felt disloyal, because Dick was helping her for no reward and after all it was his job to report things.

Dick saw all this in her face. It was something all newspapermen had to cope with when their friends became mixed up with events. And if you were half-decent there were times when you wished you were not a reporter, because all professions tend to mould people to their ethics and journalism was no exception. It was not a pleasant mould. Nor an ethical one. The most successful tabloid reporters could only be described as s***s.

'It's almost as bad as being a politician.' he said. 'But not quite.' That made her smile; he wanted to cheer her up. 'I promise to keep you out of what I write. That's the best I can do.'

'If only I could get back to the island quicker.' She knew she could take a flight. Bother the cost this time, and she'd have to cope with the fear. It was only fifteen minutes, after all.

'You wouldn't get there by air today.' Dick had quite a knack of reading her thoughts. 'The airport's fogbound.'

Almost to her own surprise she gave Dick a kiss on the cheek when he said goodbye. She had taken to him instinctively as a soulmate and hoped he would be sent across, though Quinn would immediately get wildly jealous. Quinn practically went berserk if she patted a dog. Needless to say, any affection he himself displayed to other women was totally different, reasonable, justified. Yet again she wondered if he was not at this moment being altogether too reasonable with Lavinia.

The hydrofoil slipped gently out of St Mary's harbour, past the 'four knots maximum' speed sign, past a pair of stone pillars bearing red and green navigation lights, out into the broad channel and was soon slicing through the sea as though on skis. Anna found herself a seat by a window in the cabin and prepared to open the diary package. It was now three days since she had last been on this ferry, three days out of her eight, and what had she achieved? Not a lot. She had failed to trace her uncle and was far from sure where she stood with Quinn. She might as well see what Dick's contribution had to offer, though she had no great expectations for it.

The diary was indeed small, of a size that could be slipped into a handbag. It was German made, with the year '1943' in faded gold Gothic script on the front cover, and was bound in stained and scratched red leather. Gold corners had helped preserve it. The entries were in French, in a handwriting which must normally have been open and demonstrative, but here was compressed to fit the small pages. Even so the entry for one day often ran on over several.

The opening page had 'Personal Notes' printed in German at its head. A single notation in strong capitals announced its owner as 'Marianne', but with no other details at all. Was this going to be the Holy Grail of her research? Who was Marianne?

Anna began to flip idly through the pages, waiting for something to catch her eye, conducting a sort of fishing expedition. However the thought of Tad in hospital was distracting her badly and what with the motion of the boat she was unable to concentrate, especially on crabbed writing in a foreign language.

Suddenly she did find herself wide-eyed at a description.

'That crazy Grundmann' it read 'has fixed up a wicker cradle hanging on a rope from the ceiling over the bed. I have to squat in it, he twists the rope tightly round and round, then he enters me from below and grunts with delight as the contraption rotates me on his erection. He likes to order "basket" as if I am dog and expects me to squeal with pleasure. Mon Dieu, what will he dream up next for his "House of Joy"!'

Anna giggled irrepressibly, everything else forgotten. So that was what used to go on in the fragrant Lavinia's bedroom! She would die if she read it. If only she could! Thank God for some humour in this depressing scenario, though it might be best not to show it to Quinn, in case he started getting ideas.

A change in the noise of the engines made her look up. The hydrofoil had slowed and was enveloped in fog. She could only see a few yards through the window. The boat's captain was edging ahead cautiously and sounding the foghorn. In the cabin a loudspeaker clicked and a woman's voice regretted that due to adverse weather conditions their arrival would be delayed.

And late they were. The vessel finally nosed up to the quay, still in fairly thick fog, over an hour late. Anna got off, clutching a shopping bag full of French cheese and bread and other goodies she had promised to bring, as well as her sack, only to find that Quinn was not there. What to do? Idiotically she had not got the phone number of the Moroccan room and Quinn was ex-directory – another silly conceit of his.

She found a bench, by the end of an old stone quay which must have formed the island's original dock, but had long been superseded by a commercial quay, and sat down to wait, gradually getting more angry. Okay, she should have noted his phone number, but for Chrissake he should been here, whether she was late or not. She desperately needed to get to the hospital.

The fog lay heavily damp in the early evening air and clung to her hair and clothes, making her chilled and depressed. Having dressed for a hot sunny day she began shivering. Why wasn't Quinn here? She knew Lavinia was determined to destroy what was left of their marriage. Had she prevented his coming?

The bench faced towards the bay, the largest bay on the island, with a half moon of sandy beach with on the far side a rocky headland and yet another squat Victorian fort. That much she remembered from her arrival.

But the scene was almost completely hidden now. The fog drifted around as aimlessly as it always did in a light wind, which Quinn had told her was not enough to clear it away, only to stir it up. Sometimes it was a blanket closing the rest of the world out, at other times it thinned and she could discern indistinct outlines of the wide bay and see the houses close by where she sat.

They were handsome old houses with high pitched roofs, which had historically lined an 18th Century quayside, now lost beneath the sand since the new harbour had been constructed, or so Quinn had explained. Looking to her right she could see the gabled end of the nearest house, while straight ahead of her was the much less distinct outline of a small steamer in the bay.

This is absurd, she thought. I can't call him. I must go to the see Tad. It's a very long walk to the fort and I would probably get lost. Then, forcing herself to be philosophical, he decided she could see just about enough to do some sketching to kill the time. It might even help her feel less cold. She fished out her gear, checked that she had a sharpened pencil, balanced the pad of art paper on her knee and began.

Whether the fog did drift away a little, or whether her imagination strengthened the vague shapes in the bay, the scene she was watching became clearer.

The steamer was a fair size, though almost a period piece. Its bow was straight edged, not raked like a modern ship's, and its stern projected back in an elegantly period kind of way. It had a single upright funnel between two short masts. There were probably some fairly ancient cargo vessels operating around here, she thought, and this would be one of them. The islands were the sort of place where they would end their careers before their last voyage to the scrap yard. But, oddly, there didn't seem to be any crewmen on board.

With a small sense of shock, perhaps more of surprise, she realised that the way the steamer lay in the water wasn't quite right. The bow was down and the stern up, so that the deck was not level. Suddenly she understood. The ship had gone aground – she had seen jagged rocks out there at low tide when Quinn drove her past on her arrival – and been abandoned. That was why there was no-one on board. Being only a few yards from the beach, they would all have got away safely. Not too much of a loss, Anna reckoned, it being such an old ship, as she filled in all the detail she could, making the most of the fog clearing a little. She had never seen a shipwreck before, even as undramatic a one as this.

The fog continued drifting lazily across the bay, briefly revealing, then concealing again, and she noticed that there were people on the beach. They looked like soldiers and they were standing around idly in small groups, their rifles slung over their shoulders. A couple of more smartly dressed men, with high peaked hats and an air of authority, were standing with their booted legs firmly apart, studying the ship through binoculars, as though something was about to happen.

She roughed in the soldiers at the edge of her drawing, putting them closer to the ship than they really were, because the ship was the focal point of her sketch. But they were part of the overall scene, so she wanted them in.

A rowing boat began making its way across the water to the steamer, coming from somewhere not far from where she was sitting. She sketched that too. Its oarsmen, who were recognisably sailors, stopped near the stricken ship and Anna saw them begin pulling something like a heavy sack out of the water, though it was impossible to make out what. Then the little boat headed back towards her.

Moments later men appeared on the deck of the ship, seeming to surge up from nowhere. She could see they were jostling and pushing each other, until several tumbled over the side into the sea and began struggling to reach safety among the rocks.

The two officers on the beach lowered their binoculars and started gesticulating at the soldiers, some of whom raised their rifles and to her horror began firing at the escaping men. Others just stood there, uncertain what to do. She could see that the officers were shouting at them, though their voices did not carry far enough for her to hear. She didn't hear the shots either, though she saw several of the escaping men collapse into the sea.

This terrible sight made her jump to her feet, knowing she must stop this wanton killing, thinking she might run down to the beach between the soldiers and the ship. That would force them to stop. Dropping her pad, she ran towards a ramp leading down to the beach, then realised the men were actually quite a long way away, in the centre of the bay, and already the fog was sweeping back in. The steamer disappeared, as quickly as though a curtain had been drawn across it. Everything was hidden: the beach and the soldiers and the rowing boat.

However the rowing boat emerged from the fog soon after she abandoned her effort, its sailors slowly sculling towards the stone quay to her left. She saw that what they had retrieved was a body, which lay limp across the gunwales. They must have heard the gunfire, but even though they had already turned their dinghy round to return, why hadn't they attempted to rescue the men who had surged on to the deck and jumped despairingly overboard? And why were the soldiers shooting them? None of it made sense. She decided that the shipwreck must have occurred earlier in the day, or there would have been boats all over the place. The rowing boat must have been making a last attempt at rescue. It came back.

The oarsmen did not row directly towards her, but diverted far out to her left, where for the first time she noticed there was a long ironwork extension to the main quay of the harbour, just like a section of the Brighton pier she knew so well. She squeezed a side view of this into her sketch, although that was cheating too, since when she had been drawing the steamer, the pier-like construction had been out of sight. Quinn would have justified it as 'artist's licence'.

She had not quite finished the sketch when she heard the familiar clunking, grinding noise of the Land Rover. Its door slammed and Quinn came running, panting and embarrassed.

'I'm terribly sorry,' he gasped, 'Lavinia thought.....' he cut that dangerous explanation short, though not quickly enough......'that is, I thought the fog.....'

'Well, it didn't.' she was quietly angry at first, then really let go. 'You mean Lavinia thought. Were you in bed with her?''

'No, we....' Quinn's reply had all the hesitation of a man with a guilty conscience.

'You mean "yes" don't you?'' Anna accused him. 'Why can't you be honest with me! What's the matter with you? Why can't you keep your wretched dick inside your trousers?'

Quinn retreated from her fury, backing up against the side of the Land Rover as if it would protect him.

'We didn't. I promise.' he was like a schoolboy caught raiding an orchard.

'We! You and your bloody Lavinia. For goodness sake just take me to the hospital.'

'What on earth for?'

'Tad is there. Didn't you know?'

This was another embarrassment, because Quinn did know. The police had rung him several hours ago. But he had done nothing about it, not daring to tell Lavinia.

Totally defeated, he opened the passenger door for Anna and drove her straight to the hospital, not a great distance because the small modern building overlooked the coast near the harbour. In the waiting area by the entrance, supervised from a glass enclosed nurses' office, was a Police constable

He was in dark blue uniform, standing upright and holding his helmet in one hand and when Anna went to the office he constable stepped forward to intercept her.

'Are you Mrs Quinn?' he asked politely, but firmly. 'I'd like a word with you, please.'

CHAPTER TWELVE

'I've come to visit the Polish man.' Anna said, shocked at being confronted by the constable with his notebook, and instinctively fearful. What on earth could Tad have done? Had Jack Mackinnon been right? Had he turned dangerous? She must be extremely cautious. 'Can I please go in?' she asked.

'I'd like a word with you first, Mrs Quinn.' The constable insisted. Quinn himself said nothing, just standing there in the vinyl tiled hallway, absolutely mute.

A white-uniformed nurse emerged from the office, a traditional fob watch pinned to the front of her uniform. She knew how distressed the old man was, especially and inexplicably about the hospital pyjamas he had been given. When Jack Mackinnon could not be found, he had insisted on their calling Anna. And now the constable was firmly blocking her from going to the ward.

This was tricky for the nurse. The hospital staff had a duty to patients. At the same time it was important to maintain a co-operative relationship with the police. Theirs were the two services which sorted out the aftermath both of road accidents and the occasional violent crime. But the nurse found it hard to believe that the old man had really committed an assault: and she knew how the woman complaining about him enjoyed a drama. Possibly letting Mrs Quinn see him would be half way to having a lawyer.

'The old man is very upset and refuses to take a sedative,' the nurse temporised, 'it might help if he could talk to Mrs Quinn.'

'Hmm,' the constable considered this, then said to Anna 'I'd still like a word with you.' he only seemed to have one phrase. In reality, he had almost added 'if you don't mind', thinking of his Chief Officer's belief in community policing.

But community policing had its limits when up against the islanders' version of the Sicilian 'omerta'. They always clammed up after an incident, seldom gave evidence. However these people were not part of the local community.

'The Pole is a friend of yours?' he asked Anna.

' 'I really don't know him very well.'

'Can you tell me anything at all about him, Madam?'

To Anna this insistence had the unpleasant ring of forthcoming interrogation. 'Helping with enquiries' they always called it. She didn't trust the police.

Police forces were organisations she had never been able to make her mind up about. If you did confide in them they were quite likely to double cross you and she simply could not believe that Tad had been a serious threat to anyone with that ancient and broken knife. So what was this really about? She was going to have to find out and stop him being falsely accused.

Another nurse came through from the ward to say that Tad knew she was here and was begging to see her.

'Listen,' Anna said firmly to the constable, 'I must see him. He's all by himself in a strange place. He came here for the memorial service on Sunday. You can listen in if you must.'

'He's not well enough to be officially interviewed yet.' The nurse interjected to the policeman. 'In the morning probably.'

The constable knew better than to argue with the hospital staff. No-one had actually been hurt and he would need co-operation here in the future. He stood aside to let Anna past.

Leaving the embarrassed Quinn behind to entertain the constable, which she reckoned he deserved, Anna was taken through into a general ward. Because the beds were only curtained off there was no privacy of speech. Tad was propped up on pillows in the metal-framed bed, looking as if he had had a terrible fright, which Anna realised he undoubtedly had.

'We'll give him a sedative when you've gone,' the nurse said in a whisper. 'A good night's sleep and he'll be as right as rain.' She brought Anna a chair, partially drew the curtain again and stood to one side, watching. She had been ordered not to leave them completely alone.

Tad was wearing blue striped cotton hospital pyjamas. Deprived of his cloth cap and leather jacket he looked more frail than ever, the tendons in his wrinkled neck standing tautly out and his head skeletal. He tried to smile.

'Is good you come. Thank-you.'

'Are you all right?'

'Besser.' He slipped into German. 'But why this?' he gestured at the striped pyjamas, sounding extremely worried.

Anna was flummoxed, aware that the nurse was curious too. What was he talking about? Then she remembered Jack telling her that the slave labourers, like Tad, who had only the clothes they had been rounded up in, were known as the 'shaggy', while the SS prisoners were issued with boldly striped pyjama-like jackets and trousers, as in all concentration camps. That was what her grandparents must have been forced to wear. She had shuddered when she had learnt that and Mackinnon had shown her old photographs of those skeletal pyjama-clad victims. Now she understood. She had to re-assure Tad that he was not a prisoner.

'Don't worry' she said with an urgency that mystified the nurse 'you're safe here. Tell me what happened.'

'Would you like me to go?' the nurse asked 'I was told to listen to everything, but bother that.'

Anna saw from Tad's face that he would like to be alone with her, though he probably hadn't understood what was said.

'For a few minutes.' she suggested and the nurse smiled understandingly.

When she had gone Tad began to relate in slow, awkward phrases how he had returned to the cave and how the barking of the woman's Labrador had catapulted him back into the past.

'Did you do anything to her?'

'Nein, nein. I fear dog.'

'But the knife?'

'Is fur hunde nicht frau..'

Anna had already been certain of this. 'I will tell the police that.'

'They take me away?' He pulled at the striped pyjamas, trying to rip them off, but lacking the strength.

'No, no. I promise.'

In reality how could she promise anything, with a constable waiting outside? And exonerating Tad could easily become a full time job. All too easily. With only so few days left for her own mission, she had no time for this distraction.

'I visit cave again.' Tad asserted strongly.

'The cave?' she could barely believe that he wanted to.

'Is vital.' He pronounced the word as in German and Anna wondered why, as the stress mounted, he was lapsing more and more into German 'I think we kill man. And Miki dead. I know this. Not why. Nicht kennen.'

Tad shook his straggle-haired head despairingly, reminding Anna forcibly again of the sepia photographs of concentration camp inmates. The shaggy and the striped. If it sounded a bit like a joke now, it had not been then. Could Tad have murdered someone when they escaped?

116

'Are you are sure you killed a man?'

'Maybe was Miki. Germans kill escapers. We escape.'

Tad looked at her, beseechingly, desperate to be believed. 'I must go again. The day,' he struggled for the word 'different. Not like other day. Ship is wreck. Cave tell me.'

'Would you like me to go with you?' she made the offer from immediate sympathy, as rapidly wondering if she was completely out of her mind and, for the first time in this curious relationship, feeling seriously frightened. Had Tad threatened the woman with the dog? It was only his word against hers. Anna thought of Mackinnon's warning. What if Tad did go berserk? Would she be able to hold him off? Almost worse, what else might he find in the cave? Would the police let him go back there?

The nurse returned and said that she would have to leave now. After promising to fetch Tad from the hospital in the morning, because he certainly could not afford a taxi, Anna reluctantly left the ward.

A different policeman was waiting at the reception, with Quinn sitting silent on a chair, looking as resentful as only he could. Evidently their small talk had run out. The new arrival was a man in his mid-30s, tall, solidly built, with a sergeant's three chromium chevrons on his shoulder, but still with that plodding and methodical manner typical of a certain kind of officer.

'Mrs Quinn' he stepped forward. 'I have taken over from my colleague. Can you spare some time now?'

Anna quickly deduced two things. First that a more senior officer had been brought in and second that this one was not wanting about just a few minutes chat. Bloody fuzz, she thought.

He asked her to come through into the glass enclosed hospital office, which the remaining nurse tactfully vacated.

'Please sit down. I am Sergeant Price. I would like to ask you a few questions about the gentleman you've been visiting.'

'I really hardly know him.'

'You were with him when he found this?'

It sounded like an accusation and the sergeant took out a notebook and pencil, before showing her the rusty kitchen knife, protected within a transparent plastic envelope. She saw at once that Tad had wrapped a strip of cloth around the iron spike of the handle and the blade had been rubbed down so that a sharp tip emerged from the rust.

117

'He appears to have intended using it.' the sergeant said.

'But I'm sure he never would have done against a person.' Anna protested, trying to counter the damning evidence in front of her. 'He's not that kind of person.' Why should he have sharpened it and made the handle usable, she asked herself? 'Perhaps he wanted to be able to defend himself.'

'Against whom, Mrs Quinn?'

'He's terrified of dogs. He was hunted by guards with Alsatians here during the war.'

'That was many years ago.'

'For him it was yesterday. He's not been back since then.'

She decided not to mention Tad's visions. And if either he or Miki had really killed a man, perhaps he could still be like that, which she definitely did not want to suggest. She was beginning to feel like Tad's defending counsel.

'You knew about this cave?' the sergeant was making notes now with his stubby pencil: presumably, she thought, in pencil so it could be altered later.

'Me?' She didn't need to playact horror. 'I've never been here before! How could I? He said he hid there when he escaped. Finding the knife confirmed that it was the right cave.'

'I see, Mrs Quinn.' the sergeant's tone made it clear that he did not see, not at all. 'And?'

'When he was hiding there he was attacked by an Alsatian. He killed the dog. In the war, that is.'

'The lady states that he threatened her with this knife.'

'And immediately collapsed in front of her?' Anna didn't say 'what a ridiculous lie', but implied it. 'Have you seen how frail he is?'

'The staff have asked us not to interview him until tomorrow morning.'

This had evidently aggravated Sergeant Price, who recounted it in a severely condemnatory voice. 'He was in possession of an offensive weapon.'

'And he says the woman's dog attacked him. Isn't failing to control a dog an offence? It's her word against his. And I've told you how he found the knife. It's not as though he deliberately bought it or anything.'

'But he was expecting to use it.' The sergeant was insistent. Carrying an offensive weapon was a crime.

'I'm sure he had a reason. He was very scared of what he might find on the island.'

She spoke as determinedly as she could, still without saying anything about Tad's visions. If she did do, the Social Services would have him in a mental ward within hours. And they were accountable to no-one.

The sergeant closed his notebook. 'We may need to talk to you again, Mrs Quinn.'

He was clearly still not satisfied and made no attempt to thank her.

'I'm staying at Fort Rocquaine with my husband.'

He ushered her out of the office and she rejoined Quinn. 'Let's go.' she said with undisguised disgust, adding to the nurse 'I'll be back tomorrow morning. Please tell Tadeus.'

Going out to the Land Rover she turned to Quinn, needing someone to talk to. 'You know, that copper really believes Tad tried to attack the woman. Who is she? What can she have said?'

'Search me.' Quinn was still in full retreat.

'I asked you. Who is she?'

'Another widow with nothing to do except walk the dog and gossip.'

Quinn said it bitterly and Anna guessed he had not enjoyed a smooth ride with Lavinia during the day, damn the woman. She would get to the bottom of that later. Meanwhile she wanted answers.

'You still haven't explained why you weren't there to meet me!'

'To be honest, I forgot the time. Truthfully.'

Should she accept that at face value? He knew the ferry time. He could have rung the harbourmaster. She felt a disorienting mix of emotions, intensified by poor old Tad being accused of an assault he could never possibly have committed.

'I suppose I have to believe you.' she said, wishing Lavinia dead, as Quinn drove away from the hospital. But inside herself she did not believe him at all.

Something had changed outside. It took her a few moments to realise what. The fog had cleared completely, gone as if it had never gripped the island. The gloom had turned into a beautiful evening. A pale blue sky had a few high up mare's tail streaks of cloud in it. The light was reflected in a calm sea.

The hospital, she now realised, was on a hillside overlooking a bay, a real 'get well soon' vista for patients. Her mother had told her about the former cottage hospitals in England; small manageable places that had belonged to the community. They'd been abolished decades ago in favour of monster ones serving whole areas. This was what those friendly cottage hospitals must have been like. It was a consoling thought that the old man was in one. Damn the fuzz and damn Quinn too for being so useless.

As they passed the harbour and the wide bay she saw that the grounded steamer was no longer there and asked him about it.

'There hasn't been any shipwreck.' he assured her.

'But I drew it while I was waiting. A small boat was collecting bodies. And there were soldiers on the beach.' she shuddered from the memory, but instinct told her not mention the shooting.

'What on earth are you talking about?' he tried to make a joke out of it. 'No is possible. There is a wreck out there, sure. From years ago. At low tide you can see its boiler among the rocks. You've been imagining things again.'

'When did that ship go on the rocks?'

Quinn slowed down on a bend and glanced sideways at her. 'During the war.' he tried to joke again 'Don't start telling me you saw it!'

CHAPTER THIRTEEN

'So who was this reporter bloke?'

'The moment they were back at the fort Quinn began an inquisition into Anna's trip, oblivious of how upset she was by his failing to meet her and by the hospital visit.

'As a matter of fact Mr Carey was very helpful,' she tried to keep herself calm and controlled and emphasised the 'Mr Carey' bit. 'He saw me off, which was how I knew about Tad. And you didn't even manage to meet me!'

'I told you why! And while you were junketing around with your "Mr Carey" I was working!'

Anna just looked at him. How could he convince himself that he'd been hard at work, when she'd bet her socks he'd actually been lunching with Lavinia? And he had. What was to be done with so emotionally obsessive and jealous a man? Challenge him? Invite the aggro? At that rate she might just as well go straight back to Brighton. Anyway, why should she have to defend her actions?

'Carey and me had lunch together,' she went on 'which was nice, because the morning had been so frustrating.' she had to make Quinn understand things had changed since they separated. She was her own woman now. 'We went Dutch, by the way.'

'Sorry.' he mumbled, unexpectedly yielding and going to the kitchen fridge. 'White wine? Let's both have some and you can tell me all about your day.'

'That's a bit better.' she accepted the wine, though not acknowledging his apology. He had behaved appallingly and she was not about to let him forget it. She settled herself down on one of the enormous sofas. 'There's a not a lot to tell. The archivist thought my uncle must have been here during the war itself.'

'In the German army?'

'Presumably. He was still only 18 by 1945.' she left out her fears about the SS. 'The man was helpful, but the military records are all in Germany.' She spread her hands in a gesture of futility. 'So I gave up and went shopping in St Mary instead. Retail recovery. What a lovely place!'

'The big smoke, so far as we're concerned.'

'And what about you?' she tried to keep her tone neutral, though it wasn't easy. 'How did you get on with Lavinia?'

'So, so.' Quinn temporised, but hesitated a little too long before adding 'She gave a lunch party.'

'And that was the end of work for the day?'

'Wish it had been. She gave me a hard time.'

He got up and went to fetch the project paper, allowing Anna to speculate on what precisely being given a hard time by Lavinia implied.

'Look at this,' he said, thrusting the document at her, 'look at this load of bull. "Interpretative empathy" Holy cow!'

'Did she write it?' Reading the text made Anna feel a sudden twinge of sympathy for Quinn. Her college was a hothouse of interpretative empathy.

'No way.' he saw her expression soften and hastened to exploit it. 'Some creep must have cooked it up for her.'

Anna shook her head in commiseration. The Mission Statement had probably come off the internet. It was just the sort of jargon her College Director used.

'The artist must employ whatever technology is appropriate to address the central metaphysical issues of our time' was one of his favourite, studiously non-gender-specific pronouncements.

Metaphysical issues had enabled one street-wise student to win a cash prize with a pile of untidily folded, flea infested blankets, exhibited inside a sealed Perspex case (for which all involved were grateful), and captioned "Homeless". But who was homeless? The absent owner of the blankets, or the fleas without their host? And what happened if the fleas died? Was the metaphysical integrity compromised? No-one ever had the courage to ask.

'Your problem,' she said to Quinn, only half teasing him, 'is that you're not metaphysical enough. You can actually paint a recognisable subject. You're out of date.'

'At least I paint what people want.'

'What Lavinia wants, you mean.'

She immediately regretted being so caustic, because she did feel sorry for him, in an almost motherly way, knowing how wretchedly his mediocre talent was trapped. How could he not welcome a patron, even if the patron was a marauding widow? In Brighton he made a living from advertising, trapped 9 to 5. Here he was in a similar bind, with Lavinia replacing the agency.

'Can I see what you've done today?' she asked, now remorseful in spite of her anger and not mentioning Lavinia's lunch.

'It's in the studio.' he became moodily dismissive, which was the sure prelude to a tantrum, and Anna knew there was something else on his mind, something he resented, just as he used to resent doing illustrations of chocolate biscuits.

Leaving her drink behind – she didn't want more alcohol anyway after the wine at lunch – she went up the stairs to the studio, not at all sure that she really wanted to, yet feeling under an obligation to try and admire Quinn's latest efforts.

The easel was draped with a white cloth, while a variety of historical sketches were propped around the walls and she saw that Quinn had a substantial new subject. This was a panoramic view of Drake Bay, seen from the castle battlements on the hill above, but with no causeway or fort in the bay. A senior officer was giving orders to a subordinate. Quinn had pencilled in below 'Major General Sir Richard Petty demands more guns, 1810.'

Petty must have been famous in his day. Even so it was curious that Quinn, the least militaristic of men and so bitter about what the German army had done here, should concentrate so heavily on the island as a fortress in the past. Perhaps Lavinia liked men in uniforms. Very probably. She was the sort of woman who would. And Petty was depicted in full fancy dress, with cocked hat, gold epaulettes and all the braid trimmings. But although she might joke about it, the series worried Anna, because they displayed an island always pre-occupied with war.

Somehow linked with this was the worrying realisation that she herself was occasionally visualising scenes from the German wartime occupation. Visualising, she had been telling herself, visualising, not seeing. And always when there was fog with its attendant mystery. She tried to take her mind off that.

Looking around she realised there was something beneath the cloth covering the easel. She lifted it and found herself gazing straight at a head and shoulders portrait of herself. She was completely stunned and stood there in shock, the white cloth trailing from her fingers. The painting was magnificent, the colours subtle, the brushwork deft, the whole composition arresting. She was wearing the yellow smock which Quinn particularly liked, her hazel eyes clear and appealing, her features soft, her hair glowing. When could he have done this? Not since her arrival, not possibly.

She tried to be critical, instead of overwhelmed. Of course he had borrowed the overall composition from Van Gogh's portrait of a Breton girl in a yellow smock. The picture had the same confrontational directness. But in no way was this a manipulated copy. It was sensitive and original and what caught in her throat and made her want to cry was that it radiated love. This portrait said all the things that Quinn was so hopelessly bad at putting into words. She was still mesmerised when he came up the steps to join her.

'Are you all right?' he began to ask, then saw the unveiled painting and was embarrassed. 'I did it from an old photo.'

'Oh Quinn, it's beautiful!' She turned and instinctively hugged him. 'I had no idea. Why did you hide it?'

'Lavinia….'

'To hell with bloody Lavinia. It's a fantastic picture, quite the best thing you've ever done.' she hugged him again, all her anger forgotten. 'Oh Quinn!'

'The subject does make a difference.' He still had his arm around her, attempted to sound offhand and utterly failed, so tried to kiss her instead. 'Even more if you're in love with it.'

'You're a fool!' she said lovingly, but began to slide out of his embrace none the less. 'Where did you find the photo?'

'I took it in Greece.'

'Oh.' she didn't take her arms away completely, but did stand back a little. 'How odd.'

How could such an unhappy time have given birth to such a happy painting?

The painting holiday in Greece had killed their marriage. The plan – or deliberate lack of one – had been inspiring. They would wander with a minimum of possessions, stay in tavernas, eat grilled fish by the beach and liberate themselves from all the inhibitions of English life. It hadn't worked out quite like that.

The liberation had only been for Quinn. In so far as he thought about her holiday at all, it had been as a travelling companion who would bargain in the markets, cook, admire what he did and be available in bed whenever he felt the urge.

Then he discovered that because of some hang up he couldn't paint out there – 'the muse has left me' – he had bought a cheap camera and busied himself with that, pretending it was for taking visual notes. The tension had grown and grown. They could not afford to return early because they had unchangeable charter flight tickets. She left him two days after they got back.

'Spetsai wasn't really that bad a place.' Quinn suggested, reflectively and sadly. 'We had problems before.'

'It was utterly awful.' Anna gave him a little peck of a kiss on the cheek. 'But that is a marvellous portrait and I shall never, ever forget it.'

'I did it mainly from memory. Loving memory.'

He was completely serious, but the words broke the atmosphere and made her laugh.

'Anyone would think I was dead. "Loving memory" indeed!'

'You know what I meant. I love you, Anna.' He tried to take her hands and lead her to the sofa, which she let him do, but avoided being too close.

'Please stay.' he pleaded.

'Oh Quinn.' She gave a sigh, almost of irritation. 'I love you too. But you're impossible to live with. You know that. And I'm not at all sure about this place.'

'The island will grow on you.'

'I'm not sure it would. There's something sinister about it. An undercurrent of...' she tried to find the right words 'of violence, well not only that. Perhaps of evil.'

She had been thinking about this on and off throughout the afternoon, in the way that ideas go in and out of one's mind when doing other things. The contrast between the cheerful bustle of St Mary and the gaunt loneliness of this island had reminded her of all that she would miss about Brighton: the galleries, the restaurants, the curio shops in the Lanes, the theatres, the whole feeling of get up and go. And get up and go you could, with the West End of London only an hour away by train. Whereas here!

The island did have a cinema show once a fortnight and audiences went to the pub while the reels were changed. There was an amazing community spirit, with a volunteer lifeboat, fire service, ambulance – Quinn had not hesitated to boast about them. But how would she occupy herself, apart from keeping house for him? Joining committees, like the dreaded Lavinia? Doing the church flowers?

She had been reminded again of Simone de Beauvoir's words on middle class women, introduced to her by the lecturer at those evening classes on 'Gender Studies', which she had gone to after breaking up with Quinn. In the end the classes had not helped one bit in restructuring her life, because the female tutors ferociously ruled out attempting any kind of emotional relationship with men. So she stopped going, but remembered de Beauvoir, even though the translation made the phrases sound more archaic than they were.

De Beauvoir had written in 'The Second Sex' about the middle class woman as if she had personally known Lavinia. 'She is most likely to seek relief in social life' and, regarding benefits, 'She expects special favours….. the policeman will let her through without a pass.' It might be dated, but it was wickedly accurate.

Okay, so de Beauvoir had been writing in the late 1950s, since when women's lib had revolutionised society, even here. Anna assumed that many island women worked, as they likely always had. But for the middle class tax exile settlers the island was in a time warp and de Beauvoir's words remained spot on. There would always be what she identified as 'the ridiculous problem of how to kill time'.

'You really would get to enjoy life here.' Quinn insisted, interrupting her thoughts.

'I told you, I'm not sure. There is something I can't put my finger on about the island. Something, well, spooky.' She began to be irritated again 'Please give me time.'

But she could put her finger on it. Not precisely. Not exactly. Even if she succeeded in exorcising the ghost of her uncle, would the sense of foreboding and evil that she had felt on her walks with Tad dissipate with time, like mist cleared slowly by the sun? Or would the feeling of menace never disappear?

The answer had been provided by being fogbound on the way back this afternoon and the events she saw in the harbour, the men trying to escape, the troops firing. In the end that strange disquiet would probably drive her off the island.

Quinn guessed what she must be thinking. 'Surely you can forget about your uncle now?' he said 'You've done all you can and he probably wasn't here anyway.'

'I'm afraid he must have been.' she slipped her hand into his, as if to console him. 'But that's not it.' She had to be honest, even when she had been feeling so close to him again. 'It's just so confining here.'

'But I'm here!'

'Couldn't you paint in England, now that you have some money of your own?'

'Now it's you who's missing the point.' Quinn's inborn argumentativeness surfaced and she let go his hand. 'This is where I've found my true self. This is where I've become really creative. I couldn't have done that portrait anywhere else. I need to be here.' Fearing this sounded self-centred he made it worse by adding. 'And, my love, I need you with me.'

'Yes. As your life support system. What about my life?'

Those evening classes might have been too aggressive, but one thing had become fixed in her mind: women always had to fight for their rights against men. They'd had to fight to end their husbands legally acquiring everything that was theirs in the Victorian era. They'd had to fight over only 'coming of age' at 40. They'd had to fight for the vote.

Quinn recoiled, as if she had physically lashed out at him. 'What bloody nonsense! I've always supported you!'

'I didn't mean financially.'

This was hopeless. She would only win this argument by walking out, which would be an admission of defeat. She didn't want to do that yet. Not yet. At the same time she could not, absolutely could not, revert to being his emotional crutch for 24 hours a day. 24/7 as people said.

'Perhaps if we had slightly separate lives....' she began, then cut herself short. If he really did want them to get together again, they must discuss where they were going to live. 'Listen,' she said, knowing this was a retreat, 'it is only Tuesday, we still have time to talk.'

'You're always saying that.' The petulant way in which he spoke nullified further argument and he made it worse by changing the subject. 'So who exactly was this reporter you met?'

'A friend of Jack Mackinnon's.' She wasn't going to get into a spat over a man she had never met before and might not meet again, even if he had been attractive. 'Which reminds me, I must telephone him this evening.'

'It's all yours.' But Quinn's tone had a hard edge of sourness.

The brief interlude of intimacy and understanding was broken. She rang Jack and arranged to meet in the morning. He had already spoken to the police, who were now unlikely to press charges against Tad, who could be fetched tomorrow.

'Still the good Samaritan?' Quinn asked.

'Somebody has to be. Well, I suppose I don't have to, but someone should. The old man had a pretty tough time here.'

'I'll take you to the hospital tomorrow.' he offered, with a spark of helpfulness, 'but then I have to....'

'Meet Lavinia?

'She is being rather demanding.'

'So what exactly happened at the lunch party? It's obvious that something did.'

'The President told me about some German murals there. Rather fanciful ones. Her house used to be the officers' brothel.'

'Colonel Grundmann's House of Joy?'

'How on earth did you know that?'

'It was in the archives.' A white lie, but pardonable. She did not intend telling him about the diary. 'And while we're on the subject of research, what did you do after lunch?'

Quinn did not exactly squirm, but she saw the discomfort in his eyes. 'If you must know, she made a pass at me.'

'What a surprise! And you had a problem holding her off.'

'I had to kiss her once before I could get away.'

Even as he spoke Quinn knew he had made a bad mistake. Honesty with women is seldom the best policy. In a single, sweeping movement Anna stood up, took her glass from the table and threw the wine in his face. He jerked back as it splashed into his beard and all over his shirt.

'Had to kiss her! You protest undying love to me and you kiss her. Good night, Quinn.'

'Anna, please!'

'You can cook your own bloody supper tomorrow and I'll walk to the hospital.'

She ran off to her room, locked the door and burst into tears on the bed. When Quinn knocked and tried to make apologies she shouted at him to go away.

Later he knocked again. 'Mackinnon is on the phone.' he said through the door.

'Say I'll be there at eleven. Now GO AWAY.'

But anger and a sense of betrayal kept her awake most of the night. And to make it worse sometime after midnight the wretched foghorn started its mournful bellowing again.

CHAPTER FOURTEEN

When she got up on Wednesday morning Anna was still seething at Quinn's kissing exploits with Lavinia. How dare he do that? How dare he tell her about it with that helpless, little boy, 'what could I do?' expression on his face. She knew he would argue that his lame confession was being deeply honest with her.

But in the pub he would probably boast about having got away with it. She felt grievously humiliated, not least because at heart she was still in love with him. Relationships! Men!

She was also becoming acutely aware that she only had four full days left. And being in a completely contrariwise mood, had nonetheless lain awake during the night considering whether to cut the visit short, but ended up deciding it was important to be at the memorial service on Sunday with Tad.

There was no logical explanation for her feeling so protective towards the old man, only the emotional one that he had been through experiences she would rather not even guess at and that he was so friendless here.

It looked like being a nice day, but just in case she rang the phone number which issued a local weather report. There was a comforting feeling about that, as though somebody actually cared about this small community.

'Here is the forecast at six o'clock' the baritone male voice told her 'The weather in the northern isle will be changeable, with sunny periods and the chance of a shower. The wind north westerly light force three. High pressure is expected to dominate until tomorrow with some patches of sea fog.'

And, she added to herself, the micro-climate in the Moroccan room will be moody with outbursts of temper and occasional tears. At least Quinn would be pre-occupied most of the day with keeping the foul Lavinia content and not, she trusted, by dint of too much kissing. That admission really had got into her, upset her more than she would have thought possible. Why, oh why had the idiot man told her about it anyway? Perhaps because Lavinia would not be above insinuating it herself if she had the opportunity.

I shall do my own thing completely today, Anna decided. I will walk to the hospital, even if he offers to drive me. Besides, she wanted to look at the harbour bay again and she could see that the tide was on its way out, so the wreck of the steamer would be exposed. Could it be the one she had sketched in the fog? She was both apprehensive about discovering and anxious to know.

She fixed herself juice, toast and coffee, whereupon Quinn appeared, full of contrition and ready to drive her to the hospital, just she had known he would be. Adopting a tone of sweet reasonableness more suitable for persuading a ten year old to let the cat out of the washing machine, but with an undertone of anger which surely even he must have picked up, she explained her plans. Then, with her sketching materials and Marianne's diary safely inside her sack, she set off.

The walk was only a mile and half and not a stiff one, but she intended to spend time examining things which Quinn always drove past without stopping. One of these would be the memorial, located a few hundred yards beyond a holiday campsite with a number of concrete slabs and walls. The site was protected from the sea by high dunes, largely covered in coarse dune grass. It being early in the season, even if it was a school holiday, only a few tents were pitched there.

She clambered down a grassy slope to it looking more closely at a partially overgrown water storage tank, which she recognised as dating from the Occupation. She was getting used to identifying such relics now. The grey German concrete was unmistakable and bore the horizontal outlines of the wooden shuttering planks into which it had been poured. It was extremely solid, hardly weathered after so many decades.

Turning to go back to the road, she noticed a granite lined tunnel with an impressive entrance arch, which led from the campsite to another bay. This must be much older, possibly Victorian. What was it for? The sand of the path through it was strewn with broken glass. Both the tunnel and the concrete tank gave her a sensation of spookiness, totally at odds with this being a holiday site, complete with shop and café. Could it have been a labour camp in the war, where slaves were starved and beaten? What would today's holiday visitors think if they knew?

By contrast the memorial was straightforward: a semi circle of neatly cut granite blocks, with little flower beds built into the walls, and bearing a series of commemorative plaques. The central, shield shaped one had the inscription 'In memory of all foreign workers who died here 1940-1945'. The others were in various languages: Russian Cyrillic, French, Hebrew, Polish, Spanish. And each was dedicated to the dead citizens of a different origin, some with small coloured carvings of national flags. The Spanish one was dedicated to the 'victimas del Nazismo'. No Germans were commemorated, although Mackinnon had mentioned that disaffected Germans had been imprisoned here too.

All of them, she realised, with a shiver, must have been labourers along with Tad. The difference between him and all these others commemorated here, probably thousands of them, was that while they had died, he had somehow escaped and lived. More than ever she understood why he so badly needed to know how, just as she wanted to unearth the truth about her uncle.

Leaving the memorial Anna continued past some whitewashed cottages and the single track railway line, past a rough gravelled road leading up to a huge fort commanding the harbour bay, and so on to the bay itself.

Laid out before her in perfect clarity – in the light that Quinn so enthused about - was the reverse of yesterday's fog-obscured scene. There on the far side where she had sat sketching were the harbour sheds and the commercial quay, with a crane lifting loads out of a ship half hidden by the sheds. Strangely the ironwork quay extension projecting out to sea which had reminded her of Brighton pier was missing. She stared across the water, thinking she must be looking in the wrong place. But, as obstinately as a fugitive dream refusing to let itself be recalled, the ironwork quay extension simply wasn't there.

The rocks in the centre of the bay very definitely were there. They poked up out of the shallow water in a jagged group hardly fifty yards off the crescent-shaped beach. At anything much less than low water they would be invisible, as sharp as sharks' teeth, waiting for the unwary sailor. And lying among them was the round black shape of a ship's boiler, plus, when she looked more carefully, the broken skeletal spars of a hull.

She fished out her pad and swiftly drew this alternative version of the scene, lit occasionally by shafts of sunlight through the clouds. There was no problem discerning the details this time. The low tide shoreline, the nearby rocks and the barrel shape of the boiler, the row of pastel painted old houses, the small and partially silted up stone quay, close to which she had sat before, the new commercial quay beyond with its buildings and cranes.

She was glad to get all this down on paper, albeit from a different angle to yesterday's sketch in the fog. She even felt a sort of morbid triumph at having done so, as if she had exposed two opposite sides of the same truth. Then she continued on her way past the harbour to the hospital.

The nurses had the old man ready to leave in a day room for patients, which looked out splendidly over the sea. What a good thing, Anna thought, what a blessing for people who have to be in hospital.

'He's a bit shaky still,' the nurse commented as she led Anna through, 'he ought to rest for a day or two. Are you his daughter then?'

Anna hesitated 'Just a friend He doesn't know many people here. I'll be taking him back to his guest house.'

'He does need looking after...' the nurse hesitated, as though it might be a mistake to be discharging him '....and the doctor prescribed these. They're a mild sedative. He should take two at night. And better not to drink any alcohol.'

'I'll do what I can.' Possibly the guest house owner would deal with the pills. Or his wife. They had seemed decent enough people. And Tad was hardly likely to squander his savings on drink. 'Can I order a taxi?'

Tad was indeed shaky and had to be helped up from his chair when the taxi arrived, while the other elderly 'care' patients - Anna knew you weren't allowed to say 'geriatrics' any more – murmured encouragement and farewells. It was not every day that they had a foreigner here, let alone one under police guard. They had all been pleased when the policeman went away. Tad hadn't looked like a criminal to them. 'A bit past it, I'd say.' an even older patient quipped.

So Anna escorted him up to the guest house in the town, handing him and the pills over to the obliging owner, together with the doctor's orders about resting

'I thank.' Tad said with dignity, as she bade him goodbye, 'I thank very much.'

'I promise I'll come to see you tomorrow.' she wanted to re-assure him, in case he tried to go off by himself again. 'You just stay indoors for a day. Have a rest.' She smiled conspiratorially at the owner, uncertain if Tad fully understood her actual words, but quite sure he had got the message. 'Be a good boy for a change.'

After that she walked down through the town to Jack Mackinnon's house, managing the timing extraordinarily well, only ten minutes late. Being on time was not her big thing: that could safely be left to men.

Mackinnon was as welcoming as before. His wife brought them coffee and then tactfully retreated to another part of the house. Anna sank into the wide chintz covered sofa, realising that their talk was going to be much more relaxed without Quinn, and this stimulated Mackinnon's opening remark.

'So Quinn's busy with his project? Not a bad thing. I need to talk to you seriously about old Tadeus. What on earth was he doing with a knife? Mark you, that lady walking her dog has a very fertile imagination. A regular drama queen. Luckily I was able to remind the police sergeant of various unsubstantiated accusations she has made against men before. But they were wise not to give him back the knife.'

'He would never have used it!'

'There are no such certainties when a man is pursued by demons. No-one really knows what goes on in their minds.'

'I'm still sure he must have been badly frightened by the woman's dog' Anna insisted. 'Whatever happened down that valley during the war traumatised him. And I'm sure he did kill a dog that had cornered him then.' Well, she knew he had.

'I did warn you,' Mackinnon said quietly, 'that the old man might behave strangely. The past plays curious tricks on people. I was deliberately understating the risk. I wanted to warn you, but not quite put you off helping him, because the truth might emerge. I hope you don't mind. To be honest, it was a difficult call. There was a risk. He strikes me as being genuine, but also obsessed. Memories can play devilish tricks on people.'

'He's certainly desperate to know what happened on that day. One of the oddest things is that the guards don't seem to have searched for him until long after he and Miki did a bunk.'

'Ordinarily they would have been pretty quick off the mark. Grundmann emphatically did not like escapers and even the most junior ranks knew it. I suppose Tad has no idea of the date?'

'In 1943 some time. Late spring.

Mackinnon pondered this. 'There were distractions. Allied air attacks were one. And small commando raids. The Germans got very jumpy when our commandos came ashore, took prisoners and then got back successfully to a submarine. They were just pinpricks raids, really, to damage morale. But our friend Grundmann was always worried about being accused of negligence.'

Anna decided to take a small plunge into waters she had not yet charted. 'Did the Colonel have a French girlfriend called Marianne?'

'How on earth did you know?' Jack was surprised. 'He did indeed. And, unrealised by Grundmann, the name Marianne was an undercover taunt. Her real name wasn't that at all. "Marianne" has long symbolised the spirit of France. She must have adopted it deliberately, possibly when she first met him. How did you know?'

Anna didn't answer, posing another question instead. 'But why? I mean why go with a German at all, if she was so patriotic?'

'Ours not to reason why. The necessities of survival can shift overnight in a war. Did you ever see Brecht's play "Mother Courage and her children"? Set during the Thirty Years war. It's about adapting to events. And, if you'll forgive my saying so, what man can ever know why a woman does what she does?'

This was a touch chauvinist for Anna, but she reminded herself that Jack was of a much older generation and laughed politely. After all, he was her only true friend here. It would have been completely counter-productive to object.

'I may have the answer to a lot of things.' She decided to reveal her treasure. 'May I show you something? Dick Carey lent me this' She retrieved the carefully wrapped up diary from her bag. 'This was Marianne's.'

Mackinnon devoted some minutes to examining it. 'It does look kosher. Where did it come from?'

'Inside the roof of Lavinia's house. A decorator found it.'

He exploded with laughter. 'Then it must be okay. The kind of evidence every investigator dreams about and seldom finds. Quite amazing. I have no doubt you will come to love and respect Lavinia Wildeblood as much as we all do. But she might not welcome this! Is it revealing? Would she want it burnt?'

'I expect so.' Anna laughed delightedly at being so exactly on the same wavelength. 'I've only dipped into it, just enough to know that it isn't only about goings on in the House of Joy. Marianne recorded day to day events as well.'

'Then you might stumble on something worthwhile. Grundmann may be in his grave, but this could be a voice from it.'

'It was very trusting of Dick Carey to lend it me. I'd had no luck in the archives.'

'He's a good boy, Dick. I'm his godfather, by the way.'

Encouraged by these reactions, Anna raised the subject of the steamer in the bay by asking what the old supply boats had looked like.

'That's easy.'

Mackinnon rose and trawled quickly through a bookcase, picking out a slim volume called 'A Short History of the Ancient Isle.' He flipped through the pages, found the section of black and white illustrations, and handed it to her. There the steamer was, with its upright bow, cantilevered stern, thin straight funnel and pair of masts. There could be no mistaking it. Anna felt a great wrench of fear. This was the ship she had seen and drawn yesterday, the ship of which all that remained today was a blackened boiler and a skeleton of ribs among the rocks.

'What happened to it?' she asked.

'For many years it carried freight and passengers between here and St Mary once or twice a week, depending on the weather. The Germans renamed it "The Horst Grundmann" in honour of our enthusiastic Colonel.'

He paused, almost thinking aloud. 'Then there was a disaster, around the time old Tadeus was here. The ship hit rocks in fog in the Spring of 1943. The loss of life was terrible. At least three hundred slaves, mainly Russians, were battened down in the hold. They'd been on board a day and a half, coming from France, with barely room to stand, no water, obviously no toilet facilities. The stench must have been appalling. Their only food had been buckets of soup lowered to them on ropes. And they drowned where they stood, when the ship went aground, because no-one opened the hatches.'

Anna listened appalled. This was what she had seen and drawn, the wrecked steamer, the men some of whom Jack didn't know had broken free and been shot. And it was starting to dawn on her that she heard no sounds. No cries for help, no shots. Why? Should she tell Jack? Would he just assume she was inventing it?

Mackinnon looked straight at her, misinterpreting her uncertainty and, for a few seconds, she again saw the steel in him.

'My superiors wanted to indict the Naval Commander for murder. But he had been off the island that day and strictly speaking Grundmann, as the Land commander, couldn't be blamed. It was not easy investigating such a crime when the perpetrators had long gone. However, our Department found most of them. And the ship's captain went on to be embraced by Madame Guillotine.'

'Seriously?' The flippant reference to the guillotine was scary. 'He didn't get away like Grundmann?'

'I was a witness to the execution some years later.' Mackinnon made a slight grimace of dismissal. 'An unnerving experience for a young officer. But one learns.'

'Do you know the date of the shipwreck? Or doesn't that matter?'

'To our friend Tadeus? If that was the day of his escape, it might. Who knows what goes on in his troubled mind. I can look it up. But first I have an idea.'

Mackinnon excused himself, springing out of his chair - he was very agile for his age - and left the room. Anna heard a sotto voce consultation in another room. Then he returned. 'My wife would be delighted if you can join us for lunch. Unless Quinn is cooking for you, of course.'

'He might just not be.' Anna smiled at this somewhat sideways sense of humour. 'Yes, I should love to. But I must phone him.'

'We'll do that for you. Would a quarter to one be convenient? Meanwhile I shall look up that date.'

With over an hour to kill, and the shopping street not alluring enough for retail therapy – the island really was a backwater fashion-wise – Anna walked up to the grassy plateau, past the eyesore of the ruined hotel, sat herself down on a bench facing the harbour below and took out Marianne's diary.

She skipped straight to the year 1943, scrutinising each entry, sometimes laboriously. She was going to have to buy a French dictionary from the bookshop. Marianne wrote colloquially and was not always easy to understand. However, Anna did understand enough for a picture of her life to emerge.

Socially Marianne had been a cut above the girls in The House of Joy, most of whom were lower class French or Algerian and lived as well as 'worked' out there. However Marianne herself lived with Grundmann in a small house on the town's only residential square, effectively as his wife, and he called her 'his little gazelle' - when, that is, he was not ordering 'basket' down at the House of Joy.

Their house sounded like a 'two up, two down' terraced one, though with an important refinement. A stone walled shed at the back had been turned into Grundmann's personal air raid shelter, with a thick concrete slab as a roof and access from the living room. When the air raid alarm klaxons sounded, Marianne retreated there, although not often, because British air raids were few. They didn't seem to have worried her, but she made scornful diary references to Grundmann's fears when planes were overhead. Anna resolved to go and find the house.

Other bitchy diary entries mentioned the Colonel's real wife, a fat hausfrau in Frankfurt, whom he visited on furlough in January 1943, carrying with him Marianne's most fervent private wishes for a seasick boat crossing, filthy railway carriages and freezing cold. She wanted him to loathe going home.

The truth now, in this month of May 1943, Marianne confided to her diary, was that all this basketwork had left her with a familiar problem, or rather two problems.

The first was that it was three months since she had begun missing her periods. Horst was fond of calling her his 'little gazelle', but soon she would more resemble a cow, and she was terrified that the gallant Colonel would want to duck the family complications of an illegitimate child. He had many important responsibilities, as he never ceased telling her. He was unbelievably boring about them. He had also been insensitive enough to tell her that his superiors would disapprove of a child.

So she was scared stiff of being sent back to France, alone, to bear the baby. The situation was complicated by the danger that if Grundmann starting doing his arithmetic, he might suspect that she became pregnant while he was on leave. Marianne was essentially a free spirit and free spirits exploit absences.

As Anna worked her way through these intriguing diary pages, she realised that both of Marianne's problems had been far less threatening than a third one.

Earlier in May Marianne had accidentally witnessed an atrocity in which Grundmann himself was involved. She had recorded what had happened in her deliberately tiny, space saving, handwriting. She had witnessed a murder, the gunning down by the SS, of an escaped slave.

'What I saw walking back from shopping before lunch was so bad I hardly dare not write it down. But I must. Someday it may matter. I have plucked up courage and told Horst it dishonours all Germans. He agrees, but insists he can do nothing against the SS. It would be more than his own life is worth. But I am determined to record these appalling doings, which I hear about, but don't usually see.'

As Anna read on the scene came to life.

CHAPTER FIFTEEN

Marianne's morning routine was to dress demurely, like a good hausfrau going shopping, then set out across the cobbled square to the *Soldatenheim*. This was a high and impressive Georgian building, of the island's ever-present granite, with a garden in front. Originally built by the island's Governor, it had been a Catholic convent and school before the war. Indeed the desks and English schoolbooks had been left intact when the locals were evacuated.

Under German ownership the building served as a recreation centre for the soldiers, with a canteen where they could buy ersatz coffee, artificial honey, bread and a few 'luxuries' like French bottled beer. Although the Colonel's official rations were adequate Marianne liked to supplement them with anything newly available there and make their meals a little more interesting. She was after all a Frenchwoman.

She was authorised to shop at the *Soldatenheim*, but was in a stormy relationship with the formidable manager, Schwester Olga, because the Sister despised her as a prostitute and this loathing was heightened by Marianne's French nationality. Even so, she usually made some purchases, leaving them for later collection by their soldier servant from the canteen.

This Tuesday was turning out to be a difficult day. Supplies were often erratic and all Marianne could get was bread and nothing else, except ersatz coffee made from God knew what, possibly burnt breadcrumbs, plus a lot of chicory. With luck she would find a few home grown vegetables in the town, sold 'under the counter' The Colonel liked to be properly fed. Good German food, none of your French muck. She kept her mouth shut when he said that kind of thing. Tact was not Grundmann's strong suit.

She continued along a narrow street with the island's former courthouse, now used as the army ration office, on one side and the tree shaded expanse of the churchyard on the other, set with old gravestones.

The church itself was large enough to be a small cathedral, massively built of granite. Since the occupation it had been a storehouse for the garrison. The pews had been burnt for firewood. Marianne knew its stores included wine and tinned food, but had never ever dared ask to see inside.

Anyway Grundmann could get all the wine they needed.

This morning there were a number of SS men in the churchyard, which made her hurry past. Their black uniforms and death's head badges scared her, quite apart from their reputation for brutality. They weren't seen in the town very often.

The narrow street past the churchyard led to the main cobbled thoroughfare, still lined with the facades of the island's empty shops and banks. At the forces' bookshop she had recently bought a pre-war tourist map of the island, overprinted in German. She dropped in now because it was a good place for gossip and she was curious about the SS men being around, even though questions were dangerous. An assistant told her, in a whisper, that one of the SS concentration camp trusties had escaped.

'They think he's holed up in the church. He was a *Kapo*, but he'd got into trouble.'

The *Kapos*, Marianna noted briefly, were prisoners who kept order among their fellows, usually with whips, and were allowed privileges in proportion to their brutality.

'I wouldn't want to be him.' the assistant remarked. 'They'll string him up. Or worse.'

This conversation changed Marianne's mind about shopping. She decided to return home at once. But as she walked back towards the churchyard she heard shouting.

'Run, you bastard, run!'

Down by the church an SS man was beating a fugitive in striped clothes with a nightstick. The escaper tried to run up the path from the church to a gate on the street, hardly ten metres from her. A shot rang out and he stumbled.

'Run!' bellowed the SS man, whom she now saw was a corporal, still thudding blows on the man's shoulders.

The *Kapo* had reached the gate when other SS men fired low at his legs. He clung to the gatepost. Several men closed in on him, forcing him to the ground, kicking his head, his ribs, his groin. He screamed, blood seeping through the blue striped pyjamas on to the pavement.

Marianne did not know what to do. She glanced round for a way to escape. The street behind her was swarming with soldiers. So she pressed herself tight against the corner of a house, which had the date 1929 incised on it, a detail she remembered and recorded, while the fugitive struggled and screamed.

Then she heard a car. The soldiers in the street gave way for it. The car came slowly past then stopped. She saw that it was Grundmann's official car, with his soldier driver and the swastika flag fluttering above the bonnet on a stubby chromium pole. Surely he would do something! For God's sake please do something, she thought. He stepped out of the car.

The SS men stopped their beating of the *Kapo* when the staff car drew up. The .fugitive struggled to stand, blood streaming from his head and legs, staining the path. 'Help me, Sir!'

But Grundmann waved him aside and went into the Ration Office opposite the church gate; a building which Marianne recorded in her diary.

The man was still clinging desperately to the low wooden gate. The SS corporal brutally knocked his hands away. He rolled over on the pavement and begged for water in a croaking voice, which Marianne thought she would never forget. The SS men gathered round and contemptuously watched him writhe in his agony. Finally the corporal drew a revolver and shot him in the head. An SS truck arrived and stopped behind the staff car.

Marianne shrank even more closely against the wall and covered her face with her hands. She knew such things happened here, but until this moment they had been in a parallel and hidden world. Horst never spoke of them. As soon as the corpse had been thrown into the back of the truck, the SS men jumped in with it and the staff car driver prudently pulled up on to the kerb. Once the street was cleared, she hurried past to the square. On the way she encountered another officer coming from the *Soldatenheim.*

'How can a civilised nation do this!' she screamed at him.

'What are you talking about? You mean the shooting?'

She told him, graphically, adding 'They are animals.'

The officer gently took her by the elbow. Marianne was well liked, quite apart from her occasional availability. 'Go home,' he urged, 'and tell no-one what you saw.'

Safely back in the small house on the square, still swabbing her tears with a handkerchief, Marianne began writing this account, swearing she would see the corporal punished if it was the last thing she did. But first she had to find out his name.

Later she was told by her lover that he had encountered an SS lieutenant outside the churchyard, as the corpse was being removed and was himself outraged, but for a very different reason.

The lieutenant had been tall and young, his high-peaked hat bearing the silver death's head, the buttons on his black serge tunic glittering and his black jackboots highly polished. Grundmann had demanded to know what was going on.

The SS officer had saluted, but replied arrogantly. 'That is our business, Herr Oberst. We are not under your command.' He had saluted again and turned away.

Grundmann also told Marianne to forget everything she had seen. Instead she wrote every detail she could remember down and vowed to do the same on any such bestial future occasion. It was a resolve to be tested all too soon.

CHAPTER SIXTEEN

Anna closed the diary, feeling sick. Could this be true? She had to know if it had been and she still had time to spare. She walked back to the shopping street, trying but failing to imagine it semi-deserted during the Occupation, and took Marianne's route along the side street to the churchyard gate. The street was tarmaced now, but must have been cobbled then.

The churchyard gate itself was a low wooden one, relatively new, supported between two stone pillars. Anna looked around nearby carefully, noticing the standard military headstone for a British soldier who had been blown up clearing mines after the war. She recalled Mackinnon telling how, after that, prisoners of war were made to test their own minefield clearance

Next she walked the length of the path from the church door up which the trustie had been chased. Finally, she examined the stone gateposts, undoubtedly unchanged since the war.

Two shallow cavities in the stone, weathered now and grown with lichen, showed where bullets could have struck the granite pillars. Anna gazed at these little testimonies to a brutal death and wondered if she was right. Surely these must be where the bullets had struck, chipping the hard stone, during the killing. The cavities could be due to nothing else. Marianne had not invented the dreadful incident. It really had happened.

Asking herself why the past should be revealing itself to her in this way, and getting no satisfactory answers, Anna walked abstractedly back again to Mackinnon's cottage. She had a growing certainty that her discoveries were all as inevitable as one day looking death in the face would be. And it was macabre for this to happen to her in a peaceful churchyard, in a far off island., where for some reason she had become a witness to the past, not only through her sketches in the fog, but also through Tad.

Explaining this to Jack Mackinnon was gratifyingly simple, once she had gathered up the courage to tell him. Behind that cherubic, yet urbane, exterior there lurked a very perceptive person. Mackinnon was nobody's fool and nobody fooled him. His reactions gave her new strength.

'I absolutely believe what you are telling me.' he said 'Totally. Why you are having these experiences I do not know. But reflecting on it, I equally don't think you resist them. And,' he

144

laughed gently, 'you might easily do me a personal favour by explaining events which I have been trying to understand for many years. To use a modern expression, just go with the flow.'

The lunch was informal, though not casual. Jack's wife, Phyllida, possessed the gift, which a thousand 'easy ways to cook' books could never impart, of making the production of a meal appear effortless. It wasn't the menu, it was the person: and Phyllida was the perfect foil to her husband, quiet, thoughtful and one hundred percent in control. Impressive, Anna thought, especially since Jack clearly trusted her judgement in other ways.

Against this backdrop, conversation was easy and unforced and Anna accepted a celebratory glass of wine as well, because Mackinnon said she was filling gaps in his knowledge, which as he put it, had been in his pending tray a very long time. She took this as a serious compliment, knowing he was one of those tenacious people who never give up once they are on a scent.

'To my mind,' Jack said emphatically, 'this diary is completely kosher, as I said before. I've checked my files and the churchyard shooting was on 17 May 1943, as Marianne records. The SS corporal was never identified. He might have been helped to do a flit to South America after the war, as the officers were, with money and a new identity. He might not. For a mere corporal everything would have depended on the friends he had, even though the *Totenkopf SS*, the Death's Head boys, was something of a club. A large and not very exclusive one, but still very influential even long after the war, while who you were helped by depended on who you had either helped or had the goods on.'

'So the shooting in the churchyard really did take place.'

'Unhappily, yes.'

'I saw what might have been bullet holes.'

'They were. I examined them myself when I first came here soon after the war, when they were relatively fresh. A former army ration clerk admitted when he was interrogated that he'd seen the killing through a window. But Marianne tells us what the officers thought about it, which is better.'

'They sounded horrified.'

'I think most of them were. They weren't all sadists. Nor were the men. Around 3,000 prisoners of war were interrogated and most were perfectly ordinary conscript servicemen, appalled at the atrocities, but too scared to say anything.'

Anna prayed inwardly that her uncle had been one of those.

'There's something else the diary might tell you. A week later there was the shipwreck we discussed this morning. On the 26th of May to be exact. Marianne might have known about that.'

Anna hesitated, full of doubts. Should she tell Jack that she had drawn the shipwreck? Witnessed it, effectively. Would he believe her? She decided he would, and was about to start explaining when Phyllida, listening quietly and sensing her confusion of mind, intervened.

'Why don't you wait until after we've eaten.' She suggested. 'Your chicken's already getting cold.'

This gentle rebuke discouraged further exploration of the past, until they were back in the sitting room having coffee. Then Jack discovered from the diary that Marianne had indeed reported the shipwreck, but not in any detail because it had been close to dawn when the alarm klaxons sounded.

'I do wonder,' he said, 'whether that wasn't the same day old Tadeus and his friend escaped. There was the thick morning fog that caused the shipwreck.'

'He did mention hearing alarms go off.' Anna confirmed. 'I'll read some more of the diary before I see him. Anything which helps him remember things might help me. But right now I'm finding this all rather overwhelming. I ought to be getting back to the fort.'

'Why don't you run her there.' Phyllida suggested. 'Emotionally she's had quite a day.' She gave Anna a quick kiss on the cheek. 'Do come again, my dear.'

Mackinnon obligingly took her to the bookshop first, where she bought a French pocket dictionary, then drove her back to Rocquaine. Walking up the lawn above the fort's courtyard, Anna prayed that this would not be a repetition of Monday's sparring match. She wasn't sure she could cope with that. But neither Quinn nor Lavinia were there.

Then she realised it was only mid-afternoon and they might be at the Museum. Or, of course, at Lavinia's house: the one and only House of Joy. She made herself coffee and decided to sit outside in the sun and tackle more of Marianne's tempestuous life.

What she guessed, following up a clue in the diary entry for 17 May, was that Marianne had written a fuller account which

146

was concealed somewhere else in the book. She fingered through the whole diary, page by page, until she realised that the back cover was thicker than the front.

Fetching a sharp pointed knife from the kitchen, she very gently prised off the back endpaper. It had been glued along the edges, but she was able to ease it off gradually, until it hung loose from one side. And there, concealed, were several folded sheets of very thin paper, entirely covered in Marianne's handwriting. The author had headed it 'Personal and Private', but surely no-one who had penetrated this far would hesitate. Certainly Anna did not. Aided by what she knew already, more of the activity of 17 May came to life. But would it of the shipwreck a week later?

CHAPTER SEVENTEEN

'Marianne, kaffee!' Grundmann shouted as he returned from his office to the little house on the square, where she had been prudently keeping out of sight for the hour since the shooting. He slumped into an easy chair, the springs of which creaked. My God, he complained to himself, the furniture one had to put up with here! Stuff that would be sent to the scrapheap in Germany. And junior officers think he is lucky. 'Coffee, Marianne! Kaffee. Schnell!'

Very quickly Marianne appeared with the coffee she had kept ready. She wore a diaphanous black negligee, as if she had been resting. She kissed him and knelt on the floor to pull off his jackboots. The heels are too tight and give him cramp in the right foot. He winced. Once they were off he wriggled his toes in relief. and sighed. 'Thank you, meine liebe. My God, what a day.'

She handed him the coffee cup, nestled on the floor by his knees and waited for him to recover himself.

'The problem with being Commandant is that there is no-one to talk to.'

'You have me, my darling.'

'This is a hell of a day' he reiterated. 'I have told my officers that what the SS does behind its own barbed wire is its own affair. Nothing to do with us. The SS Commandant is answerable only to Berlin. I told them, this incident must be held to have taken place within the SS jurisdiction and witnessed by no-one else.'

Grundmann sipped his coffee and felt better for getting this off his chest, momentarily forgetting the question of Marianne's fidelity.

'The Medical Officer had signed the *Kapo's* death certificate. "Heart failure." I agreed with him that gunshot wounds can have that effect.' Grundmann sighed. 'What else could I say? "You appreciate," the medic said, "that we have no post-mortem facilities. It was therefore a waste of time to inspect the body." Of course I agreed. One must be practical in these matters.'

Grundmann sighed again. 'I told him "A non-person alive is no different to a non-person dead. It is a question of timing, not physical condition." He agreed with me. It is necessary to have common ground on these questions.'

But Grundmann's display of cynicism was undermined by the uncertainty in his voice. Marianne could tell he was worried, perhaps even frightened.

'Meine liebchen,' he put his arm around her, 'between ourselves, I am ashamed. But what else is there to do?'

'It is not your fault, my darling.' she moved on to his lap and stroked his cheek. He smelt of cigar smoke, which she always found disgusting, but no matter. She could feel him getting an erection, which was what it was really all about. His swelling penis thrust against her thigh through his serge trousers. He was not saying what he meant to and she was memorising every word.

She asked calmly, while shifting her naked butt towards his erection, 'Do you think I like witnessing murders?'

'Gerhard tells me you were hysterical. That could be dangerous for both of us.'

'Sweetheart, women are allowed to be emotional.'

'That doesn't play well with our friends in the black uniforms. They'd rape you as soon as look at you.'

'And wouldn't you, my love?' She wriggled her backside against him some more.

'Be serious.' Just thinking about the SS made his erection start to subside. 'They are certain to interrogate you. The sooner we get you out of the island the safer for you.'

This was highly disingenuous and Marianna knew it. The real issue was her pregnancy, but she wasn't going mention it until he did. His erection ha now totally collapsed. He was plain scared.

'So, what should I say to them?' She asked.

'You were too far away to see anything clearly.'

'I saw that corporal's face. I shall never forget it. Who was he?'

'How could I know? Don't ask insane questions. Forget the whole thing.'

'Alright, my darling, I will forget it all. It's out of my mind. There!' she snapped her fingers, then kissed him. 'I need you, my love. I need you inside me.'

'Please be discreet. Don't say a thing.'

'Of course I will. What was it you said about my leaving?

Grundmann struggled to be dignified, but with her sitting on his lap in her negligee, her arms around his neck, her bare backside wiggling, it was impossible. He resorted to accusation.

'You are pregnant. Don't deny it.'

'Why should I, Horst my darling, why should I for God's sake. If the baby is like his father he'll be a fine, strong boy. I know he will be a boy.' In reality she was hoping for a girl.

'Like his father? Nicely put. Who is the father? I have been calculating dates. Were you fooling around with Gerhard when I was on leave?'

He managed to lift her off his lap and stood upright in his stockinged feet. She noticed a hole in one sock. It provided an ideal distraction.

'I must mend that.' She said in a motherly voice. 'We can't have the Colonel with holes in his toes.'

'Have you been fooling around with Gerhard? Answer me!'

'He takes me riding. On horseback.'

She thought of the basket and almost laughed out loud, remembering demonstrating it to Gerhard. Riding! That had been quite a ride. But now she had to playact outrage. And how much did Horst actually know?

'You're so virile. You have three children.' She flattered him some more, 'And you always come in floods.' She embraced him, oh so spontaneously. 'My darling, you are a very virile man.'

'Either way, liebchen, this is no place for a baby.'

Her flattery calmed him down a trifle. He became less authoritarian. But it would be most embarrassing to have a baby around. Altogether too dangerous domestically and it might affect his next posting, which he earnestly hoped would be far away from this hellhole. Not too far away though, not to the Eastern Front in the snows of Russia. Plenty of only mildly disgraced officers had been sent there as a disciplinary measure

'You will have to leave the island.' He insisted.

'So that's it! You're embarrassed.' Now she was genuinely angry. 'An embarrassment am I? Perhaps I should ask the SS about that.'

'For your own sake be careful.'

He dared not say more and subsided into the armchair again. If she spilt the beans to his superiors about what she saw this morning he could end up posted to the Russian front, sentenced to deprivation, defeat and very possibly death. The army commanders had very ambivalent attitudes towards what went on in the island. They knew about and condoned the atrocities, yet wanted them never mentioned. They knew about mistresses, but did not welcome babies or angry *Hausfrauen* back home.

'I must get back to headquarters,' Horst snapped 'help me with my boots.' He had a wooden bootjack, but preferred to watch her to do the work. He got a kick out of that. She knelt to get his feet into the long glossy boots, then leant across him to pull them up. It was no accident that her breasts brushed his face.

'You'd miss me.' she said, darting a kiss at his mouth.

He dodged the kiss, knowing he was being made a monkey of. He wouldn't trust her not to unload his confidences elsewhere, but he'd thought of a solution. Quite a neat one.

'If there are any problems at all,' he warned her, 'Schwester Olga will look after you. Don't forget Schwester Olga if the SS do come round.'

This was a serious threat. Schwester Olga was that boot faced army nurse, with a figure like a beer barrel, who obstructed Marianne whenever possible at the *Soldatenheim*. She frightened the hell out of everyone. Even the SS men respected her.

'Thank-you,' Marianne said, with as much sarcasm as she could muster. 'But hers is the kind of help I do not need.'

Grundmann barely heard. He was tugging at his well-cut, grey-green tunic to straighten it. He adjusted the high black collar and the Iron Cross on his breast pocket, buckled his dark brown leather belt and settled his gold braided peaked hat on his head. He was dignified and self-important once again. Now would come a performance for the benefit of anyone passing.

'Wiedersehn, liebchen.' he said in the doorway and gave a stiff Heil Hitler salute to her before he walked out into the cobbled square.

'Fuck you,'' said Marianne in French to his retreating back as the door with its flaking paint closed. She wasn't going to be run out of the island like some common whore. And she was going to get the name of that SS murderer. Obviously Grundmann reckoned that the SS would send someone round to interrogate her, probably straightaway. Maybe she'd be able to wheedle the name out of whoever it turned out to be, though not with the techniques she employs on Horst. God, no. She was not a fool.

She went upstairs and changed into the most demure and ladylike clothing she possessed, or rather that the owner of the house's wife used to possess. It was a tweed suit, surprisingly soft and light, coloured in a subtle blend of oatmeal and light blue. It carried a French designer label from just before the war and, perhaps because Marianne had as yet a neat, slim figure, it fitted her well. The owner must have treasured this suit. Too bad.

Marianne had heard that the inhabitants left in such a hurry that they only took one suitcase of possessions each. *Tant pis.* A girl had to seize her chances in war. The suit was a small example. The departed owner of this house had good taste, though not in the terrible English furniture and cream painted walls.

She made up her face very lightly, slipped on her only pair of silk stockings and a pair of dark blue court shoes, which she also found in a cupboard and which just about fitted, and prepared to wait. Whoever came would be expecting a tart. They were going to find a patriot and a lady. She did not have to wait long.

A heavy hammering on the door announced visitors. She ordered the soldier servant, who was just back from the canteen, to answer the door. Then she settled herself composedly on the sofa in the small sitting room. This was a pantomime really, because the house was too small to play the hostess in. The visitor was the well-turned out SS lieutenant who had been so brusque with Grundmann earlier. As planned, he was immediately taken aback by the sophisticated woman who rose to greet him.

'Obersturmfuhrer Vogelsang.' He clicked his jackboot heels together and gave a small bow, just the slightest inclination of the head, as an aristocrat would. SS officers might be tough, but they liked to demonstrate how they understood social etiquette.

'May I offer you coffee and cake, Herr Obersturmfuhrer?

She had already ordered the servant to bring it whenever the visitor arrived. 'Please sit down.'

Vogelsang was only 22 years old and recently promoted to officer rank. He was impressed. The Colonel's mistress had class. She had not asked what he wanted and showed no sign of being frightened. Mentally he gave her points for that.

Dealing with a male suspect, he would respond to such implied resistance with threats, if not blows. He had been taught that not to show fear of the SS was a form of insolence. But it was clear that that this was different. This woman might deserve respect. He took off his black peaked hat, with its silver death's head badge, revealing thick blond hair above his closely shaven neck, and accepted a chair. The soldier servant brought the coffee on a looted silver tray. Marianne poured it, smiled graciously and finally asked how she could be of assistance.

'There was a small incident this morning, Frau…?'

'Hausmann.'

When she had needed a new surname in a hurry she taken it from the famous Parisian boulevard. It had the advantage of sounding German too.

'We require witnesses of that incident.'

Marianne was not fooled. He was concerned about how much she might have seen.

'Near the church, you mean?'

'Richtig. I myself arrived after it was over. But you were there.'

This was a factual statement, not a question and Marianne quietly and politely corrected it.

'Only just. As I walked along the street after doing my shopping I heard firing. Naturally I stopped.' She sighed and fluttered her eyelashes in apology. 'I am not very brave, I confess. I took shelter in a doorway. Then when the shooting ended, I continued.'

'But you saw what took place.' Again a statement, not a query.

'Very little of it. There was a car which blocked my view. Thankfully.' She parodied aversion to violence. 'But one thing I did observe!'

'Jah?' Her emphatic, even enthusiastic, tone surprised the lieutenant.' What was that?'

'The bravery of one of your young men. In spite of all the danger, he chased the gunman across the street to tackle him. That was all I saw, because of the car, but I was thrilled.'

'And then?' He might be young, but Vogelsang was well trained and persistent.

'There was one more shot. Who fired it I have no idea.' The shot had been the corporal's brutal summary execution of the fugitive 'But I will never forget that young man's heroism.'

'That would have been Rottenfuhrer Eberhardt.' The lieutenant nodded appreciatively. 'Yes, he is a good man.'

'Please congratulate your brave Rottenfuhrer Eberhardt.' She deliberately repeated the name in order to remember it. 'That is really all I can tell you. Very shortly afterwards I encountered another officer, Hauptmann Gerhard, who told me to go home.' She smiled persuasively 'And here I am.'

'Sehr gut.' The lieutenant smiled back, but nonetheless took a notebook out of his tunic pocket. 'Just a few personal details, Frau Hausmann, and we are finished. Your nationality is German?'

'Unhappily not. I am Italian by birth. One of your allies.' She laughed confidently, 'But the Herr Oberst believes I am French. It suits his romantic ideas. And for various reasons I adopted the Parisian name when the war began.' The reason had been problems with a Gestapo interrogator at a railway station, but Marianne twisted it into a hint of difficulties suffered by an Italian in France after the invasion. However, this was lost on the SS man, who perhaps knew nothing of such details of the Axis pact..

'May I see your papers, Madame?'

'Of course.' Life under the Nazis was one long round of demands for "papieren, bitte" She reached for her handbag, which was on the carpet beside the sofa, and held the documents out to Vogelsang, forcing him to stand up. He examined them and handed them back.

'Alles in ordnung' he conceded, a little stiffly she thought, before sitting down again. 'Now, about your relationship with Oberst Grundmann.'

'Keine probleme, Herr Obersturmfuhrer. I send regular reports.'

'Reports?' She had him foxed.

'Naturlich! Why else would the Gestapo in Paris have authorised my papers? Surely you noticed?'

She thumbed through her papers and displayed the swastika sign of the Fuhrer's secret police stamped in the corner of her passport. He realised he was out of his depth.

'My sincere apologies, meine liebe Frau.' Vogelsang's embarrassment showed in his young face. 'I did not know.'

'Nor does anyone else. But since our organisations are so close....' she smiled discreetly, hinting at endless conspiracies 'I can surely trust you. Necessarily the Colonel must never know.'

'Fully understood.' Vogelsang rose to leave. 'I am most grateful, meine Frau. This has been a pleasure.'

'Mine I assure you, Herr Obersturmfuhrer.'

She extended her hand graciously, without getting up from the sofa. He bowed and planted a kiss in the air, the regulation two inches above her outstretched fingers.

'So nice to meet an officer with perfect manners' she breathed. And, come to think of it, he was a good looking boy too. 'The servant will show you out.'

Vogelsang clicked his heels and replaced his hat. The thick blond hair above his close-cropped neck was concealed in the regulation way.

'If I can assist at any time.'

'Thank-you, I will not forget.' She wouldn't either, although the danger would be that he was probably spied on all the time himself.

The very moment he had gone Marianne ran upstairs, choking with laughter, and scribbled the name 'Eberhardt' on a scrap of paper. One day that animal would get his come-uppance. And if she needed to manipulate Grundmann she might be able to do so now as well, though she was wise enough to appreciate the risks, even if her lover was terrified of the SS.

Not for the first time, she congratulated herself on 'borrowing' the Gestapo stamp. That quick and surreptitious act when its owner was briefly out of the room had been an inspiration when she was being interrogated on the trickiest day of her life: the day she was detained by the Gestapo at a railway station in Brittany, the day that sent her scurrying to St Malo in the hope of getting away somewhere, anywhere, and ended with meeting Grundmann in a bar when he was waiting for a ship.

That stamp with its eagle symbol had saved her more than once since then. And she had reckoned Vogelsang was far too wet behind the ears to question it. After all, the Gestapo's network of informers does extend everywhere, though was no office here.

Marianne changed out of the tweed suit into an ordinary skirt and blouse, then wrote down the day's events on several sheets of the thinnest airmail paper she could find. She opened up the endpaper of the diary, inserted the folded pages, glued around the edges and pressed the endpaper back in place, smoothing it with a handkerchief, so that the enlarged binding was barely detectable. Finally, she added a note to her 17 May page, which anyone astute enough would understand. 'There is more to this than meets the eye.'

CHAPTER EIGHTEEN

Anna stared at the pages extracted from the diary cover with something close to disbelief, in fact of sheer horror. The SS corporal had the name of her uncle. Eberhardt. Could it be him? Could these things really have happened? But then, closing the diary, she knew that they had. Marianne's story was totally convincing. The atrocities she had recorded must have been real. And she had seen the bullet marks at the churchyard gate herself. Was her search over in the most distressing way possible?

She sat there out on the battlements, while the sunshine outside had become almost blinding. The fog had completely cleared and it was a glorious late spring day, while the light on Rocquaine Bay now possessed exactly that painterly clarity which Quinn so enthused about. Here was another of the island's abrupt changes of mood, from fog to sunshine, from gloom to light. But no amount of sunshine could outweigh the hard truths of Marianne's narrative. Corporal Eberhardt, she had written. No first name. Had it been Johann?

Any decent person who read the full doings of that 17th of May could only be horrified and worse. Words like 'obscene' and 'barbaric', weakened by over-use, failed to convey what Anna felt. Marianne had called the SS men 'animals', but the most savage animals, except perhaps cats, lacked their extreme malice. Even the other German officers had been ashamed of them.

And there was Marianne herself, taking huge risks to record the truth and never once asking her unknown future readers for sympathy. Marianne had been quite a woman. She had seen Eberhardt cold-bloodedly execute a fugitive, then managed through an extremely hazardous subterfuge to find out his name and preserve it. Anna felt physically sick at thinking the corporal might have been her uncle. Did she have to believe it?

The only possible escape from this appalling possibility lay in Mackinnon's belief that her uncle would have been would be too young to be in the SS. True he could have been 19, rather than 18, but the officer in Marianne's account had been very young. So how old might a corporal have been? How important was a corporal? She had no idea. Presumably less important than an officer, but possibly with longer service. Her lack of knowledge made her head spin. She would have to ask Mackinnon.

But there was no escaping the name being the same. Marianne, so determined to see him brought to justice in the end, had spelt it out in capitals: EBERHARDT. Anna felt more and more sure it must have been her uncle. Why did she feel such certainty? Perhaps it was because of the island's violent past, which Quinn was so anxious to sidestep, but which she had found more and more oppressive with each successive day. Did her uncle link her to that past whether she liked it or not?

'You must be psychic.' Quinn had half-joked at one point, then backtracked because he believed strongly in intuition. But this whole scenario was beyond a joke: it was a nightmare. It made her less and less sure of everything about herself, her relationships, her real family. It undermined her very identity.

What had begun as a simple, well, she admitted to herself, a relatively simple, voyage to discover whether she wanted to re-unite with Quinn, plus a minor family history incentive, had developed into a full-blown emotional saga. And was Tad's own journey of rediscovery pure co-incidence, or was it somehow linked to hers in ways she did not understand?

These unhappy musings were cut short by Quinn returning, accompanied by Lavinia. Anna saw them walking up the lawn in the luminous afternoon sun, Lavinia close at his side, as close as if hand-in-hand. She quickly composed herself for whatever unpleasantness was about to come her way. Quinn's patron seemed to have only two operational modes; seductively authoritarian and out and out bitchy. It was ninety to one she would now shift from the one to the other.

'Hello, there!' Quinn called out loudly at the door of the Moroccan room, as if it was he who might catch Anna out.

She answered quietly. 'Jack Mackinnon gave me a lift.'

'Oh, that man.' Lavinia appeared behind Quinn. 'I didn't think he had a charitable thought in his head.' she came into the room. 'Feeding you a lot of nonsense about the war, I suppose.'

'He has been very helpful.' Anna said, then to emphasise the point added 'Extremely helpful.'

'Well, Quinn,' Lavinia changed tack, like a sailboat avoiding a rock, though she was more of a galleon than a dinghy, Anna thought. 'What are you going to offer me after all that work?' she looked meaningfully at Anna. 'The time I devote to helping this man! You wouldn't believe!'

'A glass of the usual?' Quinn tried to defuse the tension.

'The usual is the answer.' Lavinia emphasised the 'usual' to show how at home she was at Rocquaine.

'It's a little bit early for me.' Anna said, recognising Lavinia's reply as intended to imply intimacy and denigrate her own standing.

'It can never be too early on this island.' Lavinia said. 'But newcomers learn in the end.'

'Two thousand alcoholics clinging to a rock in the Atlantic,' Quinn said 'that's us.'

He laughed uproariously at this obviously well-worn joke and went in search of the white wine, while Lavinia settled herself in one corner of the big sofa with an air of prior possession. Just like Germans with beach beds, Anna thought.

'So you're a bit of an artist, too?' Lavinia said, 'I should love to see your, er, what is it, watercolours?'

'Drawings.'

'You've been out sketching already, Quinn tells me.' This was half-way to an accusation. 'Well, they always say that artists are awful, novelists are worse and reporters are the end.' Except, of course,' Lavinia dispensed her most regal half-smile, 'that artists contribute so nobly to our heritage. True artists, that is, which is more than those wretched reporters ever do.'

Quinn must have told her about Dick Carey, the bastard. Not that he actually knew anything about Carey. Not that there was anything to know, but that wouldn't calm down his uncontrollable jealousy. He had never physically assaulted her, but Anna had always been afraid that given the right trigger, he might. Even allowing that Lavinia would have wormed things out of him which he had not intended to tell her, this cutting allusion to reporters was infuriating: and solely designed to underline how Quinn confided in his patron, without baldly stating it.

If Quinn wasn't careful he'd be left flat with her, period, as the Americans said. And then what a volcanic fuss he would make! There would be tantrums and protestations of love and threats of suicide. There were times when being in love with Quinn was like intentionally speeding through traffic lights at red.

'You really must show me what you've done.' Lavinia insisted, now the knowledgeable patron on the watch for talent and speaking with precision. 'Quinn tells me it is very imaginative.'

'I draw what I see.' Anna said. Lavinia could take that any way she wished.

Quinn returned with two glasses of wine. 'Sure you don't want anything?' he asked Anna, with a small show of concern.

'I'll just make myself some instant.' she got up to go to the kitchen.

'I absolutely demand to see these drawings.' Lavinia tried to be humorously autocratic, but succeeded only in being shrill and sounding her age.

'Please bring them out.' Quinn begged.

'If you really must see them.'

Anna abandoned the coffee idea, went to her bedroom and returned with a single drawing, the one she had done of the bay this morning in sunlight, the one of the present day. Looking at it again, she realised how detailed and factual it was, every feature from the treacherous rocks to the distant harbour quayside in precise relationships. She knew, but of course Quinn did not, that it was the counterpoint to the fog scene of the afternoon before.

'Very nice.' Lavinia said, damningly. 'Is this what you teach? In Brighton, is it?'

'Oh no! I teach how to fold blankets. Creatively.'

For the first time Lavinia was nonplussed. She had very little sense of humour.

'Conceptual art.' Anna explained. 'Not quite your style, I imagine. Except for .the interpretative empathy bit.'

'Anna's talking nonsense.' Quinn cut in, angry at his patron being teased. 'Where are those other ones you did?'

'I tore those up. You said they were all wrong.'

She had done nothing of the sort, of course, but she wanted to end this interrogation. Lavinia would have made a passable SS officer. A very passable one, in high heeled jackboots.

'Well, my dear,' Lavinia recovered herself, 'I'm sure you could sell them to tourists.'

'I don't do it for money. I paint for myself. I only wish Quinn did the same.'

This was virtually unanswerable, except to someone of Lavinia's hippo-hided self esteem. 'Quinn's heritage work is extremely fulfilling.' She said, 'Isn't it my dear?'

'Some of the most exciting I've ever done.' Quinn knew which side his bank balance was buttered on.

'Yes, he really has caught the essence of interpretive empathy.' Anna suggested, amazed at her own nerve.

'Exactly,' Lavinia snapped, striving for matching jargon and getting it slightly mixed up. 'Interpretative sympathy. Quinn takes a completely holistic view too. Holisticity is so important, isn't it? Now I really must be off. Sir Edward is coming to tea. Such a distinguished man.' She swept to the door. 'I can find my own way out. It's not as though I haven't been here before.'

'What the hell are you trying to do to me, Anna?' Quinn demanded as soon as she had gone. 'Lose me my job? You're being as tricky as she is.'

'That's just not possible.' Anna said with spirit. 'No-one could be. And you're pretty tricky yourself. Now I am going to make some coffee.' When she came back she told Quinn to sit down. 'Just listen for a moment. You asked me what I'm trying to do, right? Well, I'm trying to discover who I am, okay?'

'Don't you want to be with me?'

'Not on this island. I've made a terrible discovery, Quinn, a really frightening one. My uncle was here. He was here in the war. He was in the SS. And he gunned down an escaping slave in the churchyard.'

'How on earth do you know that?' A note of serious alarm came into Quinn's voice. If this was true she would never agree to live here.

At long last Quinn did wake up to her being really distressed, though in a purely selfish way. This was a brutal threat to everything he had dreamt of, everything he had planned. He had always assumed that, eventually, Anna would agree to live here.

'How did you find this out?' he demanded

'In an archive.' She dared not reveal the existence of the diary and Marianne's testament.

'It's that bloody Mackinnon!' Quinn exploded. 'Lavinia's dead right about him. He has Nazis on the brain.'

'Don't blame the messenger for the bad news, Quinn.' She was trying to keep as calm as she could. 'The past is not Mackinnon's fault. It was his job to excavate it.'

'Haven't I told you. So far as the island's concerned the war is a non-event.'

'You mean that because the islanders weren't here, it didn't happen?'

'Of course not. But they'd rather it hadn't.'

This prompted Anna to raise a question which had occurred to her on that first day at the harbour, when Quinn had been so matey with the locals.

'How well do you really know them? I mean, aren't they a bit of a closed society? Do you get asked to their homes?'

Put like that Quinn had to admit that he had very seldom been a guest in an islander's house. 'We have a few pints in the pub, though.' he said defensively.

'They must be rather inbred, aren't they? I mean, being so cut off. When they were fisherman and pirates, would there have been much new blood? And what do they think of tax exiles like Lavinia?'

'She's never going to be one of them. Never in a hundred years. Wouldn't want to be, either.'

'Thank God you realise that at least. And you, Quinn. How about you? Your parents or grandparents weren't evacuated and they didn't have to come back to rebuilding an island that had been comprehensively wrecked.'

'I suppose not.' he conceded, suddenly weary of argument. He had not had an easy day with his patroness. 'Unless you were born an islander, and I don't just mean born here, I mean educated and raised, you can't be one. Never. It's a refusenik situation. Even the husbands of island girls are only half accepted. They may seem to be, but come the crunch they'll be shut out.'

'I don't think I'd like being a permanent outsider, quite apart from the business over my uncle.'

'You have to understand their point of view.' Quinn argued. 'They rejected the mainland, came back from it after the war to great hardship, rebuilt their island. Or rather their grandparents did. Perhaps in their imaginations the time before the war was a golden age, when they were independent, even though they didn't have electricity or mains water. Now they have to go to St Mary for funding and they need tax exiles and tourists to bring in extra revenue. Their pride has been assaulted. They feel diminished. And they always were an unruly bunch.'

'They don't appreciate what people like Lavinia bring? Spending in shops and all that.'

'They despise the tax exiles; perhaps because they know they can't manage without them, yet don't want to admit it.'

'And do all the tax exiles wish they weren't marooned here? I suppose widows like Lavinia are pretty well stuck?

'Quite a few go away again after a year or so, leaving very few ripples on the pond.' Quinn admitted. 'So the islanders remain a controlling minority and fight to keep the old ways. Oh, they want a decent hospital and a school and an airport and a harbour, facilities they can't pay for themselves, so they're always over in St Mary with the begging bowl. At the same time they're fiercely independent.' he shook his head in aggravation, then grinned like a schoolboy. 'But you don't have to be an islander to enjoy living here.'

It struck Anna that perhaps the islanders ought to be subsidised for staying in their timewarp, like the reindeer-herding Lapps in Norway were. She wondered if they had picturesque traditional costumes too. If you were going to play the threatened lifestyle game you had to act the part.

'Listen Quinn,' she said firmly, because in a way this was the crunch, 'I also have a life, which I also want to enjoy. A timewarp may not be the place. And at this moment I also have a serious problem. May I please telephone Jack Mackinnon?'

'Sure.'Quinn heaved himself out of the chair and slouched through to his studio. He was only forty four but he felt a hundred. Anna might be through there, lifting the telephone, but emotionally he had lost her. She was gone, a wraith from a former life, a will-o-the-wisp as uncatchable as the drifting fog outside. Incautiously he followed her through.

'I'm so sorry to bother you,' Anna was saying, 'and thank you again for lunch. Please tell me, how old would an SS corporal have been?'

'Strictly speaking Eberhardt was only a lance corporal, a Rottenfuhrer.' Mackinnon explained. 'The ration clerk thought he was aged about 20. But he could have been younger. By the Spring of 1943 Hitler was losing his campaign in Russia. They recruited younger and younger men into the services, boys almost, though things became even worse in 1944.'

'So we can't be certain?

'Not without the Christian name. And I hope to have it soon.' His merely saying so made Anna feel sick and her feeling communicated itself back to him. 'Would you like to come here tomorrow?' he suggested.

'Very much. I promised to see Tad in the morning.''

'Midday perhaps? Unhappily we are going out to lunch.'

Anna put the phone down, not needing to tell Quinn, because he had been standing within earshot.

'Do you have to meet the Pole again?' he protested. This visit was getting further and further out of control as far as he was concerned. 'Can't you cancel?'

'I can't quite say why, but yes I do.' She tried to rationalise it. 'He's alone and he needs help.'

'Which you never cease telling me.' Quinn moved round to face her, motivated by a concern that he could not quantify either. 'Why did you tear up the other drawings?'

'Didn't you dislike them?'

Suddenly it was a question of who was going to admit the truth first and Quinn flinched away from it.

'Was it,' Anna asked grimly, 'because in the fog I drew scenes from the war, like the labourers building the wall? You said I must be psychic. I've never thought I am. Did you mean that?'

'You've, well you must have been looking at one of those Occupation books and your sub-conscious did the rest.'

'Yes, I suppose that must be it.' she said meekly.

It was easier to fall in with Quinn's explanation than argue. Anna gave up, she would save her energy for the real search. The only such book she had seen was the one Mackinnon showed her after she had already drawn the shipwreck.

'I must have remembered the scenes as if there were my own idea,' she continued obediently, 'like those plagiarists in the Saatchi collection.'

'It's the obvious explanation.' Quinn didn't try to hide his relief. If the truth be told he was worried by Anna's visions and his own apparent lack of perception. 'Definitely auto suggestion.'

'But I still desperately need to talk to someone about my uncle. Can't you understand that?'

'Then I suppose it has to be Mackinnon.' He turned away her appeal instinctively, not wanting to be involved, then realised he ought to be conciliatory. 'I honestly don't know how to help.'

She was about to say that she didn't need to know any more about the war, all she needed was willingness to talk through a possibly extremely unpleasant episode of family history, when the telephone rang. It was Tad.

'For you.' Quinn said, resentfully.

Anna listened to what the old man had to say in his broken English, then agreed to meet him, though reluctantly.

'I'll come to your guesthouse at ten.'

'No, no, please. By bay. I take bus.'

'Alright, then. At ten.' she rang off.

'You've had a bad day.' Quinn observed in an ostensible show of sympathy. 'Would you like a drink now?'

'A glass of Lady Lavinia's special would go down quite well.' Anna finally abandoned attempting to talk through her dilemma with him 'And then I must think about supper.'

Quinn positively beamed through his beard, delighted at the resumption of domesticity. This was what it was all meant to be about. Woman looks after needs of man. The two of them in a comfortable domestic relationship, with no unwelcome intrusions.

Inevitably, much later, after they had eaten and were having coffee, he assumed she would be compliant in other ways. Declaring how much he loved her, he tried to persuade her into bed. She firmly refused, though a curious notion had come into her head. Perhaps, if she did finally decide she had no future here, she would sleep with him on her last night, and enjoy his lovemaking for the last time. Quinn had many faults, but very few in bed.

'No, my dear,' she said, kissing him on the cheek, 'there's just too much going on inside my head at the moment.'

Then the dull boom of the foghorn began again and seemed to echo around the fort. She went to the windows. There was no fog outside, at least not between them and the house on the next headland, where the lights were undimmed.

'Probably just out at sea.' Quinn said, wondering if she might change her mind.

'I'd like to listen to the forecast, if you don't mind.' She picked up the phone and dialled the number. The friendly voice of the weatherman clicked on.

'And the forecast from six am tomorrow, Thursday. The wind light south westerly, the sea state slight, visibility poor to very poor at first, but clearing gradually later, with a fine sunny afternoon.'

So it was going to be another of those foggy days which haunted Tad's memories and, like it or not, she was morally committed to revisiting 1943 with him again.

164

CHAPTER NINETEEN

Once or twice during the night the foghorn had woken Anna and she felt chilled and lonely, as if there was a ghost out there circling the fort, against which she had no protection. She thought of waking Quinn, but then the complications deterred her. Men always jumped to conclusions, usually the wrong ones.

When she did get up, shortly after seven and well before Quinn would appear, the fort was completely encompassed. The fog blanketed it, delaying the advent of morning, even preventing the gulls from flying. She saw a group of them marshalled on a rocky outcrop, all facing towards the temporarily inhospitable sea, waiting not very patiently, she thought, to be able dive after fish. Gulls were voracious predators with their own definite agenda.

As always she made herself coffee, the lifeblood of waking up, the essential precursor to the day, more vital than the minimal make-up she wore. Without coffee the day could not properly begin.

After the second cup she decided that, since she was going to be meeting Tad, she ought to read more of Marianne's diary. Just in case. There would probably be no connection. The likelihood of Grundmann's mistress hearing about the escape of two slaves must have been minimal when there had been a shipwreck with hundreds dead. And after accidentally witnessing the churchyard shooting she would have been kept as far as possible ignorant of anything to do with hunting down escapers. But Anna knew the date now and leafed through the coarse, wartime paper of the pages to the entries for 26 May 1943.

The field telephone by Oberst Grundmann's bed erupted with a tinny jangling as the operator at the military exchange furiously wound a handle to activate its bell. He reached for it, cursing and causing Marianne to roll over sleepily beside him.

'Grundmann' he answered, fully awake in an instant. 'Ja, ja. Ich kommt.' He put the instrument back on its cradle and nudged Marianne's shoulder. 'There has been an accident.' As he spoke they heard klaxons blaring in the town.

'What has happened?' Marianne asked sleepily, inwardly cursing the klaxons, one of which was mounted on the

Soldatenheim roof across the square, so that all the military quartered in the town would hear it.

She tried to sound concerned, which was difficult before seven in the morning, even though the early morning light had been percolating through the thin curtains since six. She had argued for thicker ones, but Grundmann liked to be woken naturally by the dawn. She hated that. Then she remembered that today was her last day. This evening she would be leaving..

'You will not be on the ship tonight.' Horst announced, getting out of bed fast. 'I suppose for you that is good news.' The implication was that only a particularly silly woman would think so. 'My ship', a sincere note of pride and of sorrow entered his voice 'has hit the rocks in the bay. I must go down at once.'

He was already pulling on his carefully pressed grey-green uniform trousers as he spoke. 'I don't know when I'll be back. The Naval Commander is in France. I have to take charge.'

Surprisingly quickly, because Grundman could shift his bulk when he needed to, he was gone. Marianne had to make her next decision herself: back to sleep or get up too. The soldier servant would not come on duty until seven, but that would be in a few minutes. Normally he made the coffee and then cooked the Herr Oberst's breakfast. She decided to make the coffee immediately herself, but would dress and get herself presentable first. If here had been a disaster anyone at all might come round.

In any case she did not want to be in her underclothes and alone in the house with the servant. He had slipped her various suggestive compliments about her breasts when Horst was away. That was the problem about being thought of as a tart, when anyone who knew the truth would appreciate that she was really just a survivor, albeit a survivor expecting a baby.

She made the coffee, from bitter tasting ersatz grounds that she was sure included burnt breadcrumbs as well as chicory, and sat at the scrubbed wood kitchen table to consider her position.

She was in a serious bind. Since the dreadful morning of the shooting in the churchyard Horst's attitude to her seemed to have changed, without his being honest enough to explain why.

'It is not good to have a baby here.' he had told her a few days ago, very soon after the shooting. 'There is not the right food for a baby.'

'You may not have noticed,' she had replied smoothly, 'that mothers often feed their babies themselves.'

'This is not a suitable environment, meine liebchen. You must go and live in France for a while. I will make arrangements and pay for you.'

Whether he was worried that his *hausfrau* in Frankfurt would hear of it, or that he was afraid of being laughed at, or more likely that his superiors disapproved, she did not know.

Then two days ago he had told her to pack. When the ship named after him came on 26 May, bringing a cargo of labourers, she would leave with it. Supply ships always sailed at night, to avoid enemy attacks, so it would dock early in the morning and depart in the evening.

'I shall miss you, my little gazelle,' he had insisted, 'but it is for the best. The baby can be adopted in France and then you will come back.'

With my figure restored, she had thought, and ready for more sessions in the basket. Can he not understand that I may love my child, even if it was fathered by a German, and that I may want to keep it?

This war could not go for ever. Even the carefully censored radio reports and the soldiers' magazine, 'Signal', which Horst received, revealed that Hitler's army was in trouble. When you read about 'heroic battles to the last man' you knew it meant defeat in the snows of Russia.

When this nightmare was over she and her child would live in France and somehow she would find her parents again. She would have survived. That was what mattered. Anyway she knew that Horst's talk about coming back to the island was just flannel to keep her happy. He would never bring her back because of what she had seen. That was the reality. She was a civilian, one of only a handful here, and she had witnessed an SS execution. By accident, but she had seen it. Men had been shot for less.

If the pages glued into the binding of her diary were ever discovered by a German, that would be the end for her too. She hoped they would be found when the true owner of the house returned after the war, where she planned to hide it. Also, being sent to France had a positive clandestine advantage.

She would be able to get information to the Resistance, with which she had worked for a long time. She had been lucky last year when she was detained. Incredibly lucky. Her arrest had been by chance, due to a collaborationist policeman being suspicious of her actions at a railway station, not as a result of betrayal. The Gestapo interrogator had believed the explanation for her journey. Being lucky mattered more than anything else. That was what Napoleon used to say. She would pass on that luck to her child. It was a simple and sustaining credo. She was not the complaining kind; all she asked for was to continue being lucky.

The soldier servant arrived late and, if she had not been fully and modestly dressed, would undoubtedly have made some sniggering suggestion. She headed off that possibility by asking what was going on. If you needed to know the news fast, she always said, ask a driver or a servant. They had none of the inhibitions of officers. In her diary she later paraphrased what the soldier told her.

Edging its way into the bay to dock at the new steel girder quay extension the local cargo ship re-named as the 'Horst Grundmann' had strayed off course and met with disaster. Her captain was bringing her in just before dawn on a dark night, with very few navigation lights permitted, and when the bay was enveloped in thick fog. Although the tide was going down the rocks in the middle of the bay were still under water: hidden and fatal, if a navigator was careless.

'Couldn't hardly see your bloody hand in front of your face.' was the soldier servant's description.

His billet was in a house just above the harbour and he'd run straight down there to help.

'They say there was three hundred Russians locked in the holds. They'll all have been drowned. Only the crew and the guards were rescued.'

The servant had stayed to watch the drama. By the time he finally did leave there were servicemen swarming everywhere, small boats going out and troops on the beach, but nothing was being done for the labourers trapped in the hold. With the tide going down, they could easily have been rescued. He'd heard someone saying they ought to be. A naval officer had intervened to stop the attempt Why bother? No one had to account for *Untermenschen*. Instead he had ordered renewed searches for any remaining Germans. *Kriegsmarine* sailors had rowed out in small boats and brought a few more survivors to shore.

Now, the servant explained with ghoulish delight, the eels and octopuses would soon be slithering in through the rents in the hull to tear at the slaves' bodies, followed by crabs and lobsters. And where would the crabs and lobsters go, he asked rhetorically? To the dining table at the Officers Mess in the big house overlooking the harbour, where the Herr Oberst presided over formal dinners.

'Where have all the Russians gone,' he sang softly, 'gone to salads every one.'

'That's enough, thank-you, Kurt.' Marianne cut him short. 'Please prepare breakfast.'

She knew something of the German army's anxiety complex about Russians. On the one hand they were non-persons, on the other these serfs had inflicted the terrible Stalingrad defeat on the mighty Wehrmacht. The worst disciplinary threat that could be made to a soldier was of a transfer to the eastern front. Perhaps that was why the Russian labourers here were particularly savagely treated and why fears were sublimated into crude jokes like the one Kurt had just made. But she still wasn't having him talk like that. She watched him depart sullenly for the kitchen.

Marianne was almost as disgusted by the shipwreck rescue failures as by the churchyard shooting. But she had learnt her lesson. When eventually Grundmann returned in mid-morning, his uniform soaked with seawater, loudly demanding the breakfast he had missed plus some schnapps, she asked no questions. He told her all about it anyway.

The Russians had been shipped from the French port of St Malo. They had been on board since the night before last. When no rescue was attempted some had succeeded in breaking out of the hold and tried to escape by jumping into the sea.

'My orders from Headquarters are clear.' Grundmann explained. 'all attempts to escape are punishable by death. Troops deployed on the beach carried out the orders.' Noticing Marianne's look of dismay he added. 'A regrettable necessity, liebste. Discipline must be maintained.'

'What about those who didn't try to escape, my love?' she asked sweetly. 'Were they rescued?'

'Too dangerous. The bodies will be retrieved in due course and taken for burial near the wall at Long Bay. We can't risk burying them in the sand where they drowned although it would be easier. We don't want to have corpses floating around the harbour.'

Through further discreet questioning as Horst tucked into his delayed breakfast, Marianne learnt that eventually the tide at Long Bay would wash them out to sea. No-one knew for sure who the men were, because although they had been documented in St Malo, they had not been through the arrival procedures here, when each would have been photographed like a convict with a number hung around his neck and had his name recorded.

'As for the captain, he ought to be court martialled for hazarding his ship.' Grundmann emphasised to Marianne how serious it was to lose a supply ship. Especially, she thought, one named after him.

'And now,' he added, coming to the subject she feared most, 'since all the arrangements have been made for you to leave here, I think you should move down to the House of Joy.'

He made a feeble attempt to re-assure her, because to live there with the common prostitutes would be a terrible debasement, even though she often visited it for 'entertainments' and parties.

'Purely temporarily, just until another ship departs. There will be one soon.'

'Do I have to?' Genuine tears came to Marianne's eyes. Already she was being sick in the mornings. 'Can't I stay here with you?'

'Meine liebste, I would like nothing better. But higher authority has been informed.'

She guessed this was an abject lie. The very last thing he would discuss with the General Staff were the arrangements for his mistress, whose status had been queried several times already.

'I am so sorry, my love. It is out of my hands.'

When he had returned to his duties Marianne broke down into tears at last. She was going to need all the luck in the world for her and her child: and all the courage.

CHAPTER TWENTY

Anna had begun to feel a considerable bond with Marianne. Even though they lived more half a century apart and Marianne would by now be eighty, if she was alive at all, she had – in a phrase she would not have recognised – 'what it takes'. She reminded Anna, as Mackinnon had suggested, of Brecht's Mother Courage, although Anna could not remember much about the play. Still Marianne had been the ultimate survivor. She took out the faded photo of Marianne which been in the diary.and studied it again. Marianne had not been conventionally pretty at all, no English rosebud, but dark and fine featured and, she guessed, probably as sexy as hell. What a truly attractive woman.

Wars were truly hateful. 'Men are war', the lecturer at the Gender Studies class had always told them, with a vengefulness which hinted at a failed affair. But men certainly had been war in this island.

These reflections were interrupted by Quinn appearing with only minutes to spare before he had to meet Lavinia. He gulped down the coffee Anna provided, wolfed the toast and hardly had time to say more than 'See you later' before he was off, rampaging the Land Rover down the drive. Anna concluded that the rush was deliberate. He wasn't yet able to cope with last night's revelations. Well, she thought, I was only being cruel to be kind: and my uncle's past is not his problem.

At nine thirty the fog was a little less dense, but she still allowed herself more than enough time to walk to Drake Manor. She had dressed in jeans, trainers and a sweatshirt, anticipating fighting her way through undergrowth again and took her sack with the sketch pad, though in these conditions even the battlements of the fort itself were only shadows. She could not see far enough to draw anything properly and was somewhat relieved that she could not. She was on the verge of ceasing the sketching.

Altogether Anna was more and more apprehensive about what scenes she might conjure up when she next began to draw. Marianne's mention of Russian corpses being shovelled into the sand at Drake Bay added to the fear. She emphatically did not wish to witness that.

Why she should suddenly have acquired this unwanted and uncanny ability to visualise the past, she could not work out. It was not susceptible to reasoning. But she did vividly remember her mother describing how, when working as a nurse in a military hospital, she had distinctly seen a young man in a white hospital dressing gown walking down the ward. That man had been brought in severely wounded and died in theatre the night before.

Her mother made nothing much of the experience, in fact had only mentioned it after watching a TV programme about the paranormal. Her mother also had an acute sense of when a place was permeated with evil, as when they had visited a film star's mansion where the chapel had been converted into a bedroom and a double bed replaced the altar. Most people would have merely thought that sacrilegious. Her mother had known better. Possibly, Anna thought, scientists would eventually identify a protein in the brain which gave second sight, like the inherited ones that carried a propensity to cancer.

For now her only certainty was that, as yet, she only 'saw' these 1943 scenes when she was sketching and it was foggy. With Mackinnon's warnings about Tad echoing in her head, she was frightened of getting any closer to atrocities. Meanwhile Quinn was reacting as if she was trespassing on his divine right to depict the island's history, which was why she had pretended to have destroyed those drawings. In fact it might be altogether better to do no more sketching, except in very clear weather, when as her later harbour sketches proved, everything was of the present day.

She walked slowly on around the bay in the thick fog, not exactly worried about accidentally falling over the low bank on to the rocks, but being cautious. The low outline of the slaves' memorial took shape only when she was five yards from it, reminding her that the service there would be on Sunday, her last day. Did she want to attend? Quinn certainly wouldn't and she was already framing a plan, if the weather proved sunny, for their seeing only the happiest side of the island on that last half day together. Lavinia would do her best to prevent it, of course, but even she could not insist that Quinn worked on a Sunday.

The glistening tarmac of the road took her between two rows of cottages, whitewashed like ghosts, and then across the neck of the island to Drake Bay, crossing the curious railway line. She never had got around to asking what the line was for. Meanwhile the slight descent down to the bay only brought an intensification of the fog, if that was possible.

Anna could barely make out the end of the long concrete wall as she reached the track to the restaurant, which now lurked among mist-shrouded trees and bushes, as if trying to conceal itself. It was closed. She should have known that ten o'clock would be too early; and Tad was not there either. She returned to the main road and sat on a bench, huddling against the chill.

She heard the bus long before it came into sight, grinding down the hill where Tad claimed that he and the other boy had made their escape. Before the episode in the cave she had not believed his story one bit and she still found it hard to credit. Then the period piece of the 1960s bus arrived and she realised Tad was the only passenger. As he clambered stiffly down the awkward step the driver leaned across and shouted at her.

'If he weren't so bloody old I'd not have made this trip, schedule or no schedule. Not worth doing on a day like this, eh. No bloody visitors.'

The driver vented his annoyance by accelerating away noisily into the fog, discharging oily exhaust smoke into their faces.

'So sorry.' Tad said unhappily, although it was hardly his fault that the bus had been late and the driver rude. 'He not want come. Want not.'

'And I'm afraid the café's closed too. What would you like to do?'

'We walk again.' Tad said decisively. 'Another way.'

This turned out to mean approaching the wooded valley from the Drake Manor end, instead of from the top. He showed her the rough-hewn rock tunnel opening in the cliff face, with its narrow railway line and abandoned chassis, then regained the path and began questing slowly though every clump of bushes and saplings on the same side, as if he was some veteran detective seeking clues in the most old-fashioned way. She noticed some pleasant things this time, like clumps of bluebells and tall white cow parsley, but the fog hung heavy in the trees and it was intensely gloomy as well as unusually still.

After fifteen or twenty minutes Tad seemed to find what he was searching for. Hidden behind a thick screen of vegetation was another tunnel entrance in the cliff face, which Anna had not observed before, further down from the cavity where he had faced the dog. He struggled to make his way to it, while she held the branches back. This entrance was smaller, being partially blocked with heaps of earth. He stood by it, panting, and tried to explain how the two were joined, forming a U in the air with his hand to indicate a horseshoe shape. But how did he know? How could he possibly know?

'This is second door.' he said. 'I want knife.'

But the knife had been confiscated, which he seemed to have forgotten. He started to scrabble at the side of the entrance with his hands until Anna found a thick stick and he used that to dig with, painstakingly excavating up against the rock. She found a large piece of pointed granite and began helping him, just as if they were Stone Age cave dwellers.

Half an hour later, having unearthed nothing, she suggested they should stop. It was a fruitless search for something which he could not find the English words to describe. None the less he absolutely refused to stop, saying 'Is here. I know.'

Eventually he did dig up a thin and heavily rusted chain from the earth and leafmould in the tunnel entrance. It had a round piece of metal attached. Triumphant, he demonstrated that it was a soldier's identity disc, a military dog tag that had hung around a man's neck. Anna tried to decipher the name, but it was so corroded that she would have needed a magnifying glass. And even that might not have been enough.

They stood there, their hands caked with wet earth, their finger nails encrusted. Her sweatshirt was soaked by drips from the trees, her jeans were stained and her white and red trainers dark brown. As for Tad, his once respectable trousers would have to go to the cleaners. As rapidly as he had been triumphant, he now collapsed into seeming despair.

'Now.' he said mournfully. 'I know.' Then he told her.

CHAPTER TWENTY ONE

As the fog dissipated and the sky above them slowly brightened the boys realised they could not stay in the tiny cave much longer. Sooner or later, probably sooner, the dog handler would return and find the Alsatian's pawprints in the muddy ground by the stream.

Having so laboriously buried 'Caesar' would be of little use to them if a guard decided to search where the pawmarks ended. Nor would the broken knife. At the same time, they had to hide somewhere until evening, until after the working parties had marched back to camp from the wall. Then they had to get past Long Bay and reach the boat somewhere beyond, kept there so that the prostitutes could be taken sailing.

'You reckon there are other caves?' Wolf asked, very quietly. They were still worried about being heard.

'Could be.' Miki felt little certainty. 'This hill has quarries all over.'

'When do the guards stop to eat?'

'Midday.' Miki whispered 'You know that.'

But looking up at a sky in which the sun was not visible was no help in telling the time.

'They blow whistles sometimes.' Wolf remembered.

The beginning and end of the half hour break for *Bunkersuppe* was announced by both whistles and loud shouts, while the guards often stood in for each other to allow themselves a longer break. Any soldiers down at the vehicle park by the ruined barn could be expected to do the same. The boys hunkered down at the back of the rock recess and waited. Whether it was imagination or nor, it seemed to them that a fetid stench from the dog's carcase began coming up from its leafmould grave, adding to the overall smell of rotting vegetation and damp.

Distantly, the boys heard the meal break whistles and shouts from the bay, deadened by the fog and the trees, although the wall was only six or seven hundred metres away. They cautiously looked both ways along the path, pushed out through the bushes and started walking slowly downhill. They had barely gone a hundred and fifty metres before they both froze.

A sentry was advancing up the path towards them from a tunnel entrance in the sheer rock face to their right, previously unseen by them because it was masked by small trees. They shrank into the nearest bushes, holding their breath. The sentry turned about in a most unmilitary way and they saw from a curl of smoke that he had lit a cigarette.

'What now?' Wolf whispered, asking for Miki to decide. He did not know what to do. In fact he was too scared to think.

'Walk towards him, surrender, hold up your hands, somehow get his back turned to me.'

'You think he's alone?'

Miki spent half a minute scrutinising the sentry through the foliage. The man was wearing regulation field grey army uniform, not the khaki of the camp guards, and he had a rifle slung casually over his shoulder. Although he wore a standard army steel helmet. he was not an impressive soldier, probably a reluctant conscript. Miki knew regulations said sentries must work in pairs. The other man must have gone down to the barn to eat.

'He is by himself. Go!' Miki ordered.

Slowly, and shaking, Wolf pretended to amble down the path, as though he had been in the bushes to relieve himself.

'Halt!' The sentry shouted the order, but was so taken by surprise himself that he dropped his cigarette.

Wolf immediately raised both hands above his head, at the same time continuing as far as he dared down the path, which here was much broader.

'What are you doing?'

'Going to the work party.'

Possibly, with all the confusion caused by the shipwreck, this soldier had not been briefed about a labourer escaping. Or if he had, not that a pair had got away. Pointing his rifle loosely at Wolf's belly, he asked more questions. While answering them, Wolf shifted his position further. The sentry seemed not to notice.

'Where is your work?' he demanded.

'On the wall. Can I go on now?' Wolf asked with great politeness, edging further down. He could see Miki approaching behind the sentry's back.

'Ja,.ja.' The sentry wasn't sure, changed his mind. 'Nein.'

He saw that this unarmed labourer was no threat, but being alone at his post, the sentry could not escort him anywhere. The tunnel was an ammunition store. His orders were strict on the subject of guarding the entrance at all times.

'Stay here.' he ordered. They were his last words.

In almost a single movement Miki hooked the loop of wire over the sentry's helmet and down round his neck, then clasped one hand over his mouth, getting bitten for his pains. Wolf dived for the rifle and wrested it away. The next moment the sentry was on the ground, with Miki forcing his face into the earth. A croaking scream had to be stifled and then, with a brutality either inborn or learnt from the camp guards, Miki stamped on his head. Then Wolf knelt on his back while Miki garrotted him.

When the body ceased to twitch, they both stood up. What Miki had planned privately in the small cave, but not spoken of, had been achieved. Now they had very little time before the fellow sentry might return. But they did have a loaded rifle. And, once they had brushed the dirt off it, they had a uniform.

They carried the corpse into the tunnel. Unlit electric bulbs hung from the rock ceiling, linked by a cable which disappeared into the darkness. Once inside they stripped the body and tried the uniform for size against each other.

'I speak German better than you.' Miki argued. 'And I'm bigger.' He might be younger, but he was also stronger.

The uniform was too large for Wolf anyway, so Miki put it on. They found identity papers in the tunic pocket and Miki memorised the name – Wolfgang Holtslag, born Minden 1925. So he was aged 18, two years older than them. Had been.

'Died on active service for the Fuhrer.' Miki remarked. He possessed a slightly deranged sense of humour which worried Wolf, who was very literal minded. 'I am escorting a labourer to......' Miki's imagination died. 'Where am I taking you? Think.'

'The lighthouse?'

'Okay, the lighthouse, for a repair job. You're a technician.'

'But we can't go yet.'

'Not yet. Now let's get shot of this lump.'

Together they pulled the body, stripped to only its underclothes, into the darkness of the tunnel. They found a roughly hewn alcove and stowed it in there.

'Better take the identity disc.' Wolf suggested 'Put it on.'

Miki disagreed. 'Throw it.' he stamped it into the earth.

In the end Miki did keep the identity papers. They were better than nothing and in the dullness of evening anyone who

177

stopped them might fail to see that the small photo was not his. But in a way it didn't matter. If he was challenged, the bluff failed, and a guard saw that the photo was not his, they would be shot anyway. There would be no second chances.

They cautiously spied out the land from the cave entrance, and again prepared to wait, with Miki parading as the sentry outside. If a genuine sentry returned, they would have to kill him too. This time Wolf took the garrotte, since Miki had the rifle. But its use had revolted him. Miki might be younger, but he was much more ruthless and Wolf realised that he was quite afraid of him. As they waited and the afternoon wore on the fog cleared.

CHAPTER TWENTY TWO

During Anna and Tad's exploration the Drake Manor had opened and when they got back there they ordered some much-needed coffee at a table in the garden. The abrasive owner, Brian, had taken one look at their clothes and refused to allow them indoors.

'What d'you want? Have me chair seats filthy and a bloody great cleaning bill. Visitors!'

However, Anna's money had been acceptable enough and he had relented to the extent of letting them use the washrooms, for a fee. Besides, he fancied himself as an expert on the war and intended to ask questions of this old man.

The account Tad had given Anna of the sentry's murder was fragmentary. He not only lacked the language capability, he was also cautious about admitting to such ugly violence in case he frightened her, even though he would be totally incapable of it now He realised that she was badly worried about this whole exploration of the past. So he modified the story, saying that they had been arrested by a soldier and forced to kill him because he was about to shoot them: which was not far from being true.

Anna, for her part, appreciated immediately that this was a sanitised version and suspected that he feared retribution might yet be exacted by some unspecified authority, even though the real war crime had been inflicted on him, not by him. Anyone who had been a slave here would have had a terror of authority imprinted on him for the rest of his life.

Tad was exhausted now. After finding the dogtag he had needed to sit down on a rock by the path and rest for a few minutes. Watching his face she saw a sequence of emotions which would have done credit to an actor in the old silent films. His successive expressions told her as much or more than his eventual verbal account.

'With uniform we can go Long bay.' he had concluded. 'Miki guard, me prisoner.'

After hearing Tad's rather disjointed account, Anna needed to sit down herself and think about it. Worse, the wretched Brian was hovering in the background throughout, listening to every word and waiting for an opportunity to join the conversation. That was the last thing she wanted to encourage.

'I must take you back,' she said briskly to Tad, 'you're soaked and I need to get changed myself.'

She asked Brian about the bus. He did his best to cheer them up further by announcing that there would be no more buses until the afternoon, then seized his chance.

'You here in the war then, eh?' he demanded of Tad and when the old man only muttered a reply, added 'Wish you'd get rid of that bloody wall. We don't want it.'

He and the bus driver were what he himself would have called 'a right pair.'

Anna thought of taking Tad back to the fort, but was afraid that he could not walk that far. And Quinn might cut up rough. So she ordered a taxi to take them both to town and as they left revenged herself mildly on Brian for being so unpleasant.

'This gentleman nearly died building that wall. He did more hard work in a year than you've done in a lifetime. And he was not a bloody visitor.'

She hustled Tad to the taxi, while Brian scowled at her. Bloody islanders! she thought. What was it that got into them? They coined money from tourists and hated them for being here.

At the guest house, where the very much more pleasant owner allowed her to have another go at cleaning herself up, she said 'goodbye' to Tad. She meant it. The strain was too great.

'I can't come for any more walks.' she said 'I've too much to do before I leave myself. Maybe I'll see you at the service.' If she hadn't decided to leave earlier before then.

'Sunday?' he asked hopefully, brought pathetically low by her decision. 'I hope.'

'If I can.'

She had to catch a ferry to St Mary on Sunday afternoon in order to connect with the overnight one there to Portsmouth if she was going to be at work on Monday. This would be cutting it fine, allowing how chaotic the trains could be. So she didn't want to make any promises, even though she was already feeling a heel for not going through to the end with him.

But the end could only be his final escape in a boat and, if his vague memory was correct, it had involved the death of Miki. Another violent death was not an experience she wished to share, even in the oblique and second hand way she had helped Tad relive the murder of a soldier this morning, let alone by witnessing it herself. When the Germans counted them up, the total of Tad and Miki's crimes, from escape to murder to impersonation, would have merited the most extreme and unusual punishment. She didn't even want to guess at what that might have been.

When she walked down to Mackinnon's house after leaving Tad the sun had bloomed in a cloudless sky and it was a perfect day, although as she crossed the Plateau recreation ground she noticed a line of haze lying on the sea and obscuring the horizon, as if it was waiting to return and reclaim the island.

Quinn had explained to her about the fog in meteorological terms, which had pretty much gone into one ear and out the other. Men's explanations were always too long-winded and serious. What she remembered was that warm cloudless days produced thick fog in both mornings and evenings. On that basis there would be fog again tonight.

As before, Jack Mackinnon welcomed her warmly and Phyllida swiftly offered coffee.

'Unless you'd rather have a drink.' Jack said. 'It is midday.'

He was definitely a 'now the sun's over the yardarm' kind of host, though it was unimaginable that he would ever drink too much himself. He was far too controlled. Feeling that the morning had earned her something stronger than coffee Anna asked for white wine.

'A la Lavinia?' Jack asked, mischievously. Their dislike of Quinn's patron was mutual.

'If you mean dry, yes.'

'How's Quinn's historical project going?'

'All absorbing.' She was dry as any wine. 'For Quinn.'

'I rather imagined Lavinia would keep him busy during your visit.' he gave her a shrewd glance and after he had brought the wine, and a cordial for his wife, he came to the point. 'So, what can I help you with? You found the name?'

'The corporal was called Eberhardt. So was my uncle.'

'No first name?'

'Not so far.' Anna recounted Marianne's story as briefly as she could, though that took some minutes. 'I haven't reached the end yet.'

'She'd be unlikely to have learnt the name at the House of Joy. Officers don't usually refer to corporals by their first names and anyway I doubt if Grundmann would have welcomed the SS as guests. Certainly not after Marianne's little adventure.'

'Is there any way to check? Any way at all?'

'Not without going to Germany, as I said. And the SS old comrades association – yes, there is one – might not be helpful.'

'Must I assume the worst? Could a, what was it called, a Rottenfuhrer have been so young?

'Easily. If he was both efficient and brutal. As I told you, they recruited younger and younger men. They had to.'

Anna sighed. This reminded her of the first day here, when every door had slammed shut in her face. She ventured on to the subject of Tad and told Jack about the morning. 'He and the other boy murdered a soldier and he remembers that they got past Drake's Bay, which they called Long Bay.'

'We must assume they did find Grundmann's little sailing boat.' Mackinnon reflected. 'That could be in Marianne's diary. She might have seen something. She would probably have been taken out in the boat quite often. Unless Grundmann was too busy honouring one of the other girls with his undoubted energies while she waited at home.'

'I've decided not to continue walking with Tad, though I do feel sorry for him.'

'You're right not to go. I'm sure you are.' Mackinnon was firm in his advice. 'Call it a day. You've done your bit. More than your bit, in fact.'

He sipped his own wine. He did indeed drink only sparingly, unlike most of the locals. He seemed to be mulling something over in his mind, then came out with it.

'That diary is an extraordinary find. An explanation of one of the most eventful days of the island's entire Occupation. I began investigating 26 May nearly fifty years ago, when I was a newly joined officer. The department never secured the criminal convictions we would have liked. And was it co-incidence that the boys chose that morning to make a run for it? Or did they hear something about the disaster?'

'I really don't know.' Anna was getting less enthusiastic about this research. But then she was not a professional Nazi hunter like Mackinnon. For her the big question now was whether to go home early, which she explained. He was as balanced a counsellor as she could hope to find and sympathetic.

'Is it finally over with Quinn? I'm so sorry. I don't know him well myself, but mutual friends tell me he had high hopes. Of your getting together again, I mean.'

'Oh, Jack! You must see he hasn't really changed. In a way I love him, but he's impossible. And if the Eberhardt does turnout to have been my uncle. Well I couldn't ever live here.'

'May I make a suggestion?' Jack temporised, 'the long range weather forecast is pretty good, why not forget about your uncle and try to see some of the more agreeable aspects of our island? There are plenty. Cliff walks, marvellous wildflowers at this time, bird watching, it's a bit chilly for swimming in the sea, but you can sunbathe. If Quinn can't take you, hire a bike. A pushbike's the best way to get around, in spite of the hills, because you can explore where cars can't. You'd go back fitter too.'

Anna laughed. His enthusiasm was appealing. 'You've talked me round. I'll give it a go.'

'And give Tad a miss from now on. He's close enough to finding his own answers.'

CHAPTER TWENTY THREE

Why indeed waste a beautiful day? Anna decided within seconds of leaving Jack Mackinnon's house that she would follow his advice – immediately. She would hire a bike and explore, completely by herself. She would do it unburdened with Quinn's prejudices, or Tad's dangerously introspective searches, or one single breath of Lavinia's holistically empathetic insights. She would see the island for herself, as a total and unrepentant grockle. No insights. No emotional baggage. If she liked what she saw, then she would stay until Sunday.

But first she did have to contact Quinn, in case he had already organised anything. And where would he be? Ninety to one with Lavinia, but not, she trusted, at the House of Joy. She decided to try the Museum and set off up the main street. On the way, passing the Victoria and Albert pub, she glanced through the window and there to her surprise he was, standing at the bar regaling friends with anecdotes. At least she assumed this was what he was doing, since he was laughing and they were not. She went inside.

'Darling, how lovely to see you.' Say what you might about Quinn, he was capable of reacting fast. 'Are you going to join us? Please do.'

'I assumed you were hard at work. Where's Lavinia?

Quinn gave her a conspiratorial wink. 'Redecorating her house, probably. I told her the labourer was worthy of his beer and as she doesn't much like pubs, she released me. 'What's your poison?'

'I'm off to hire a bike.'

'You're not serious?'

'I'm going to explore the island. All by myself.'

'You'll only get lost.'

'You'd better get a shift on either way.' one of the men said, not unkindly, 'the hire shop will be closing. Three hours in the morning and two in the afternoon's as much as the shopkeepers here can manage. Any longer and they have stress related illnesses.'

Anna looked round doubtfully, but the others nodded agreement. Evidently running a shop here was exceptionally stressful, possibly due to the lack of customers.

At this moment a youngish, tousle haired man in dirty jeans and a frayed blue fisherman's sweater swayed across the bar towards them and shouted at Quinn. He was very drunk.

'Taking our bloody fish, you are! Bastards. Get back where you bloody came from.' He looked round at Quinn's friends. 'Who do you lot think you bloody are?' He waved a fist in Quinn's face. 'Fucking so called fucking anglers.'

The barman acted fast, leaning across the bar. 'They're not doing you any harm Darren. Lay off.'

Someone else tried to take the drunk by the arm, which was a mistake, because he wrestled himself free, lashing out wildly, then staggering across the floor, headed for the exit, cursing.

'We'll get you!' he shouted as he left.

Anna looked around her, not knowing what to do until one of the other men said quietly. 'He'll be hanging around outside, as like as not. You stay here, Quinn and I'll take your wife to the bike shop.'

'Is that alright?' Anna asked, feeling shaky. 'Then I'll see you for supper, Quinn.'

'Lavinia's asked us for drinks. You must be back by six.'

'If you say so.' she fled with Quinn's friend, noticing that the drunk was indeed waiting outside, supporting himself against a wall. 'Should you call the police?' she asked.

'Not much point. The landlord'll let Quinn out the back way. Darren's not as bad as that all the time. Only when he's had a few. Calling the cops would only make things worse.'

The bicycle shop was about to close. Thanking the friend profusely and still feeling shaky, Anna was given a bike with a wire basket on the front which conveniently held her sack, paid three days rental, and asked for directions to the cliffs. The owner gave her a simplified line drawing map – far too simplified she would discover – and off she went. She was profoundly glad to be away from the pub. The fisherman's antagonism had been frightening. Would she ever be able to feel relaxed here?

The tourist map soon proved itself an example of 'disinformation' worthy of a political spin doctor. However, with advice from various helpful people, Anna eventually pedalled her way to a cliff top location above Semaphore Bay. Back from the cliff edge stood the Semaphore Tower, which the notes on the map told her was used in the past for signalling to St Mary's. Not in fog, perhaps.

A precipitous path with steps down the cliff led to a sandy beach far below on Semaphore Bay, but a sign warned that it was unsafe. So why bother? The flowers which had delighted her on previous walks were all here, hugging the coarse turf, like the alpine flowers she'd seen illustrated in books.

A circular stone tower excited her curiosity, too. It had windows, so was presumably occupied, while alongside was parked a largish fishing boat, with a faded blue clinker built hull and white painted cabin. They'd have problems launching that from here, she thought, and made her way across the tussocky grass to the tower itself.

As she approached a man came out from the rather incongruous wooden porch. He was slim and tall, with a mop of pale blond hair. In for a penny, in for a pound, she decided, and asked him about the boat.

'My kids' playroom.' he explained. 'I had a time getting it here, but nothing like the battle with the Planning Officer over keeping it. Some bureaucrats have zero imagination. She didn't want to understand how much the kids enjoy it. But we won. She's gone back to the mainland now and the boat's still here.'

Anna was delighted by this unconventional attitude. It was exactly what she had hoped to find on the island; and the man was dead right about civil servants. They chatted a little, then he pointed out the best walk to take.

'The Wildlife Trust's cleared a path all along the south cliffs. Don't take any notice of the map. You'll just get lost. Follow the small signs painted on stones.'

None the less she was roughly able to equate the path with a dotted line on the map and, after thanking him, set off again.

She wasn't consciously looking for signs of the Occupation, but was pleased that, apart from one small pillar of suspiciously solid concrete, Hitler did not seem to have left his mark up here. Later she would learn that she had been within two hundred metres of the SS concentration camp site. However, at this sunlit moment she was unaware of any such horror. Pushing the bike along a narrow footpath was laborious, but worth while.

The gulls, which previously Anna had thought of only with dislike, wheeled and soared along the cliffs in a perfect flying display. Being an artist, she studied their movements. They controlled their flight with minimal adjustments of their wings and reacted to the air currents faster than she could follow.

Down at sea level black cormorants took a quite different path close to the water, their wings beating fast all the time, until they settled on rocks and spread out their wings to dry, like heraldic birds. She was captivated and decided that Quinn's old wives' tales about every bird deserting the island during the Occupation could not be right. She sat down on a convenient wooden bench and contemplated the view.

The cliffs which she had found so intimating from the ferry seemed spectacular now she was on them, although she could not see the coast of France, except as a shadow across the water. 'Where every prospect pleases', she thought 'and only man is vile.' The hymn of her young childhood was politically incorrect these days, but still true. Then it struck her that this was a nice quiet place to dip further into Marianne's diary.

She extracted the diary carefully from its plain wrapper – a precaution against curious eyes – and tried to take up again where she had left off, which was on the 26th May when Marianne had been told by Grundmann that she must move from his town house to the House of Joy and had, very reasonably it seemed to Anna, burst into tears. But for whatever reason, the account then just stopped.

The front binding was an unlikely hiding place. Not when the back had been used already. Fingering though the pages, Anna found the answer. Marianne had continued in the pages designated for addresses, making her entries look at a casual glance as though they were indeed addresses. Possibly there had not been many real ones worth recording on a prison island. At all events, there the account was staring Anna in the face.

Marianne had been so distraught at being evicted from the house on the square that, even on this day of shipwreck and drama, Grundmann had come down in the late afternoon to comfort her and take her sailing. She told the story well, though economically.

Grundmann's driver brought Marianne down to the House of Joy in the late morning of 26th May. The other girls giggled at her fall in status, although luckily for Marianne she had never turned her nose up at them in the past. She had even participated in some of the striptease 'entertainments' at parties herself, while the others all had to perform in the basket, which Grundmann generously allowed his subordinate officers to enjoy when he was not using it.

In consequence the other girls' amusement was mixed with sympathy and there was no opposition to her being given a sunny bedroom upstairs, looking across the sea towards France. A print of a Toulouse Lautrec painting of a brothel in Paris, liberated from another house, gave it a touch of class.

'Who knows,' one of the girls said, 'the old goat may want to stay here overnight now.'

Even if they did not know officially, they could all guess why Marianne was here and enquired tactfully when the baby was due, though not about the father.

'Of mixed parentage' one girl joked, when Marianne was upstairs, though it went little further than that. By definition she was now head girl. In a proper commercially run establishment there would have been a Madame in charge. But this was no ordinary brothel. The girls were all paid salaries by the Todt Organisation and, not at all frivolously, referred to themselves as a 'workers co-operative'.

They also had a problem suffered by few normal brothels, namely obtaining new clothes. A search of the island ladies' abandoned wardrobes had been disappointing. The clothes left behind were plain dowdy by French standards, while demands for a workers co-operative representative to be given passage to the French mainland for a spot of shopping had been refused. Now Marianne stepped nobly into this gap.

'Give me your sizes and I'll send a caseful of dresses back from St Malo.' she had offered, only to be inundated with requests for bras, knickers, stockings and blouses as well.

This sympathetic offer from a mistress who was being abandoned tipped the balance of approval overwhelmingly in Marianne's favour, especially as she made no mention of money. She reckoned Grundmann would pay, if she could exploit his sense of guilt effectively enough.

To Marianne's surprise the womanising Colonel displayed his sense of shame almost immediately. In spite of the day's dramas, he took her sailing in the boat he kept beached near the cove. This was something she had often asked for, but somehow he never found the time to do. Not being an experienced sailor himself, he could only venture in the sailboat on calm days. This afternoon was ideal, with the fog largely dispersed and only a breath of wind disturbing the waters near the shore.

'You see, meine liebling,' he assured her, assuaging his guilt, 'at heart I like to please you.'

He led her down the path through the house's extensive garden to the shoreline, then explained about the signs and barbed wire fences by the shore.

'Because of the enemy threat, we have to mine the coast.' He pointed to one of the skull and crossbones signs attached to a stake in the turf. 'But inside the barbed wire there are safe paths.'

The razor wires were stretched between metal stakes and backed up with rolls of ordinary barbed wire. Marianne knew all about these, but pretended she did not. She knew about the minefields behind the wire fences too. However, she was gratified that the path directly from the garden gate was protected and joined a narrow coastal track which led to Long Bay.

She had long ago observed a concrete slit trench with mountings for machine guns on the small headland overlooking the cove, artfully concealed alongside an outcrop of whitish rock. Sometimes this post was manned, sometimes not. Now it was not. Grundmann noticed where she was looking.

'Owing to today's events' he did not refer specifically to the humiliating shipwreck and could not avoid sounding pompous 'we withdrew most personnel from this sector. But have no fear, they will come on duty later. You are as safe here as in the town.'

He debated whether to tell her about the escaped labourers. Because of the 'events' their absence had only been reported to him this afternoon and he felt uncomfortably sure that a missing tracker dog was involved. Escape was treated extremely seriously. But the escapees were unarmed and unlikely to get this far, if they had come in this direction at all.

'Two workmen have gone missing, 'he compromised by telling her, 'it is not a problem. They will be found long before dark and you will be well guarded.'

He helped her scramble over rocks and shingle to the cove, where the boat lay safely secured above the high tide level.

The oars and sail were in it. Together they heaved and slid it down to a little patch of sand. After he had clumsily set the sail, she got in and he pushed the boat into the water, jumping in at the last moment and getting his jackboots wet.

'Can we go to Long Bay?' she asked. 'I should love to see that fort at the end of the causeway close up.'

'I will try, my love.'

However, as soon as he manoeuvred the boat away from the cove with the oars, Grundmann realised that the tide was flowing in the wrong direction and he was likely to make an unscheduled landing on the rocks by the round towered fort. Not being a sailor, he had paid little attention when navy men mentioned tides flowing at 15 or 16 kilometres an hour past the island. Now he understood. Luckily this tide running east towards the lighthouse must have been on the verge of changing, so was not so fast, and he contrived to bring the boat back under sail near the cove, a somewhat frightened man. Then he laboriously rowed it to safety.

'Wunderbar!' Marianne praised his skill and bravery. 'You were brilliant.' though why bother, she thought, it was too late for flattery to work, but it had become instinctive.

'Next time we shall succeed.' Grundmann assured her, absorbing the praise, whilst knowing as well as she did that there would never be a next time. Later he would tell her that the replacement cargo ship was arriving early tomorrow and would leave that night. But in the end he flunked it and she learnt through a driver. Nor did he have sex with her.

'Now I know it is definitely all over.' she confided to her diary 'Normally he is like a dog with a bitch on heat when he comes down here. I can only wait for tomorrow.'

The time had flown while Anna perused the diary. Suddenly she realised it was four o'clock and she was, relatively speaking, a long way from the fort. Not all that far, the island being so small, but she first had to find her way back to the town. She followed a track passing the end of the airport runway, where an aeroplane passed so low in landing that she thought it would take her head off and instinctively ducked as it roared over.

190

After that the map was confusing. However, again helped by local people, who had a quite different attitude to visitors from the bus driver's, she found the road to Drake Bay and indulged herself in a long and relaxed freewheel ride downhill past the golf course. From there it was easy. She reached the Moroccan room well before Quinn was likely to have begun panicking. Her few hours of freedom were over, but she would continue the experience tomorrow morning, even if she did decide to catch the afternoon ferry at the last moment. She was, in her old step-grandfather's army phrase, 'playing it by ear.'

CHAPTER TWENTY FOUR

The prospect of seeing the House of Joy in the flesh – a dreadful pun – left Anna with very mixed feelings. It would have been greatly changed since Marianne's time and she would be unable to ask any of the obvious questions: just be required to pretend to admire Lavinia's probably doubtful taste. That was not an entertaining prospect.

On the other hand, she might also contrive to have a look at the coastline and the little cove where Grundmann had kept the sailboat for his women. That did appeal. So she changed quickly into the nearest thing she had to a cocktail party dress, which was a cream linen trouser suit, draped a raincoat over it, and asked Quinn to drop her round there early, thankful that the weather wasn't wet, even if it was misty.

'Why on earth?' he asked. 'do you suddenly want to go for a walk there?'

'You yourself said the house has fantastic views. I thought I might risk a sketch or two.'

She had said 'risk' as a throwaway line. But Quinn didn't take it that way. He took it literally.

'Risk?' he was instantly wary. 'Not another of those sketches?'

He had never before directly confronted her over what she sometimes saw and drew. So now was he creating an unexpected moment of truth? Should she back off? It was she who had used the word 'risk', if only jokingly. But it was a real risk in a way. The question was whether the scenes worried her, or only Quinn. Following Jack Mackinnon's advice she had refused to walk with Tad again, but this was hardly the same thing. And she resented Quinn's interference. She decided to sidestep the question.

'It would be a risk only because Lavinia will demand to see what I've drawn and equally certainly won't like it.'

'I suppose so.' Quinn did not want to find himself pig-in-the-middle again and backed off. 'You don't have to tell her.'

'I haven't even started yet, Quinn. I may not even find a subject. Why can't you just drive me round there now and then collect me at six so we arrive together? Why complicate things?'

Reluctantly he agreed and dropped her off beyond the far end of the long wall, from where she could take a coastal path past

Lavinia's house. Leaving the hideous concrete wall behind her, she walked through tussocky grass sprinkled with those same tiny blue flowers she had admired on the high cliffs. And there were amazing bright red and purple flowering kaffir figs, their fleshy stems hugging the ground, which she had so admired before. She noted from a signboard that the stretch of coast was protected by the island's Wildlife Trust.

About the scenery Quinn had been right. It was fantastic and in a quite different way to their afternoon's high up cliff walk. Here she was right down by the sea, on a shoreline protected by jagged rocks, while a low round-towered fort stood sentinel on an islet. The gaping arch of its gateway showed that it was abandoned. The sea seemed incredibly rough beyond the fort, with foaming overfalls, whirlpools and all the signs of a very fast flowing tide, but there was calmer water closer in.

Right opposite the abandoned fort she recognised the green-painted garden gate of the House of Joy from Quinn's description – 'green is so ecological' Lavinia had told him - and knew that the cove close by with its tiny beach must be the one Marianne's diary described. That gave her a very odd feeling.

So this was the house to which Marianne had so feared being sent, this little stretch of shoreline was where all the women walked when not providing sex and it was from this little secluded strip of sand that Grundmann used to take them sailing! But the ferociously choppy waves driven by the tide and fighting the wind meant he could only have chosen very calm days. As it happened today would have been near-perfect for him.

Two low headlands overlooked the cove, each with a wooden bench for passers by to pause and admire the view. Anna settled herself on the first one she reached, a little anxious not to crease her suit, fished out her pad and began to consider the possible make-up of a picture. She noted, but without being concerned, that the fog had closed off the horizon and was now creeping back in around the picturesque round-towered fort, which she had decided should be the focal point of her composition.

She was not apprehensive because Quinn had assured her there had been no atrocities committed here, unlike at the wall and the harbour. So she dismissed any possible fears about what she might see. In spite of his annoying intervention, she was still in the sunny mood of her earlier walk.

In case the fort disappeared totally in the fog, she sketched it first, positioning it in the distant centre of her picture, while the tiny cove at the foot of a long slope of weathered stones would occupy the left foreground. In fact the cove was a good way off, so she drew it nearer than it really was. Then, sure enough, the fort did diminish to a mere shadow and when she turned her attention to the cove, she realised a small sailing boat had sailed in with two people on board, who were now trying to manoeuvre it out towards the open sea again.

Perhaps they had decided against landing after all, because on another headland opposite were two more men gesticulating at them. Although human figures were not her strong point, and the sailing boat was not all that close, she decided to make use of it. Human action was always more interesting than scenery.

By five thirty the fog had closed right in and she could not see what had become of the boat, so she decided to pack up for the day. She was better satisfied with the outlines of this drawing than with most of her previous ones, partly because it was more impressionistic than specifically detailed, which wasn't so easy to achieve with sketches. With a little time in hand she meandered back along the path to Drake Bay and the long wall.

Quinn was already waiting there, the Land Rover parked on a sandy slope behind the wall. He was impatient to go and did not ask to see what she had done.

'Lavinia hates to be kept waiting.' he scolded Anna. 'Let's get going.'

'We're not late, darling, not at all.' She checked herself. She had a truly bad habit of calling him 'darling' when in fact she was irritated, didn't mean it and was feeling the opposite of affectionate. 'Anyway I thought it was diplomatic to be five minutes late.'

Quinn said nothing, but drove off too fast, as if to punish her, rattling along the main road to Lavinia's turn off. When he did speak it was only to issue a warning.

'For God's sake don't ask about the murals. They're a very sensitive subject. Completely unmentionable.'

'But you can show me where they were?'

'No way.'

Quinn was still markedly short-tempered when he ushered Anna in and helped introduce her to the dignitaries. Gathered in

194

the off-white walled drawing room, looked down on by the portrait of Lavinia as a young trophy wife in that ice-blue ballgown, were what she liked to call 'the who's who' of the island. This evening she was wearing the diamond necklace in the portrait.

With carefully contrived casualness Lavinia presented Anna to the President, Charles Cabot, then to the ever-elegant Sir Edward, to a short, rather fat retired industrialist who was also titled, and to a select few of the local Parliament, known as Deputies. And of course all their wives, plus various highly respectable and over-dressed female friends who were widows like her. The coven at full strength, Anna concluded. Try as Lavinia might, and she did strive mightily, she could not avoid the island's greatest social curse – a lack of presentable single men.

Once Anna had adjusted herself to the industrialist's less than electrifying small talk about power generation, which meant making encouraging remarks without actually absorbing anything, and she could look around, she appreciated that the assembled great and good might be distinguished, but the house was not. It was just a much extended 1930s bungalow, though with superb sea views and lots of wide windows to take advantage of them.

Perhaps Grundmann had considered fresh air and freedom essential to a House of Joy, especially in such a constricted military environment. She imagined Marianne gazing out of this long window and wondering what the hell to do next, then realised that she might be getting far too hooked on her alter ego's predicament, affecting as it was. As a result her uncle was being pushed into the back of her consciousness, like trying to disregard an incurable long term disease. Tad would presumably resolve his own problem eventually. Her uncle's name remained a challenge, which more of Marianne's diary was not helping to resolve at all.

'The real snag about nuclear power is the protest lobby.' the industrialist was declaring, as though the French nuclear reprocessing plant's tall chimneys were not omnipresent on the horizon. 'Those Greenpeace people are a menace.'

'I'm a member of Greenpeace.' Anna said, though not especially confrontationally, forcing hastily herself back into the present. Up to now she had just been remarking how right he was every now and then, without actually listening.

'You're what!' The retired industrialist exclaimed.

'They're a terrific organisation. At least I think so.'

'Can't say I agree.' The industrialist's normally rubicund face reddened further, then he remembered he was talking to a newcomer and a female one at that. 'You mustn't go spreading ideas like that around, my dear.' he said patronisingly, as though reproving a teenager.

Anna stifled a retort – after all this was a cocktail party – and excused herself to 'powder her nose', which seemed the correct period phrase for the occasion. Something told her she might not be an instant success with the island's 'Whos Who'. In any case she need a few moments by herself. When she came back she was immediately snaffled by Lavinia.

'My dear you're not leaving us early I hope?'

'I wouldn't think of leaving until Quinn does.' It was an odd sort of question. How otherwise would she get back to the fort? 'I like walking,' she replied 'but not after a party.'

'Leaving the island, I mean.'

'Oh.' Anna was caught off balance. How could Lavinia know? Why should she know? What had Quinn been saying? Was everything that she told Quinn immediately retailed here? She felt a rush of anger.

'My plan is to catch the ferry to St Mary's on Sunday. Does it matter?'

'Merely a question of our progress. Charles Cabot,' with a slight movement of her head Lavinia indicated the tall figure of their amiable President across the room, 'is quite concerned about the paintings He's a CBE you know and must be in line for a "K". We have to keep him happy.'

Anna had heard this spiel before from Quinn. But Lavinia was now being dangerously direct.

'I'd love to meet Mr Cabot.' she said, wondering how he would respond. 'Please introduce me.'

'Later, my dear. He's busy talking to Sir Edward at the moment. Now, the thing is – forgive my speaking plainly – this is a week when every second of Quinn's time is precious.'

'He did invite me to come across and I'm hardly seeing him, Mrs Wildeblood. He begged me to come. My time's valuable too.'

'I believe there is a ferry tomorrow, if you don't like flying.' Lavinia pressed on, as if she was a country house hostess

196

coldly saying that the butler would pack a misbehaving guest's suitcase and a taxi was already ordered for the station. 'It sails on Tuesdays, Fridays and Sundays. The travel agent can change your booking.'

'Thank you for the advice.' Anna flushed with real anger at this woman's sheer nerve. And it finally made up her mind for her. She bloody well would stay until Sunday. 'But I shan't be changing anything.'

'I see.' Lavinia was not the kind to admit defeat easily, so she made a flanking attack. 'How fortunate that you have your own artistic interests. Didn't I see you sketching by the foreshore earlier?'

'That probably was me.'

'Rather dull this afternoon, I should have thought, what with the fog coming in and no boats around. I do think boats enliven a seascape. One of Quinn's best is going to be of Admiral le Mesurier winning a naval battle off the Spanish coast in 1812. The only snag is that it took place on a dark night with no moon. But I expect he will manage.'

Normally Anna would have laughed out loud at the thought of Quinn struggling to illustrate a pitch dark night, if it hadn't been for the reference to boats.

'But there was a sailboat' she insisted, 'it was leaving the cove. And two men were waving from the shore.'

'My dear,' Lavinia reverted to being regal, 'I was watching you and there was absolutely no boat, nor anyone else on the shore.'

Lavinia would very likely have been watching her through binoculars. This carried distressing conviction

'So now you see why Quinn is so pre-occupied.' Lavinia reverted to her subject. 'He has to research the details of the warships individually and I really can't imagine how the scene is to be illuminated. Sir Edward thinks they would have had flares.'

If she emphasises anyone's title again, Anna thought, I shall scream. But she kept calm and, noticing that the President was momentarily talking to no-one, announced that she would now introduce herself, forcing Lavinia to do it for her.

'Ah,' Cabot said welcomingly, 'the lady we've all been hearing about. The artist's muse.'

Lavinia looked furious.

'Well, let us say his better half.' Cabot temporised.

'I have been telling Mrs Quinn what a critical stage we are at with the pictures.' Lavinia said.

'Not as bad as that, I hope.' Cabot gave Anna a quite unexpected wink 'If I were you, Mrs Quinn, I'd tell that husband of yours to damn well pay you more attention.'

Quinn, who had joined this conclave of his patrons, was neatly skewered.

'I expect you're right, Sir.' he said smarmily, amazing Anna because he never in his life called anyone 'Sir', and then had a convenient inspiration. 'I know what, darling, we'll go to the Friday night meat draw at The Salutation. Show you a bit of local life.'

'There are you are, Mrs Quinn.' Cabot joked. 'I've made him take you out to dinner. Don't go letting him off the hook.'

'Personally speaking,' Lavinia was manifestly not invited as well, so needed to have a cutting last word. 'I find those meat draw evenings at the Salutation desperately common.'

'Really? Cabot remarked, now skewering his hostess in turn, 'even though all the millionaires on the island show up?' he smiled at Anna. 'It's the hope of getting something for nothing, you see. The rich can't resist it.'

But as Quinn drove her away afterwards Anna was perplexed about the little sailing boat. Whatever Lavinia might say it definitely had been there, with nothing ugly or untoward going on either.

CHAPTER TWENTY FIVE

'I can't do it, Miki.' Wolf twisted the loop of wire nervously in his hands, as if it was already around another soldier's neck. 'Sorry.' he said. The killing of the first sentry had made him retch uncontrollably into the undergrowth.

'You need a uniform.' Miki insisted.

He was feeling physically ill himself, though for a different reason. The raw dog's flesh, swallowed into a stomach that had only known thin vegetable soup for months, was causing him digestive agony. It was hard to even stand upright, which in his sentry role was essential. He did not know that a man in his weak state could die from too much food.

'I don't like it.' Wolf reasoned. Not having eaten and having stomach cramps he could think more clearly than Miki. 'A soldier marching a labourer along looks okay. Two soldiers walking by themselves doesn't. What if we're stopped?'

'And what about the next sentry?'

'We hide in the trees.'

'And he raises hell?'

It was all speculation, not that they would have known the word. They tried to guess what the time was and when a soldier might come. The sun, now visible in a hazy sky, was past its zenith. It could be two in the afternoon. Not much later. It would be four hours before the working party on the wall was marched back up the hill and they could try to get past the bay. Why hadn't the relief sentry turned up?

Minutes later he did. Another conscript, judging from his slack way of marching, he came up the path and greeted Miki. Wolf had dashed into the dark shelter of the tunnel.

'Gruss Gott.' The replacement was a Bavarian. 'You new?'

'Ja. Heil Hitler.' Miki made a parody of a stiff armed Nazi salute. 'Ready for handover.'

'Fuck the Fuhrer.' The Bavarian said, then regretted it. 'For God's sake don't say I said that. Anything going on?'

'Fuck all. But you check around while I'm still here. I heard something in the bushes.'

As the Bavarian obeyed this suggestion and turned towards the undergrowth Miki clubbed him in the back with the rifle butt. He fell forward, his head and neck still protected by his steel helmet. The helmet extended low down the neck. It was a good design. The Bavarian groaned and tried to get up, crying. He did not understand what was going on. Miki rolled him over and was about to smash his face when Wolf shouted from the tunnel.

'Stop!'

Wolf ran out and tried to seize the rifle, while the Bavarian looked up at them from the ground, terrified. There was a demon in Miki. He wanted to kill Germans. He would have battered the soldier's head to pulp inside his helmet. Wolf hated violence, had hated the brutality of the camp guards even more than fearing it, now he hated this. The conscript was an ordinary boy like them, not a thug.

Miki struggled to keep the rifle and succeeded, though he calmed down a little in the process. The Bavarian lay on the ground and covered his face with his arms.

'He'd have done it to us.' Miki argued, standing over the man, his cheap grey uniform muddied and torn.

But Wolf knew this Bavarian would not have. He was not an OT guard, nor an SS man. Not even a professional soldier. Just another conscript sent to the 'arsehole of the world' to die in futility. Not that Wolf thought this through clearly like that. He just knew it. He was older enough than Miki not to want to become an insensate killer. And there was another reason.

'Listen.' Wolf almost said 'idiot' but that would have been stupid in Miki's aggressive mood. 'This guy must know who's guarding the bay. We must get it out of him.'

The commonsense of this advice convinced Miki. He put the rifle down and helped the Bavarian to sit up. The Bavarian had heard everything they said. He took Wolf for a friend.

'Help us and we won't kill you.' Wolf said. 'What's going on?', while Miki suddenly doubled up in a spasm of pain and gasped for water.

The Bavarian had a water bottle attached to his belt. He fumbled in taking it off. His back hurt badly and he was scared stiff, lying by their feet on the ground, even though these were teenagers like himself. He handed up the bottle.

'Gut!' Miki drank noisily, he had never known such stomach pains, but the water helped. Meanwhile Wolf began an interrogation.

'What's going on at the bay?' he asked in a friendly voice. Instinct told him that if Miki was the hard man he had to be the softie. 'What was happening early on?'

'A ship's been wrecked at the harbour.' The Bavarian was only too happy to tell them. 'They say hundreds of Russians were drowned. Didn't you hear the klaxons? Even our vehicle depot had to send men.'

'Which depot?'

'The main one's at the top.' he pointed up the path. 'The second's by the ruined barn.'

'What about the bay?'

'In the day they are building the wall. At night, nothing. But there are machine gunners 24 hours a day at the island fort. And searchlights.'

'You have a watch?' Miki cut in harshly.

With gloomy reluctance the Bavarian took it off his wrist. It was cheap, made in Leipzig, but it was the first he had ever owned and a conscript's pay was poor. Miki took it. The hands showed ten to three.

'Sorry comrade,' Wolf said 'we need it. So after six they're not many soldiers around? That right?'

'Up near the observation tower there are.' The Bavarian was eager to save himself. 'That's with the ack ack guns. But there's minefields between them and the bay. And the crews don't live there.' He thought of more things. 'There's wooden posts wired up with mines to stop planes landing. And a rifle range at the end of the bay, but no-one will be firing come the evening. And I told you about the island fort.'

It took the boys more than a moment to digest this. Although Miki seemed unimpressed, what was being revealed were far wider defences than they known. Labouring on concreting the wall they had seen things like the posts and the minefield signs, but without appreciating the extent of the defences. Trying to pass the bay by day would have been impossible. It wasn't going to be a walkover at any time.

'The small fort further on has machine gunners too.'

'We heard.' Miki said brutally. He would still have liked to kill this man, in case he gave them away.

Wolf wanted to ask about the prostitutes' house and the sailing boat, but dared not for the same reason. That would reveal where they were headed. The next problem was how to silence the Bavarian without murdering him. Again Wolf took the softer approach.

'Listen.' he said. 'We can't have you giving us away, but we don't want to kill you. We're going to tie you up and leave you. But we need rope.'

The Bavarian required no prompting. 'There's a small store.' he said. 'Just inside.'

Wolf found it while Miki stood over the soldier, returning with a coil of thick rope, thicker than was suitable, but all they were likely to find. Like crooks dressing up an informer to look as though he had been a victim, they bound the Bavarian, gagged him with his own handkerchief and then carried him a short way into the cave, though not as far as his predecessor's corpse. They didn't want that found too soon. If they were captured that corpse would guarantee torture as well as death for them.

The Bavarian struggled to speak, but only a muffled noise came out.

'Listen mate,' Miki said toughly, 'I'll be outside as the sentry. One sound out of you and we'll finish you off.'

'You're lucky.' Wolf emphasised and as he disappeared into the gloom of the tunnel. 'Goddam lucky. You could be dead.'

Time dragged on, not helped by the possession of the watch, which only emphasised the slowness of the minutes. The Bavarian had told them he was due to be relieved after four hours, at six. The night stints were the worst, he told them. Reliefs were sometimes late coming on, as he had been. The vehicle depot was badly disciplined.

'Mechanics don't like being ordered around.' he had explained before they gagged him. The boys hoped he was right.

At a quarter to six they began listening for the working party. Kranke was a stickler for timing when it involved himself getting off duty. Punctually at six some ragged shouts came from the direction of the bay. At ten past they heard the tramp of boots and sabots coming up the road above.

'Links, zwei, drei, rechts, SINGEN!' Kranke's voice rang out, followed by a subdued scream as he struck a labourer not singing well enough.

'We're off.' Miki announced. 'Wiedersehn.' Wolf said, not unpleasantly, to the trussed up Bavarian. 'They'll find you soon. And don't split on us! If your luck had been different you'd be where we are.'

The Bavarian bundle nodded its head in the gloom. He might change his mind later, when he knew they couldn't harm him, but thus far he intended to say they had gone up the valley, not down. And the nicer one had more of an argument than he knew. The Bavarian was, well, a Bavarian, and had twice nearly ended up in detention for being insubordinate.

They marched as planned, with Miki holding the rifle loosely pointing at Tad's backside, as though he anticipated no problems with this particular prisoner. Going down the rest of the valley they passed no-one, except the sentry at the more important tunnel entrance, ten metres back from the path, to whom Miki threw a colloquial greeting. Evidently the Bavarian's relief was late getting on duty.

Skirting the vehicle park unchallenged they joined the main road along which they had so often tramped. Here there were more soldiers around and the guards with the last working party leaving the wall made some jocular remarks. So far so good. They said nothing, having agreed it would be out of character to get into conversation: and too dangerous.

Everything the Bavarian had described came into view, although becoming slowly obscured by fog drifting in from the sea. The high concrete observation tower, on top of the hill near the anti-aircraft gun pits, was already invisible. Coils of barbed wire and skull and crossbones signs cordoned off much of the ground to the left, although there was a clear track to the place where they knew dead Russian labourers were taken for burial. They knew about the cemetery because Kranke was fond of joking, as he whipped his men along, that they would be there soon themselves if they didn't work harder.

There were no minefield signs on the wall side of the road, because of the on-going work. The rifle range was further on against rising ground near the wall's end. But although the range was short, it posed their first serious dilemma. The vehicle track to it from the road passed between barbed wire fences, then divided, one track going to the left through a gap in an old stone wall, the other forming a narrower path to the right close to the shoreline.

They opted for the wider first one. They had to stay close to the shore, but once they left the main road their story of repair work at the lighthouse would begin to fall apart. Possibly the wider track led to the lighthouse as well as to the prostitutes' dwelling and the boat. They hoped so. And then came their first setback.

As they neared the gap in the wall, an officer appeared from the other side of the rifle range and shouted out to them. Miki halted, shouldered his rifle and executed a perfect Heil Hitler salute.

'What are you doing?' the officer demanded, after returning the salute. They did not recognise his rank.

'Escorting a labourer to Oberst Grundmann's house, Mein Herr.' Miki chanced his arm with this change of objective and the officer was immediately suspicious.

'Identity.' he snapped.

Miki produced the dead sentry's papers from his tunic pocket and held them out, while Wolf pretended to be too scared to budge. The officer, who was young and probably junior, examined them in the lessening light. He appeared satisfied and handed them back.

'What job is this man detailed for?

'I have not been told, Sir. We come from Scharhorne Camp.'

There was no point in lying about Wolf's origin, since it was evident from coloured patches sewn on his clothes. But it was a risk, because the officer might know about the escapes from the Scharhorne labour force. He looked them both over again.

'The Herr Oberst is there?' he asked, perhaps as a trap, perhaps because he was considering a visit himself and would prefer to avoid the Commandant.

'I do not know, Sir.'

'You know the building?'

'No, Sir.'

'It is opposite a small cove. There is a green gate.'

'Thank-you, Sir.'

'You may continue.'

Miki stood stiffly to attention, the rifle on his shoulder, and released another stiff-armed Heil Hitler', which the officer returned in a more casual way, before walking on briskly.

'Phew!' Miki muttered under his breath, then shouted loudly. 'Raus! Quick march!' and hurried Wolf along the path, now lined on both sides with barbed wire looped over jagged metal stakes and with minefield signs. The fog was drifting across the shoreline. Thank God they knew about the green gate being opposite the cove.

CHAPTER /TWENTY SIX

'You ought to go around the lighthouse,' Quinn suggested 'they do a guided tour. Then I could meet you back here for lunch. It's only a short walk.'

The President's strictures at last night's party had struck home. Quinn had been much more considerate since, helping Anna cook their supper last night and discussing where she should explore today. And the beauty of it was that Lavinia could not easily intervene. She might be Quinn's patron, but Charles Cabot was hers and he had seen how she was manipulating the project to push Anna aside and spoil her visit.

'As long as it's cheerful.' Anna insisted, 'I want to see a happy side to the island. What is it the tourists come for?'

'All sorts of things, like Jack Mackinnon told you: watching birds, cliff walks, bucket and spade holidays for kids in summer, fishing, golf, what they call wildlife. Very little aggro.'

'Not many yobbos like the fisherman at the pub? I could do without men like that.'

'Very few.'

'Look, there's no need for you to bother about lunch.' Anna wanted to respond to his new-found helpfulness. 'I'll take sandwiches. The bike has a basket.'

'Going walking with the old Pole again?'

There was a hard edge of hostility in the remark, part of an attitude she did not want revived.

'No. He's had his fair share of my time. More, in fact.'

'And given you enough aggro.'

'I told you, Quinn,' she was nettled at his harping on this 'I have no plans to meet him again. Nor look at any more of that beastly Nazi concrete.'

He provided her with a better map, an ordnance survey one, before retreating to his studio to grapple with the new problem of depicting warships under full sail battling in the pitch dark. He suspected Lavinia of having chosen this naval exploit, which actually took place off the Spanish coast, five hundred miles away, purely to make things more difficult for him while Anna was here. Nor could he expect much sympathy from Anna herself. He was beginning to fear, to coin a phrase, that Lavinia had pretty well cooked his goose with his wife.

More Hitlerian relics were emphatically not what Anna wanted to see. So she pedalled round to Drake's Bay, past the now familiar concrete wall and on to the black and white striped lighthouse at the eastern tip of the island. She reckoned she must have gone near the House of Joy, but it was hidden by trees.

The lighthouse was a straightforward visitor attraction. If she was going to be a grockle, then she would be a proper grockle. She waited twenty minutes for the next guided tour, climbed the 120 steps to the lantern at the top and duly marvelled at the intricacy of the four sets of three sided prisms comprising a lens 10 feet high, which weighed four tons and concentrated its light into a narrow beam reaching over 20 miles out to sea. Facts and more facts. Good solid grockle-pleasing facts.

The Germans had maintained the light well, she was told, only one prism was found to be broken after the war, though they had reduced the sector it shone through from 360 degrees to make it face solely towards France and they only switched it on when ships were due. Now of course it shone through the full arc again. The other tourists 'oohd' and 'aahd' and so did she. If Quinn wasn't careful she'd soon know more about the island than he did.

When she had descended again she inspected the black foghorns which so disturbed her sleep. They stood like monstrous guardians of the underworld at the tower's foot, strangely menacing when their function was simply to save life.

Opposite the lighthouse, inland, there stood a huge, high, yet somehow squat looking concrete tower on the top edge of a quarry's cliff, with three long horizontal slits one above the other: presumably windows. She had seen it before, but refrained from asking Quinn its purpose.

'What on earth is that?' Anna asked one of the blue-uniformed lighthouse keepers.

'We call it the Odeon, madam. It was an observation tower for gunnery. After the war they wanted to demolish it, but the explosions would have broken every window in the island.'

'So it stays?'

'It stays, madam, it stays. I wouldn't bet on the Odeon being gone in a thousand years. Those Germans built to last. Well, they had plenty of free labour, didn't they, eh!'

These wretched Nazi fortifications were inescapable. Every inch of the island seemed to be riddled with them.

As it was still only midday Anna decided to try another walk along the shore where she had been sketching yesterday before Lavinia's party, approaching it from the other end. The sandy track went round past the little cove to Drake Bay.

She reached the shore opposite the round-towered fort and the bench on the nearer side of the headland in fifteen minutes, even though she was pushing her bike rather than riding it. The first bench she came to would be a nice place for her picnic lunch, with a rather different view of the cove from yesterday's. The bench she had sat on then was on the opposite little headland.

As she munched through a salami baguette – Quinn had gone slightly overboard when he drove out early for provisions this morning – she decided to read some more of the diary. This was an appropriately empathetic place, as Lavinia might have said, except that she would have been appalled at what Marianne had recorded. With luck, if she actually was hard at work with Quinn, she would not be sitting by her window with the binoculars.

Anna gazed at the house and wondered where the famous basket might have hung? There hadn't been a chance to look last night. There must have been a hook in a beam or a ceiling. She scolded herself for being prurient.

Yet surely Marianne would have recorded more than just her day of arrival before finally departing? Of course she would have, because the diary had been found in the house's rafters, so any last entries must have been recorded here. Looking across at the House of Joy Anna could guess where. The cedar shingled roof was interrupted by the two large dormer windows of upstairs bedrooms. Marianne, as the Colonels 'lady', would have been allocated one of them. And a compulsive diarist like her would have gone on recording what happened. But where?

Anna re-read Marianne's account with mounting alarm, noticing details she had previously missed. And they referred to exactly the headland she was now on, not yesterday's opposite. She left her sack on the bench, propped her bike against it, and walked some fifty yards to the point of the headland where she had seen the two distant men gesticulating yesterday. She guessed what she was going to find and she was dreading doing so.

An outcrop of grey-white rock slanted up out of the turf and heather at quite an angle, about 40 degrees she guessed. All the rock formations round here did that, witnesses to an immeasurably powerful pushing upwards and folding of the earth's crust aeons ago. There was a much larger one on a slight hill behind her, called 'Le Rocher Pointu' on the map. This smaller one had no name, only the printed words 'Def Wks'.

And sure enough there the defence works were, all but hidden alongside the outcrop. They consisted of a snaking concrete trench, with an underground bunker at one end. At the other was a small round concrete pit, just deep enough for a man to stand in and be protected up to his shoulders, yet still able to fire down at the cove.

So the men she had drawn were soldiers and, inescapably, the boat had been Grundmann's. But the crew had not been the Colonel and Marianne, it had consisted of two men. She realised with a pang of horror that yesterday she must have witnessed Tad and Miki making the final stage of their escape. And the men here at this concrete emplacement had not been waving at all. They must have been shooting. So what had happened next?

Why, oh why, had her mother not warned her that this kind of visionary sensitivity might be hereditary? Why instead of recounting her own encounter with the dead man walking through the hospital ward as if it had been a close to normal event, the kind of thing she had come to expect, had she not given her daughter a health warning with it?

Anna returned to the bench near the sentries' concrete emplacement   and collapsed on to it, feeling totally drained. She had sworn to avoid anything to with the Occupation yesterday and today. She had wanted to relax. She had believed that nothing much had gone on down this end of the island during the Occupation, except in the House of Joy. In the sunny mood of yesterday she had disregarded the fog creeping in and the risk of whatever of the paranormal it might bring. She had been wrong.

Worst of all, she now knew what perils the boys faced, but with no means of warning them. In any case, how could you warn people of an event that took place fifty years ago? Even if she saw Tad again, what could either of them do? Nothing: except wait for the end to unfold and give Tad his probably gory answers.

Feeling weary and depressed, she continued along the narrow footpath which in Marianne's time had been protected by barbed wire fences. Many of those curious triangular sectioned metal stakes, with jagged tops to hold the wire, were still in place.

Occasionally she scratched her arms squeezing between shoulder high patches of bracken and ferns. During the war there had been minefields on both sides of this path. She had been told that. It would have been a hazardous route for Tad and Miki.

When she reached the top of a slight rise facing Drake's Bay and looked down at the curving length of the beach and the great concrete wall, she was shocked to see Tad himself. He was walking more like a cripple than a healthy old man and he was stumbling straight towards her.

She spotted him well before he saw her, so had a little time to prepare herself. It would be out of the question to avoid him, if only because that would be so hurtful. Instead she dissimulated a little, saying she had hoped to meet him somewhere.

'I glad.' he said, in that heavily accented and very limited English of his. 'I take bus. This time okay.'

'I'm glad too.'

'I know what happen here with Miki. Some things,' he gestured at the wall and at the Odeon 'are same. I remember.'

How do I get away from him without being rude? Anna asked herself. 'I can't stay long.' she said, making a show of consulting her watch.

'I tell you.' Tad insisted, moving towards another of the memorial benches with which the island was so liberally equipped, this one dedicated to a couple whose favourite spot this had been. 'Tell you now.'

Reluctantly Anna sat down and, in order not to prolong the session, said almost nothing for the next twenty minutes. What he had pieced together of his and Miki's escape was certainly a gripping story, though only the penultimate act of a drama that remained a mystery to him, even if guessed at and feared by her. About one detail she was curious.

'Why did you use the name "Wolf" when you're really Tadeus?'

'May be someone think I am Jew.' he shook his head, as if admitting that he was not a strong character. 'I not wolf at all. Miki is wolf.'

'I see.'

Anna didn't actually see at all and anyway details like that were going to have to wait. As soon as she could she said goodbye

210

and pedalled off towards the neck of the island and the fort, trying to consign this encounter firmly to her mental backburner. First things first.

Today was Friday, she had irretrievably missed today's ferry and would have to abide by her irritated reaction to Lavinia's outrageous hints and stay until Sunday, with no likelihood of unearthing more about her uncle. Eberhardt. But what was the first name? That aspect of her visit was a dead end and a failure.

And she still had to sort things out finally with Quinn, which was after all why she had come here originally. Quite strangely, probably as a result of the problems with Quinn, she felt her common cause with Marianne even more keenly. They were both trapped in empty relationships with men whose futures were to be determined here; although in Grundmann's case unwillingly. Both of them were here at the whim of unreliable men and drawn into deep emotional turmoil as a result. But she was going to have to deal with her own predicament before she learnt the resolution of Marianne's, if she ever did discover what it had been.

Having excused herself determinedly to Tad – she felt in danger of losing control of her own destiny again – Anna cycled back to the fort. She had not expected Quinn to be back and he wasn't. Most likely Lavinia was detaining him as long as possible in revenge for being defeated yesterday. Hell hath no fury etc..

She was going to have to get the diary back to Dick Carey before she left too. Anna had a strong conscience about returning borrowed books and this was a very special one. But she would have to finish reading it first and she put this off, partly because of the labour of translating the French and partly because she needed to digest what Tad had just told her. But she did make a mental note to telephone Carey and find out if he was coming across to interview Tad. If not she would have to meet him when changing from one ferry to the other at St Mary's. Arrangements! Blasted arrangements all the time, though that was one she'd be able to look forward to. She very definitely liked Dick Carey.

Quinn did return very late, well after seven, but she stifled her recriminations, assuming this was an inevitable price for achieving a free weekend. In fact she didn't even question him, simply asked what time they needed be at The Salutation.

'It's an unusual name for a pub, isn't it?' she suggested, after he said eight o'clock.

'John Wesley, the Methodist founder, came and preached here, standing on a wooden box in the square in front of the pub. Afterwards he ate there. It was immediately renamed and so, eventually, was the square itself.'

'What sort of people go there?'

'The regulars are locals; labourers, fishermen, fairly rough. But the restaurant is a more up-market, especially on Friday nights when they do the meat draw for charity. You'll see how it works. It can be good fun.'

'What do I wear?' The eternal question.

'Anything you like. It's not even smart-casual.'

Given this typically male lack of interest in what she wore, Anna plumped for a clean pair of jeans and an embroidered jersey top to add a bit of class. Since no-one was likely to notice her feet in a crowded pub she wore trainers. Later she would be glad she had not put on flimsy shoes.

The Salutation stood facing a cobbled square, with a round ended cattle trough a few yards in front of it. Many years ago the farmers had made constant use of the trough, but now all it held was a few discarded bottles and cans, although it was kept painted neatly in white, being a designated historic monument.

The pub's front door led straight into the bar area, with a long bar and a darts board. From there an archway on the right led to the restaurant, with tables round the walls and also in the centre. Quinn greeted various friends as they were shown to their table. The atmosphere was friendly. Quinn advocated the fish pie, so Anna went for that, plus a carafe of white wine.

The meat draw operated through people buying one or more playing cards out of a full deck, with winners being drawn from another.

'Ten millionaires in here if there's one,' the organiser joked, recognising most of his clientele. 'Don't let the tax man catch you winning!'

The prizes were generous, ranging from chicken portions to steak. Anna's second card landed her a leg of lamb. The first hint of trouble came when Quinn went to collect it and a man standing in the doorway shouted at him. It was the young fisherman called Darren who had confronted them in the Victoria and Albert, this time wearing a grimy beige baseball cap worn the wrong way round. And he was drunk.

'What d'you need that for then? He shouted. 'Eat yer own bloody fish, eh?' Everyone in the restaurant swung round.

'Give over, Darren.' the organiser said firmly, edging the man back into the bar and turning to Quinn. 'Take no notice, Sir, he's had a few too many.'

'What did he mean about fish?' Anna asked, disturbed by this unexpected hostility.

'A few professional fishermen have a gripe against us anglers.' Quinn explained 'Nonsense really, if anyone's fishing out the stocks it's they themselves, not us catching a few bass off the breakwater. Excuse me a moment.' He heaved himself up and went through to the bar, before she could stop him.

She heard an immediate altercation through the archway.

'You bloody "anglers"!' It was a different voice, a woman's voice, with a load of hate in the word angler.

'I have a licence.' Quinn was more on the defensive than challenging, though Anna thought it extremely stupid of him to say anything.

'It's our fucking fish mate.' That was the fisherman who had started this.

'There's enough for everyone.' Quinn insisted.

'And it's our fucking island.' The drunken young man again. 'Fucking settlers. We'll be waiting for you, mate.'

Quinn came back, distinctly shaken. 'They're pissed out of their minds.' he said unhappily.

When the waitress came to take their dessert orders she said quietly 'The boss says if you want to leave by the back afterwards, he'll open up for you.'

Quinn's rejection of this was not quite instant. 'It only leads round into the square anyway.' he said after a moment's thought. 'But my wife might like to.'

'Just tell me if you do.' the girl said and went off to fetch their coffees.

'Is there going to be a punch-up?' Anna asked anxiously. The naked aggression in the face of the fisherman and the overheard threat had seriously alarmed her.

'Bluff, I think.'

'Well, Quinn. I'm not running out on you. I wouldn't do that.' She rummaged in the sack down by her chair and felt a re-assuring shape. She was a much faster thinker than he was.

213

'If you'd rather go out the back way, I wouldn't blame you. I can look after myself.' Quinn assured her.

There was a lack of confidence in his voice which worried Anna as much as the fisherman's threat, even though one of his hobbies was judo, so he could indeed look after himself. These men were, presumably, the same kind of islanders whom Quinn chatted and joked with at the harbour. Where had the antagonism suddenly come from? He had seemed so at home before and so well accepted. Perhaps that was what was undermining him now.

When he had paid the bill, Quinn led Anna out through the bar. The young drunk had gone.

But he was there outside waiting, sitting on the edge of the cattle trough, and as they came out he ostentatiously reached down into the trough, brought up a bottle and smashed its neck off on the coping. Then he advanced on them, thrusting this jagged weapon ahead of him, arm outstretched, though unsteady on his feet on the cobbles.

Again Anna reacted faster. She pulled out her idiot camera, the one she used for taking reference pictures, and photographed the drunk. The flash illuminated the venom in his expression. He yelled 'bloody bitch' at her. She snapped him again, now aware that a crowd was encircling them, leaving them and the fisherman enclosed, as if in a boxing ring.

When the man lunged at Quinn, waveringly because he was so drunk, she snapped him again and after that everything took on a surreal speed.

The fisherman jabbed the jagged bottle hard at Quinn's face, but Quinn was already moving and the glass only caught the side of his neck above the shoulder. It did not stop Quinn getting a judo hold on him, throwing him off balance and sending him thumping flat on to his back on the cobbles. The fisherman groaned and tried to get up. Quinn shot out a kick that sent him sprawling again. Blood was coming from Quinn's throat and on to his shirt, though not in a great flow.

People in the crowd began shouting abuse, though Anna was not sure it was at them. Anyway she photographed everyone, swinging round the whole circle. She was going to make the whole lot of them identifiable. She dared them to react. They yelled abuse at her but nothing more. Perhaps some inbred instinct held them back from attacking a woman.

214

Very soon the wailing seesaw notes of a police siren came from along the street. Immediately the crowd broke up into small groups, running away along the several roads which came into the square. By the time two policemen jumped out of their Land Rover, Anna, Quinn and the fisherman were alone outside the pub. A small group of watchers in the front doorway retreated inside. Everything was quiet, except for the running of the vehicle's engine.

'Give me your hankie' Anna ordered and began trying to stem the flow of blood from Quinn's neck. The policemen hauled the fisherman to his feet, forced his hands behind his back and handcuffed him. Then they half pushed, half threw him into the back of their vehicle. One of them returned, gingerly picked up the broken and bloodied bottle and placed it in a transparent plastic bag. Anna saw that he was the same sergeant who had interviewed her at the hospital about Tad.

'I take it he attacked you.' The sergeant asked Quinn. 'They set me up.' Quinn swayed, holding the bloodsodden handkerchief to his neck. 'He's very drunk.'

'Not for the first time. We shall need you to make a statement. And Mrs Quinn.'

'We must get my husband to a doctor.' Anna insisted. Miraculously there was not as much blood as she expected.

'D'you want the ambulance?' the sergeant asked.

'We can use my Land Rover.' Quinn said, though shakily, and moved towards where it was parked on the other side of the trough, then saw that its tyres were flat. All four had been slashed.

'We absolutely do need the ambulance.' Anna almost shouted, becoming angry. 'He can't possibly drive himself.'

The sergeant called up on his radio. 'Won't be long.'

'You'd better have this.' Anna said, handing him her camera. 'I photographed it all. I should think everyone who was here is on that film. So are pictures of mine that I need.'

Now it was the sergeant's turn to be surprised. Weekend violence outside the pubs was commonplace, in fact standard. Getting witness statements was not. In fact it was extremely difficult and there was no lack of intimidation backing up the silence. To have those responsible so positively identified was something new.

'What happens next?' Anna asked.

215

'We'll hold him for the weekend. He'd likely interfere with witnesses. Special sitting of the court on Monday.'

'And the charge?' Quinn asked.

'Wounding, most likely, under the Offences against the person Act, 1861. But the case will go to the Crown Court in St Mary. Too serious for our magistrates.'

'Isn't it grievous bodily harm?' Anna suggested.

'If he'd glassed your husband's face it might be GBH. The law officers will tell us.'

The familiar noise of an emergency siren came towards the square and the ambulance stopped beside them. After a brief discussion with the police both Quinn and Anna were taken down to the hospital, where a doctor was already waiting.

Half an hour later the doctor returned to where Anna was sitting in the lobby area, making a vain attempt to be interested in an out of date woman's magazine.

'I've stitched him up okay.' the doctor said cheerfully, 'but there was glass in it. He's lucky. Just missed the carotid artery. He's more shocked than he realises. He ought to stay in overnight.'

'Will he be alright?'

'Oh yes. It'll take time to heal and he'll have a scar, but nothing worse. If the artery had been severed it would be a different story. He could have died.'

'Thank-you very much. Very much indeed.'

Suddenly Anna realised that she had no transport and was feeling pretty shaken herself. Who could she turn to? She didn't want to be in the fort alone.

'Do you need a taxi?' the nurse asked.

'Can I see my husband?'

'I'm sure you can.' the nurse looked enquiringly at the doctor.

'Not for long. I've just given him a sedative.'

'I think I'll make a quick phone call first.' Anna said.

She knew who to call and it was Jack Mackinnon. Despite its being after ten, he offered to fetch her and put her up for the night, as she had never doubted he would.

When she told Quinn he had not the energy to object. He was already sleepy and looking dead white. She didn't realise why at first, then realised that his beard had been shaved off to allow for the neck stitching. Poor Quinn! He was so proud of his manly beard. She promised to come down first thing in the morning.

Twenty minutes later she was in Mackinnon's car and on the way to hot chocolate and a welcoming bed. When she related the day's extraordinary events Mackinnon commented that Marianne's diary explained a great deal that had previously mystified him.

He seemed less interested in Tad's latest wanderings

'There's nothing more you can do for him.' he suggested. 'Tadeus is on his own, poor man. Don't interfere.'

CHAPTER TWENTY SEVEN

Breakfast at the Mackinnons was just the well-organised, yet unceremonious, occasion Anna had expected.

She came down at eight thirty after a gloriously comfortable night in a chintzy bedroom, with a window which gave a view of the harbour. Not that the 'glassing' of Quinn outside the pub was forgotten, in fact it was so totally outside her previous experience that it never would be. And she had still to make her statement to the police and see Quinn out of hospital.

However, the solicitous care of Jack and Phyllida last night had soothed her greatly. She realised that she simply could not have slept alone at the fort even though the friendly doctor and his wife were nearby, because they lived in a separate part of the huge building. She would also have been worried about reprisals. In fact overall she would have been completely spooked all by herself, especially with fog drifting around the fort.

'I hope you slept well?' Phyllida enquired when Anna appeared. She gave the required answer of 'Marvellous, I slept like a log.'

There was an unspoken etiquette in these ritual exchanges, whether the reply was true or not, and she was sure this was Phyllida's style. It was a nice change from Quinn's.

After they had finished the bacon and eggs, coffee and toast, Phyllida made an unobtrusive exit, leaving Jack to her.

'I'll phone the hospital about Quinn being discharged.' he offered. 'And I'll have the Land Rover tyres replaced.'

'I'll pay for that.' Anna knew tyres were expensive and Quinn probably didn't have the money. Not that she could really afford them either. But the evening had been such an all-round disaster for him. 'Do they take credit cards?'

'I'm sure they do.' Jack gave her a reassuring smile, telling her that he understood exactly. 'And I'll take you along to the police to make a statement. For what its worth I'm a magistrate here. Not that it will make any difference, since three of us sit on the bench together and a crime is a crime.'

'I still can't believe what happened. It's as though there's an evil spirit around. So much violence.'

'In the past, mainly, thank God.' Jack poured her more coffee, then said reflectively. 'Sometimes I think there is evil embedded here, just as there's permanent radiation in the granite. Very low level, but irremovable, with us for ever.'

'So the Occupation was an explosion of it?'

'You could say that. An extreme manifestation.' He changed the subject. 'Was the fisherman very drunk?'

'Very. And aggressive.'

'Well, we'd better get you down to the police while it's all fresh in your memory. Don't worry, we'll come back here afterwards. My day is yours.'

He went off to make the arrangements, returning to say they could go straightaway.

The small police station, with its traditional 'blue lamp' outside, plus a precautionary CCTV camera, was close to the churchyard gate, in the same building that had once been the German ration office. If stones could talk, Anna thought, not very originally.

'The fisherman will be in our two man jail.' Jack explained. 'Pretty basic at the best of times. At the end of the war it was in such a filthy state that a German officer was ordered to clean it up. He objected strongly, that was an orderly's job, until he was told he would be locked up in it himself if he didn't.'

Anna laughed. This epitomised Mackinnon's no-nonsense approach, which made her doubly glad to have him as a friend.

She was interviewed in a tiny upstairs room, where the sergeant made meticulous notes with a pencil, finally asking her if she could identify the assailant.

'But you have my pictures?'

'To avoid any doubt we'd like an identity parade.'

This was arranged for the afternoon, although she was not happy about being brought face to face with the fisherman again. It meant that he would be certain to recognise her in the future, which the camera flash and his drunken state might have prevented. Then she remembered that he must have had many friends in the crowd last night. She had the chilling feeling that whatever happened Quinn would be a marked man after this. And she would be marked out too. It could be the end for Quinn.

The sergeant had been unwilling to speculate on the eventual charge. It might be Grievous Bodily Harm, it might not. It was on the margins. On Monday morning the court would probably hear a holding charge.

'Will Quinn be forced to leave the island?' she asked, as Mackinnon drove her back.

'I seriously hope not. He's not the criminal. But that particular thug is a vindictive so and so. Always in trouble. And a ringleader. Jailing him would set an excellent example. But, to be honest, relations between the islanders and the settlers are becoming unwelcomingly polarised, poisoned even. I don't quite know why.'

'Crime is cool.' Anna suggested.

'Cool?' he had to absorb the meaning. 'Oh yes. If you haven't been taught any differently it probably is. Lack of education is the problem. The school is there, but not the desire to learn, at least among some of the boys. Possibly I ought to be pursuing that, rather than old war crimes.'

This was a long speech for Mackinnon and redoubled Anna's feeling that the island was not the place for her. In Brighton there were muggings and vandalism, all the time, but you didn't have to say hello to the troublemakers on the shopping street every day, or live next to them. It was as bad as being on a housing estate. So the island being relatively crime free was itself relative.

'Let's go to the hospital.' Mackinnon suggested. 'The official visiting hours don't start until three in the afternoon, but I'm sure they'll be considerate.'

The duty nurse, who knew Mackinnon well, scolded him gently, then took them through to the ward. Quinn was sitting up in bed in those striped hospital pyjamas, bandages around his neck. His complexion was very pale.

'He lost a bit of blood,' said the nurse, 'didn't you Mr Quinn?'

'Must have.' Quinn conceded in a croaky voice and looked up at Anna. 'I can't thank you enough, darling. Incredibly brave. The police are coming down after lunch. Is my Land Rover okay?'

'It's being dealt with now.' Mackinnon assured him,' the garage will bring it down here for you.'

Quinn looked hugely relieved. Although he would never have admitted as much, the Land Rover was his most significant possession and defined his lifestyle. They talked a little more, in the constrained way that hospital wards induce, then the nurse said the doctor was due on his rounds any moment and they must come back in the afternoon.

When they returned to the Mackinnon's cottage Phyllida asked if Anna would like to stay another night, if Quinn had not been discharged. If he was, this being her last day, she would pretty well have to return with him to the fort. Then she felt she had to tell Jack more about yesterday's encounter with Tad by the long wall.

'He's reaching the climax of his search,' she said 'and he's looking terrible.'

'I strongly advise you not to go with him to the end.' Mackinnon said. There was no need to explain why. She knew.

'I didn't mean to meet him yesterday.' she protested 'he just turned up.'

'I'm still afraid there could be actual violence. The episode with the woman and her dog came dangerously close.'

'Then I promise not to. By the way, have you heard anything from Dick Carey?' she suddenly wanted to know.

'He's coming across for the memorial service and hopes to interview Tad. Then he'll go back on the ferry.'

'The one I'll be on?' she was delighted. It would be a melancholy journey alone. And she liked Dick.

Mackinnon chuckled. 'I thought you'd be pleased. And he wants the diary back. Now, if you don't mind I have a few things to do. Shall we see you for lunch?'

'That is really nice of you. Yes, please.'

When he had left she retired to the little library to be out of Phyllida's way and unwrapped the diary. It was time to read the rest of Marianne's narrative. There was not much of it. The diary entries concluded on 27 May, though the crabbed handwriting spilled over on to the page for the day after.

'It's all over,' Marianne wrote, after Grundmann had left the House of Joy. 'I can only wait.'

Anna suspected this could not have been entirely true. She sensed that something else had taken place over which Marianne was being uncharacteristically reticent. But what?

'Horst mentioned the escaped workmen,' Marianne noted 'but he played it down. I suppose he thought I'd be frightened.

Idiot! I don't scare easily. He said we would be well guarded. But the shipwreck put them all in such a panic that the machine gunners on the headland didn't even come on duty until seven. If only they hadn't come at all!'

'Tiens! I'd better face up to it.' she continued, 'this time I am in the shit for sure. Horst's not being promoted last week makes him even more terrified of putting a foot wrong than he was already. They're all afraid of being sent to the Eastern Front. And now I've stepped straight in it. But anyone with a grain of pity would have done the same.'

Here Marianne must have paused, because there was a stain which might have been a tear falling on the page and which had blotted a word, so that she had only resumed writing after leaving a tiny space.

'It was bad enough seeing the churchyard shooting by accident. But this will finish me. I have no choice now. I have to get on that ship tomorrow. Once he hears about it, Horst will be down there to see me on board himself. And he hasn't given me a centime yet for the future. What do I have? Just a small wad of those filthy Reichsmarks that I've saved.'

Here there was a further tear stain. Obviously Marianne had entertained hopes of staying on, but whatever she had done had destroyed them. Anna pictured her writing this in the upstairs bedroom, dabbing her eyes and gazing out blindly towards the sea.

'This horrid fog! Why couldn't it have come in properly when it was needed. Mon Dieu, how I hate this island.'

After this she must have forced herself to be brave, because the few remaining lines were strictly practical.

'I am completely packed – I never unpacked actually. I have all the girls' dress sizes written down and of course I am safe in St Malo. I have memorised the name that matters. So now I must hide this in a safe place where someone will find it after the war.'

Putting the diary down, Anna guessed that Marianne must have done something impulsively brave on her last evening on the island: some action which had been certain to appal Grundmann. She would probably never discover what it was, but it made her wonder even more keenly what Marianne's final fate had been.

Had she ever reached St Malo? Had she managed to pass on the name of Eberhardt to the Allies after the war? If she had, then surely Jack Mackinnon would have heard about it? Anna found this a far more intriguing mystery than pursuing her uncle.

This reverie was terminated by Jack asking if she would like a drink before lunch. He was ever the good host. She asked for a white wine spritzer, dismissing the associated memories of Lavinia, and told him about the last entries in the diary.

'The memory's just clicked into place, the programme's running.' he said, adopting the metaphors of a new age to which he did not really belong. 'I realise now that I did meet Marianne. I interviewed her in St Malo in 1946. But her name wasn't Marianne, it was Yvette.'

'Not as exciting.' Anna said.

'Typical French provincial.' Phyllida added.

'Which had been her whole upbringing.' Jack explained. 'Her father was a commercial lawyer in St Malo and they lived in the smart suburb of Parame, by the sea. In 1944 old St Malo was bombed to hell by the Americans but that hadn't happened yet in 1942. What Yvette did was extraordinary, not paralleled by many others in France. It would make a make a good movie.'

Her father regularly needed to send documents to Paris, Rennes, Orleans and other centres. So did the French Resistance, because St Malo has a fine secure anchorage and was used by a lot of German shipping. So she became a courier, often carrying unnecessary legal papers as cover, and using the name Marianne Hausmann with forged identity papers.'

'I reckoned she was brave.' Anna remarked.

'The inevitable happened. Her father had clients in other centres, but not as many as all that and someone informed on her. The Gestapo had a thousand ears, most of them French. People often used denunciations to settle old scores and most lawyers acquire a few enemies. Yvette's father was no exception. She was arrested on a railway station. By good luck the legal documents with her that day were relevant to her journey. She bluffed her way out of the interrogation, but was too intelligent to imagine she was safe. A second Gestapo interview could have been fatal.'

'I don't see how that brought her here, though.'

'Yvette/Marianne operated on the margins, with lovers and with life, and she was quick off the mark. A week or two later

223

she was having coffee in a St Malo bistro when Grundmann, hanging around waiting for a night sailing to this island, picked her up in the café. He'd just completed a week's leave with his fat Frankfurt hausfrau and probably felt like going a little wild.' Mackinnon paused. 'You can guess the rest. Through discreet probing, Marianne learnt that there were no Gestapo on the island. She sailed with Grundmann that night.'

'A very fast operator.' Phyllida observed, though not admiringly.

'Girls will be girls.' Jack said indulgently, making his wife frown. 'And Grundmann wasn't bad looking. Furthermore he wasn't a thug, he wasn't a Prussian, he wasn't even a Nazi. He was an ordinary army officer. Better still, and this was what decided her, he was the Fortress Commandant and so an ideal protector. She was very frank with me about it. I found the notes of my interview with her this morning. Her father didn't like the idea much, when she hurried home to pack and told him, but she was in what our American friends call clear and present danger.'

'And the baby?' Anna asked. She had hoped Marianne would have had the courage to keep it when the crunch came.

'She kept it.' Jack said. 'A very pretty little girl at the time I saw her, of whom Yvette was intensely proud. I felt she might have not have kept a half-German son. Undesirable genes, you might say. But a girl she could cope with and educate.'

'I thought she would, I'm glad for her. What happened when she got back to St Malo?'

Anna could hardly forget that she was half German herself and that her uncle, though only 17 or 18, might have been capable of horrible violence.

'After the war ended she was recognised as a Resistance heroine and of course ceased to be Marianne. She had passed on to the Resistance valuable information about the island, including military details that I would not have expected. And,' Jack glanced at his wife, not exactly seeking approval, but perhaps hoping for it, 'because she was essentially a decent person, she had sent a packing case of clothes to the House of Joy.'

'Those girls can't have had much of a time when they were sent back home.' Phyllida suggested, still disapproving.

'One hundred percent not,' Jack confirmed, 'they were paraded around French towns as Nazi whores with their heads shaved. By contrast Marianne –Yvette – was lionised, as I said. Quite soon after she married a local businessman, who was prepared to adopt the daughter, but with whom Yvette was, I imagine, reticent about her experiences. I never met him.'

'What was she like?' Anna asked, intensely curious..

'Vivacious. Very feminine. Aged about 30. Well-dressed because her father could afford good clothes, such as they were after the war. And intelligent. A lively, pretty and intelligent woman is never going to lack a husband for long and she was something special by anyone's standards.'

'Even so,' Anna asked 'wouldn't being a German colonel's mistress have made her new husband wonder?'

'Although she told me about the House of Joy, she might not have felt obliged to give her new man too much to think about. Never tell a man more than you have to, was Yvette's motto. I never met him.' Mackinnon smiled. 'I suspect she did not tell Grundmann that Marianne represented the spirit of France either.'

'Sensible girl.' Anna applauded that.

'And she hated the Germans. They liked that attitude in St Malo, which had suffered so badly in the Allies efforts to dislodge the Wehrmacht. De Gaulle had not yet given France back her self-esteem. Marianne seemed to epitomise French pride.'

'Was it the churchyard killing that really got her going?' Anna asked, trying not to think about her uncle..

'It haunted her, she told me.'

Anna counted the years. 'She would be in her eighties now? Still alive?'

Mackinnon laughed. 'Frenchwomen are tough old birds. And they rule the roost. She would still be in St Malo and highly respected, I imagine. You'd have no trouble finding her, though I can't give you her married name.'

'There are ferries direct from England aren't there?'

'Daily.'

Over lunch Anna realised that her last whole day on the island was evaporating fast.

'After the hospital, would you mind if I go walkabout on my own?' she asked 'Or rather bikeabout.'

'Whatever you want. The weather's all set to be sunny,' Jack said, 'though more of our accursed fog is expected in the late afternoon and evening.'

'Will you be here for dinner?' the ever-practical Phyllida needed to know.

'If I may.' Anna intended to get them a present and decided to do it right away, since they could not go to the hospital until three.

She bought a box of Belgian chocolates, though not huge because of the cost. She reckoned Jack's travels would have introduced them to these especially rich favourites.

'Belgium may be a small country, but she has big-hearted chocolates.' he joked when she presented them later. Then he drove her down to the hospital.

Quinn was holding court in a small public ward. Literally so. There was no other way to describe it. President Cabot was standing near the foot of the bed. Sir Edward had arrived a moment earlier and was hovering, holding a bunch of grapes. There were bunches of flowers in vases on the bedside table and on the window sill. Lavinia occupied the only upright chair and had positioned herself at Quinn's right hand, half way down the bed, neatly controlling the access of rival visitors. Patients in the other beds stared unashamedly at this swarm of notables.

'Hullo, darling.' Quinn welcomed Anna. 'Lovely to see you again.'

'Again?' Lavinia asked waspishly, 'I thought visiting hours began at three.'

'I was allowed to see my husband.' Anna said 'So were the police.'

'Frankly,' Lavinia said, 'I think it was most unwise of you to confront that crowd, and especially with a camera.'

'It was they who confronted us.'

'Did you photograph them?' Cabot cut in. 'I heard a rumour. Damned brave of you. If we could nail the ringleaders we might end this thuggery.'

'Well I still think it was asking for trouble,' Lavinia insisted, 'it's incredibly lucky that Quinn's painting arm hasn't suffered.'

'Only nearly had my throat slit.' Quinn said, but the cheerful exaggeration fell flat. Sir Edward laughed perfunctorily. He had been a career diplomat.

'I did warn you, my dear,' Lavinia hammered on at Anna, 'that The Salutation is not a nice place.' she gazed soulfully at

226

Quinn, seeing herself as the new Florence Nightingale. 'How soon will the doctors let you out?'

'They say tomorrow.'

Now it was Anna's turn to be concerned, but genuinely so. 'Not today?' she asked, feeling guilty for not spending her final night with him at the fort.

'Don't think so. Apparently the neck is tricky.'

'Don't worry about Anna, old chap.' Jack Mackinnon said. 'We'll look after her.'

'I'll be there to see you off at the ferry,' Quinn said stoutly, 'whatever the quack says.'

'Oh,' Lavinia affected surprise to Anna, 'so you're not staying to look after your husband then?' Following on quickly before Anna could answer she added 'Of course, he will be in the best of hands here and everyone will rally round to help at the fort. I can promise you that.'

'I'm sure you will.' Anna disregarded the 'everyone' bit.

Quinn sat there in his striped flannel hospital pyjamas, propped up by pillows, his beard lost from being shaved for the stitches. His utter frustration was visible and audible.

'Damn that bloody Darren.' he said loudly.

'Well,' Charles Cabot spoke, not liking the recriminatory direction this was taking, 'you have everyone's good wishes and I'm sure many people will come to commiserate. Can't afford to have our tame artist out of action. Better keep that arm flexed!'

The President laughed and moved towards the door. Everyone else obediently trooped out after him, except for Lavinia, who was determined to have the last word.

'If we don't see you again before you leave, Anna my dear,' she said 'bon voyage. I would say give my regards to Brighton, if I knew where it was.'

She made a carefully elegant exit, leaving the other patients enough to talk about for a week.

'Bitch.' Anna said under her breath 'She'll be round you every hour of the day once I've gone.'

'Can't you stay a bit longer?'

This was Quinn's final plea, his last attempt to persuade her. And he was compelled to make it with five other pairs of ears straining to catch every word he uttered. Anna felt seriously sorry for him. But she had made her decision.

'My love, I have got to leave tomorrow. I simply can't stay. My classes start again on Monday.'

Quinn recognised the determination in her voice, but was not going to give up completely.

'Give me a call this evening, please. I might have good news after the doctor's ward round.'

'I'll come tomorrow whatever happens.'

Mackinnon took her arm to guide her gently away. 'We have to be at the identity parade, remember.' he said, as much to Quinn as to her. 'I'll come down tomorrow too, Quinn.'

As they left the hospital Mackinnon said to her. 'I realise how difficult that was. But I think you're doing the right thing. This place is not for you.'

'Is it right for him?'

'Less easy to say. I imagine there's a past history.'

'There is.' she admitted.

She was starting to feel terribly weary again. She had imagined many ways of making her escape from the island, plotted one of them even, but not through Quinn being injured or incapacitated. Not that.

'He thought he would find himself as an artist here on the island. And as a person.' she told Mackinnon. 'Last night must have really hurt him. Not so much physically. But it's the end of a dream. Or the beginning of the end of it.'

'I don't know your husband at all well' .Mackinnon said 'but I can understand what his hopes were. This place seems so full of promise to newcomers at first, yet it can be very cruel.'

He drove her up to the police station and they went through the unnerving ritual of confronting a line up of fairly similar island men. Not as similar as they might have been, but there was a stubborn resistance to assisting the police over any accusation against one of their own.

Darren the fisherman was immediately recognisable, even without his baseball cap and dirty blue sweater.

'That's him.' Anna said unhesitatingly

Afterwards she gave the police her Brighton address to send her any of the developed film they didn't need.

As they left a wildly overweight young woman in bulging jeans launched herself across the pavement and spat at Anna.

'You wait!' she screamed 'We'll get you.'

'They're not always as friendly as that.' Mackinnon said sardonically, guiding her away and protecting her with his arm.

'Who was she?' Anna realised it was the same woman who had screamed abuse at her outside the pub.

'Live in girlfriend. She supports him most of the time. Light fingered too. We've seen her all too often in court.'

'I do hope they don't have another go at Quinn.'

'He'd be wise to keep out of the pubs for a time.'

But that's where he enjoys himself, she thought. What a mess. His island! Except that it wasn't. It was theirs.

When they got back it was already teatime and Anna felt grotesquely cheated. This had been a lovely sunny day, though it was already becoming hazier, a day when she could have finished exploring the enjoyable side of the island. And where it had it gone to? Dissipated in the aftermath of a vicious, drunken assault. If Jack Mackinnon had not been around, she would have been unable to cope.

After another delicious cream tea, with jam and scones and cake, which Phyllida must have assembled to cheer her up, she told Jack that she was going for the planned bike ride and a last look at the lighthouse end of the island and the fort. While she was there she would pack as well.

He gave her a quizzical glance. 'Marianne?' he asked.

'Something she wrote in that diary is still puzzling me.' she admitted. 'And I shall to give it back to Dick tomorrow.'

'Take care.' Phyllida said and she did not mean it in the casual, throwaway sense everybody used. She was of an older generation to whom the words meant precisely what they said.

'I'll be back for supper.' Anna assured them.

CHAPTER TWENTY EIGHT

But by the time Anna had cycled down to the fort and packed her case, so that they would not be in a rush tomorrow, and put a few extra oddments in the bicycle basket for tonight, it was nearly seven. The haze had thickened and wisps of fog had begun to entwine the fort, drifting as always like smoke across the landscape. It was hardly thick enough yet to be classified in her mind as proper fog, although the lighthouse was already booming away its warning to ships.

Because it was nearly seven, and chilly, although still in the strong light of a May evening, Anna nearly abandoned her idea of cycling across the neck of the island for a final visit to the cove and the House of Joy, then decided she could just fit it in.

She had become more and more intrigued by those concluding diary entries of Marianne's: 'This time I'm in the shit for sure. But anyone with a grain of pity would have done the same.'

Presumably unless she started sketching in the fog, nothing bad would be revealed to her. And she didn't want it to be either. She had been scared enough when she realised what her drawing of the boat and the men on the headland had revealed.

Nonetheless, wilfully disregarding Jack's advice, she did hope Tad would be there now. If he could recall the climax of his escape, then she might learn what acute sense of pity had excited Marianne to do whatever had landed her so firmly in *la merde*. It had to be connected with the boys. Just had to be. And thanks to the endless delays of today this was around the time when Tad and Miki would have progressed from the bay along the path to the cove and the sailboat.

If Anna's thinking been more reasoned and had she been less disoriented by the attack on Quinn she probably would not have done as she did. As it was she cycled past the memorial, past the cottage, across to Drake's Bay and then, pushing her bike, along the narrow path through the high ferns and bracken towards Lavinia's house. She should not have gone there, but she did.

There was another emotion driving her too. The diaries coupled with Mackinnon's recollections had left her with a huge admiration for Marianne. If the Frenchwoman had done such things for real in the past, how could she, Anna, be so cowardly as to retreat from bearing witness to them now, if that was what she had to? Whatever transpired could not be more distressing than the 'glassing' and the woman's threats outside the police station.

The bench from which she had sketched the first time was a short distance from the cove, set on a grassy slope beyond banks of ferns, which was why she had only seen the figures in the boat and on the headland indistinctly. If Tad arrived where she had been before he would be closer to the cove, in fact where she herself was headed now. She parked the bike and ventured further along the path. No sign of him. But she did see men on the low headland where the trench was, well off to one side of the path.

As she progressed she noticed that the path had been fenced in since yesterday, which struck her as odd and a bit sinister. She was walking between barbed wire linked posts which lined the banks of ferns. As before, she could only just see over the vegetation. She needed a vantage point and found another fenced track leading to the other headland enclosing the cove where she had made her original drawing. From there she would be able to see much better.

There was still no sign of Tad. And the fog was creeping in. The round towered fort became hidden and wraiths of mist trailed around the headland opposite her, drifting in and out, first obscuring then revealing the slanting pale rock outcrop.

Offshore the water was surprisingly rough, fairly calm in the cove, but disturbed by white crested waves further out as far as Anna could see. Not that she could see far. The ocean had disappeared, obliterated by fog. Yet the echoing boom of the lighthouse foghorns had ceased. A fact about the lighthouse clicked worryingly into place. During the Occupation the Germans only turned on the light and the horns when they had a ship arriving. Marianne's ship was not due until tomorrow. With a sickening mental shock Anna knew that, willy nilly, she was witnessing the past yet again, sketching or no sketching.

There was movement in the cove below. Two men came into view dragging a small boat down across the white stones towards the sea. They reached the strip of sand and struggled to raise a sail on the short mast, before launching it. The boat was out of a children's story illustration, only just large enough for two people, with one sitting in the stern holding the rudder, the other working the thin ropes to the sail.

As soon as the dinghy was afloat it was clear that the men were not sailors. The boat teetered in the water, almost capsizing, until they hastily shifted their positions to distribute their weight more evenly. The boat began to move slowly out towards the open sea as the sail filled and bulged. There was just enough wind to drive it along. The fog drifted closer in as Anna watched, simultaneously enthralled and scared to death. Now she knew exactly what she was seeing and Tad could not be watching because he must be in the boat. But which of the two was he?

The fog began drifting away again. The whole cove was revealed. The men on the headland by the outcrop had a long black gun on a tripod, larger than a rifle. They must have been standing in the trench, as their legs were not visible. Anna knew when they opened fire. She saw the bullets splashing into the sea around the boat.

Quite suddenly she noticed, out of the corner of her eye, someone standing by the green garden gate that led up to the House of Joy. It was a woman, watching the machine gunning, just as Anna was herself. The woman had dark, curly hair and was wearing a red print dress. Everything happened very fast. The machine gunner hit the man standing by the boat's mast. The man had been trying with his hands to spread its sail to catch the wind. As he was shot his back arched and he fell completely overboard, though on the shoreward side.

The woman reacted instantly. She ran frantically down the short path between the barbed wire fences to the cove, her thin dress flapping against her legs, her arms flailing. For a moment she disappeared from Anna's sight beneath the cove's overhang of turf, then re-appeared, stumbling over the rocks in her haste to get to the man. She reached the beach and dashed into the water.

The machine gunner stopped firing. He must have known this was one of the Colonel's women. Anna could see that he was now only watching. As the woman waded in to pull the gunner's victim to safety the wind gathered a little more strength, the boat's sail filled and it edged towards the open sea and into the fog again, with the other man in it. Within seconds it was lost to sight.

The woman, her dress soaked and clinging to her legs, was dragging the wounded man on to the shore. She found it extremely difficult and ended up pulling him with her hands gripping his armpits. He appeared completely limp. But she did not give up. The soldiers, still watching through binoculars, took no action.

Eventually, in a desperate triumph of determination against the obstacles of the rocks and the steep shingle, the woman levered the inert body up to the turf above the cove. She was panting and exhausted. Her dress was sodden and her hair wild. Anna knew who this was. It could be no-one else.

Marianne was only yards away from Anna when she reached the grass near the garden gate. She lifted the man's head to cradle him in her arms, for he was dying. Anna saw the intense compassion in both her actions and her face. She was as gentle with him as with a child. Then Anna realised that he was not a grown man at all, merely a teenager. She could not see his face, because Marianne was bent over him. But it could not be Tad. It had to be Miki.

CHAPTER TWENTY NINE

'We were beginning to get worried.' Phyllida said solicitously, as she answered the doorbell and found Anna standing outside in the fading light with her bicycle. 'Park the bike and come in. It should be safe enough.'

In fact the front door was not locked. Most other people used not to lock theirs either, although they were starting to. The creeping advance of petty crime and vandalism was something they disliked acknowledging. It shouldn't be happening here, not in this small community. But it was and now they had to lock up.

Anna left the bike propped up against a wall and entered the narrow hall, just as Jack Mackinnon, hearing voices, came through. He took one look at her and knew what was needed.

'A brandy should steady you a little.'

For once, although she very seldom touched hard liquor, Anna was grateful. She was in shock. It was not only witnessing the killing, but a host of other things.

Recognising Marianne had been one of them. Another was the appreciation, as she cautiously left the cove to retrieve her bike, the fog beginning to disperse, that the lines of barbed wire had gone and she could hear the foghorn's insistent moan again. Then she realised that the whole scene at the cove had been silent, just as previous visions had. She had seen bullets splashing into the sea around the boat, seen the boy fall, but heard no shots. Marianne must have spoken to Miki, trying so desperately to keep him alive, but although they were only yards from her, she had heard nothing.

'Anyone with a grain of pity would have done the same.' Marianne had said in her diary. This had been true grit courage, like she had shown when interrogated by the Gestapo. She really had deserved to end up feted as a heroine; even if after the war she had not revealed the exact circumstances to her new husband.

Anna told Jack Mackinnon about this, when he had brought the drink and its burning strength had begun to revive her. He made almost no comment, except to ask if he was right in remembering that her mother had experienced some kind of psychic vision.

'Yes, when she was a hospital nurse. A man who had died the night before walked through her ward. Didn't I tell you?'

'Stranger things have happened. But will you have to leave without tracing your uncle?'

'To be honest,' Anna took a larger sip of the brandy, feeling better already, 'the idea that he might have been in the SS was so unbearable that I just put it out of my mind. Except that one can never do that completely, can one?'

'Your grandparents had been sent to a concentration camp for being opposed to Hitler, is that right?'

'Yes. But Johann had done nothing.'

'He existed. That was enough in the mad world of the Nazis. Even at fifteen or sixteen he would have been a political risk, unless he had denounced his parents, unless he somehow proved his loyalty.'

'Suppose he had proved it in the SS?' Anna found this was not a pleasant idea, so she dismissed it and turned to a less important mystery.

'I am puzzled about Miki. Tad seems not have believed he was Russian.'

'Possibly he was Jewish. Or even German. The Russians were *Untermenschen*, but that was preferable to being in the SS concentration camp called Neuwerk, which took some dissident Germans. Or with the 300 Jews in the Nordstrand camp. I think both boys would have been aware of that.'

'How many of these camps were there?'

'Four. All named after North Sea islands. And Tadeus did escape, even though we ourselves, after the war, thought that would have been impossible. Did he show up last night?'

Anna shook her head. 'I expected him to, but no, he didn't.'

'Can't have the ghost and the original at the same time, eh?' Mackinnon was making a joke of it to help Anna back to normality. But he was not joking at all.

At this point Phyllida came in and apologised for their having already had supper themselves.

'We eat rather early these days. But yours is in the oven. Would you like it now?'

Jack sat with her while she devoured her steak and kidney pudding, accompanied by new potatoes from their garden. The cycling had made her hungry and Jack took that as a good sign. Although he had joked about being psychic a few minutes ago, he took any additional knowledge of Marianne's activities very seriously, because of the light it shed on the Occupation, even though he had met and interviewed her after it was all over. If challenged he would have admitted to being somewhat obsessed by the subject. He had never really retired as an investigator.

'May I borrow the diary to read tonight?' he asked.

'If Dick Carey comes tomorrow I must give it back.'

'Well,' Mackinnon said dryly, 'he might just agree to lend it to his godfather. Incidentally, he's going to be at the memorial service hoping to interview Tadeus. And he will be going back to St Mary on the same boat as you.'

'I'd hoped he would be.'

That felt like a ray of light in a dark scene. She might be in a fairly depressed frame of mind by the time she left and someone to talk to would be welcome. Nor did she want to be stuck throughout the voyage with Tad. Just as she had finally shut her uncle out of her thoughts, so she intended shutting out everything about the island once she had left.

Sunday morning dawned as clear as a bell. Anna drew the curtains to see a perfect early blue sky reflected in a calm pearly sea. Even on the far horizon, where merchant ships passing by looked much larger than they possibly could be, presumably due to some refraction of the light, there was no trace of fog. For the first time everything boded well. Holidays were often like that, glorious on the last day, though anyone who called the past week a holiday had to be joking.

At breakfast Mackinnon told her the hospital expected to discharge Quinn after the doctor's round at midday.

'Which dictates when we need to be having our own lunch.' He commented. 'The easiest plan would be to collect your bags in my car, go to the service, have a quick meal ourselves, then fetch Quinn and take you to the two o'clock ferry. At least he'll be able to see you off.'

'He won't like being kept waiting.' Anna said.

'It is the simplest solution.'

'No use arguing, my dear,' Phyllida said, 'when Jack has a plan he has a plan.' she smiled indulgently at her husband. 'I wouldn't say he's difficult, just immovable.'

Once breakfast was over Anna unveiled her second 'thank-you' present, or rather handed it over, wrapped up in tissue.

'I'm so sorry it isn't framed,' she apologised. 'I didn't know where to find a framer yesterday. I hope you'll like it.'

Phyllida carefully removed the tissue and held up the new present for her husband's inspection. Jack Mackinnon was overwhelmed. It was Anna's sketch of the shipwreck in the fog.

'You've already given us superb chocolates,' he protested 'Are you sure you want to give this away. You do realise it's unique?'

'I thought it would add to your collection.'

Phyllida kissed her on the cheek. 'That is a very dear thing to do. We'll have it framed next week. But you must sign it.'

Anna had forgotten that she hadn't, then experienced a moment of doubt.

'I'd better not,' she half-joked 'It might suddenly change back to the present day and then it wouldn't be anything at all.'

At ten twenty, allowing themselves almost too much time, Mackinnon drove Anna round to the fort to collect her case. However brief, it was a strangely melancholy experience to be there without Quinn.

Before they left again she wandered around in a rather disorganised way, casting her eyes over all sorts of minor objects that dated from their previous life together, a glazed earthenware jug that used to hold flowers, an ashtray: and she looked at the works in progress in his studio. His passionate portrait of her was under a cloth on the easel, safely hidden from Lavinia's sarcasm. She lifted the cloth and felt a great welling up of emotion, just as she had before. If ever there was a painting illuminated with love, this was it. She replaced the cloth with great sadness. All the absentee adoration in the world wasn't going to make Quinn more satisfactory to live with, nor ever outweigh her fear and mistrust of the island which he had made his habitat. She thought of taking the painting with her, but dared not.

Something of this wistfulness must have remained in Anna's expression when she wheeled her trolley case down to the entrance, because Mackinnon immediately remarked on it, even as he took the case and told her to have no regrets.

'There are people for whom this island will never be right,' he said, 'and women for whom Quinn never will be either.'

The memorial service was a very different experience, mourning the past without – so it seemed to Anna - much hope for

237

the future. A straggling line of people stood along the road near the monument, while a small group of priests and dignitaries, including Charles Cabot, were gathered facing it. A Union Jack and another flag Anna did not recognise flew from a double flagpole, forked half way up. The sun beat down indiscriminately on bald heads and black clerical cassocks, on circular Jewish skull caps and shirt-sleeved passers by.

The memorial being on the route to several beaches a few tourists stopped and snapped away. Local customs, they told each other, never see anything like this again. Anna noticed a plaque for the island family whose inspiration the memorial had been. Their ashes were interred here too. Anna was unexpectedly touched by islanders having created this; those same people whose homeland had been ravaged paying tribute to those forced to ravage it. Maybe there was more good here than evil after all.

'We are come together' the Minister intoned 'to remember before God those deported to this island and into forced labour during the years of the Occupation; to remember those who died and those who suffered through deprivation, degradation and the cruelty inflicted upon them by their fellow men.'

The small roadside congregation sang a hymn in French, then another in English, followed by prayers and the laying of wreaths, an address and the Jewish prayer for international understanding.

'Help us all to put the good of our fellow men above our own ambitions.' the prayer ran.

Very few former slaves had been fit enough to travel here. They were grouped at the front. Anna thought their ageing faces were still marked by their experiences. Tad stood among them, his flat cap removed in respect, but looking infinitely worn out. There won't be any of them left soon, she thought.

Dick Carey, fair haired and young in complete contrast to the survivors, stood to one side, waiting to catch Tad and probably the President. He gave her a smile and mouthed 'see you later'. She nodded and smiled back.

In fact Mackinnon didn't wait to talk to Dick Carey, but reminded her that the timetable was tight and hustled her home.

'We must get down to the hospital soon. Quinn will be...'

'Doing his nut.' Anna cut in cheerfully. 'And he looks so bereft without his beard.'

Despite hurrying, when they parked outside the single storey hospital they found Quinn about to leave and as Anna entered the lobby she heard a familiar voice.

'I really don't know about any other arrangement,' Lavinia was saying imperiously to the duty nurse, 'so far as I am aware I am taking Mr Quinn home.'

'We were told by his wife....' the nurse tried to explain, then she saw Anna come in, followed by Mackinnon. 'Oh, Mrs Quinn' she exclaimed with relief. 'I was sure you were coming.'

The nurse was used to defusing family confrontations, which took place often over one thing or another, though not usually over who was going to take delivery of the patient.

Jack Mackinnon stepped forward towards the desk, noticed Quinn himself sitting on a chair at the side, like a nervous schoolboy outside the headmaster's study, and spoke to the nurse, ignoring Lavinia.

'Does anything have to be signed?'

'I have already dealt with the formalities.' Lavinia said coldly. 'Quinn, dear, we must be on our way.'

He stood up a little shakily, intensely embarrassed. He was face to face with Anna in the confined space of the lobby and had no escape route. A woman patient waiting on another chair stared at them with rapt interest.

'I have to catch the ferry, darling.' Anna said. 'Are you coming to see me off?' This time the 'darling' was strictly for Lavinia's benefit.

The nurse told her colleagues afterwards that it was better than a TV soap. There was a complete stand-off for about half a minute, exactly as there could have been in a drama.

'Quinn!' Lavinia said eventually in a voice like a pistol shot.

He looked all around, knowing he was consigned to the slaughter either way and feeling far less authoritative and confident without his beard.

'Sorry Lavinia,' he said weakly, 'I must see Anna off.'

Lavinia hoisted the strap of her initialled Gucci bag over her shoulder, gave Anna a killer glance and said to Quinn. 'I hope you won't be off sick next week', with a lot of emphasis on the 'next'. She stalked out through the door and they heard a car start up, followed by the screech of tyres.

'Let's go.' Mackinnon said, thanked the nurse and picked up Quinn's small overnight bag. 'I wonder which theatre school gave Lavinia her diploma.'

'The Widows' Academy.' Anna said.

'You suppose you realise this has lost me my job?' Quinn finally found his voice.

'As toy boy or artist? Anna was furious at his having allowed this to happen and when they reached the harbour she kept the goodbyes short, although inside she was completely churned up.

Beardless and without his Land Rover, which had to be delivered to the fort for him, unable to heft Anna's bag on to his shoulder, Quinn was sadly diminished from the hearty, self-confident man of a week ago. A stevedore came up to them.

'Darren didn't ought to have done that, Quinn. Pissed out of 'is bloody mind, he was. Don't let it get you down, eh.'

'They're not all against me,' Quinn said to Anna, but without spirit.

'I'm sure they're not. Seriously.'

She tried to sound soothing, but did not succeed. She had been too angry too recently. As for mentioning her chief purpose in coming here originally, that was impossible. She would never come to live on the island and Quinn knew she would not.

'See you later, then.' he said in an attempt at bravado, kissing her on both cheeks. 'Brighton next time.'

'We'll see.' she returned the kiss in the formal continental way, on both cheeks and then the right side again.

Finally she shook hands warmly with Jack and impulsively kissed him on the cheek too. 'You've been marvellous.' she said 'You absolutely saved my life.'

She could have been nearer the truth than she thought, Mackinnon reflected as she descended the gangplank and waved for a final time before disappearing into the cabin. She had been very close to some very dangerous events.

They saw her face at a salt smeared window and waved again.

'I'd better get you home.' Jack said to Quinn. 'Have you got any food at the fort?'

CHAPTER THIRTY

Anna waved to Quinn one last time though the smeared windows of the ferry, the boat jolted, then edged away from the stone quayside. Finally it backed out into the open water of the bay, turned and headed for the sea, past the end of the long granite breakwater.

She had deliberately chosen a seat on the left hand side, so that she would have views of the island as they went round. All traces of the week's intermittent fogs had vanished. The sky was a clear pale blue, flecked only by a few puffy clouds as the scenery of her arrival unfolded in reverse.

The isolated white cottages near the shore slipped past, then the Victorian fort which she had confused with Quinn's, then the cliffs. The cliffs were every bit as gaunt and crumblingly impressive as before, guarding more lifetimes of secrets than she could have ever guessed, or anyone living was likely to know. The island had accumulated too much history, too heavy a burden for its tiny population. She suddenly felt quite weepy.

The visit was conclusively over. With the boat's departure the island retreated into the past, even though her one week here had felt like a lifetime. She had failed to solve the mystery of her uncle and now she was consumed with regret at leaving Quinn in such a poor state, despite being so angry with him.

Had she been responsible for destroying his new-found image of himself? Perhaps. Perhaps partially. Certainly she had been unable to respond as he had desired and hoped. The competition from Lavinia on the one hand and her own ever increasing absorption with Marianne and her uncle's actions had seen to that..

Perhaps one day she might write an account of this strange adventure. She distantly remembered a book of her mother's about two English ladies' experiences at Versailles in the early 1900s, when they had recurrent visions of Marie Antoinette's courtiers in the park on the day the ill-fated Queen was forced to leave Versailles forever. What the ladies saw were a series of scenes from that single day, from different perspectives. They saw garden features long since replaced and walked through doors that were no longer there. They were even spoken to by a passing courtier. Certain conditions seemed to have triggered their visions.

The authors were both well-known and highly educated women, one the Principal of an Oxford college indeed. They had subsequently researched and corroborated the events and costumes they had seen. Whether, in spite of their book's huge sales, anyone truly believed them, was quite another question. Probably not. Who would believe Anna's own story now?

For sure, one person who would believe it was sitting behind her: Dick Carey. He was just trying to interview Tad. Anna knew she must talk to both of them, though not for too long to Tad, she hoped. True, he had shown himself, when only a boy, as both compassionate and hating violence. But the whole affair was so mixed up in her mind with her uncle that she would have preferred to avoid him. She couldn't, so she got up and swayed her way back to them, holding on to seat backs as she went.

'Did you like the memorial service?' she asked Tad. He had travelled a great distance for it. 'I'm sorry not to have talked to you.' she smiled at Dick, who smiled back.

'Was good.' Tad said simply. 'I glad I come. My wife agree.'

He had achieved his mission of retrieving the past, though he looked completely exhausted as a result. At this moment Dick interrupted their conversation.

'Listen,' he wasn't about to let go of a good story. 'I know you had some extraordinary experiences with Tad. Would you be willing to do an interview for the paper too? We could do it now.'

'I'm not so sure about an interview.'

'Okay then. Listen, you have to wait for the Portsmouth boat tonight. How about over dinner?'

Anna glanced at him. A nice looking man. Probably a delightful dinner date. She pretended to consider, knowing what she had already decided. She wouldn't mind going to St Mary again some time, either.

'That would be nice. But no to the interview. The time for that is never. Now look, I must finish talking to Tad.'

She turned back to the old man and tackled the tricky part, the crucial connection. 'Did you go down to the cove yesterday?'

'Not. I remember boat and Miki is killed.'

'It wasn't your fault. It was the machine gunner.'

Dick looked across at her, his interest aroused. 'Say that again.' he asked.

242

'Tadeus was carried out to sea in the fog.' Anna said. 'The tide must have taken him to France. He did escape.'

'I....' Tad made rowing motions with his gnarled and brown blotched hands. 'Sail not good.'

'So you are happy now?' she asked.

'Yes. And tired. Very tired.'

Dick interrupted again, edging towards his interview. 'How did you get on with the diary Anna?'

'The diary was sensational.' she said, while Tad sat silent. 'Jack Mackinnon wanted to read it too. So I left it with him. I hope you don't mind.'

'I wish the hell I could read French. What have I missed?'

'If you ever feel like writing a book, then there's one in the story of Marianne.'

'And your uncle? Didn't you say you have a photo of him? May I see it?'

'I suppose so.' The request merely reminded Anna of her defeat, but she reached for her sack and took out the folder in which she kept the old photograph. 'That was him when he was about twelve.'

She displayed the picture of her uncle between his parents, standing stiffly to attention in his Hitler Youth uniform. Tad looked at it too, then took it from her and studied it closely, peering at it as an old man with failing eyesight would.

'Is Miki.' he said simply 'is Miki.'

Printed in the United Kingdom
by Lightning Source UK Ltd.
120955UK00002BA/1-6